P9-DSZ-348
TERMINAL
MERCY

Tyndale House books by Ed Stewart

◆ ◆ ◆

Terminal Mercy
Vote of Intolerance (with Josh McDowell)

A NOVEL BY

Ed Stewart

Tyndale House Publishers, Inc.
WHEATON, ILLINOIS

Visit Tyndale's exciting Web site at www.tyndale.com

Cover designed by Dennis Hill
Interior designed by Melinda Schumacher
Edited by Rick Blanchette

Library of Congress Cataloging-in-Publication Data

Steward, Ed.
Terminal mercy / Ed Stewart.
p. cm.
ISBN 0-8423-7039-0
I. Title.
PS3569.T4599T47 1999
813′.54—dc21 98-32136

Printed in the United States of America

05 04 03 02 01 00 99

9 8 7 6 5 4 3 2 1

acknowledgments

◆ ◆ ◆

Two wonderful gentlemen, along with their gracious wives, contributed significantly to the development of this book and deserve special mention.

Over the past ten years, my involvement with Dave Bellis has evolved from a project-focused work relationship to a deepening friendship forged from appreciation for each other's gifts. As a project manager in Christian publishing, Dave needed a competent, dependable writer. Someone happened to recommend me. As a freelance writer, I needed a source of steady work. Dave called at just the right time. We have been working on books together ever since.

More recently, however, my admiration for Dave as a person and my respect for his significant contributions to our industry opened up a new dimension to our relationship. When I asked Dave to become my literary agent, he took the matter seriously. Knowing my abilities like few people do, Dave gave himself to matching my skills and interests to projects that were both fulfilling and profitable. Far beyond the nuts and bolts of contracts and schedules, Dave became my coach, critic, and confidant, spending untold hours reading my manuscripts and sketching out scenes and dialogue. His vision and passion for what I could do fired my vision and passion for getting it done.

This book is a perfect example. Dave was there when we

brainstormed the story. He and his wife, Becky, gave significant input at various stages of the outline and drafts. They dug into my characters and helped me experience what they were thinking and feeling. Dave kept gently nudging me back to what he calls the "golden thread," the life-touching impact of the story. His passion for the relational message of this book will be felt in every chapter.

Dave, the title "agent" falls far short of summarizing all you have contributed to my work and to this book. Thank you for lending me your wisdom, expertise, encouragement, and inspiration. Thank you for investing yourself in me as a coworker, adviser, and friend. And Becky, thank you for joining Dave by sharing your valuable insights. Carol and I deeply value our relationship with both of you.

This book is also a reflection of the ministry and personal testimony of Dr. David and Teresa Ferguson, directors of Intimate Life Ministries. Dave Bellis hooked me up with the Fergusons so I could assist them with ministry writing projects. As a result, I became submerged in Intimate Life's profound, life-changing message, and Carol and I were enriched and blessed by participating in David and Teresa's conferences. This couple's ministry to the body of Christ has significantly energized and influenced my story.

David and Teresa, thank you for imparting to us not only the gospel but your lives as well. And thank you for reviewing the manuscript and supplying invaluable insights to the finished product.

I must also acknowledge a number of others for their contributions to this book.

David N. Weiss, who refers to his role as "borrowed brain cells," provided very helpful creative guidance to plot, story line, and character development.

Being neither a physician nor the son of a physician, I am indebted to the following members of the medical community who provided needed technical assistance: Gregory Beagle, M.D.; Kris Wike, R.N.; Craig H. Rabb, M.D. When the medical terminology and procedures in the book are correct, these people deserve the credit. When the details are erroneous or obviously fictionalized, I will take the blame.

Ron Beers, Ken Petersen, and Rick Blanchette at Tyndale House Publishers have been encouraging and supportive throughout. I cannot imagine a more satisfying publishing relationship.

Finally, someone once remarked that marriage with peace is this world's paradise. The peaceful, pleasant environment in which I live and write is largely the product of the commitment, partnership, friendship, and fun Carol and I share. Honey, thank you for thirty-five years of heaven on earth.

ONE

"Coming through, coming through! Give us a break, people!" The urgent order of a female intern penetrated the rhythmic roar of the Life Flight helicopter lifting off the helipad just outside the double glass doors.

The gurney glided swiftly along the short hallway between the elevator and the Emergency Room. Two trauma interns provided the push power while an ER nurse in blue scrubs steadied the patient, who lay strapped to a body board and head brace. A few hospital staffers hugged the walls as the gurney passed.

Those who risked a glance at the comatose patient—a woman in her midtwenties—grimaced or shook their head. Large smears of blood stained the white sheet that had been hastily thrown over her torso. The exposed left hand and forearm were scraped raw, with two fingers severely dislocated. The left side of what once had been a pretty face resembled a slab of cube steak prepared by a mad butcher—shredded flesh, blood, bone, and hair matted together. Two feet protruded from the sheet—one still wearing a scuffed, black, steel-toed boot, the other bare, twisted at a grotesque angle, and swollen.

The nurse aboard the inbound chopper had called ahead with the preliminary details of the woman's injuries and her vital signs. The trauma team was summoned by beeper from throughout the sprawling hospital while Life Flight was en route. Most had already scrubbed, gloved, and assembled outside trauma slot 4 as the gurney approached.

"What's on the menu today?" a late-arriving team member asked, tugging on his gloves.

"Looks like a large order of broken bones and scrambled brains," another answered wryly. "A Harley and a Buick got into it at seventy miles an hour on I-5 south of Woodburn. This gal was a passenger on the bike."

"What about the driver?"

"Her boyfriend hit the Buick first. Heard he didn't make it."

"Alcohol related?"

"No, but the nurse said their clothes smelled of pot."

"Bet this lady wishes she'd strapped on a helmet."

"She *was* wearing a helmet. They said it split open like a honeydew on the first bounce."

"Then we'd better put her back together so she can sue the helmet manufacturer for twenty million."

"It works for me."

As the gurney wheeled into trauma slot 4, the team—three trauma residents, a respiratory therapist and assistant, a trauma nurse, a recording nurse, a radiologist, and a fourth-year med student—swarmed in to assess the damage. Other specialists, such as an on-call neurosurgeon and orthopedic surgeon, would be summoned if needed. The Life Flight nurse had radioed ahead that this critically injured patient would likely need both to survive. An ER staffer had already called to secure an operating room.

The nurse with the gurney parroted the data obtained from the chopper nurse: "Young Latino female, motorcycle passenger in MVA. Unresponsive since the accident. Unknown head trauma, fractured left tibia and fibula, severely dislocated left ankle . . . for starters." Then she cited the declining blood pressure and compensatory increase in pulse rate. Armed with the foreboding particulars, everyone in trauma slot 4 knew they were in a battle for the life of a young woman they had never seen before.

An intern quickly removed the bloody sheet, then retreated while the trauma specialists went to work.

The trauma team leader orchestrated the team's skilled, time-critical activity. Today's leader, sixty-seven-year-old Bertram Waller, M.D., Ph.D., also happened to be the head of Surgery at Portland Mercy Teaching Hospital, a 460-bed facility nestled in the wooded hills of Oregon's largest city. Had the patient, twenty-eight-year-old Trudy Aguilera, been able, she could not have scripted her care any better. Portland Mercy Hospital, known to those who served there simply as Mercy, boasted one of the best trauma units and medical training facilities in the three-state area. And Dr. Waller was the best surgeon at Mercy.

"Give me new vitals and respiratory status," Dr. Waller directed firmly from his station at the foot of the gurney. "Replace cold IV with lactated Ringers to run wide open, and get a second access." As he spoke, the trauma nurse, a man in his early forties, checked the patient's vital signs and called out the numbers. The med student and a resident worked around the nurse to cut apart and peel away the patient's bloody jeans, denim jacket, shirt, and underclothes. The last item snipped from the woman was the gold chain around her neck. Attached to the chain was an ornate, bloodstained crucifix.

"Airway is clear, but breathing is rapid, shallow, and labored," came the report from the resident physician hovering over the patient's head. "I hear nothing on the left side."

Assimilating the data provided by the team, Dr. Waller said, "Pneumothorax, I expect."

He ordered plane films of the cervical spine, chest, and pelvis. The X-ray tech navigated the portable unit into position and exposed several films. In minutes the images were on the view box. The chest radiograph confirmed a large, left-side pneumothorax.

"Chest tube," Waller directed. "Dr. Vo, you're on." A third-year, Vietnamese-American trauma surgery resident inserted the chest tube to release the air from the chest cavity.

With the patient's breathing and heartbeat stabilized, Dr. Waller turned to the next crisis: the head trauma that had rendered patient Aguilera comatose. Dr. Waller ordered immediate transport to the CT room for a scan of the head.

Following the scan, Waller reviewed the pictures with two trauma residents, Drs. Favouri and Coe. "What do you see, Dr. Favouri?" probed Waller, ever the teacher.

"Subarachnoid hemorrhage over the right cerebral convexity and in the Sylvian fissure," Favouri said, touching the affected areas on the film.

"What else?"

Favouri looked closer, then put his finger on two more areas. "Looks like an epidural hematoma—left temporal—and a temporal bone fracture."

Coe whistled. "Worst I've ever seen."

"I should page the neurosurgeon," Favouri said, looking at Waller for confirmation.

"Absolutely. Who's on call?"

"The new guy from L.A.," Coe answered. "Kelly or Klein or Katz—some *K* name."

"Keyes," Waller said, nodding with recognition. "Page Dr. Keyes and his team. Get them down here—stat." Dr. Favouri moved to follow through.

"What about family?" Waller asked. "Does the girl have family here yet?"

"They're on the way," Coe responded. "They live down by Eugene. Could take them a couple of hours."

Waller frowned. "Ms. Aguilera can't wait." Then he motioned to the broken body on the gurney. "Get her to the OR."

◆ ◆ ◆

Dr. Jordan Keyes was momentarily lost again. Having been at Portland Mercy Teaching Hospital for two months, he still regarded the campus as a baffling maze of buildings and pathways spread over one hundred acres of hilly terrain. He was tired of asking others for directions. But the beeper vibrating on his belt demanded that he do so once again in order to find the fastest way back to the Trauma Center.

Jordan did not need to check the readout on his pager. He had heard the chopper thunder in and then depart minutes ago. Life Flight shuttled in only critically injured patients, many of them the victims of motor vehicle accidents. Safety belts and air bags notwithstanding, MVA victims nearly always arrived with life-threatening head or spine injuries. Not only was Dr. Keyes the on-call neurosurgeon for the April rotation, but brain trauma was his specialty. Somebody had likely cracked open a skull, and Jordan was being summoned to fix it.

Even after two months at Mercy, Jordan sensed an adrenaline jolt with every code call. Part of it, he knew, was from the sheer excitement of a new challenge. "Whenever the human head forcefully collides with the ground, a cement curb, the dashboard of a car, or another head," Jordan often explained to med students, "the brain ricochets against the inside wall in random fashion. You never know what kind of serious brain trauma will result. So every case presents a new and somewhat different puzzle to solve. Add to the puzzle the pressure of life-and-death urgency, and you have a totally captivating challenge. It's like racing to defuse a time bomb before it blows up in your face. And if that doesn't kick your adrenals into action, nothing will."

The thrill of the challenge was not the only reason for the surge Jordan felt just now. The skilled neurosurgeon hated to admit it, but he knew that anxiety was another reason for the sudden knot in his stomach. He was the new guy on a prestigious surgical staff. The anxiety was about first impressions, proving himself, earning his stripes in a new unit. Only one person at Mercy Hospital knew how desperately Jordan needed to make the most of these first opportunities. Dr. Jordan Keyes was that person.

Jordan was nearly half a mile from the ER in the Biomedical Information Center when the page came. Traveling at a jog, he found his way outside after only one wrong turn. He crossed the street and cut through Bernardi Hall to stay out of the spring drizzle. But then he couldn't find his way out the rear without asking directions and backtracking. Finally outside, Jordan covered the last hundred yards to the Trauma Center at little less than a sprint.

Once inside, Jordan wiped raindrops from his face with a handkerchief, hoping it didn't look like he was perspiring. Tiny beads of sweat immediately seeped from his pores to replace the rain. A trauma resident in green scrubs and a rumpled lab coat joined Jordan in stride, pointing him toward the elevator and a ride to the surgery floor. Dr. Favouri had CT films in his hand.

"Twenty-eight-year-old female MVA in OR 2," Favouri recited. Shorter than Jordan by four inches, the resident labored to keep up. He summarized his findings from the films. Hearing the complexity of the injury described, Jordan felt another mild flash of excitement and anxiety.

The two men approached the wall-mounted film viewer outside OR 2. Favouri fumbled with the films, trying to separate them. Jordan deftly collected the films and mounted them on the viewer. "Thank you for your help, Doctor," he said, giving full attention to the images before him.

Favouri took the cue and headed back toward the ER. "Good luck, Doctor," he said.

Luck has nothing to do with it, Doctor, Jordan corrected him silently. *Only God's grace and the diligent application of God-given skill will save this girl's life.*

Jordan absorbed the films in several studied gazes. Moments later, a third-year neurosurgery resident joined him at the viewer. Dr. Webster Chen had assisted Jordan on a few craniotomies since his arrival at Mercy. Jordan appreciated the man's skill and professionalism. He would be an excellent neurosurgeon.

"What do we have?" the lanky Chen asked, slipping out of his lab coat. He was slightly out of breath also.

Jordan had already assessed the multiple injuries, prioritized them for attention, and charted his surgical course. "Acute epidural hematoma, potential uncal herniation. I will evacuate the hematoma; then we can check out the fracture and see what else is needed."

"Very good, Doctor," Chen said. Jordan also appreciated the respect the young doctor afforded him.

"Let me know when the patient is prepped," Jordan said as he left to change into surgical scrubs.

Alone in the locker room, Jordan slipped into clean blue scrubs and a cap. Then he sat down for a moment to focus his thoughts. The procedure ahead of him was by nature difficult and demanding. But the task was certainly not uncommon to him. During six years as a neurosurgery resident and a two-year fellowship, Jordan had done more temporal craniotomies than he could count—perhaps an average of six a month. He had already performed three of them in his two months at Mercy.

But he had no reason to be cocky or casual about this familiar procedure. Even after thirteen years of training and six years of practice in his chosen field, Dr. Jordan Keyes recognized his limitations. He was not considered the seasoned veteran that many people his age were in less complex occupations. Even at the ripe old age of thirty-nine, he was only six years removed from his "apprenticeship": residency. Schoolteachers, auto mechanics, and bankers had mastered their craft by age forty and were halfway to retirement. Jordan was just hitting his stride.

Jordan was pleased about where he was in his career, especially considering what had happened in Los Angeles. The sudden, unpleasant memory prompted him to get off his chair and move around. The patient would be ready for him momentarily, so he hurried to the sink outside OR 2 and began the thorough, methodical process of scrubbing his hands and arms.

As a young neurosurgeon, Jordan had viewed his first job in L.A. like a kid sees Disneyland for the first time. Big-city population, big-city action, big-city violence. Where could he get better trauma care education and experience in his chosen specialty of brain trauma? So Jordan had applied—and was accepted—at USC Medical School after graduating summa cum laude from Santa Clara University with a degree in microbiology. *I'll be watching from heaven, Jordan; make me proud.* His mother's words, spoken from her deathbed when he was only nine, had motivated him to excel in every academic endeavor. Prestigious USC Med School, which welcomed him gladly, had been no different.

Jordan had marched through med school with honors. Then he had excelled for seven years as a general surgery intern and neurosurgery resident at Los Angeles County General Hospital and the University of Southern California Medical Center. LAC+USC, as it was known in the medical community, admitted a staggering three-thousand-plus major trauma patients a year. After a two-year neurosurgery fellowship at New York University, Jordan had returned in triumph to LAC+USC to begin what he knew would be a long and illustrious career saving brain-damaged patients in one of the country's busiest hospitals.

He never dreamed he would be exiled in shame to a comparatively small hospital in Portland, Oregon, after only three years of living out his dream career.

Thankfully for his patients, Jordan was more at peace and focused in surgery than at any other time. Hovering over critically injured patients who were only hours if not minutes from death, he was acutely aware of his keen mind, steady hand, and uncanny skill—and equally aware that these raw talents were God given. How could any surgeon deny it?

Another skill he recognized was the ability to thoroughly detach himself from the emotions of the moment. Physical tragedies seemed to swamp patients and their families in grief, terror, and despair. Jordan could not allow the emotional hurts of others to interrupt his delicate work, so he had trained himself to block them from his focus.

More important to him, Jordan could also shut out disturbing thoughts of personal failure that nagged at him most of the time. It seemed that life and people and problems outside the OR ceased during his hours in surgery. He had often mused since arriving in Portland, *If I could do surgeries all the time, all day every day, even through the night, perhaps I would forget about—*

"We're ready, Doctor." Dr. Chen's voice was a welcome interruption from a familiar but uncomfortable train of thought.

Jordan nodded, lifting his sterilized hands from the sink and holding them high. "Let's do it," he said. Then he followed Chen through the OR doors to receive his gown and gloves.

TWO

"Good afternoon, everyone," Jordan said in a businesslike monotone. His team of assistants today was in place and ready. Dr. Chen, a scrubbed nurse, a circulating nurse, an anesthesiologist, and a surgery intern returned his greeting. Jordan was sure he had worked with all of them before, but he knew only Webster Chen on sight. He did not mind the anonymity suggested by surgical masks, caps, and gowns—in fact, he preferred it. The names and backgrounds of the people around the table were immaterial. All that mattered was their skill and diligence in the task at hand.

Jordan calmly reviewed the procedure he was about to undertake: a left temporal craniotomy and evacuation of the epidural hematoma. "We also have a right cerebral subarachnoid hemorrhage, but we'll cross that bridge only if we have to. The hematoma is immediately life-threatening, and the patient has several other injuries working against her. So let's be on our toes."

Stepping to the table, Jordan saw the patient for the first time. Trudy Aguilera was completely draped except for an opening over the left side of the head, which had been shaved for the procedure. The brilliant overhead lights seemed to bleach her Hispanic skin white. From what Jordan could see, she could have been male or female, old or young, white, Hispanic, or Asian. It did not matter to him. The patient's anonymity was even less of a problem than the namelessness of those assisting him. Only if Jordan was unsuccessful at saving this girl's life would her name become important to him.

Looking down at the freshly shaved scalp swabbed with antiseptic, all Jordan saw was a person who would die today if he did not intervene quickly. As was his custom, he received the scalpel and paused. Eyes wide open and fixed on the patient's head secured in the Mayfield holding clamp, Jordan silently prayed. He recited a prayer he had composed in his last year of med school, after he had asked the Great Physician to be his Lord: *I have no wisdom or ability apart from yours. I yield my mind to your counsel and my hands to your skill.* Then he deftly sliced open Trudy Aguilera's scalp with his number 10 blade.

As Jordan began to work, the strains of the overture from the *Messiah,* performed by the London Philharmonic, rose above the rustle of surgical gowns in motion and the clicks and beeps of life-support apparatus. He smiled to himself. Every surgeon chooses his own background music, providing the ambiance for maximum efficiency. The type of music each surgeon selected became his or her OR signature. Jordan had heard everything in the OR during his residency, from rock and roll to country to rap to alternative to show tunes—most of it played loud enough to seemingly rouse the sedated patient.

Shortly after arriving at Mercy, Jordan had brought in several CDs from his own collection—largely classical: Mozart, Handel, Schumann, Debussy. Even before he became a Christian, Jordan was most inspired by classical music, especially pieces originating in the church sanctuary. To him, this was "God's music," and he determined early in his residency it would be his signature in the OR. He was quietly pleased that someone had taken care to put one of his favorites into the OR's CD player.

In less than twenty minutes Jordan had applied hemostatic Raney clips to the scalp edges and reflected the scalp with surgical "fishhooks." By the contralto aria, "He Shall Feed His Flock Like a Shepherd," he had drilled several burr holes into the skull at the point of the fracture. It took another twenty minutes to tack up and open the dura mater, the tough fibrous membrane enveloping the brain and spinal cord.

As the films revealed, Jordan found the middle meningeal artery lacerated in two places and actively bleeding. It took nearly half an hour to evacuate the buildup of blood and repair the artery. Then he called in a radiologist for an intra-operative ultrasound. He had to make sure that no contusions or subdural hematomas had formed since the time of the original CT scan.

As the radiologist prepared the instrument, Jordan stepped back for a moment for a breather and to appreciate his work. The patient's blood pressure was already stronger, and the brain swelling was only moderate. The soprano aria "I Know that My Redeemer Liveth" pouring from the speakers momentarily transported Jordan back to Los Angeles and a pleasant but distant memory. A string quartet had played this piece, along with other selections from the *Messiah,* during the prelude to his wedding.

Jordan remembered standing in the anteroom to the sanctuary with his best man and five groomsmen—all medical students like himself. To distract himself from the mounting emotional pressure, Jordan had begun singing along with the instrumental in exaggerated, comic vibrato—until one of the ushers burst in to report that the wedding guests could hear the ruckus from the sanctuary. The groom and his amused friends barely pulled themselves together before the processional began.

That was the day Jordan had taken the captivating Della Maria DiCarlo to be his wife. They had no business getting married at that time, not with Jordan about to begin his grueling six-year residency. But they were in love, and Della was convincing. "Darling, if we wait until after your residency, you'll be well into your thirties. I know these years will be difficult, but they will be more enjoyable for both of us if we're together. Besides," she had added with a twinkle, "I want to start having kids before we're too decrepit to take care of them." And so they were married the summer Jordan graduated from USC.

They were hard years, but reasonably good years, Jordan recalled as the aria played on. A daughter, Katarina Suzanne, and a son, Jeffrey Jordan, came along much sooner than Jordan and Della had planned. The young doctor had little time for his family until he completed his neurosurgery fellowship and accepted a staff position at LAC+USC. He considered it ironic that things began to turn dark for them just when they were beginning to live like a real family.

"Ultrasound looks good, Doctor," the radiologist reported. "The contralateral side is out of our view, of course, but I find no new lesions on this side."

Jordan stepped in to verify the doctor's observation. He studied the monitor carefully while the transducer surveyed the left side of the brain. "Very good," he said after a thorough exam. "We're out of the woods, at least for the moment. Let's insert an ICP and close." The intracranial pressure monitor measured the swelling inside the skull after surgery. A high reading would indicate additional swelling, requiring anti-inflammatory drugs or another emergency surgery. "Dr. Chen, will you do the honors?"

Under Jordan's watchful supervision, Dr. Chen inserted the ICP. Jordan was aware that other surgeons left the OR while their assistants closed. He had never been able to do so. Rare though it may be, he was not about to allow an underling to botch his excellent work and thus taint his reputation in the OR. "I want you to hover over her in Recovery like a mother hen," Jordan admonished as the young resident tied the last suture. "I don't want a right temporal hematoma to ruin our good work on this side."

"I'll stay right with her through recovery, Doctor," Chen promised.

Jordan followed the patient out of the operating room as the contralto and tenor exulted "O Death, Where Is Thy Sting?" The CD would be snapped off before the chorus "But Thanks Be to God." Jordan thought these closing selections to the *Messiah* were particularly appropriate to the end of another arduous two-and-a-half hour surgery. He breathed a thankful prayer that God had used him to remove the imminent sting of a tragic death from patient Aguilera.

Jordan was met outside the OR by a nurse. "The Aguilera family is here, Doctor. Can I tell them something for you?"

Jordan shed his gloves, mask, and gown. "How many are there?"

"Three—the mother, father, and an older sister. They're in the surgery waiting room."

"What do they know?"

"We told them the patient was in surgery, that it was pretty serious, and that the doctor would talk to them soon."

He moved to the sink to wash. The nurse followed him. "How do they seem?" he said.

"The women are pretty emotional. They know the boyfriend is dead. The dad is sucking it up and trying to hold them together."

Jordan patted his hands and arms dry as he thought. "All right, I'll talk to them," he said, dismissing her with a nod.

Jordan did not hurry to the waiting room. First he dialed the hospital dictation number and described the just-completed procedure in detail. His dictation would be transcribed and transferred to Trudy Aguilera's permanent computer chart by the end of the day. Then he waited until the girl was settled in Recovery under Dr. Chen's care. Finally, he left for the waiting room.

This was a job he would rather leave to someone else. Early in his practice he realized that bedside manner was not his strong suit. He treated patients and family members the way he felt they should be treated, giving them the information they needed as clearly and concisely as possible. An inoperable brain tumor is not "a problem I need to chat with you about"; it is a terminal condition. It was only fair to be realistic and pointed with people, whether the report was good or bad. False hopes and platitudes compromised the truth.

But in a noble pursuit of honesty, a few colleagues had told him, Jordan came across as cold and blunt. Maybe so. Once, very early in his career, he had been moved to share one simple sentence of concern with a traumatized family. But before he could finish the comment, Jordan was caught up in his own emotion over a dying patient. He quickly excused himself before he broke down. He vowed to himself never again to compromise his professionalism in that way.

Jordan was a role player. He could not be neurosurgeon, chaplain, and counselor to his patients at the same time. His job was to be thorough, truthful, and as kind as possible under the circumstances. How people dealt with the information he brought them was not his responsibility.

"Dr. and Mrs. Keyes, it's leukemia—advanced and aggressive. Your son probably will not reach his eighth birthday."

The haunting words echoed in his memory as he walked, and Jordan caught his breath for an instant. *Dr. Dan Rocco did it the right way,* he reaffirmed for the umpteenth time. *Slap all the cards on the table faceup.* Bam—*this is reality. The sooner we know the facts, the sooner we can get to work on a solution.* How vital Jordan's firm grip had been at that moment in light of Della's difficulty with the startling news.

Pushing through the doors to the large OR waiting room, Jordan spied his patient's family immediately among four small clusters of people in the room. The Latino couple in their late fifties, with their thirty-something daughter, sat tentatively near the back of the room. The mother wore a simple housedress and apron under her threadbare car coat. Her husband was dressed in the stained khakis and rubber boots of a nurseryman. Jordan guessed from the younger woman's gray suit that she had left an office job to rush her parents to Portland.

The moment Jordan turned in the direction of the trio they stood, clinging to each other as if braced against a strong wind. "Mr. and Mrs. Aguilera," Jordan said, approaching them. The grim-faced father nodded stiffly. At the sound of her name, the mother covered her mouth with a handkerchief, and fresh tears spilled onto her cheeks. "I'm Dr. Keyes. We removed a blood clot from your daughter's brain, but she is still in critical condition. There may be other head injuries, so we are watching—"

"May we see Trudy?" the daughter interrupted, biting her lip to hold back the tears. She clasped a simple rosary in her hand.

"In an hour or so, when she is out of Recovery."

Mr. Aguilera cleared his throat. His Latino accent was thick. "Is my daughter's brain going to be all right?"

Brain damage. Next to death, it was feared by a victim's loved ones more than anything else. *Lay the cards on the table, be up front with the truth, and be as kind as possible,* Jordan coached himself. "With such a serious injury, brain damage is possible," he said. At his words the older woman groaned, and her knees buckled slightly. Her husband and daughter held her fast on either side. Jordan continued, "We won't know for twenty-four to forty-eight hours. We can only wait . . . and pray."

Mrs. Aguilera's audible grief turned a few heads in the waiting room. These people were dealing with their own worries and fears, waiting to hear the fate of their loved ones in surgery. But there was another man in the room who was here for another reason. And Mrs. Aguilera's visible grief attracted more than a curious glance from him.

Buster Chapman had just wheeled his custodian's cart into the waiting room to empty trash receptacles. He was about six feet six, and his husky frame filled out his neatly pressed, dark blue, cotton twill hospital uniform. When Jordan had first seen him nearly two months ago, he had assumed Buster was a football lineman working his way through college. But after only one brief encounter Jordan realized that Buster was far from college material. He soon learned that the hulking janitor had barely finished high school on a special education track. His odd-shaped, prematurely bald head and homely face prompted coldhearted staffers to refer to him as "the missing link"—mercifully, never to his face.

Now in his early thirties, burly, nearly hairless, Buster had been a janitor at Mercy since graduation. Jordan had found him to be affable, helpful, and hardworking. Another neurosurgeon had once commented to Jordan, "Buster Chapman may be the first viable candidate for a brain transplant, but he has an extra heart to give in trade."

Buster left his cart and approached Jordan and the Latino family. Lowering his head in order to catch Mrs. Aguilera's eye, he said, "Would you like a soda, ma'am?" His words came a little slowly, but the concern on his face was unmistakably clear.

Mrs. Aguilera's tear-filled eyes flitted from the doctor to Buster and back to the doctor, silently asking, "Who is this man and what does he want?" In two short months Jordan had become accustomed to the puzzled look and the unspoken question. His early impressions of Buster had been negative, judging the janitor's interruptions into the lives of patients and their families to be unprofessional and uncalled-for. But the big man was already growing on him. Buster was just a teddy bear trying to help people the only way he knew how. His childish antics still embarrassed Jordan a little, but he was harmless. Jordan had grown to appreciate Buster's interruptions because they provided enough of a distraction for him to back away from emotion-laden conversations.

"This is Buster, and he's on our hospital staff," Jordan explained evenly. "He would be happy to get you a cup of water or a can of soda."

Before the woman could respond, her eyes were drawn past him to the door leading to the surgery suite. "Dr. Keyes." The nurse's voice was urgent. Jordan turned quickly. "Recovery—stat!"

Jordan bolted for the door without a word. Behind him the terrified mother wailed, but he did not turn around. *Work your magic, Buster,* he urged silently. *I have my own work to do.*

THREE

An urgent call to the recovery room could mean only one thing: Trudy Aguilera was failing. The prospect soured his stomach. The craniotomy had been difficult but successful. Jordan had left nothing undone. But major injuries and major surgery might have taxed the patient's vital organs to the breaking point.

As he ran, the penetrating comment of his superior, Dr. Bert Waller, sprang to his consciousness. *Absorb yourself in saving head trauma patients, Dr. Keyes, and you will get along just fine at Mercy.* The words had been spoken on February 15, his first day on the job in Portland. Jordan was indebted to the man who knew about his past and welcomed him anyway. Waller's unspoken words that day rang just as clearly in Jordan's memory: *Keep your nose clean here, play by our rules, and people will forget all about L.A.*

Jordan had been abruptly dismissed from LAC+USC just before Thanksgiving, following the last in a series of clashes with the hospital's assistant director over procedure. Jordan had been in the wrong, he knew, and he had tried to make amends. But the damage was done. A dismissal, even if not for negligence or malpractice, is still a dark blot on a résumé. So only a few years into his career, Jordan had found himself without a position and with no prospects for one.

Jordan's father, a retired general practitioner, and Bert Waller had been medical school acquaintances at the University of Washington. The elder Dr. Keyes begged a favor from his old classmate, who in turn had convinced Dr. Taylor Sheffield, the hospital's director, to interview Jordan for the vacancy in Mercy's Division of Neurosurgery. Throughout the process, Waller was thoroughly professional, with no sign of favoritism. Had his curriculum vitae not been so impressive, Jordan was sure Waller and Sheffield would have sent him packing despite his father's request.

In view of his recent "difficulties" at L.A. County General, Jordan had been appointed to the position at Mercy on probationary status—which, thankfully, had not been publicized to the rest of the hospital staff. Portland Mercy Teaching Hospital was a far cry from the day-and-night thrill ride of a big-city trauma center. But Jordan thanked God for the second chance, and he had pledged to God and his benefactor, Dr. Waller, that he would make the most of the opportunity.

Jordan burst into the recovery room. "Cranial pressure is way up," Dr. Chen reported gravely. "Anesthesia is starting to wear off, but she's not responding to voice commands."

Jordan studied the monitor and the escalating pressure in Trudy Aguilera's brain. Every slight increase brought her seconds closer to a fatal uncal herniation. Jordan paused a moment longer, processing every shred of data about his patient. The solution was quickly evident. It was the right hemisphere, the relatively insignificant subarachnoid hemorrhage. "I want another CT—stat," he said at last.

"Do we have time for another CT, Doctor?" Chen reacted.

Jordan glared at his young assistant. "Get her to the scanner—now!" he snapped, angered by the resident's momentary insubordination.

"Yes, Doctor," Chen said, flushing at the rebuke. Motioning to the waiting aide and a recovery nurse, the resident began preparing the patient for a quick trip down the hall.

Jordan turned to another recovery nurse. "Make sure an OR is available," he ordered crisply. The nurse was moving before Jordan had spoken the last word.

As soon as the CT image reached the monitor, Jordan winced. His expectations were correct. Turning to Dr. Chen, reading the image over his shoulder, he said, "One hundred cc's of mannitol—stat."

As Chen hurried to comply, Jordan pulled a tiny, digital recorder from the vest pocket of his lab coat and activated it. Heading back toward the OR, he spoke into it, "Large intracerebral hematoma in the right temporal lobe, with mass effect and impending uncal herniation." Words he hoped not to deliver to the Latino family in the waiting room came to mind but remained unspoken: *While we were treating the first blood clot, a larger, more serious one developed on the other side of her brain. It shut off her respiration before we could get to it.*

Remembering the family, Jordan turned to the nurse who had hailed him in the waiting room. "Please tell the family that the patient is going back into surgery for another blood clot. I'll talk to them in a couple of hours." The nurse nodded and left.

Dr. Keyes and his hastily reassembled team were scrubbed and into gowns, gloves, and masks by the time Trudy Aguilera was rolled back into OR 2. A large dose of mannitol had been administered to slow the brain swelling. The patient was quickly sedated and subjected to her second major brain surgery in the span of two hours. The shock and trauma of such treatment to a healthy human body was significant. The risk of mortality to someone having suffered other serious injuries was enormous. No one paused to put a CD into the player. Jordan's silent prayer was reduced to a few simple words: *God, keep her alive until I get in there.*

Working with unhesitating precision, Jordan opened the right side of the patient's skull. His breathing came in short, silent gasps, as if helping the woman ration precious oxygen. Rivulets of perspiration coursed down the skin inside his shirt. The only voice in the room was that of the anesthesiologist, quietly reporting vital signs every two minutes, as ordered by Dr. Keyes. An inner voice kept Jordan riveted to his task: *I'm watching from heaven, Jordan. Make me proud.*

Jordan found what he would later report as "frank hematoma and severely contused and necrotic temporal tissue"—extensive bleeding and dead tissue. The right side of the patient's brain, which at first appeared to be the least of her head injuries, had sustained violent contact with the skull during the accident. Grateful that the patient was still alive, Jordan petitioned God to sustain her through the next step of the procedure.

Jordan explained his actions as he began. "We will evacuate; then I will do a temporal lobectomy from the upper border of the temporal gyrus superiorally, medially about a half-centimeter short of the tentorial incisura, and posteriorly five centimeters from the temporal pole." It would be entered on Trudy Aguilera's chart as a right frontotemporal craniotomy and partial anterior inferior temporal lobectomy. The surgeon's team was silent and responsive to his orders.

Three hours later Jordan tossed his gloves, mask, gown, and shoe covers into the trash and slumped down in front of the phone. His thin shirt seemed glued to his skin from perspiration. What he wouldn't have given for a trained masseur to rub out the huge knots in his upper back and neck. Instead, he arched his back and rolled his head a few times with little relief.

Retrieving the microrecorder, he listened to the diagnosis and then dictated the details of his procedure for transcription. He added the last line after blowing a long sigh. "At the conclusion of the procedure, the brain was relaxed and pulsing well. Prognosis: Patient should be alert and neurologically intact within twenty-four hours." Tapping off the machine, he dropped his head and added in a whisper, "Thank you, Lord."

Jordan glanced at his watch: 6:35 P.M. His body complained of hunger and fatigue. It had been seven hours since he had eaten a granola bar and cup of yogurt, and fourteen hours since he had slept. He had totalled just over four hours of sleep for the two nights of his on-call shift, which had officially ended thirty-five minutes ago. He would round on two other patients and wait until the Aguilera woman was stabilized in the Surgical Intensive Care Unit. Leaving the hospital by eight was a hopeful possibility. One more task awaited him here. He slipped into his lab coat, raked his thick, wavy brown hair into place with his fingers, and headed toward the surgery waiting room.

Several other relatives and friends had joined Mr. and Mrs. Aguilera in the vigil for their younger daughter. Buster Chapman, sitting at the fringe of the group, looked starkly out of place next to the smaller, darker Latinos. The janitor's shift had ended at five, but he remained on guard with the family like a loyal collie. Someone once mentioned to Jordan that Buster had been known to spend half the night in the waiting room if someone needed company. The tears were absent from the Aguileras' faces, restrained by the stifling fear of the unknown. But the small cluster of family members held its collective breath as Jordan approached them.

Jordan addressed the parents. "Your daughter needed a second brain surgery, this time on the right side, to repair more damage from the accident. She is still in critical condition, and we will be watching her closely through the night. But she appears to be out of immediate danger. You should be able to see her in about an hour."

The two Aguilera women broke down again, this time with tears of joy. Jordan backed away as the loved ones drew together to share the happy moment. Buster Chapman was right in the middle, towering over the small throng. "Oh boy, that's good news," he said, his voice quavering with emotion. "The doctor fixed the bleeding. That's very good news. Oh boy, I'm so happy for you, ma'am. I'm so happy for you, mister. Oh boy." Tears trickled from his eyes as he rather clumsily embraced the parents. To Jordan's surprise, the Aguileras received his childlike affection and returned it, their eyes also leaking tears.

Jordan glanced over his shoulder as he retreated toward the doorway. Buster was making the rounds, hugging each person, weeping, and saying repeatedly, "Oh boy, that's very good news. I'm so happy for you." Pushing through the doors, the surgeon shook his head in wonder. He didn't know which puzzled him more: why Buster did what he did, or why people let him do it to them.

"He's a piece of work, that Buster, isn't he?" Dr. Waller followed Jordan through the doors and joined him in stride.

"Good evening, Doctor," Jordan said, surprised at Waller's sudden appearance. "Yes, quite a piece of work." Then the question just on his mind found its way out. "But don't some people get a little . . . nervous . . . with him so emotional and touchy-feely?"

"Nervous? Yes, I suppose they do," Waller answered with a gentle chuckle. "Can't say I'm all that comfortable when he hugs me. Buster is just a little boy in a man's body. I think most people recognize that and let him be. Besides, most of the people in that waiting room need a teddy bear to hold onto."

"I guess," Jordan answered without conviction.

Jordan regarded the short, stocky man walking beside him. Had he not known at their first meeting that Bert Waller was head of Surgery at Mercy, Jordan would have never guessed him to be a man of such skill, responsibility, and influence. Waller looked more like a country doctor from a previous generation. His bushy mustache and brows were mixed brown and gray. Generous shocks of gray hair were carefully combed from ear to ear to cover the top of his head, which had stopped growing its own covering twenty years earlier. The shirts, ties, and sport jackets Jordan had seen him wear would likely be back in style again someday. And Waller's brown wing tips from the sixties, Jordan had heard, probably held the world record for number of times resoled.

Dr. Bertram Waller's looks were deceiving, Jordan knew. He had read a little about his father's onetime friend before the move. The unassuming Waller held the most prestigious position in a hospital renowned in three Northwest states for its trauma care. A lifelong bachelor, Waller was married to medicine. Where other physicians did well to stay up with the journals and conferences in their field, Waller never stopped learning. Even after earning his Ph.D. back in the '70s, the sixty-seven-year-old kept taking graduate courses on topics of all descriptions: archaeology, paleontology, international economics, and all fields of medicine.

Among the various degrees and honors framed and mounted in Waller's office was a "membership in good standing" certificate from what Jordan knew was a very liberal church denomination. Waller did not attend church, however, and had not displayed evidence of a vital Christian faith. Jordan was somewhat chagrined that his problem in L.A. was a rickety platform for sharing his own faith with his boss.

Waller said, "How did it go with your last patient, the poor girl on the motorcycle?"

"Good, good," Jordan said, inflating his response with confidence. "That's her family back there with Buster." He summarized in two long sentences the procedures and the prognosis for Trudy Aguilera.

"I knew you would fit in just fine, Jordan," Waller said with a hint of fatherly pride.

The words could not have been more timely. "Thank you, Doctor," Jordan said quietly.

Waller stopped before turning off the main hallway,

touching Jordan's shoulder to make him stop too. "Now don't forget the clambake tonight. My place at eight. Do you need directions?"

Jordan groaned inside. He *had* forgotten, probably on purpose. He was dog tired, and he wasn't much for parties, especially those in his honor. Dr. Waller had scheduled the reception to welcome several new members of the surgical staff. "You e-mailed us a map as I recall," he answered weakly. "Council Crest Drive?"

"That's it. Just up the hill from your apartment in Northwest."

"I'll see you at eight then," Jordan assured him.

"Any chance we will meet your wife and daughter tonight?"

Jordan shook his head. "No, they're still in L.A."

"I wish they were with you, Doctor."

Jordan agreed with a nod. "Soon, I hope. Della has to close her business, and Katy is in school. They may not move until the end of the school year."

"That's over a month away," Waller lamented for Jordan's sake.

"I'll be looking at some homes tomorrow. If I find something special, maybe I can get them up here sooner."

Waller gave Jordan a final pat on the shoulder. "Let's hope so. You'll be an even better doctor when your family is here." Then he disappeared into an office, leaving Jordan standing in the hall.

Jordan took his words to heart. He would do anything in his power to become a better doctor.

FOUR

It was 7:45 when Jordan hurried into his small apartment to shower and dress for the reception. He knew he would be late, but he did not want to leave the hospital until Trudy Aguilera was moved from Recovery to SICU. The young woman had other injuries that would need attention in a day or two, but Jordan was assured she would be neurologically intact. The two emergency craniotomies had been successful.

Jordan was back in the car and on his way in twenty-five minutes. Not spending much time at home was no great loss to him. He hated living alone, even though he was rarely in the apartment except to sleep and shower. His long hours at Mercy were nothing new. In twelve years of marriage, Jordan had spent the majority of his evenings in a hospital treating patients. But when it was time to go home, he went home to someone. Even if Della and Katy were asleep when he left in the early morning and when he returned late at night, Jordan was content to know he was not alone.

It was important to him that his wife and daughter join him in Portland as soon as possible. He only wished Della was more excited about moving north. He understood how difficult it was for her to leave Los Angeles, her business, and her circle of friends. That's why he would spend several hours tomorrow looking at homes with a local Realtor. Della might be more amenable to the transition if he was able to find her a dream house. At least that was his hope.

Guiding his leased Lexus through the hillside streets of posh, vintage Northwest homes, Jordan came up with several reasons he would rather skip the reception. Parties in general were a waste of time, and receptions were the worst kind because they seemed to lack any structure at all. In Jordan's mind, free food and beverages were poor compensation for the inane small talk he had to endure with people he knew only on a professional level.

A reception to welcome new surgical staff seemed especially pointless. Nearly half the staff, including many of the new hires, were on duty at the hospital tonight—or at least that would be the excuse for skipping the party. Jordan might have used that excuse himself had he not been so indebted to his host and boss, Bert Waller. The fact that Della was not here to attend with him was no excuse either, since physicians were notorious for socializing without their spouse. No matter how Jordan looked at it, tonight's event was a command performance for him.

Jordan was also not looking forward to being a featured newcomer tonight. The stated purpose of the gathering notwithstanding, partygoers tend to seek out familiar faces in these settings. Several new colleagues would grab Jordan by the hand and say a hearty "Welcome aboard." Then they would spend the rest of the evening clustered with their buddies, leaving him alone by the onion dip to fend for himself.

He was also uncomfortable because of the absence of Dr. Will Kopke from tonight's festivities. Kopke had been Jordan's predecessor in the Neurosurgery Division, the brain trauma specialist Jordan was hired to replace. An avid outdoorsman, Kopke had been killed in a skiing accident on Mount Hood just before Christmas. Jordan disliked the idea of being on display tonight as the "new kid on the block," and he winced at the prospect of being compared to Kopke, a popular member of the neurosurgery team. Kopke no doubt left a legacy of being a party animal who kept everybody in stitches at Waller's clambakes, Jordan surmised wryly.

Jordan straightened his tie and put on a happy face as he rang the doorbell of his boss's large, opulent Council Crest Drive home. Dr. Waller shepherded him through a number of introductions, mentioning to a few people, "Keyes is doing a great job for us. We're pleased to have him." Jordan had seen many of these people around the hospital during the past two months. He had even worked with a few of them in surgery. Everyone seemed cordial and pleased to welcome Jordan as a colleague. And thankfully no one said, "Oh, you're the guy who took Will Kopke's place."

Having filled a plate with a variety of delectable finger foods, Jordan was herded by Dr. Waller into a huddle of guests. Jordan knew two of them fairly well. Dr. Taylor Sheffield, well into his seventies, was the director of the hospital. An orthopedic surgeon in his younger days, Sheffield moved into administration when arthritis encroached on his dexterity. Dr. Sheffield had been a vital cog in the machinery that had brought Jordan to Portland.

Dr. Philip Ettinger, a tall, lean, and very proper Ivy Leaguer of fifty-two, was the cerebrovascular surgery specialist in the Neurosurgery Division. Philip had been especially helpful at the hospital during Jordan's first weeks. The doctor with the rich Boston accent always had a ready answer for Jordan's who, what, when, and where questions, even when they were asked for the second or third time.

"You've been with us almost a month now, haven't you, Keyes?" Dr. Sheffield said, jiggling the ice in a glass of ginger ale.

"Almost two months, actually," Jordan replied after a bite of cheese canapé. "I started February 15."

"And how do you find our weather, Jordan?" The question came from Mark Sutherland, the only African-American in the cluster and in the room. Jordan had seen him a few times around the neurosciences building. Sutherland was a spinal cord specialist, he recalled.

Jordan had been warned that Oregonians didn't take kindly to Californians ragging on their rainy winter weather. The warnings were mostly tongue-in-cheek, he assessed, but he decided not to test the point. "I've been so busy I haven't even noticed the weather."

"We only have two weather reports here in Portland, you know," Sheffield inserted with a mischievous grin. "They say if you can't see Mount Hood, it's raining. If you *can* see it, it's *going* to rain." The old gentleman laughed heartily at his own joke, and the others in the circle joined in, including Jordan, who had heard the quip twice before.

Dr. Waller stuck his head into the circle. "Good, you're getting acquainted with Dr. Keyes. Be sure and tell them about your family, Jordan." Then the host scurried on to another group.

"Does anyone really want to hear about my family?" Jordan shrugged, a little embarrassed at being put on the spot.

"Yes, we want to hear about them," said the only woman in the huddle. "I'm Maggie, by the way," she said, extending her hand. "I'm a nurse in SICU. And this is my husband, Sam." Jordan shook hands with the couple.

Thirty-something, bleached-blonde Maggie Rusch had been at Mercy only a month longer than Jordan. She had cared for a few of Jordan's patients, but he had spoken to her only briefly at the hospital. Maggie explained that Sam, who looked to be ten years her senior, ran his own small remodeling and construction business.

"Well, I've been married to Della about twelve years," Jordan said, intent on sharing the basics and being done with it. "We have a daughter, Katarina—we call her Katy—who will turn eleven next week. That's about it."

"Is your wife a career person?" Maggie asked without seeming to probe. Dr. Sheffield quietly backed out of the circle and headed for a ginger ale refill. But Maggie, Sam, and four doctors—Sutherland, Ettinger, a pediatric orthopedic surgeon named Sid Kaplan, and a trauma surgeon named Otto Gebhardt—stayed to listen to the obligatory family vitae.

Jordan explained with a tinge of pride that Della was resurrecting her home-decorating business after being a stay-at-home mom for nearly eight years. During the brief story he inadvertently referred to their "kids."

"You have more than one child, then," Maggie deduced aloud. Then she laughed and said, "Don't hold out on us, Jordy. There are no secrets among the surgery staff—right, gentlemen?" The doctors played along. Sam nodded and smiled, obviously enthralled with his wife's humor.

"We had a son, but he died two years ago," Jordan said evenly.

After three long seconds of silence, Maggie spoke. "Jordy, I'm so sorry," she said contritely. "Please forgive my insensitivity."

"It's all right, really," Jordan said.

"How old was your son?" Sam put in, his tone respectful and inoffensive.

"J. J. was eight when he died."

"J. J.?" Sam said.

"Jeffrey Jordan—we called him J. J."

"Was there an accident?" Maggie continued, seeming genuinely interested. Sam's expression mirrored her concern.

"Leukemia."

"That had to be difficult for you," Ettinger put in sympathetically.

Jordan nodded. But before they could ask another question about his son, Jordan said, "We're still trying to sell our home in West L.A. I hope to have Della and Katy up here by June at the latest."

"June—I believe that's when we get to see Mount Hood again," Kaplan quipped, provoking another laugh to lift the momentarily somber mood. It was the segue everyone seemed to be waiting for. The doctors drifted away to other conversations. Sam and Maggie restated their cordial welcome, then excused themselves. They said their good-byes and left the party arm in arm, leaving Jordan with a pang of loneliness for his wife.

Dr. Waller brought a few other people to meet him, but the conversations degenerated into the small talk Jordan despised. Having stayed an hour, Jordan felt he had fulfilled his social obligation. He cordially thanked his host and began working his way toward the door.

Stepping outside, Jordan sucked a long breath of cool, damp air. Relieved at surviving the social ordeal, Jordan hurried to his car before anyone came after him. Driving down the hill he realized he had a phone call to make. He hoped he would fare as well in this conversation as he had at the party.

FIVE

Jordan dialed his cell phone as he drove to the apartment.

"Hello," came the familiar voice in the receiver.

"Hi, Dell. How are you?"

"Hello, Jordan. I'm fine. How are you?" Jordan could not read Della's mood from her tone of voice, and her stock response told him nothing.

"Good. Doing fine. Sorry I haven't called for a couple of days."

"I know. You're really busy," Della said, stealing his standard line.

"Yeah, it's been a madhouse around here." He mentioned a few of his recent cases, including Trudy Aguilera. "We're still without a permanent department head, so everyone in Neurosurgery pulls extra duty."

"That's what you have been saying."

Silence. As usual, keeping the conversation alive seemed to fall in Jordan's court. "I just left Dr. Waller's place. He had a reception for all the new people in Surgery. Lot of nice people."

"Mm."

Reflecting on his discomfort at being on display and feeling pangs of loneliness during the party, Jordan was surprised by words that begged for expression: *I wish you were here; I miss you.* But he fought off the sudden urge. After an awkward pause, he said, "You would have enjoyed it."

Jordan pulled into the parking lot of his small apartment complex, navigated the Lexus into a covered parking space, and turned off the engine. "I thought you'd like to know that I have an appointment with a Realtor tomorrow."

"They actually gave you a day off?" Della said, seeming more animated.

"Well, I probably can't take the whole day off," he explained, "but I have blocked out the morning to look at several homes."

"Really?" Della's mild amazement seemed more provoked by the hours off Jordan had arranged than by how he intended to spend them.

He decided to take advantage of the interest she displayed. "Three of the homes sound just like you, Dell. They're all suburban, all on the warmer west side, but close to the city and the hospital." He dropped his head back to the headrest and rubbed his tired eyes as he tried to recapture the glowing descriptions from the Realtor. "The one in Lake Oswego has lots of glass in the living area and a view of the lake. Huge trees on the property. Big stone fireplace. There's another one in an area called Skyline. Nice view of the west side. Big—nearly four thousand square feet. Great for entertaining. The last one is in West Hills. It's smaller and older than the others, but the Realtor says it has a spectacular view of downtown and the Willamette River. And if we don't like these, she has plenty more."

After a silent moment, Della said, "I'm sure you'll find something. Whatever you think is best."

"But what sounds good to you, Dell? I want you to have something you really like—a dream house."

He heard a long sigh. "It doesn't matter to me, Jordan. They all sound fine. Whatever you decide is OK with me. I . . . I just don't want to think about it right now."

This time the long sigh was on Jordan's end. Finally he said, "OK, I'll check them out tomorrow. They may not look as great as the lady makes them sound. I'll let you know what I find out. Maybe I can bring some pictures next weekend."

"Sure, fine," Della said.

Jordan asked if the real estate agent had shown their west L.A. home in the last few days. Della said no. He questioned her about the leaky faucet—had she replaced the washer; the lawn—had the neighbor spread the weed and feed for her; the screen doors—had she sprayed WD-40 in the hinges to stop them from squeaking. Della provided the information, then mentioned two other maintenance-related issues he needed to know about. Jordan explained how he wanted her to deal with them.

Then she said, "Katy wants to talk to you before you hang up." The phone changed hands.

"Hi, Dad."

"How are you doing, Katy?" Jordan said, a smile suddenly in his voice.

"You're still coming home for my birthday party, aren't you?" she pressed. She had asked the question at least once a week when they talked on the phone.

"Yes, one week from today. I have my airline tickets. I'll be there."

"And we're still going to Catalina on Sunday—the three of us?"

Jordan smiled at her insistence. "Absolutely. We'll have a great weekend."

Katy babbled on excitedly about her upcoming party—the friends she had invited, the games they would play, the ice-cream pies she would help her mother make. Then she reminded her father of several items on her birthday gift list. Jordan made a mental note of them.

"Are we really going to Catalina?" Katy asked again. "And are we all going, even you, Daddy?"

Jordan winced at her petition for assurance. Katy was not mature enough to disguise her apprehension. More than presents or a party, Jordan knew, his daughter was looking forward to being with him. He sensed that she was suffering not only from the physical distance but the emotional distance of living away from her father.

"Yes, Katy, I'm going to Catalina with you," he insisted. "You can put it in the bank."

Katy cooed her delight, then said good-bye and turned the phone back to her mother.

"I'm really ready to be home for a couple of days," Jordan said. "I miss you." It had been over a month since he flew down for a twenty-four-hour visit.

"It will be nice to have you here, Jordan."

He waited to see if she had anything else to say. Finally he said, "I'll call you tomorrow night and tell you about the houses."

"We'll be at the Drummonds for a potluck at six—you know, our church care group."

"Right, I'll wait till after nine to call."

"OK."

"I love you, Della."

"Take care, Jordan."

He tapped off the phone and sat for several minutes in the semidarkness of the carport. The sound of rainwater dripping from the flat roof to the pavement surrounded him.

Della's lack of enthusiasm was obvious every time Jordan talked to her. He knew she did not want to leave L.A. for Portland. It was not his first choice either. But he was lucky to have a job and an opportunity to get his career back on track. Why couldn't she see that? After a few years at Mercy he would be established. He had superior skills—even in his darkest days in L.A., no one had ever denied that. His success in Portland would cause everyone—even him—to forget the humiliating circumstances of his dismissal from LAC+USC. Perhaps then he could write his own ticket at the hospital of his choice, even back in L.A. And no matter where they ended up, Jordan would be able to provide for his wife and daughter and bring them the happiness they deserved.

But until then, he had to make it in Portland. And that meant Della had to make it in Portland. If she would only try harder, the transition neither of them wanted would go more smoothly, and the future they both yearned for could be theirs. Yet she seemed so resistant, even angry.

The thought of going up to his tiny, silent apartment left Jordan cold. So he fired up the engine and left the complex, turning in the direction of Mercy Hospital.

It was almost ten when he walked into Trudy Aguilera's softly lit room in Surgical Intensive Care. He had reviewed her chart on the computer at the nurse's station outside. All the numbers were positive. She was going to make it and resume a fairly normal life. The duty nurse had informed him that the patient's family had left the hospital less than thirty minutes ago. Trudy had awakened briefly to her mother's voice at least once during the evening, prompting fresh tears of joy from the Aguileras.

Jordan stood at the foot of the bed and studied the still form. The patient's face—what he could see of it beneath the bandages encircling her head like a turban—was swollen and discolored from the crash. She would likely need plastic surgery to repair the side that had been scraped raw from skidding across the pavement. An orthopedic surgeon would repair the broken bones in a day or two, when her system could withstand the trauma of another surgery.

Jordan marveled again at both the frailty and resilience of the human body. This young woman had teetered on the precipice of eternity for nearly four hours. Apart from swift medical intervention at the accident scene, in the Emergency Room, and in the Operating Room, the Aguilera family would be making funeral plans tonight. Instead, Ms. Aguilera would be out of the hospital in seven or eight days and back to a fairly normal life in a couple of months.

Jordan realized that his role in the process was comparatively small. The craniotomies, the evacuation of two hematomas, and the lobectomy merely removed the imminent danger. From this point on, Trudy Aguilera's body assumed the primary role of repairing itself. Tissue temporarily sutured together would permanently bond without external intervention. Brain function temporarily dulled by the trauma would be restored. As miraculous as the surgeon's skill appeared to the common observer, Jordan knew that he was only an instrument in the Master Engineer's blueprint for human healing.

Jordan moved to the side of the bed to inspect the site of the ICP. He gently tugged at the head bandages and decided that the next dressing should not be as tight. He lifted the patient's wrist to check the pulse. She stirred and moaned softly. Puffy eyelids parted to slits, revealing dull, dark brown eyes trying to focus on the figure standing beside the bed.

The heavily sedated patient would not remember his visit, but Jordan spoke to her anyway. "Ms. Aguilera, I'm Dr. Keyes. The surgery went very well. You need a lot of rest, but you're going to be fine." The dark eyes disappeared behind heavy lids without a glimmer of recognition. Noticing the rosary and crucifix pinned to the sheet near her head, Jordan added, "God bless you—*Dios te bendiga.*"

Returning to the nurse's station, Jordan opened the patient's chart on the computer and entered a note about the bandages. A nurse stepped to his side. "I almost forgot," she said, presenting an envelope. "The woman's parents left this for you."

Jordan turned over the envelope and smiled at the misspelled inscription: Doctor Kees. He pulled out a greeting card with a glitter-strewn flower print on the front. Skipping the four lines of rhyming sentiment printed inside, his eyes fell to a handwritten note. "Dear Doctor, Thank you, thank you for saving our Trudy. We are so happy. God bless you. Roberto and Esther Aguilera."

The exhaustion overtaking him suddenly seemed worthwhile. This was payment enough for the grueling years of study, the tens of thousands of dollars of expense, the punishing schedule, the relentless pressure of split-second, life-and-death decisions. He read the message again, wishing somehow his mother could read it. This was what she had seen in him during their eight brief years together. This was what she had urged him toward with her dying breath.

This is for you, Mom, Jordan thought. Then he went home.

SIX

It was all Jordan could do to keep from canceling his 9:00 A.M. appointment with the Realtor and going to work. Up and dressed for the day by 6:30, he spent two hours reviewing patient charts and sending orders via modem on his laptop. He had promised to dismiss two surgery patients around noon if they were eating and voiding successfully. Four others under his care needed continuing attention, especially Trudy Aguilera, Jordan's only patient in SICU today.

According to the chart, Ms. Aguilera fared well through the night. There was no sign of infection, and her vitals were holding well. By early afternoon she should be fairly alert and neurologically intact. Jordan would be there to make sure of it.

The Realtor, an ebullient woman in her early sixties, seemed a little put out that her client would not ride with her during their tour of Portland homes. But by having his car with him, Jordan could immediately race to the hospital if paged. So the physician in his white Lexus tagged after Virginia, the agent, in her silver Lexus, who kept a close eye on her client in the rearview mirror.

Jordan would not allow himself to discount the importance of this task. The size, style, and location of a home meant little to him, being admittedly task focused to a fault. But finding the right home could make all the difference in

Della's willingness to make the transition from Los Angeles to Portland. Until she grasped the importance of his position at Mercy Hospital to his career and their future, he would captivate her with the home of her dreams.

Virginia marched Jordan through seven homes in less than three hours. Only two of them were worthy of photographing with the 35 mm point-and-shoot camera he had purchased for the occasion. And only one deserved a return visit and another roll of pictures. The Lake Oswego house combined the features he knew Della would most appreciate: beautifully landscaped lot on a small lake, spacious great room with stone fireplace, plenty of windows and skylights, three bedrooms, a den and an office for her decorating business, and a great school district for Katy. He thanked Virginia for her time and said he would think about an offer.

Jordan arrived at the hospital shortly after noon. He went straight to the room of the first patient he hoped to release. The burly, middle-aged steelworker, from whom Jordan had removed a blood clot after a work injury, sat on the edge of his bed, dressed and ready to go. Jordan was glad the big man checked out all right; he thought he might have a fight on his hands if he had to keep the steelworker another day. He also quickly examined and released a second patient in a nearby room. Jordan left the fourth floor for the Surgical Intensive Care Unit.

Maggie Rusch was on duty at the nurse's station when he arrived. Jordan nodded a greeting, and she returned a wave. Then he went straight to the monitors for Trudy Aguilera's room. They were all switched off. Puzzled, he glanced across the hallway to room 6. Unable to believe what he saw, he crossed the hall in several quick strides and entered the room. All personal effects had been removed. The bed was neatly made. Trudy Aguilera was gone.

The only explanation was that Trudy had been moved to another SICU room for some reason. No one would dare schedule her for orthopedic surgery or transfer her upstairs without Jordan's approval. Besides, Ms. Aguilera would not be ready to leave SICU for at least two days. He made a hasty visual check of the other eleven rooms in the unit. Trudy Aguilera was in none of them.

"Did someone move this patient?" Jordan all but demanded of Maggie Rusch. He was standing in front of the vacant room 6 again.

The nurse studied him curiously. "Yes, about an hour ago," she answered, sounding as if he should have known.

"She is *my* patient," he said indignantly, his voice a little loud for the ICU. "Where did she go, and who authorized it?"

Maggie came around the counter to speak more privately. "They took her to the basement, Doctor, over an hour ago," she said, wondering why he needed to ask. "To the morgue."

Jordan fell back a step. "The morgue?" The words caught in his throat.

Maggie read the shock in his face. "Nobody paged you about the death?" she asked in disbelief.

"When did she die? What was the cause?" he demanded, ignoring her question.

"Heart monitor went off at just before ten. We were in there doing CPR in seconds but—"

"You and who else?" he interrupted.

"Dr. Sutherland was in there—he was seeing a patient in 8 when the alarm sounded. Dr. Amundson was there too. They tried the paddles, even a straight shot of epinephrine, but nothing. Dr. Sutherland called it at about ten after."

Jordan turned away and stared at the ceiling, hands on hips, barely breathing. His gut suddenly ached, and it seemed like a set of giant pincers had him by the back of his neck. "It shouldn't have happened," he said to no one, stunned. "She was fine. She was going to make it. Heart failure? I can't believe this."

"I'm very sorry, Doctor," Maggie said from behind him. "I assumed you had been told."

Jordan spun around. "Where is Sutherland?" he snapped with a give-me-answers-not-apologies tone.

Maggie hunched her shoulders. "I haven't seen him in an hour or more," she said, clearly not taking his attitude personally. "I'd try Surgery."

Jordan whirled and took three large strides toward the hallway before Maggie snagged him with, "Doctor, wait."

He turned with a stern look. "Yes?"

Maggie approached him, again to speak more privately. "Don't you want to see the family?"

Maggie's question sobered Jordan. He was focused on solving the problem, righting the wrong. He had forgotten that a grieving family was likely still on the premises. "Yes, you're right," he said, slightly chagrined. "Where are they?"

"I think they're still in the chapel."

Jordan nodded. "Thank you," he said, hoping she knew he was referring to more than the information she had provided.

"No problem, Doctor." Her smile revealed that she knew.

As much as he disliked dealing with his patients' families—especially after a death—Jordan knew he had to express his condolences and answer their questions to the best of his knowledge. It was proper protocol. It was right. But it just was not his strength.

He found Roberto and Esther Aguilera in the small chapel across the hall from the surgery waiting room. The couple was huddled together on a kneeling bench in the second row of pews, facing a large, ornate carving of Jesus on the cross. The room was quiet except for an occasional sniffle. Jordan was relieved to have missed the first wave of mourning. He disliked outpourings of grief, especially those that accompanied a sudden death.

A family member who saw Jordan enter approached the praying couple and whispered a message. The couple rose, crossed themselves, and shuffled to the rear of the tiny sanctuary.

Jordan greeted them with an outstretched hand, hoping to

avoid an emotional scene by keeping the family at arm's length. "I'm very sorry about your daughter," he said. "I just arrived at the hospital and found out."

Roberto took Jordan's hand and held it warmly while his other arm remained wrapped tenderly around his wife. "This is a hard thing to us, Doctor," he said. There was great sadness in his voice, but no blame.

"It was a great shock to all of us," Jordan said. "Her recovery was proceeding so well."

Esther Aguilera gazed at him, her face drawn with grief. "Why did my Trudy die? Was it the marijuana? I told her not to smoke marijuana."

"No, it wasn't the marijuana," Jordan assured. The real answer sprang to the front of Jordan's mind. *She died because she experienced a violent impact greater than her body was created to sustain. Your daughter should never have climbed on the back of that suicide bike.* But he provided the standard, more diplomatic response, one he was not sure he fully believed himself: "Her severe injuries were more than her system could handle. Her heart just gave out. I'm very sorry we could not save her." Jordan intended to know the exact cause of death after the autopsy. Depending on what he found, he might offer the Aguileras a more detailed explanation later.

Having performed his official duty, Jordan eased toward the door. The couple and their supportive loved ones followed him, each in turn shaking his hand and thanking him for his effort. But when the small group reached the hallway, Jordan spied his way of escape. Buster Chapman was coming down the hall with his large cart of custodial supplies.

Seeing the Aguilera family, the affable janitor could not resist inquiring about their daughter. When one of the relatives quietly informed him that Trudy had died, the big man clasped a hand to his mouth, and his eyes filled with tears. The scene to follow was one Jordan was becoming accustomed to, even though he was personally uncomfortable with it. Turning to Esther Aguilera, Buster said in a quavering voice, "Oh, you poor lady, oh, you poor, poor lady." Then Buster enveloped the small woman in his long arms and wept with her. The others joined in the fresh wave of mourning.

With the big teddy bear on the scene, Jordan was free to walk away. He went directly to his small office on the sixth floor of the neurosciences building, closed the door, and sank into the chair behind his desk. On average, he spent no more than ten minutes a day here. While in the hospital, he was consumed with surgery, rounds, mentoring a cadre of medical students under his care, and updating records. He could access his office computer and voice mail from anywhere in the hospital and from the apartment. So he only came to this private cubbyhole when he needed to disappear for a few minutes and collect his thoughts.

This was such a time. The unexpected loss of Trudy Aguilera weighed heavily on him. He had lost patients before—all surgeons do. Sometimes, even great skill and timely intervention cannot undo the havoc wreaked by horrendous injury or advanced disease. But this patient was different. Except for two patients who died during surgery from injuries too severe to repair, Trudy Aguilera was Jordan's first loss at Mercy Hospital. Although his head knew that he had done his best to save her, that indeed she would have died much sooner apart from his skillful intervention, his gut sensed that he had failed.

The last thing Jordan needed at this stage of his life was another failure. His expulsion from LAC+USC five months earlier was painfully fresh in his memory. It had not been an issue of practice or ethics. Jordan had not screwed up a surgery and caused a patient to die, nor had he violated physician-patient trust in any way. His dismissal might have been easier to take if he had. Rather they let him go for conduct detrimental to the integrity of the staff. *That's what they called it,* he mused bitterly. *How was I supposed to respond to policies and procedures left over from the Stone Age—perpetuate them in the name of staff unity? What was I supposed to do about colleagues whose calcified thinking may someday cost the lives of patients—stick my head in the sand and fail to confront them?*

Jordan had grown to admit he was not as tactful as he might be in addressing problems and dealing with people. Perhaps he resembled at times the caricature of the neurosurgeon that the rest of the medical community accepted as reality: independent, stubborn, short fused, abrasive, opinionated, task oriented, socially challenged. He may have been too picky, too insensitive, too outspoken to his superiors in Los Angeles. But somebody had to shake them up and wake them up. Unfortunately for Jordan, he had pushed the assistant director too far, and the man had tossed him out on his ear. Ms. Aguilera's death brought the foul smell of that failure to his nostrils again.

Jordan's most recent loss also kicked up another memory of failure, and the unbidden image made him so uncomfortable he had to stand. His sweet J. J.—at six years of age, still a little guy, vulnerable, defenseless—had been smitten with leukemia. Jordan recalled his son's cherubic optimism as he and Della had explained his sickness to him. "I'm lucky you're a doctor, Dad," J. J. had chirped with a proud grin. His meaning was painfully clear. A kid who has a fireman for a father doesn't worry about a fire at home because his dad can fix it. My dad is a doctor, so he will be able to fix the leukemia.

But J. J.'s dad couldn't fix it. How defeating that the son of someone proficient in the healing arts should be taken by such a dreaded, despised enemy. The children of carpenters and computer technicians and stockbrokers contracted leukemia—and physicians ministered to them and sometimes healed them. If anyone should catch a break on such a hideous disease, it should be one who knows most how to attack it and defeat it. But for all his skill and resources in the medical field, Jordan could not prevent the leukemia from taking the life of his only son.

Jordan had not failed for lack of trying. Not only had he exhausted the resources of countless American specialists in the field of pediatric oncology, he had also probed the hazy limits of cures thought to be unconventional and even quackish by some of Jordan's colleagues. He and Della had dragged poor J. J. to Mexico and Switzerland and South Africa in search of either a pharmaceutical cure or a prayer of healing. How he had cried out to God for clues, ideas, leads, direction. "Where shall I take him? Whom shall I consult?" Jordan had petitioned God. "Someone on your beautiful earth knows the secret that will save J. J.'s life. Who is that person? Where is that clinic? Where is that chemist? Please, Great Physician, tell me what I need to know before we lose the son you gave us."

Answers came in the form of advice from relatives and fellow church members and referrals from colleagues—some of them shared in confidence due to their questionable nature. And Jordan had followed every lead with the same dogged tenacity that made him an excellent surgeon. He locked onto every possibility like a missile, boring in on it until it exploded in his face, as they all eventually did. But on every occasion, before the smoke had cleared, Jordan mustered his hopes and selected a new approach, only to be disappointed again and again.

Bricklayers and corporate vice presidents might see their children cured of leukemia, but for all their effort, expense, and prayers, Dr. and Mrs. Jordan Keyes were granted only a brief remission before the fiendish disease devoured their child a scant two years after he was diagnosed. No matter what anyone said, Jordan felt like he had failed his son.

Part of what gnawed at Jordan every time he sensed his failure was the dark suspicion that God had answered his prayers for guidance, and he had somehow missed the answer. Had he taken one more step, spent another thousand dollars, solicited one more lead, he might have found the obscure pathway out of J. J.'s deadly maze. But that last step, in reality the only step that really counted, had eluded him.

Losing J. J. had fueled in Jordan a determination that bordered on obsession. He may have failed to save his son, but he would save others. How many lifesaving surgeries had he performed in the twenty-two months since they laid Jeffrey Jordan's small casket in the ground? Scores, perhaps hundreds. But it only took one failure to sweep them all away and leave Jordan staring into the plaintive face of his little boy. And that one failure was lying cold and still in the hospital basement right now.

SEVEN

A soft rap on the door interrupted Jordan's thoughts. Through the opaque glass, he could tell that it was a woman in hospital garb. Having never turned on the overhead light, Jordan stood motionlessly in the semidarkness, hoping she would eventually go away. He didn't have the time or the inclination to receive guests.

After several seconds, the visitor knocked again, just a little louder. When Jordan saw an arm reach out to try the handle to his unlocked office door, he reluctantly conceded. "Just a second," he called, stepping toward the door. If he could not prevent the female visitor from opening his door, he could at least block her from coming in.

He pulled the door open to find Maggie Rusch holding two medium drink cups, complete with lids and straws, from the hospital cafeteria. "Thought you could use something cold to drink," she said.

Jordan stared at her, not sure what she meant. "Excuse me?" he said, begging an explanation.

"I said I brought you something cold to drink. You looked a little down about your patient's dying. I thought you might like a Pepsi. It always perks me up."

Jordan glanced at the drink cups, then back at Maggie. She wanted to come inside, it was clear. Otherwise, she would have held out a cup to him so she could be on her way. Maybe she was waiting for a response first. "Thanks," he said.

"May I come in for a minute, Doctor?" Maggie said. "I'm on my lunch break."

"Well, I don't get a lunch break, and I'm really—"

"Just for a sec, I promise."

Jordan knew that he intimidated most nurses, male or female. It was not intentional. His penchant for precision and promptness cast him as a tyrant at times. But Maggie's brashness caused Jordan to guess she might have intimidated a few doctors during her career. It was a quality he would never tolerate in patient care, where a nurse's immediate, unquestioning compliance was vital. But outside the hospital he had always appreciated women who did not let men push them around. He hoped for the marriage's sake that her husband, Sam, held the same appreciation.

Jordan opened the door and stepped back. "OK, just for a sec."

Maggie swept into the small office, handing a cup to Jordan as she passed him. She sat in a chair in front of the desk and took a long pull on her drink. Jordan left the door half open and flipped on the overhead light. He was not about to enclose himself in a room with a woman he barely knew, married or not, and open himself to a sexual harassment claim. More important, he had learned early in his Christian journey to avoid temptation and the appearance of evil by keeping a door open and a desk between him and the women he encountered in his practice.

Jordan moved behind the desk but remained standing, emphasizing nonverbally that he only had "a sec" for the SICU nurse.

Maggie looked up at him with a serious expression. "Are you OK, Jordy?"

Jordan regarded the woman across the desk. Maggie had a pretty face, and even the unflattering hospital uniform could not hide an impressive figure. But Maggie was no cheerleader or homecoming queen. Jordan detected a rough edge to her appearance. Her blonde hair, combed back into a short ponytail, was a few days past needing a color treatment. A modicum of makeup did not cover all the shadows around her brown eyes. And the determined set to her jaw suggested that she had faced a few substantial obstacles in her life. No wonder she was bold enough to barge into his office and call him Jordy to his face. Only Jordan's oldest aunts and uncles called him Jordy anymore, a nickname he purposely shed when he left high school. This was not the time to argue the point with Maggie.

"What do you mean, 'OK'?"

"You know, your patient died and nobody paged you," she said. "I just want to know if you're OK with it. That's all I mean."

"It's not the first time a patient died on me, you know."

"Yes, I know. Won't be the last time either. But you looked pretty ticked about it. You're OK, right?"

Jordan thought about it. "OK" was rather nebulous, so he could truthfully agree to it if it expedited Maggie's visit. "Yes, I'm OK with it."

Maggie flashed a crooked little smile. "You might feel even better if you drank some of your Pepsi," she said, motioning to the untouched cup on his desk.

A little sheepish that he had ignored her gift, Jordan lifted the cup and took a long drink. She was right. The icy jolt of sugar and caffeine immediately refreshed him. "Thanks," he said, returning the cup to the desk. "That hits the spot, as they say."

Maggie pointed to a hardback edition of the Bible standing in a row of books on Jordan's desk. "I heard that you are a Christian."

"That's right, I am."

"How long?"

She surprised Jordan with her directness. "Almost fourteen years. I came to Christ in a Bible study group at USC during med school. My wife, Della, whom I was dating at the time, invited me to attend." Unsure of Maggie's intentions, it seemed appropriate to Jordan to bring Della into the conversation.

Maggie smiled broadly. "That's wonderful. I found the Lord just three years ago. A church near my home advertised a divorce recovery group on their reader board, so I signed up. I found out that I not only needed Christ to survive my divorce, I needed him to survive life. I've been attending the church ever since—as my work schedule allows, of course."

Jordan's words just tumbled out. "So Sam is . . . ?"

The nurse broke into a huge grin, which eclipsed the hard edge on her face. "Sam is wonderful, Sam is great, Sam is beautiful," she giggled. "We met at the divorce recovery class. His ex left him for an old high school flame. We became friends, then fell in love. Only been married a year and a half."

"I'm . . . I'm sorry about your divorce," Jordan said, not knowing what to say.

"Don't be too sorry, Jordy. Derrick was a violent, abusive man. Sam and I still pray for him. But I should have left him long before he decided to leave me."

Jordan now understood a little about the hard side he had perceived in the SICU nurse. "I'm happy for you and Sam."

"Thanks. We'd like to have you over for dinner some night, being that you're sort of a bachelor for a few more weeks."

"I appreciate your kindness, Maggie, but unfortunately I don't get many nights off."

Maggie brushed it off and continued, "Anyway, I wanted you to know that I'm a believer too. There are a couple of us in Surgery."

"That's what I understand," Jordan said. "Thanks for telling me about your . . . your journey."

"Enough about me," she said. "How did it go with the Aguilera family?"

Jordan slipped his hands into the pockets of his sport jacket. "They were holding up all right—at least until Buster arrived."

"Ha!" Maggie exclaimed. "What a sweetheart. I think he out-chaplains the chaplain in the compassion department."

Jordan shrugged his shoulders noncommittally.

Maggie studied the gesture. "Buster makes you uncomfortable, doesn't he?" she said.

Jordan flushed at the nurse's uncanny insight. "Well, he's not a chaplain, is he? He's a janitor. I just think he gets a little too emotional."

"Jordy, he's only a kid, mentally," Maggie remonstrated playfully. "When somebody hurts, he hurts with them. That's all. He may be simpleminded, but he has a big heart. And people like the Aguileras get more out of Buster's teary bear hugs than our technical explanations about what happened to their loved ones."

Jordan did not fully agree, but he was not about to engage in a debate about Buster's unconventional role at Mercy. He took another sip from his drink, then turned the conversation back to his primary concern. "What do you think happened to the patient?"

Maggie said, "You're the expert, but I think her heart just gave out. Maybe she had a defect nobody knew about. Multiple injuries from her accident—and two craniotomies in eight hours—were too much for her system. It's another one of those sad deals around here: The operation was a success, but the patient died."

"What do you mean '*another* one of those sad deals'?" Jordan pressed, intrigued at her choice of words.

Maggie gave out another wry laugh. "Just a little hospital humor, I guess. You know, SICU's reputation for losing patients."

Jordan sank to his chair, perplexed. "Reputation? What are you talking about?"

Maggie pulled a nutrition bar from her pocket and peeled

away the colored foil wrapper as she answered. "I guess you haven't heard the jokes. Some of the staff talk about 'Plead for Mercy Hospital,' where trauma patients check in, but they don't check out—pretty crude really."

"Patient mortality is a fact of life," Jordan said, catching the irony only as his words came out.

Maggie either missed the irony or ignored it. "I know trauma patients die, Jordy," she said, waving her nutrition bar. "But some of our coworkers talk like we get more than our share." She took a bite from the bar, then washed it down with a sip of Pepsi. "Like most hospital humor, it's probably groundless. I'll bet they say the same things over at Good Samaritan, Providence, and St. Vincent's."

"How many have you seen since you've been here?"

"You mean like Aguilera—apparently successful operation followed by sudden death in SICU?" Jordan nodded.

"Two that I know about. Ettinger lost a man in SICU a couple days after successful cerebrovascular surgery. Myocardial infarction was the culprit, as I recall. And the first week I was here, a brain trauma case didn't make it after surgery. I think that patient belonged to Kaplan."

"Three in three months," Jordan said, more to himself.

"Like you said, Jordy, patient mortality happens," Maggie said after another bite.

"But three successful surgeries ending in death in a span of three months. That seems awfully high. Maybe it could happen at a big hospital like County General, but not here."

Maggie finished her nutrition bar, then said, "Perhaps we didn't lose any trauma patients in the nine previous months. I don't know what the national average is, but three losses a year doesn't seem so bad. I'm sorry I mentioned it. I came here to cheer you up, not to depress you."

Jordan stood, hoping to convey to Maggie that he had work to do, which he really did. "Thanks for the drink," he said, stepping out from behind the desk. "That was kind of you."

"Glad to do it." Maggie took the cue and met him at the door, her drink in hand. "One more thing, Jordy. You've been here a couple of months, right?"

"Almost," Jordan returned, nodding.

"And Della is still in L.A.?"

He nodded again.

Maggie's brow furrowed, and she locked eyes with Jordan. "I hope you realize how difficult it is for a woman to be separated from her husband for so long." She did not wait for a response. "This kind of arrangement is not good for a marriage, even a Christian marriage. Della has emotional needs that can't be met by a paycheck and a phone call now and then. She needs *you,* Jordy. I hope you're doing your best to get her up here as soon as possible. I just had to tell you that."

A little stunned at the strong, sisterly admonition from a near stranger, Jordan considered his reply. Maggie didn't know that he had spent the morning looking at homes and that he would probably make an offer on one in a day or so. She didn't know that he would be in L.A. next weekend for Katy's birthday. And she didn't know that Della was the one dragging her feet on the transition, not him. He was doing everything he knew to do to provide for Della's emotional needs by finding her a dream house and urging her to join him. If she needed him, she was being very coy about showing it.

Jordan decided not to say anything more than, "Thanks for your concern, Maggie."

"You're welcome. Hang in there, Jordy. Sam and I will be praying for you. And let us know when you're free for dinner." Jordan nodded, and the nurse was quickly out the door and down the hall.

Jordan changed into a lab coat and left the office. He had a number of patients to see, and he hoped to catch up with Mark Sutherland and express his displeasure at being left out of the loop when Trudy Aguilera died. Jordan was more than pleased when he ran into Sutherland on the fourth floor outside a patient's room.

"Why didn't you page me when Aguilera arrested this morning?" he asked pointedly but without anger.

Sutherland was on his way to another patient's room, so Jordan walked along with him. "For one thing," Sutherland said, "I had it handled. The patient was gone in minutes. There was no reason for you to come. For another thing, the schedule said you had taken a few hours off. We try to protect each other from unnecessary calls during time off."

"But she was my patient. I should have been contacted about—"

"I left you voice mail, Doctor," Sutherland interrupted. "Did you check it while you were out?"

Jordan felt stupid for pressing the issue. "No, I didn't check voice mail."

"Well, I'm sorry we didn't connect on that," Sutherland said. Jordan knew what he meant: *It's your fault for not checking your voice mail.*

"What was your take on the cause of death?" Jordan said.

"Open and shut case: Cardiac failure due to severe head trauma. That's what I put on the death certificate."

"Wait a minute." Jordan stopped his fellow surgeon in order to speak to him face-to-face. "You already signed the death certificate?" he asked in disbelief.

"Of course. Why not?"

"What about the postmortem?"

Sutherland looked at him incredulously. "There won't be one. The mortician has probably picked up the body already."

"But—"

Sutherland interrupted again, this time with a hint of irritation. "Doctor, I don't know what it's like in Los Angeles County, but we're a small operation here in Oregon. The state medical examiner won't look at a body unless it is a suspected homicide or suicide. They just don't have the manpower. We sign the death certificate, and that's it."

"What if the family requests an autopsy?"

"We refer them to a private pathologist. The family pays the bill, and they get the results. We're out of the picture."

"What if I request an autopsy?"

Sutherland scowled. "Why would you want one?" There was a coarse edge to his question.

"Just answer my question, Mark. How could I get an autopsy on this patient?"

Sutherland blew a sigh of resignation. "If you want our pathology lab to do it, you need permission from the family and from Dr. Waller. Once we sign off on the body, you have to talk the family into a private autopsy."

Sutherland started walking again. "We may do things a little differently here, Jordan," he said, "but our system works well for us. You'll get the hang of it. Sorry, I have to keep moving."

Jordan watched him walk hurriedly down the hall until he disappeared into a patient's room. There was one more question on his mind, but he knew he would never ask it: *How do you know Trudy Aguilera's death wasn't a homicide unless you open her up and find out?*

EIGHT

Trudy Aguilera's death left Jordan disheartened. For the next two days he mentally replayed his role in the young woman's care, each time concluding that he could have done nothing more. Yet a nagging sense of failure persisted. He had done his best—all anyone could possibly do for her—and she still died. Why? Following the surgeries she was holding her own. Apart from her many injuries, she seemed to be in good health. Her heart should not have just stopped beating. So he replayed the mental tape again, looking for a reason.

Part of Jordan's discouragement stemmed from the realization that he would never know why his patient's heart stopped. His request Sunday for an autopsy was too late; the body had already been moved to a funeral home in southeast Portland. Dr. Waller sounded sympathetic to Jordan's request, but he echoed Dr. Sutherland's explanation: The nature of the patient's death did not warrant a postmortem exam by the state medical examiner or by the hospital's pathology lab. Unless the family sought an autopsy—and Dr. Waller urged Jordan not to burden the Aguileras with such a suggestion—the issue would be laid to rest along with the woman's body.

Jordan understood, and to a point he agreed. It was practically and logistically impossible to autopsy every patient who died in the hospital. And Trudy Aguilera's heart failure was at least plausible considering the extent of her injuries. But he silently contended that they could learn something positive from an autopsy. Perhaps the young woman had a heart defect that contributed to cardiac arrest. Other members of the Aguilera family should know about it and consult a cardiologist in case the condition was genetic. Or perhaps Trudy's post-op meds were somehow fouled up. An autopsy would reveal the presence of a foreign drug or the erroneous overdose of a prescribed drug.

However, the point was moot. There would be no autopsy. It was still a failure to Jordan, but at least he was not to blame for the patient's death.

Having been thwarted on this front, Jordan turned his attention to another bothersome concern as the week wore on. Maggie had intimated that Mercy Hospital had a history of losing trauma patients. Could he believe Maggie Rusch? Her confession of faith notwithstanding, was she given to sensationalism and exaggeration? Or was Mercy Hospital accident-prone in its care of trauma patients?

The answers to these questions bore significantly on Jordan's quest at Mercy. How could he reestablish his career at an institution with a slapdash approach to trauma care? How many more Trudy Aguileras would there be before he would be judged guilty by association?

Jordan reasoned that he could better predict the future if he had a better grasp of the past. One direct way to determine if prestigious, respected Mercy Hospital had a history of patient deaths was to check records. His problem, as always, was time.

Mondays, Wednesdays, and Thursdays were his scheduled surgery days in the hospital. In addition to long hours in the OR on these days, Jordan still had to round on other surgery patients. Tuesdays and Fridays were his clinic days. He began at 7:00 A.M., rounding with med students, then at 9:00 he launched into a full day of appointments with patients, consultations with colleagues, and classes in the medical school.

Jordan was blitzed with work on the Monday and Tuesday following Trudy Aguilera's death. But Wednesday happened to be a fairly light day of surgeries—only about seven hours scheduled in the OR. Arriving at the hospital at 6:15 A.M. with a twenty-ounce cup of steaming Starbucks, he sequestered himself in the tiny office to begin a preliminary search of hospital records before surgery at 8:00. He peeled off his sport jacket, loosened his tie, and booted up the computer. He had limited experience with the hospital's computer system, so he geared up for what he expected to be a trial-and-error search.

Jordan went first to the hospital's Web site to gather a few items of general information. Clicking the button for the Trauma Center, he found what he wanted: a "commercial" for Mercy Hospital's state-of-the-art trauma care facilities and staff. Opening a few more colorful pages, he reached a block of statistics. Jordan marveled at how small the numbers were in comparison to L.A. County General, where trauma patient volume was easily three times as great. Leaning back in his chair, he absorbed the section of data.

Last year Portland Mercy Teaching Hospital Trauma Center had admitted 1,278 major trauma cases. On average, three or four people were rushed to Mercy every day of the year in need of lifesaving medical intervention. Motor vehicle accidents were the major contributor to this patient base, followed by domestic and gang violence; industrial and home accidents; recreational mishaps on Oregon's mountains, trails, and waterways; and sudden, life-threatening illness.

According to the report on the monitor, 243 of these patients—about 19 percent—had not survived resuscitation. They were dead by the time they reached the Trauma Center, or they died on the table in the Emergency Room. Of the 1,035 patients who were resuscitated, 61 percent required emergency surgery to repair potentially fatal damage to organs and tissue. A few died on the operating table, and the rest were sent to SICU to recover. Last year the twelve-bed Surgical Intensive Care Unit logged 2,393 patients, 608 of whom who came through Mercy's Trauma Center.

Home free, Jordan thought. *By the time the patient reaches SICU, he or she should be out of immediate danger. The life-threatening problem has been uncovered and surgically treated. Unforeseen complications do arise, and a few deaths—like that of Trudy Aguilera—occur. But they should be rare at this point.*

Jordan wanted to know just how many deaths there had been in SICU, but the information was not here. He had to go into the hospital's archives for this information. So Jordan exited the Web site and accessed the hospital's computer using his password.

Working through the maze of menu options into the heart of the hospital's mainframe was tedious. How much faster it would have been for him to utilize one of the administrative assistants assigned to the Neurosurgery Division, someone who better understood the system and could find what he was looking for. But this search was personal, not a task related to his position at the hospital. It was better that he do the work alone and keep the findings to himself.

After ten minutes of opening subfile after subfile, Jordan clicked his way into what seemed to be the morgue in the hospital's store of electronic data. Stylized, multicolor pages had given way to color text on color background to basic black type on white background. The file drawing his attention read: In-Hospital Deaths. Jordan clicked it open to find a white screen with a list of years lined down the left margin. The number at the top was 1976, apparently the year Mercy Hospital had transferred hard copy records to electronic data. Jordan scrolled down the list, and the years rolled by, ending at the present.

Jordan clicked open the present year. Total in-hospital

deaths to date, listed at the top of the page, was eighty-two. The list of names was arranged into two categories: trauma and non-trauma. The list of non-trauma deaths was much shorter: fourteen so far this year. Jordan knew this figure represented end-stage patients who were admitted to the hospital essentially to die.

The list of trauma deaths contained sixty-eight names. There were two subcategories, headed DOA and ER-OR-ICU. The DOAs—Jordan counted sixty of them—were accident victims, shooting or stabbing victims, heart-attack victims, and the like who died at the scene or in transit to the Trauma Center. But since they were officially pronounced dead at the hospital, they were logged as in-hospital deaths.

Jordan's attention moved quickly to the much shorter list of trauma deaths that occurred in the Emergency Room, Surgery, or Intensive Care. He followed the list of eight names to the bottom. The eighth and most recent entry, dated Sunday, April 11, was Trudy Aguilera. Cause of death was listed as "Closed Head Injury—MVA." Jordan frowned. He had skillfully repaired his patient's brain injuries. She died because her heart could not handle the one-two punch of traumatic injury and traumatic surgery.

Jordan studied the other seven names on the list. In each case, as with Trudy Aguilera, hospital staff attempted heroic measures to thwart the sudden trauma of a life-threatening injury or illness. Here death appeared not as an angel of mercy but as a marauder, a thief taking a child, a teen, or an adult before his or her time. Despite the valiant efforts of the medical personnel on hand, death had won.

An unbidden thought momentarily stopped Jordan. His son's name probably appeared on a list like this in the database at the UCLA Medical Center where he had died. Jordan had never seen the entry, never even thought to look for it, though he probably could have accessed the file from his computer at LAC+USC. But for a moment his imagination added another line to the text on the screen before him:

Jeffrey Jordan Keyes, age eight, cause of death: liver failure due to advanced leukemia.

After a few seconds he pushed back from the desk and stood to break the unpleasant train of thought. He grabbed his cup of coffee and walked to the front of the desk. He was not about to let unnecessary thoughts of his dead son sidetrack him. His personal vow to himself after the funeral was to leave those dark memories in the past. So he had buried his grief with the dead body of his son. Jordan had done the same thing when his mother died of cancer when he was barely J. J.'s age. "Big boys don't cry, Jordan," his father had coached him as they left the hospital. "Your crying won't do your mother any good. Just put your mind to making her proud, like she said." Jordan had taken his father's words to heart then and again when J. J. died.

His father's counsel had seemed the only efficient response to the pain of J. J.'s death. More than that, it had also arrested an ill-defined fear that lurked just beyond Jordan's inner vision. Had he allowed himself to grieve for his son, he deduced, he may not have been able to stop grieving. Had he allowed himself to grieve, he might have become another Buster Chapman.

Jordan had often appreciated the sensibility of devoting himself to industry and achievement instead of squandering emotional energy on sad events he could not change. Where would he be today had he not channeled that energy into focused ambition, disciplined study, and tireless work? Certainly not in one of the top fields in the highly respected career of medicine.

Jordan drained the last ounces of his lukewarm coffee, crumpled the paper cup, and tossed it into the basket. Taking a deep breath to clear his head, he returned to the chair. He had to narrow his search to people like Trudy Aguilera: trauma patients who had been treated successfully only to die in SICU. To get this information, Jordan had to click open the complete files of each of the seven deceased patients listed above Trudy Aguilera.

A quick scan of the seven charts revealed that two patients did not survive emergency surgery. Deciding it would be easier to compare the other five charts if he could see them side by side, he sent them to the printer.

Rearranging the stacks of materials on his desk, Jordan laid the printed sheets of paper side by side to survey them. Here were the sad stories of five people who were the victims of double tragedies. First, horrendous, painful circumstances rudely interrupted their healthy, productive lives. Jordan studied the admittance details. Two of them—one man and one woman—were the victims of separate car crashes. A repairman had fallen from a power pole during a winter storm. A university athlete was flown to Mercy after he collapsed during basketball practice. And a twelve-year-old boy came in by ambulance with his head split open, having fallen out of a second-story window.

Each victim had suffered injuries that were imminently life threatening. But the speedy response of emergency medical technicians on the scene and the skilled trauma team in Mercy's Trauma Center spared each a certain death. Then lightning struck again in each of these five lives. Each patient died while under care in the SICU.

Jordan agreed that all five cases were tragic, especially for surviving family members. These cruelties of life could be traced back to original sin, he knew. Sin opened the door for imperfection, and imperfection included disease, poor human judgment, and unfortunate happenstance. Disease makes people sick, and some sick people die. People are injured and die as a result of poor human judgment and unfortunate occurrences.

Sin is at the heart of all human tragedy, Jordan assessed. He remembered a verse from Romans he had learned as a young Christian: "Where sin increased, grace increased all the more." God allows his sinful human creation to continually perfect the healing arts, in many cases turning tragedies caused by disease, bad judgment, and happenstance into triumphs. And in some cases, God intervenes where human knowledge and medical technology prove to be insufficient.

But in the case of Trudy Aguilera and the others represented by the sheets in front of him, the Bible verse seemed reversed: Where grace increased, sin increased all the more. Tragedy had been averted, but then the grace of medical intervention had been overwhelmed by a second and greater tragedy. It was the most difficult expression of original sin for Jordan to swallow. And as it related to his involvement with Trudy Aguilera, the overabundance of sin had left a cloud over him.

Yet it had been Nurse Rusch's contention—as well as others in the hospital, if she was to be believed—that the battle between sin and grace at Mercy was unfairly weighted in sin's favor. Too many tragedies at the hospital were explained as normal. Trudy Aguilera was a case in point. This is why he was poring over these charts, Jordan acknowledged. If there was another dark factor at work—some kind of unseen special agent for sin, it should show up somewhere. "The devil isn't that clever, nor is he very tidy," he had heard a Bible study leader say once. "If you look closely enough, you can discover his modus operandi and thwart his schemes."

Jordan retrieved a legal pad and a pencil from a desk drawer. Carefully comparing the five printouts on the desktop, he began to jot down his observations.

All patients were victims of head or spinal cord trauma.
All required emergency neurosurgical intervention.
All surgeries were successful.
All surviving patients appeared to be out of immediate danger.
All patients died unexpectedly in the SICU of heart failure related to their problems.

He reread the list. The scenario he was composing looked familiar. He added the initials T. A. to the end of each line. They were all true of Trudy Aguilera, the last name on the list of trauma patient deaths.

Jordan continued to scour the charts, adding more lines of observation. These items seemed inconclusive to him, but he jotted them down:

> One death in January, two in February, two in March.
> One patient from Washington, four from the greater Portland area.
> One autopsy performed by family request.
> Attending neurosurgeons: Boorsma, Ettinger, Andrade, Ettinger again, and Muranaka.

None of the attending neurosurgeons were primary specialists in neurotrauma. That had been Dr. Will Kopke's role until his accident in November. Now it was Jordan's role on the neurosurgery staff. Randall Boorsma focused on neuro-oncology—cancerous brain tumors. Philip Ettinger was the cerebrovascular specialist—primarily aneurysms and strokes. Johnny Andrade worked in interventional neuroradiology. Liz Muranaka was the pediatric neurosurgery and neuro-oncology specialist. But all were trained in neurotrauma intervention, as were chronic pain specialist Dr. Oscar Ortiz and five neurosurgery residents. And all rotated to trauma code responsibilities a few nights each month. Everyone had an opportunity to save brain trauma victims—and to lose them.

The phrase flitted through Jordan's mind again: *The devil isn't that clever.* It occurred to him that if there was some heinous, unearthly plot to snuff out lives at Mercy Hospital, the five former patients documented before him did not prove it. As in Trudy Aguilera's case, apparently their hearts just gave out. The one private autopsy among the five patients confirmed it. Jordan had yet to find anything to confirm Maggie Rusch's suspicion that Mercy had lost SICU patients due to negligence.

A glance at the digital clock on the monitor told Jordan he was due in surgery soon. He collected the five printouts and stacked them neatly on a corner of the desk. So much for this year's SICU deaths. Maggie had intimated that the oddity extended further into the past. A part of Jordan was ready to blow off additional forays into the hospital's archives. Why continue a wild-goose chase when more pressing responsibilities clogged his days?

But he had always been a person of meticulous follow-through. "If you don't plan to finish, don't start," his father had drummed into him as a boy. They were wise words, Jordan knew. He would not have excelled through medical school, residency, and his neurosurgery fellowship had he ignored his father's counsel and his late mother's charge to make her proud. As time allowed, he would not forsake that successful pattern now.

Jordan backed out of the hospital's computer archives until the desktop appeared on his monitor. He cinched up the knot on his tie, pulled on a clean lab coat, and hurried toward Surgery.

NINE

Jordan did not see his office again until 8:30 that evening. After closing and locking his door, he shed the lab coat and collapsed into his office chair. Two neurosurgery residents had been out with the flu all day, so the OR was shorthanded. Jordan was asked to assist on two additional surgeries, adding about five hours of work to his "light day."

He had not talked to Della since Saturday night, and he knew he must call her tonight. But their usual time to talk was 10:00, after Katy was in bed. So he nudged the computer from sleep mode and accessed again the records for in-hospital deaths. Having already examined January through the present, he highlighted the previous year and clicked open the file.

The monitor filled with the record of another year of sad stories at Mercy Hospital: 285 deaths within these walls. Non-trauma deaths numbered 51, trauma deaths 234. DOAs accounted for 206 of the trauma deaths, leaving 42 patients who had died in the ER, OR, or ICU. Jordan opened each of the forty-two charts for a quick look, but he printed only those that paralleled the deaths of Trudy Aguilera and the other five patients he had studied this morning. There were twenty-eight with a familiar variety of trauma conditions and treated with predictable resuscitation and surgical procedures. Nothing unusual here. This collection of cases could have come from any trauma hospital in the country.

He spread the twenty-eight printouts on the desk in four groups of seven and studied them as he had the five sheets this morning. About two-thirds were head or spinal cord trauma patients; the rest presented with grave injuries or illnesses threatening other vital organs. All had survived emergency surgeries—some, like Trudy, more than one. All were moved to the Surgical Intensive Care Unit. Though listed as critical, all were considered out of immediate danger. And yet all died in ICU within a few hours to a few days.

Jordan collected the twenty-eight printed files into one stack on the desk in front of him. Easing back in the chair, he processed what he had seen. Three thoughts scraped uncomfortably through Jordan's brain.

The first concerned the sheer number of patients. Twenty-eight Aguilera-type cases happened at Mercy last year—more than two a month. Even though several hundred patients came through the SICU and were dismissed from the hospital in good health, over two dozen did not make it. *Is that high, or am I just too tired to think?* Jordan pondered. *No wonder some people joke about this hospital being a slaughterhouse.*

The second thought centered on the cause of death listed for each patient. The data on the charts communicated that eighteen of them closely resembled Trudy Aguilera's case. All of these patients were head and spine cases. Potentially fatal neurotraumas had been temporarily relieved, but the patients had died anyway. Hearts gave out before the healing could take hold in the injured brain and central nervous system. Counting Trudy Aguilera, thirty-four SICU patients had died over the past sixteen months. *What is wrong with these people in Oregon? Are they weakhearted? Is there something in the atmosphere or the water? Why did so many fail to complete their recovery?*

It occurred to Jordan that incompetence among the surgical staff might be a contributing factor to the surprising statistics. Leafing through the twenty-eight charts again, he looked for the names of attending physicians and surgeons. Several were familiar to him; some he had met for the first time at Dr. Waller's reception Saturday night. Among the general surgeons and trauma surgeons, Waller and Dr. Otto Gebhardt appeared most often. Neurosurgeons were the most prevalent, including many with whom he presently worked: Drs. Ettinger, Sutherland, Ortiz, and Muranaka.

But one name leaped out at him from several of the charts: Dr. Wilfred Kopke. After a quick count, he noted that the name of his predecessor in the Neurosurgery Division appeared as the attending neurosurgeon for six of the head trauma victims—more than any other surgeon. Jordan could not miss the sobering irony: Kopke lost six brain trauma patients last year, then died from massive head injuries in a November skiing accident. *That's what I call a bad year,* he mused darkly. *Perhaps SICU deaths will diminish now that the accident-prone neurosurgeon has done himself in.* Jordan immediately chastised himself for such a disrespectful thought.

The third nagging concept had been bothering him since Sunday. It returned in force as a question while he sifted through these charts: *Why so few autopsies?* He had been told that the Oregon state medical examiner's office was small and understaffed. He also realized that natural deaths were not automatically subject to a postmortem as homicides and suicides were. But why were these people so dense about investigating SICU deaths? Did they even consider petitioning the families to allow hospital pathologists a chance to look for possible deeper causes? It did not make sense to Jordan.

Dr. Sutherland and Dr. Waller had spelled out the hospital's policy on physician-requested autopsies: Don't burden the grieving family with an unnecessary procedure merely to satisfy curiosity. But Jordan was not at all pleased with the prospect of losing more patients, especially if it could be prevented. However, if he was to identify a treatable cause for some of the SICU fatalities—if indeed there was one—he would need some help.

Jordan made a snap decision. It took him only a couple of minutes to find the telephone number he needed. Pausing briefly to wonder if 9:20 was too late to call, he lifted the receiver and tapped in the number from the monitor. Stomach churning with anxiety, he waited through two rings.

A woman with a Latino accent answered. "Mrs. Aguilera?" Jordan said.

"No, this is her daughter."

"May I speak with Mr. or Mrs. Aguilera, please?"

A pause. "Who is calling?" the woman probed with a hint of suspicion.

"This is Dr. Keyes from Portland Mercy Teaching Hospital."

"The doctor who operated on Trudy?"

"That's right. I'm sorry to call so late in the evening." Jordan referred to the family information on the monitor to verify the first names. "But I was hoping I might speak with Roberto or Esther briefly."

"Just a minute please, Doctor."

While waiting, Jordan remembered Dr. Waller's admonition *not* to bother the Aguileras. It was a strong suggestion, not an order, Jordan rationalized. He really should clear this with Waller before proceeding. But that would mean another phone call, and he would likely only reach Waller's voice mail, resulting in further delay. Some things were too important to put off. Besides, Waller might not approve. So, with some trepidation, Jordan decided to move forward and ask permission later.

The voice of Roberto Aguilera came through the phone. "Hello."

Jordan apologized for the late call and asked how the family was doing. Mr. Aguilera sounded moved by Jordan's concern. He explained that the family was holding together well as they awaited the funeral mass on Saturday. As the man spoke, Jordan labored over how he would present his request.

"Mr. Aguilera, when we last spoke at the hospital, I said I did not know why your daughter's heart stopped beating."

"Yes, Doctor, I remember."

"Do you mind if I talk to you about this for a minute?"

Roberto Aguilera did not hesitate. "No, it's all right. Did you find out why Trudy died?"

"Not exactly. But I think it is important to find out while there is still time. Do you know what an autopsy is, Mr. Aguilera?"

The Latino man related a limited understanding of the procedure. Jordan filled in a few blanks, trying to avoid medical jargon. He explained that autopsies in cases like Trudy's were important in learning how to prevent other deaths. Then he said, "The hospital does not require such an autopsy, but I recommend that you allow your daughter to be examined by a private pathologist. We may learn exactly why she died, and we may be able to help others like her. The procedure could be completed before the funeral on Saturday. I will handle all the arrangements, and there will be no cost to you whatsoever. What do you think, Mr. Aguilera?" The family generally absorbed the responsibility and expense of a private autopsy, but Jordan was ready to go the second mile for what he wanted to know and pay for it himself.

After a tentative silence, Mr. Aguilera asked a few questions about the procedure, which Jordan answered as concisely as possible. "I must talk to my family about this, Doctor," Mr. Aguilera concluded.

"Of course, I understand," Jordan acknowledged. "Why don't you talk it over and sleep on it. If you can let me know tomorrow, I can schedule the procedure so your daughter is back at the funeral home by Friday afternoon. You can call me directly when you decide."

Mr. Aguilera agreed. Jordan gave his pager number and

wished the family well. Then he tapped the phone off, lifting a silent prayer that the Aguileras would judge him trustworthy—and not mention his unusual request to anyone else at the hospital.

Shutting down the computer, Jordan was about to leave with the printouts of deceased trauma patients spread across his desk. He thought better of it. He collected them and stuffed the sheaf into a file folder. Taking the folder with him and grabbing his sport jacket, he locked the office and left.

Jordan dialed Della's number as he drove out of the parking garage into the clear and surprisingly balmy Oregon night. She answered on her cell phone, explaining that she was on the San Diego Freeway near Mulholland Drive in L.A. She sounded unusually pleasant and upbeat.

"Where's Katy?" Jordan asked.

"She's at Mother's. I'm on my way to pick her up now."

"It's a little late for her to be out on a school night, don't you think?" Of all their points of disagreement, Jordan and Della usually agreed on guidelines for Katy's behavior. Staying up past nine on a school night was a compromise.

"She'll be fine, Jordan," Della said without taking offense at his subtle criticism. "It couldn't be helped tonight."

"Where have you been? What are you doing?"

"This is so great," Della said, sounding guardedly enthusiastic. "I've been at a planning meeting for the West Valley Parade of Homes out in Agoura Hills. Jordan, I finally got a house."

"You got a house?"

"A house *to decorate,* Jordan," she said, chiding him a little for missing the point. "I'm sure you don't remember, but I've been trying to get a West Valley Parade home for the past three years and have been shut out. I'm finally going to do one! Can you imagine how many people will walk through that home and see my work, Jordan?"

Della's animation did not divert Jordan from the implications of her news. "When is the show?" he probed.

"Mid-July, for two weeks."

"Dell, you and Katy will up here with me by July," he said, a hint of frustration in his tone.

Della answered with a similar edge. "Do we have a house in Portland yet? No. Have we sold our house in L.A. yet? No. Is there a possibility the home situation will not be resolved for several months? Of course. We don't know what the real estate market will do. There may be a contingency up there, a delayed closing, or the deal may fall through—who knows how long it may take? When the move happens, it happens. In the meantime, I just can't put my business on hold."

Jordan braked behind a Tri-Met bus stopping for passengers. Watching the side-view mirror for an opening, he darted into the left lane, accompanied by a horn blast from a car he nearly cut off. "I think I found a house Sunday in Lake Oswego," he said with a note of triumph. "Really nice. I'll bring the pictures when I come down for the party."

"Sunday?" Della's inflection amplified the question in Jordan's mind: *You found it on Sunday and you're just telling me about it tonight?*

"I've been really—"

"—'really busy,' I know, Jordan," Della cut in. "That's my point. It's going to take time, and I want to stay busy in the meantime."

"Della, that doesn't make sense," Jordan said, battling feelings of defensiveness. "Even if you do that house in Agoura Hills, you won't be around for any clients you may attract."

The moment of silence communicated Della's frustration. "You don't get it, Jordan. I'm not doing this for the clients. I'm doing it for me. Even if I live in Portland by then, I will fly down here for three or four weeks and do this home. It's something I *want* to do, something I *need* to do."

Jordan's pager buzzed halfway through Della's explanation. He squeezed the phone between his shoulder and ear, freed a hand, and pulled the unit from his belt to read the message. It was a return call from the Aguileras.

"I just got a page, Dell. I'll call you right back."

Della blew a long sigh. "Never mind, I'm almost to Mother's."

"Maybe tomorrow night," he said.

"Whatever." Della suddenly sounded very tired to him.

"I love you, Dell. Good night."

"Good night, Jordan."

Pulling to the curb on West Burnside at Eighteenth, Jordan dialed the number on the pager's readout. Roberto Aguilera answered. "I talked to my family. We want you to do the operation."

"The autopsy," Jordan clarified, keeping the surge of elation from his tone.

"Yes. If an autopsy will help other families, Trudy's dying has more meaning to us."

"That's very kind of you, Mr. Aguilera, very kind of your whole family." Jordan instructed him to go to the funeral home first thing in the morning and sign a release, assuring him that he would make arrangements with the pathologist.

Jordan set the phone aside. "Yes!" he exclaimed, clenching his fist triumphantly. "Mr. Aguilera, I hope we both find the answers we're looking for."

TEN

Every spare moment between morning surgeries, Jordan slipped away to dial the office of the Portland pathologist recommended by Mercy Hospital for private autopsies. With each try he heard a female employee on the machine recite woodenly: "This is the office of Dr. Joseph Wiggins. Please leave a message after the tone. Thank you." He hung up every time without leaving a message, impatient to schedule Trudy Aguilera's autopsy with someone in person. Then he remembered that Dr. Wiggins, who was semiretired, probably kept banker's hours. It was the attractive trade-off Jordan's med school classmates had sometimes joked about. Medical examiners and private pathologists earned about half the money of other physicians, but they enjoyed evenings and weekends off because their patients never called them during off-hours.

Jordan finally got through just after nine. Speaking with the receptionist, it only took him a few minutes to set up the autopsy. Wiggins's office would pick up the body from the funeral home this afternoon after a representative from the family arrived to sign a release. The autopsy would be performed Friday morning, and the remains would be back at the funeral home in time for the Friday evening viewing, a closed-casket affair due to her head and facial injuries. Jordan gave his name and apartment address for billing, purposely leaving the hospital out of the loop. Trudy's cause of death was now a personal matter between him and the family. It would be less complicated if Dr. Waller and others at the hospital knew nothing about it.

The issue of the thirty-three other Aguilera-like SICU deaths at Mercy had been festering since last night. The deaths themselves were disturbing enough, although he fully understood that the severely traumatized human body is fragile and vulnerable to major organ failure. But Jordan was even more irritated at the hospital's protocol—or *lack* of protocol—for such occurrences, especially since Mercy's unresponsive posture shed poor light on his precarious career.

The questions had drummed in his brain through periods of sleeplessness during the night: *Why are there not more autopsies on patients like Trudy Aguilera who died over the past sixteen months? If the bottleneck is an overloaded pathology lab, why doesn't the hospital expand that department? How are they going to help more patients experience a positive outcome if they do not scrutinize closely patients who die when others like them recover?*

This storm of thoughts accompanied Jordan to the weekly Neurosurgery staff meeting at 10:00 A.M. He grabbed a cup of coffee from the machine in the hall and took his seat among the staff of faculty, researchers, residents, and fellows, many of whom he barely knew.

The meeting itself was an irritating waste of time to Jordan, as everything presented could have been disseminated via e-mail or hard-copy memo. But Dr. Waller insisted that meeting regularly was important for nurturing esprit de corps in the division. Attendance was required at staff meetings, but a few were always missing. Today Waller himself was out of town attending a conference. Philip Ettinger, the acting head of Neurosurgery, handled the meeting.

The agenda was superfluous and boring, as usual. Ettinger, a lanky New Englander whom Jordan liked and respected, was not a commanding presence. He dutifully plodded through items of policy and information that could have been handed out on a single sheet of paper. Jordan leafed through the folder of printouts from last night without paying much attention to Ettinger's droning.

The last five minutes of the meeting were generally devoted to feedback from the staff. Anyone who had a question, a gripe, an interesting case, or a good medical joke was free to verbalize it. When Dr. Ettinger tossed the meeting out to the floor, Jordan found himself on his feet. Philip nodded in his direction. "Yes, Dr. Keyes?"

Jordan had never spoken out in a staff meeting before, and he had not planned on saying anything today. But the buildup of disquieting thoughts and questions since the death of Trudy Aguilera seemed to launch him from his chair. He immediately wanted to wave off the opportunity and sit down. But the eyes of his colleagues were now on him.

"I know I'm still the new kid on the block in our division, but . . . well, I'm . . . wondering about something." He glanced down at the manila folder on the tabletop, wishing there were notes for him to follow. "I lost a patient in SICU Sunday after two successful craniotomies, one for an epidural hematoma, the second for an evolving intracerebral hematoma. Her heart arrested, and standard measures of resuscitation failed. But by the time I got here two hours later, the patient was practically in the hearse on the way to the funeral home."

Surveying the room as he spoke, Jordan noticed that Mark Sutherland was eyeing him intently. Jordan detected a hint of defensiveness in his colleague's steady gaze—perhaps he was waiting for Jordan to blame him for not resuscitating her—but Jordan had no sympathy for him.

"Cause of death was traumatic brain injury leading to cardiac arrest. At least it's reasonable to assume that's why she arrested. And it *is* an assumption. We don't know exactly because the patient's body was tagged, bagged, and shipped to the funeral home without a postmortem."

"Do you have reason to suspect your patient died from another cause?" The question was from Dr. Oscar Ortiz, who specialized in chronic pain. The forty-seven-year-old Ortiz, a striking presence with his muscular frame, jet-black hair streaked with gray, and dominating black eyes, was expected by many to inherit the vacant position of division head. Jordan had spoken to Ortiz only briefly.

"I have no such suspicion, Doctor," Jordan replied, returning his powerful gaze. "But I'm suggesting that—"

"Are you aware of our policy on such matters, Dr. Keyes?" Ortiz's question overpowered any response. Jordan wondered if the handsome neurosurgeon, usually the strong, silent type in staff meetings, was using this platform to display his qualifications as division head.

"Yes, I understand our policy," Jordan retorted with an edge he hoped added, *I may be new to Mercy, but I'm no dummy.* "The state requires postmortems for homicides, suicides, and other suspicious deaths. And internally our pathology lab is too busy to satisfy our curiosity when an acceptable cause of death is apparent. So autopsies of this nature are the responsibility of the family, not the hospital."

"You have a problem with that policy, Doctor?" Ortiz was glaring now. The undertone of his question was a challenge: *Who are you to throw stones at our policy? You're wasting our time bringing it up. This had better be good.* Jordan suspected that the stress of Ortiz's work—which everyone in the room knew from experience—and perhaps the stress of competition for the promotion were fueling his surprisingly confrontational response.

Instead of wilting Jordan, the heated comeback ignited him. "Yes, I have a big problem with this policy," he returned angrily. "I lost a patient Sunday, and nobody really gives a rip about why she died. She sustained substantial head trauma in the accident, but I repaired it. She was on the edge twice, and I brought her back twice. The odds of cardiac arrest due to injury or surgery were reduced and still falling."

A few staff members, including Ortiz and Sutherland, stirred as if to interrupt, but Jordan continued. He cited a short list of problems that may have caused Trudy Aguilera's heart to stop, including a congenital heart defect and an accidental prescription drug overdose. "These may not be as plausible as the cause of death on this patient's death certificate, but they are possible. How can we know for sure unless we investigate more of these deaths?"

He swept up the sheaf of printouts from the table and held them aloft. "And I'm not just talking about one trauma patient. Here are thirty-three more of them who died in SICU over the last sixteen months. Look at them if you want to. Some of you are listed as attending physicians in these cases: Dr. Muranaka, Dr. Sutherland, Dr. Boorsma, Dr. Andrade, and my predecessor, Dr. Kopke." Jordan tossed the stack on the table. The sheets fanned out across the tabletop. "Even you lost one last year, Dr. Ortiz," he added with a quick glance at the man.

The murmur of several private conversations rose across the room. Dr. Ettinger stood helplessly behind the small lectern as the spirited interchange unfolded before him.

Already hip-deep in venting his concern, Jordan saw no point in backing down now. He continued with a conviction that quieted his colleagues. "Homicides and suicides at Mercy Hospital are shipped to the medical examiner. But the cases on this table were not considered suspicious deaths. Their hearts apparently gave out—at least that's what the death certificates report. A couple of them were autopsied by Dr. Wiggins at the families' request. But most were buried or cremated before the cause of death could be challenged. We are doing a great disservice to their families and to our future patients by letting these deaths slide by without a closer look."

"Did you go to the trouble of checking the results of those private autopsies?" This time the challenge was from Dr. Mark Sutherland.

"Yes, Mark, and I am aware that the postmortems confirmed the cause of death entered by the physician at time of death. But two autopsies are only a sampling. What about the others? Who's to know if something else happened when no attempt is made to find out?"

"Patients die, Dr. Keyes." Sutherland was on his feet and scowling at Jordan from across the room. "Despite our best efforts to prevent it, traumatic injuries and illnesses often kill. How dare you imply that we fail to put forth our best effort to save every patient." The "we" Sutherland referred to clearly included everyone in the room except Jordan. A chorus of affirmation followed Sutherland's objection.

"I'm not impugning the effort to save these patients," Jordan said above the growing din. "My concern is that we don't do enough *after* they die to find out what happened. There may be unseen factors in these deaths we will never know about until we become diligent about postmortems on these borderline cases, perhaps illegal or unethical factors."

Ortiz stood now, and the room became quiet. "What are you saying, Doctor?" he probed soberly. "Are you saying that some of these patient deaths might have been encouraged or facilitated in some way?" Two dozen pairs of hostile eyes turned in Jordan's direction.

Jordan wished now he had never opened his mouth. Diplomacy and tact were not his strengths, and his outspokenness had hurt him in the past. But there were moral values at stake here. He had not verbalized his convictions this way before, but he saw no gain in leaving them unsaid.

In the silence, he began calmly and respectfully. "I am not suggesting that any of these patients were the victims of negligence in this hospital, either intentional or unintentional." He gestured to the printouts spread on the table in front of him. "But in the cases where a postmortem was not performed, the cause of death listed on the certificate is at best an educated guess. And perhaps that guess is correct. But we cannot know for sure because we do not autopsy them.

"Here's my concern: What is to prevent someone from

taking advantage of our policy to autopsy only suspicious deaths? In a state where assisted suicide is already legal, what is to prevent someone from taking the next step: the 'mercy killing' of a terminal patient? Worse yet, what is to prevent someone from tgaking the life of a patient whose condition is not terminal but rather conveniently critical: an elderly parent who is going to die soon anyway, a drug-addicted teenager brain-injured in an MVA?

"We all know that injecting something as simple as an overdose of potassium stops the heart just like a heart attack. But without an autopsy, who will ever know? I think we are leaving the door open for unscrupulous family members and physicians to take assisted suicide to a frightening new level: physician-assisted homicide."

As soon as the indicting words passed his lips, Jordan grabbed after them to pull them back. But they were out, and the reaction was immediate. Dr. Randall Boorsma, the neuro-oncology specialist, released a muffled curse as he pushed back his chair and stood. Then he stormed out of the room, flicking Jordan a look of disgust. Several others followed suit, including Ortiz and Sutherland. Watching the exodus, Dr. Ettinger announced, "The meeting is adjourned. Thank you for attending."

Conversations erupted in the hall as staff members returned to their duties. The phrases Jordan overheard made him wince: "Who died and made him god of Mercy Hospital?" "He's been reading too many Michael Crichton novels." "'Unscrupulous physicians'—what nerve!" "What can you expect? He's from L.A."

Philip Ettinger walked to the table where Jordan stood. They were alone in the conference room. "Sorry about ruining your meeting, Philip," Jordan said dejectedly.

"Don't worry about it," Philip returned. He added with a smile, "It wasn't much of a meeting until you spoke up."

Jordan collected the printouts and stuffed them into the

folder. "What do you think? Was I out of line? Can you see my point?"

The tall neurosurgeon's pause communicated to Jordan that he was composing a diplomatic response. "Yes, I see your point," he said at last.

Waiting for more, Jordan said, "And . . . ?"

Philip seemed reluctant to continue. "I share your concern, but to a lesser degree. This is a good hospital, Jordan, with a very professional staff. I doubt very much that we leave much of an open door for the mayhem you spoke about."

"So you don't see a need for autopsies on these patients?" Jordan asked, tapping the folder with his finger.

"To the contrary, I wish every deceased patient were subject to a postmortem. As you stated, it is the most direct path to discerning the cause of death. It just seems very impractical and, at least here at Mercy, unnecessary."

On the way out of the room, Philip said, "Have you considered asking the family of your deceased patient to seek a private autopsy?"

It was Jordan's turn to be diplomatic. He was afraid if he revealed his actions to Philip, they might get back to Waller. "I considered it. But Dr. Waller discouraged me from contacting the family." He felt a pang of guilt for passing off a half-truth.

Thankfully, Philip dropped the subject. "Don't let the meeting bother you," he said, with a pat on Jordan's shoulder. "You ruffled some feathers, but everyone will get over it." Then he took off down the hall at a brisk walk.

"Thanks," Jordan called after him, heading toward the staff elevator. He was already late for a 10:30 surgery.

◆ ◆ ◆

Twenty-five minutes later a telephone call was placed from within a private office in the neurosciences building. "I'm very concerned about the new man. He's asking too many questions, and he's sticking his nose where it doesn't belong.

The death of his patient seemed to set him off." The caller paced the room, listening to the response through the phone.

"Yes, and he even dug up charts from the last sixteen months," the caller explained. "He's concerned about the number of SICU deaths, thinks there should be more autopsies." More pacing and listening. Then the caller interjected, "No one in the building suspects anything. They think Keyes is just shooting off his mouth."

The caller listened again, then said, "The Aguilera woman will be no problem. The body is at the funeral home, and burial is Saturday. But what about the next one or the next one? I tell you, Keyes is a loose cannon. He is a threat to our work."

The caller listened intently, responding at intervals, "Yes. . . . yes. . . . I agree. . . . Absolutely." Finally the caller said, "All right, I'll take care of it. You can count on me," and he hung up.

ELEVEN

"How's it going, Jordy?"

Jordan was too busy to shoot the breeze. Had the speaker been anyone else, he would have nodded and kept working. But Maggie Rusch, despite her brash, confrontational style—and that she sometimes called him Jordy instead of Dr. Keyes—seemed like a friend. And after the caustic reception he had received yesterday from his colleagues in Neurosurgery, Jordan could not ignore her friendly greeting.

"Too busy for words, Maggie. How about you?" The two were momentarily at the SICU nurse's station on the way to other duties. Jordan's small flock of med students was with a patient in room 10.

"How does it feel being the talk of the town?" she asked with an impish grin.

The reminder of yesterday's fiasco during the staff meeting tightened the knot in Jordan's stomach. "Good news travels fast," he said wryly, scrolling through a chart on the computer.

"Unfortunately, this place feeds on juicy gossip like piranhas on fresh meat. You just happened to be yesterday's blue plate special. You're old news now. Who knows who will get chewed up and spit out today?"

Jordan wished it were that easy. He wished he could rid himself of yesterday's trouble as simply as tearing Thursday,

April 15, from his page-per-day desk calendar and throwing it away. He had incensed a number of colleagues. How? By thoughtlessly pushing his agenda, foisting his opinions, and ridiculing the status quo. His conviction on the issue of SICU deaths and autopsies had not changed in twenty-four hours. But he regretted how he had shared that conviction.

Maggie moved around so she could see his face. "Are you OK?"

Jordan glanced at her guileless, caring expression, then quickly back to the monitor. "I got a soda for answering that question last time," he said, deflecting her probe with a little humor.

Maggie smiled. "OK, so I owe you one. But are you doing all right?"

It was the second time this week she had asked him that, and it was getting embarrassing. Did he not look OK? Or was Maggie just one of those nervy Christians who weren't afraid to dig beneath the surface to check emotional vital signs?

"Yeah, I'm OK, thanks," he said. In reality, he was OK most of the time. A relentless schedule was his greatest ally. As long as he was busy, he had little time to reflect on what had happened in the neurosurgery conference room. As long as he was busy, he was OK.

Maggie's next question was even more invasive and discomfiting: "Have you told your wife about yesterday?" He could feel her eyes reading his face for an answer. Jordan had called Della last night, but he had not mentioned his run-in with the surgical staff. He did not want to remind her of the dark days at County General Hospital or suggest that they could happen again.

"I'll be seeing her this weekend in L.A.," he said, making eye contact for a moment, hoping sincerity covered his intentional vagueness. "We'll talk."

"Good. It means a lot to a woman when her husband confides in her about his problems as well as his successes. Sam is very good about that. It's one of the ways he makes me feel loved."

"I see," Jordan said, eyes on the monitor, trying not to listen.

"And when he talks about what bugs him, he often discovers a hidden layer of sadness or hurt underneath it. When he helps me see that sadness or hurt, I am able to care for him, which really draws us together."

Jordan acknowledged her with a nod. He didn't have time for another sisterly counseling session.

Maggie did not press the issue. "Since you're going away for the weekend, I guess you can't join Sam and me for barbecue tomorrow night."

"Maybe next time," Jordan said.

"Consider it a standing offer, Jordy." With a small laugh, she added, "Call it Sam and Maggie's soup kitchen for malnourished doctors."

"Thanks again," he said.

Finished with her task at the counter, Maggie left to check on a patient in room 6. "Catch you later, Jordy."

Jordan was relieved to see her go.

At eleven he rushed out of the hospital to meet Virginia. The Realtor had convinced him over the phone that he *must* see two more Lake Oswego homes before making an offer on the lakeside property he liked. Juggling appointments, he had cleared a couple of hours. Armed with the camera, he took Interstate 5 toward the Lake Oswego exit. It was an unseasonably warm spring day for Portland. Jordan could see snow-covered Mount Hood, rugged and proud, east of the city. It felt good to be out of the hospital.

Driving southward, Jordan allowed his mind to dwell for several minutes on a thought that his morning's agenda had continually pushed away: Trudy Aguilera's autopsy. He found himself praying that the pathologist would uncover something—anything—other than heart failure due to severe brain trauma. Such a finding would at least partially vindicate him in the eyes of his most vocal detractors, Dr. Oscar Ortiz and Dr. Mark Sutherland. And if Dr. Waller, attending a conference in Santa Fe, New Mexico, had already heard about the staff meeting, vindication now would make for a more pleasant reunion upon his return.

Jordan believed that God performs miracles, but he was also a pragmatist. He knew that God sometimes answered prayers in the negative for reasons known only to him. So Jordan kept tight rein on his hopes. If nothing materialized in Aguilera's postmortem, there would be other patients. He would eventually prove his point, hopefully in a way that would win the respect of his colleagues and superiors.

The pager on his belt buzzed as he exited the freeway. After a quick glance at the readout, Jordan braked suddenly, checked his mirrors, and squealed the Lexus through a tight turn toward the on-ramp. It was a trauma code call from the hospital. Since Jordan was not the on-call neurosurgeon, the summons could mean only one thing. An emergency requiring backup surgeons.

Racing up the on-ramp to northbound I-5, Jordan dialed the Trauma Center on his cell phone. An ER nurse delivered the report in a hurry: "Shoot-out during a bank robbery in Northeast. We have three badly injured cops and a civilian en route—at least two with head injuries." Jordan estimated his arrival at ten minutes. Tapping off the phone, he swept into the fast lane and accelerated.

The Trauma Center was spooling up to full alert when Jordan jogged in from the parking garage. The first Portland police officer, a female veteran of nine years, was in slot 3. Pieces of a bloody uniform and a Kevlar vest had been tossed in a corner. Doctors and nurses swarmed frantically over a pale white body on the gurney. The officer had taken a bullet in the lower abdomen and another in the neck, outside the protection of her bulletproof vest.

Trauma surgeon Otto Gebhardt, a tall, barrel-chested redhead, turned away from directing resuscitation efforts to yell at Jordan. "Incoming in two minutes, Keyes. Another officer, bullet to the head. Slot 1."

Jordan ditched his sport jacket and ordered an operating room and surgery team to be readied. By the time he had secured gown, gloves, and mask, the trauma team awaiting the second officer had assembled in slot 1. Meanwhile, intense activity in slot 3 revealed that the resuscitation of Officer Josephine Ward was not proceeding well.

Officer Eddie Beamon, a thirty-three-year-old African-American police officer, arrived by Life Flight helicopter. Beamon had taken a bullet in the head during the war scene outside a bank in a Portland shopping mall. A third-year trauma resident mobilized the slot 1 team as the comatose officer was rushed in. Jordan stood by to assist and await the results of a CT scan—if the officer survived resuscitation. Outside the ER another frenzied scene was developing. The Portland media, now fully aware of the spectacular events at the mall, circled like vultures for breaking news on the fallen officers.

Once Officer Beamon's condition was stabilized and portable life support apparatus was in place, Jordan accompanied the gurney to the CT scanner. The stark image brought a whistle of amazement from the radiologist. A .38 caliber slug had penetrated the left frontal lobe. On the film the clearly defined white cylinder appeared to be suspended in the opaque, gray background of the brain.

"How is this guy still alive?" remarked Dr. Gerald Mickens, a second-year neurosurgery resident, peering in for a look over Jordan's shoulder. Mickens had been hailed at the last minute to assist Jordan in the likely event of brain surgery on Officer Beamon.

"He won't be for long unless we get that thing out of there and stop the bleeding," Jordan said. "Let's get to work."

Five hours later Jordan tossed away his mask and cap, along with bloodstained gloves and gown. After washing his hands and arms, he buried his face in several successive handfuls of cold water. He had been informed that Eddie Beamon was a bachelor. His mother and younger brother, plus a few other family members and a Portland police captain, had been afforded a private waiting room away from the media maelstrom. Jordan patted his face dry and quickly combed his hair, then set out to deliver his report.

Finding Buster Chapman holding vigil with the Beamon contingent did not surprise Jordan. There was a childlikeness about the tenderhearted big man that was without threat and seemed to exude peace.

Mrs. Arleta Beamon, a smallish woman in professional attire, sat on the small divan with her younger son, who appeared to be in his late twenties. A uniformed captain stood near, as if on guard. He and a few other relatives—as well as Buster Chapman—moved in close as Jordan sat on the coffee table opposite mother and son.

"Mrs. Beamon, I'm Dr. Keyes."

The woman extended her hand. "How do you do, Doctor." Her eyes were somewhat puffy, but she was not crying. Jordan shook her hand.

"I removed a bullet that had lodged well into the left frontal region of your son's brain." He touched his forehead near the left temple to indicate the general area. "He is still in critical condition, and he is on a ventilator—a breathing machine. But the bleeding in the brain has been stopped, and for now he is holding his own."

A glimmer of relief moved across the woman's face. Eyes closed for a brief moment, she whispered, "Thank you, Jesus, thank you."

Jordan continued with the waiting room litany he had recited in countless severe brain injury cases: "The patient will likely remain in a coma for several days, possibly longer. It's too soon to determine the extent of the brain damage. His injuries are still life threatening. The next twenty-four to forty-eight hours will tell us more. You will be able to see him in about an hour, after he is out of Recovery." Having delivered his message, Jordan stood to leave.

Johnny Beamon stood with him. "Will my brother be able to go back to work someday, Doctor?" It amazed Jordan that people asked questions like this right after he had already answered it: It's too soon to tell anything.

"The injured area of his brain handles aspects of cognitive function—thinking, problem solving, language, memory for most motor activities. Some of these functions may be disabled by the injury. The brain has a marvelous capacity for self-restoration. He may regain much of what he has lost. He may even be able to go back to work. Our first concern is that he survives the bullet wound and the surgery. After that we can begin to wonder about any brain function that has been damaged."

As Jordan backed slowly out of the small room, the woman broke into tears. "Jesus, Jesus, Jesus," she cried softly, "Jesus, touch my son." Buster Chapman was at her side with the rest of the family. As usual, the big man was crying too. He prayed along with her, "Jesus, Jesus, Jesus, touch her son." The police captain shifted from foot to foot, not knowing what to do.

For a moment, Jordan was unable to leave. In no way did he wish for Arleta Beamon's grief. He had been there. He had lost a son of his own. He was beyond all this. But there was a magnetic warmth about the scene before him. There was something so pure and so right about the comforting arms and tearstained cheeks of the big janitor doing his thing.

A strong hand gripped his shoulder from behind. "Dr. Keyes, a word please."

Jordan turned to see the weathered face of the hospital director. "Yes, Dr. Sheffield."

Taylor Sheffield motioned him away from the door for privacy. "The police officer is out of surgery, I take it?" Jordan nodded. "There must be two hundred people outside waiting for a statement—cops, TV people, the works. Your prognosis on Officer Beamon?"

Jordan shrugged. "He's on the bubble, Dr. Sheffield. I removed a bullet from the left frontal lobe. But he's on life support, and he may be comatose for days or weeks."

"Basic line, in other words—too soon to tell anything."

"Right."

"The other two officers didn't make it, you know. One was a woman."

"I didn't know that. That's too bad."

"I'm just glad I can give these people a little good news," Sheffield said, waving toward the crowd awaiting him at the entrance to the Trauma Center. "Good work, Doctor."

"Thank you, sir."

Sheffield dropped his head for a moment. "By the way, Jordan, there are some very angry words floating around the hospital about you. Something about a staff meeting yesterday, some things you said."

Jordan winced inside. "Yes, sir."

Regaining eye contact, Sheffield said, "I'd like to hear your side of the story, maybe later tonight, after all this quiets down a little." The director gave no hint of his feelings or thoughts on the matter.

"Of course," Jordan said.

Sheffield left to perform his public-relations duty, and Jordan breathed a sigh, relieved that his boss had not asked him to go along. He retreated to a telephone in the surgery wing, dialed the dictation service, and recited the details of Eddie Beamon's surgery.

Before leaving the phone, he dialed his voice mail. Having been out of reach for over five hours, he found a string of messages. He jotted down a few notes and numbers as he listened.

The eighth message was from the office of Dr. Joseph Wiggins. The stoic receptionist reported: "Dr. Wiggins completed the autopsy on your former patient Trudy Aguilera.

He reports no findings to contradict the cause of death listed on the death certificate. A full written report will be mailed to you along with a statement for services."

Jordan hung up the phone and leaned against the counter. It was after five o'clock, and he had not eaten since breakfast. But if he stopped to eat now, he might end up thinking about what he would say to Dr. Sheffield. Since Dr. Wiggins had given him nothing positive to say, Jordan decided to get back to work and not think about it.

TWELVE

Saturday was getaway day to L.A., so Jordan was at the hospital before 6:00 A.M. His United flight to L.A. would leave at 12:50 P.M. Before leaving town he had to pick up snapshots of the Lake Oswego house from the photo shop, stop by Virginia's office to sign an offer to purchase, and buy birthday gifts for Katy. So he had about four hours to tie up loose ends at Mercy before his brief trip south.

First stop was SICU room 8 and his star patient, Officer Eddie Beamon. Jordan had successfully evaded the media last night, though a number of reporters had clamored to meet the "skilled neurosurgeon who brought the brave officer back from the brink of death." And he had become something of a hero among the Portland police. A stream of officers filed respectfully through the SICU to view their fallen comrade and offer support to his family. Arleta Beamon introduced Jordan to a few of them, and many praised him for saving Eddie's life—some with tears in their eyes.

Apparently Jordan's sudden hero status in the community had impressed Dr. Taylor Sheffield. The director had never contacted Jordan last night for a summit meeting to discuss the staff conflict. Hopefully, his public relations role on the Eddie Beamon case would keep Sheffield out of Jordan's hair until the staff issue calmed down. Best-case scenario,

Jordan mused, was that Dr. Waller, who returned from his conference later today, would never hear about it.

Jordan studied Beamon's chart on the in-room computer as his patient lay comatose. Pleased at what he found, Jordan input orders to remove the ventilator. Beamon's overall fitness would be his greatest ally in recovery. The officer was ready to assume breathing on his own, and seeing him without the life-support apparatus would be a boost to his family and coworkers. The city was in mourning over the loss of two other officers. Eddie Beamon would be a ray of hope.

The patient's chart gave signs of moderate seizure activity, not uncommon in brain-injured patients. Jordan tapped an order into the computer for one hundred milligrams of phenobarbital to be administered each hour for the next eight hours. The drug would keep Beamon somnolent through the day, but he would not likely regain full consciousness for another twenty-four to forty-eight hours anyway. In the meantime, the medication would diminish the prospect of harmful seizures.

On his way out, Jordan conferred with the charge nurse on the SICU night shift and communicated the orders orally. Eloise Sandborn, an eighteen-year veteran at Mercy with the build and temperament of a linebacker, said she would handle it.

When he returned to SICU three hours later after nonstop rounds on other patients, a few off-duty policemen were in the hall outside the unit, and Arleta Beamon sat quietly at her son's bedside. Countless bouquets and potted plants had been delivered to the hospital for the wounded officer. But since flowers were not allowed in the SICU, Arleta Beamon donated the beautiful expressions of care to other patients throughout the hospital as quickly as they arrived.

Before visiting his patient, Jordan accessed the chart from a computer at the nurse's station. Angered at what he saw, he hissed and shook his head. His order for phenobarbital was there, but the prescription had not been filled. *No won-*

der people keep dying around here, he grumbled to himself. *Nobody knows how to follow orders.* He looked around for Nurse Sandborn, then realized she had been off shift since seven o'clock. He would write her up when he got back on Monday and give her a dressing-down for good measure.

Running out of time and patience, Jordan was at a crossroads. It was highly irregular for a physician to administer meds. It was a task nurses were trained and hired for. But the night nurse had already failed him, and he could not wait around to make sure the busy SICU day crew would comply. So he made a snap decision for expedience.

Phoning the hospital pharmacy from the nurse's station, he ordered the first hundred milligrams of phenobarbital to be delivered to him stat. After a few more minutes reviewing the chart, he went to visit Eddie and Arleta Beamon.

When he entered, Arleta was softly reading aloud to her unconscious son from a well-worn Bible. He recognized the words from Jeremiah 29: "'I know the plans I have for you,' declares the Lord, 'plans to prosper you and not to harm you, plans to give you hope and a future.'" Seeing him, she stopped. "Good morning, Dr. Keyes," she said with a slight smile.

Jordan nodded his greeting. "He did well through the night," he said. Eddie Beamon looked much better without the ventilator.

"Oh, I knew he would be all right," Arleta said, placing the open Bible on the bed beside her son. "I've been praying most of the night."

"I think a lot of people in Portland have been praying for your son," Jordan said.

"And I prayed for you all through the operation yesterday. God worked through you to save my son; you know that, don't you?"

Jordan smiled to himself, aware that Arleta Beamon was subtly witnessing to him. "Yes, I know God works through me. I count on it."

"Thank you for what you did for my Eddie, Doctor," she said, holding back a tear.

"You're welcome."

The mother turned toward her son. "Eddie is a good Christian man, Doctor. He and Johnny team-teach a Sunday school class of boys at our church. Eddie never got into trouble as a kid, never got into drugs, never ran with the bad girls. His dream since he was a boy was to be a police officer. As a mother, I couldn't be more proud."

"You have every reason to be proud, Mrs. Beamon."

"He doesn't date much, but I've been hoping he would find a nice girl soon," she said with a light laugh. Then she added wistfully, "But perhaps it's best that Eddie is still single."

"A hope and a future, Mrs. Beamon, that's what God promised, remember?"

Arleta brightened at his words. "Amen, Doctor. Amen."

The pharmacy tech arrived with the vial of phenobarbital, and Jordan prepared to inject it into the port on the patient's IV line. He explained, "Brain trauma such as your son experienced sometimes leads to seizures, and he doesn't need a complication like that. Phenobarb will keep him sleeping for a while, but it greatly reduces the danger of seizures. I have ordered one hundred milligrams an hour for the rest of the day." Arleta watched with interest as Jordan dispensed the drug.

"Mrs. Beamon, I'll be away from the hospital until late tomorrow night." He recorded the injection in the chart on the bedside computer as he spoke. "But your son will be well taken care of. If you have any questions, you can contact anyone here in Intensive Care."

Maggie Rusch was on duty in the nurse's station as Jordan emerged from Eddie Beamon's room. He went directly to her. "What do you know about the night charge nurse—large woman, kind of gruff?"

Maggie nodded. "Eloise Sandborn."

"That's the one."

"Eloise may be a little light in the people skills department, but she's a very good nurse. Why?"

"She forgot to dispense an order of phenobarb early this morning. I put it on the chart, and I told her about it in person. But it never happened."

"Need me to take care of it?"

"No, no, I got it already."

"You gave the meds?" Maggie's expression was one of mild shock.

"I wanted to make sure it happened before I left. Had I known you were on duty, I would have let you do it. I'm not happy that the night nurse let it slip through the cracks. I'll talk to her when I get back."

"When do you leave?"

Jordan checked his watch and whistled. "I need to get out of here now."

"Don't worry about anything around here, Jordy," Maggie said. "We'll take good care of your policeman for you. You take good care of your family. They need you."

Jordan recognized another dose of sisterly admonition served with a friendly smile. "Thanks," he said as he hurried away.

Jordan parked in the economy lot and arrived at the United gate five minutes before departure. He was grateful to be making this short trip with only a small carry-on and a plastic bag containing Katy's gifts. He was also bringing treasures for Della: twenty-four snapshots of what he hoped would become her dream home and a copy of the offer sheet he had worked out with the Realtor. Virginia had quickly forgiven Jordan for standing her up Friday when she learned that he had cared for the victims of the foiled bank robbery. Her positive attitude had been encouraged when Jordan arrived at her office this morning with checkbook in hand.

During taxi and takeoff, Jordan was pricked with anxiety about leaving the hospital for so long. He had poured in the hours during his first two months at Mercy, so he had certainly earned a little time off. Furthermore, Dr. Waller had encouraged him to expedite his family's move to Portland—and it was certainly a primary goal for this trip. But Jordan fidgeted like a first-time flyer as the 737 gained altitude and banked south over the city of Portland. Some people who knew him would laugh and call it a typical control issue—and they might be right. But Jordan did not want to leave. He was unwilling to trust his colleagues with the care of Eddie Beamon and others, especially with Nurse Sandborn's blunder still sideways in his craw. He kept reminding himself he would return late tomorrow night to reclaim his turf.

Once the coffee was served, Jordan purposely directed his thoughts toward Los Angeles. The two gifts he had selected at Meier and Frank downtown typified his dichotomous view of his eleven-year-old daughter. Katarina Suzanne Keyes was on the threshold of becoming a teenager, so he bought her the short skirt and top she had asked for. It seemed better suited for a college girl than an eleven-year-old, but he knew she would love the grown-up style. And since she was also his baby girl, Jordan also bought her a plush toy raccoon for her stuffed animal collection. He had been buying Katy stuffed animals since before she was born.

Jordan pulled out the birthday card he had purchased, a card that better suited the young lady's outfit than the kid's stuffed toy. Reaching for a pen, he realized he had nothing with him for J. J. Jordan and Della always bought presents for both their children on each of their birthdays. The bigger gifts were for the "birthday kid," with a smaller we-love-you-too gift for the other.

In less than a tick of time he remembered: *We only buy presents for one now; J. J. isn't with us anymore.* He had not lapsed that way in several months. The sudden, unbidden memory of his son's death threatened a wave of sadness. But just as quickly, the failure of Nurse Sandborn to medicate his patient flashed before him once again, instantly shutting down the encroaching sense of loss over his son. The more he thought about the nurse's incompetence, the more irritated he became.

The flight attendant approached his row to offer a beverage. Jordan asked for mineral water, then redirected his attention to the task of signing Katy's card. Rotating the pen in his fingers, he set about to frame a sentiment just right for the occasion.

He had always prided himself on the ability to focus his thoughts and emotions. It was a skill, he had often reasoned, that allowed him to deal with a serious head injury without being distracted by the anguish plaguing the patient or the patient's family. Being judged by some patients as uncaring or aloof was a small price to pay for the "gift" of intense focus.

This highly developed skill had served him well when J. J. died. Della had been a basket case for weeks after the funeral. Jordan regarded his ability to emotionally disconnect as a strength, allowing him to be a rock of stability for his family. In light of his most recent conversations with Della, however, he had begun to question just how much of a rock his wife and daughter considered him to be.

Opening the birthday card on the small table, he wrote his carefully worded comments beneath the printed sentiment:

My Sweet Katy,

I am so proud of you, and I love you very much. Happy Birthday to my beautiful daughter.

Daddy

He reread the note, then underlined the words *love you* three times. After tucking the card in with the wrapped gifts at his feet, he reclined his seat to reclaim an hour of lost sleep.

THIRTEEN

"Daddy, you're here!" Katy squealed the words when she opened the front door. Then she plunged into her father's arms.

Jordan dropped his travel bag and the sack of gifts to embrace her. "Of course I'm here," he laughed, relishing his daughter's welcome. "You only turn eleven once, and I wouldn't miss it for anything."

"Thank you for coming, Daddy," she said, hugging him. "Thank you, thank you, thank you."

From the corner of his eye, Jordan noticed an attractive woman watching them from inside the house. He assumed the party had already begun. The woman must be the mother of one of Katy's friends. But when he looked at her squarely over the top of Katy's head, he saw that it was Della. She looked like a different woman. Her shimmering dark hair was three inches shorter, framing her face nicely instead of being pulled back with a bow. She wore a stylish blouse and slacks he had never seen. And there was a welcoming smile on her face.

Katy grabbed her father's travel bag and pulled him into the house. Jordan scooped up the sack of gifts on the way in.

"I'm not late for the party, am I, sweetheart?"

"Of course not," Katy returned with a comical I-can't-believe-you-said-that scowl on her face. "The party starts at five. You're early, just like I planned."

Jordan pulled the wrapped toy from the sack. "Then here is a little before-the-party gift," he said, holding the toy out to her.

Katy beamed with delight and gratitude as she tore away the paper. "A raccoon! How cute! I love it!"

"And here is another gift, for later," he said, producing the white Meier and Frank box swathed in a wide gold ribbon and bow.

"Thank you, Daddy. We have a table for gifts in the family room. But don't worry. I'm going to open yours and Mom's first." Then she and the gifts disappeared toward the back of the house.

Jordan turned to Della, who had watched her daughter and husband from a distance. "Hi, Dell," he said, approaching and embracing her. "You look wonderful." He kissed her on the cheek, then on the lips. The familiar softness and alluring fragrance warmed Jordan with anticipation for their first night together in over a month.

"Thank you. Welcome home, Jordan," she said, returning his embrace before stepping back. "How was your flight?"

He shrugged. "Nothing special. Just a flight."

"I could have picked you up, you know," Della said. During one of their conversations earlier in the week she had offered him a ride from the airport. Jordan had politely refused.

The idea of depending on his wife for transportation had been too confining for Jordan, who liked to have his own wheels available in case of an emergency call to the hospital. "I know," he said. "But you had the party to prepare for. Besides, a rental car just makes it easier for all of us to get around. We can take it to San Pedro tomorrow for our trip to Catalina."

"Sure, that's fine," Della acquiesced.

Jordan moved to retrieve the packet of snapshots from his bag. "Wait till you see this, Dell," he said excitedly. "Come on, sit down. You won't believe this place." Leading his wife to the sofa, he called over his shoulder into the family room. "Katy, come here. I want you to see your new bedroom."

With his wife and daughter sitting beside him, Jordan laid the pictures on the coffee table one by one with a dramatic flair. He began with shots of the lake and woods around the property. "Now look at this," he said proudly, presenting a front exterior view of the two-story contemporary home backed up to a mini-forest of mature fir and spruce. "And how about this, and this, and this." He continued with snapshot after snapshot presenting the massive rock fireplace, the spacious living room, family room, and kitchen. Jordan embellished each photo with a verbal description.

Della studied each of them carefully without picking any up. Katy oohed and aahed at each new view. And she was ecstatic over three shots of her bedroom, which featured a large window seat and a view of the lake.

"Did you already buy the house, Daddy?" Katy probed after Jordan displayed all the pictures.

"No, but I made the owners a good offer. If they like our price and can wait until we sell this place, then this will be your new bedroom." Jordan tapped the two photos displaying Katy's window seat.

"And what about J. J.'s room?" Katy asked tentatively.

"J. J. won't have a room in our new home, Katy," Jordan said without looking at Della. "There is a bedroom for you and a bedroom for Mom and me. The other two bedrooms will be offices—one for Mom's decorating business and one for me."

Katy voiced her next question with even greater caution: "So what happens to all the stuff in J. J.'s bedroom?"

Jordan drew a long breath and released it slowly. The topic of what to do with J. J.'s "shrine"—though he never used that word around Della or Katy—had not been broached. Della had insisted on leaving their son's room intact. For the first several months after the funeral, Jordan would occasionally come home to find her sitting in there. He never knew what to say at such times, so he said nothing. Whenever he walked by J. J.'s bedroom, he made sure to close the door, hoping to urge Della nonverbally to get on with her life.

"We have photo albums and videos to help us remember J. J., sweetie. I'm sure there are other little boys who would be happy to have his clothes and toys."

The answer seemed to satisfy Katy, and Della acted as if she had not heard, though Jordan knew she had. Katy turned her attention back to the snapshots on the table. "Can I show my new room to Maddie? I can't wait till she comes over."

Jordan passed off responsibility to Della with a look. "All right," she said, "but it's only an hour until your other guests arrive. Don't be long."

Katy snapped up the three photos and bolted for the door with little-girl enthusiasm. "OK, back in a few."

Jordan sat in silence for several moments after the front door closed as Della's eyes surveyed the snapshots. "What do you think, Dell?" he said at last. "Didn't I tell you it was a dream house? And the pictures don't really do it justice."

"It's a beautiful house, Jordan," she said with a modicum of enthusiasm.

"Do you see the decorating possibilities? It's like a blank canvas for someone like you. I can't wait to see how it looks after the Della touch."

Della nodded. "It will be a challenge to decorate, with all that glass. But it will be fun."

"So you like it, then?"

"Yes, I like it. It's a very nice house." As she spoke Della collected the snapshots into a stack and returned them to the envelope.

"You don't sound very excited."

Leaving the packet of photos on the table, Della stood. "Jordan, you know how I feel about this move," she said plaintively.

Jordan stood also. "That's why I want you to have this house, Dell," he said, waving at the photos. "I want things to be better for you there. You're going to love it in Oregon. No L.A. traffic. Beautiful seasons. Skiing. What's not to like about going to Portland?"

"All this is wonderful, Jordan. But a nice house and beautiful scenery and season tickets to the performing arts center—these things do not make someplace home for me."

Jordan knew she was edging back to what he perceived to be the central issue, so he went there first. "The schedule will be better, Dell, I promise. By the time you and Katy are moved, I'll be settled into a routine at the hospital."

"From hundred-hour weeks down to eighty-hour weeks, I suppose." The words came out in a playful tone, but Jordan felt the cynical bite.

"There will always be some long days; you know that. It goes with the territory. But I'll have regular days off. We can do things together."

Della smiled at him weakly. "I know, Jordan," she said, "I know."

He started to respond, but Della flashed a stop sign with both hands. "We can talk about this later if you want. But right now I have pizzas to get ready. I need you to set out folding chairs around the patio table and carry out the paper plates and plastic utensils, OK?" She started for the kitchen.

"Sure, Dell," he said, a little deflated. "Anything."

Once the little girl guests and their mothers began to arrive, Jordan assumed the role of assistant host. He kept the punch bowl filled and delivered pizzas to the patio as they came out of the oven.

During the party games, Jordan sensed a growing urge to slip away to the phone and check his voice mail at the hospital. There would be plenty of messages, some that might need his personal response. But he resisted. He was here for Katy's party, and he dared not let Della catch him on the phone to Portland during the festivities. If there was an emergency concerning him, the hospital had the number for his cell phone. There would be time later to check his messages, after the guests were gone.

Fancying himself a better-than-average point-and-shoot photographer, he volunteered to take pictures while Della helped with the games. Katy was absorbed in the attention and fun, but an occasional glance from her conveyed pleasure at having her dad on hand and involved. Jordan continued in his photographer's role through the opening of the gifts. The skirt and top made a big hit with the little girls, but Della's raised eyebrows caused Jordan to wonder if his daughter would be allowed to wear the outfit before she grew out of it.

He made sure he got candid shots of each guest interacting with Katy, the guest of honor. He always took twice as many pictures as Della did in situations like these. But he knew Katy would appreciate the large variety of snapshots to choose from when putting together her memory book from the evening.

While Katy and her friends watched a video in the family room and Della and the mothers chatted in the living room, Jordan busied himself cleaning up the dinner mess. Anything he could do to convince Della that he wanted her with him in Portland seemed like worthwhile activity.

On the way back from delivering soiled dish towels to the laundry room, Jordan detoured into the bedroom to make his call to Portland. The bedside lamps were turned low. The feminine fragrances and decorative touches in the room rekindled his desire for Della. He understood her reticence to move north. He understood her reluctance to believe his work schedule would change. But if he could persuade her to trust him, she would see that their life together would be better. Perhaps tonight he could encourage her in that direction.

Jordan dialed his voice mail on the bedside phone. The first six messages bolstered his hope that the staff he had left in charge of his patients could pull it off. Instructions for patient care were being followed meticulously, and reports from the attending nurses and physicians were comprehensive and concise.

But the seventh message rocked him. Sitting breathlessly on the bed, he tapped in the command to replay the message, hoping he had heard it wrong. The voice was familiar, but the spunk and joy he had come to expect were missing: "Jordy, this is Maggie. I don't know if you're picking up your messages or not, but I thought I should call anyway. I don't know how to tell you this, but Eddie Beamon, the police officer in SICU, just died."

FOURTEEN

In her message, Maggie went on to explain that Eddie Beamon had suffered respiratory arrest around noon. He was given emergency resuscitation for about twenty minutes without a response. Cause of the respiratory problem could not immediately be determined. The state medical examiner would perform an autopsy later today because of the gunshot to his head. Beamon's death was now a homicide charged against a bank robber, who had survived the shoot-out with minor bullet wounds.

Numb from shock, Jordan listened to the rest of his messages. None of them concerned the late Eddie Beamon. He hung up the phone and sat motionlessly on the side of the bed, head down and shoulders hunched under a sudden invisible weight. Dozens of positive, freeze-frame images flooded his consciousness: a bloody bullet fragment; a steady heartbeat; a mother's tearful gratitude; accolades and appreciation from a dozen police officers; an open Bible; the words *a future and a hope.* But one dark image obliterated them all: lifeless Eddie Beamon, draped with a sheet, being wheeled from the SICU.

A sudden urgency gripped Jordan. He had to find out what happened to the police officer. He had to be there when the autopsy results arrived. He had to defend himself in case anyone—especially Taylor Sheffield or Bert Waller—suspected him of error or negligence. He had to assure them that the death of two of his patients in less than a week was not his fault. He had to get back to Portland *now.*

No, you can't leave, he ordered himself sternly. *You promised to be here for the party. You promised to take Katy and Della to Catalina tomorrow. If you leave now, Della will throw it back in your face: "Your work always comes before your family. See, Jordan, it will never change, not here, not in Portland, not ever."*

The battle waged only for a moment. Jordan made the hard choice, the right choice: He would not go back to Portland tonight. There was nothing he could do for Officer Beamon or his family now. The autopsy would likely find the cause of death to be a complication of the man's critical brain injury. That seemed to be the way things happened at Mercy. No one expected Jordan to be back at work before Monday morning. As much as he wanted to bolt for the airport, he would follow through with his plans to be with Della and Katy.

He quickly made a subsequent decision: He would not tell Della his news. He did not want his wife to think he was playing the martyr: "Yes, my medical career might be on the line, but I have decided to stay here with you." Della and Katy needed to know nothing about Eddie Beamon or the anxiety that now chewed at the lining of Jordan's stomach. The party and the trip to Catalina would go on as planned, and Jordan would demonstrate to Della with his devotion how much better things would be when she and Katy got to Portland.

If Maggie were here right now, he pondered cynically, *she would probably say, "Sam shares his problems with me, Jordy, and when we talk about them it draws us closer together." Well, I'm not Sam, and Della isn't Maggie. Della and I will get closer when I get my career back on track. And that's something I have to do alone.*

After the guests left, Jordan and Della sat with Katy in the family room as she looked through her collection of gifts. Jordan helped her load a CD-ROM game on her computer, a gift from Della. Then Katy begged her parents to play "one more game" after "one more game." They had fun playing together, and the constant chatter and activity diverted Jordan from the pall of concern hovering over him. Finally Della announced, "We have to leave for the boat at 6:30 tomorrow, so it's bedtime for everyone."

Jordan closed up the house for the night while Della prepared for bed. When he came into their room, she was already in bed watching the ten o'clock news on TV. The room was dark except for the glow of the monitor. He showered and dressed for bed, then slipped between the sheets. It was the first time he had been to bed before eleven in months.

Della remained on her side of the bed watching the weather report without comment. When the credits began to roll, Della snapped off the TV with the remote. The room was dark, silent, and still.

"You did a wonderful job on the party, Dell," Jordan said.

"It turned out all right, didn't it?" she responded with a measure of satisfaction.

"The pizza was perfect. You had the evening well planned. Katy had a great time."

They conversed quietly for several minutes in the dark. They talked about Katy's gifts, her friends, their mothers. They discussed the day ahead—when they had to leave for San Pedro, what they needed to bring, what they would do with Katy in Avalon. Even in the same bed, Della seemed far away, as if they were talking on the telephone.

After several moments of silence, Jordan posed a question that had been nagging at him since he left Los Angeles: "Dell, do you know that I love you?"

Della seemed to analyze the question before speaking. "What do you mean, exactly?"

"Just what I said. Do you know that I love you?"

"Yes, I guess so," she said tentatively. "Why?"

"How do you know?" Jordan pressed. "I mean, what makes you believe that I love you?"

"What are you trying to say, Jordan?"

"Just tell me how you know I love you," he insisted.

The covers rustled as Della changed positions on her side of the bed. She did not answer for several seconds. "Well, you work hard to pay the bills. You take responsibility for getting things done around the house. You're helpful—like tonight in the kitchen. You tell me you love me . . . sometimes."

The room was silent again. Jordan waited, hoping for more. Enough time passed that Della could have drifted off to sleep. But Jordan asked his next question anyway. "Honey, do *you* love *me?*"

The covers rustled again as she turned to face the wall, then a long silence fell. Finally, Della breathed a quiet sigh. "Jordan, I'm sorry, but I don't know how I feel for you right now. I'm just numb inside."

Long moments passed between each succeeding exchange.

"How long have you felt this way?"

"I don't know . . . months, I suppose."

"When I moved to Portland?"

"Before that, long before that."

"When J. J. died?"

"Even before that, Jordan. Except after losing J. J., I almost lost hope."

Jordan rolled onto his side to face Della, though he could barely see her in the dark. "What happened? Did I do something?"

"I've thought about it. I've asked God to show me. I don't have much of an answer. I guess it's just that . . . you're not here."

"It's my schedule then, right? Della, we talked about this before we got married. We knew going in that my work would take a lot of time, at least in the early years. I've been trying to tell you since I moved that it's going to get better. As soon as you get to Portland, we—"

Della rolled over to face him. "Jordan, listen to me," she interrupted. "It's not your schedule. Because even when you're home, you're not really here."

Jordan could now make out the features of her beautiful face. She was less than two feet from him. He could almost feel the warmth coming off her skin. Yet the wall separating them at this moment seemed impenetrable, insurmountable.

Della went on. "I entered this marriage with my eyes wide open. I knew I was marrying a doctor. I knew about the hours, the pressure. Those first years were very difficult, especially when Katy and J. J. came along. When you weren't at the Medical Center, you were studying in the university library. When you weren't in the library, you were locked up in our basement with your medical books. You don't know how many times I put the babies to bed and fell asleep crying, just because I missed you.

"But I knew it was going to be better. Somewhere beyond the six years of residency and your two-year fellowship at NYU, there would be a regular practice, and we could begin a normal life—normal at least for a fully practicing physician. So I held on because I deeply loved you . . . and because I so desperately wanted to connect with you."

Della rolled to her nightstand to collect a tissue, bringing it back with her. Jordan lay motionless, in awe of his wife's startling revelation.

She continued, dabbing her eyes and nose. "When you went on staff at County General, I thought my dream had finally come true. We bought this house and joined our church. You had a more predictable schedule. We actually took the kids camping for a week, our first real vacation since our honeymoon. You were finally a husband and father who happened to be a physician, instead of a med student and resident who happened to have a wife and two kids.

"But . . . but between us, nothing changed." Della paused to blow her nose. "You were home more, but you weren't really here. You took me out to dinner once a week, but we never talked about us. You talked about your patients and your surgeries and your ambitions at the hospital. You rarely asked about my dreams, my feelings, and when you did, your eyes seemed to glaze over—you mentally left the room. After about six months I realized that there was someone else in your life."

Jordan rose on one elbow. "Della, there has never been another woman, never," he insisted. "I can't believe you would—"

"Not another woman, Jordan," Della cut in. "Another passion. A higher priority. I always knew there was room inside that handsome, intelligent shell for something else—a soul mate, a confidant, a lover. I thought it was going to be me—I hoped it would be me. But even in our deepest conversations, our most intimate moments in bed, I never feel connected with you, Jordan—not the real you. When we buried our son, I guess you buried what was left of the real you. The man I married isn't here anymore, Jordan, and I don't know how to find him."

Jordan dropped onto his back, staring up at the dark ceiling. The room was still again and silent until his cell phone sounded from the dresser top. He would have pretended not to hear it, but he knew Della heard it. In a way, the call was a welcome relief. So far tonight he had lost a patient and exposed his wife's broken heart. Solving a medical crisis over the phone should be a piece of cake.

Jordan slipped from the bed without speaking or turning on a light. Collecting the phone, he plodded to the kitchen in his pajama shorts and answered.

"Dr. Keyes?" No "hello," no "Mercy Hospital," just his name.

"Yes."

"This is Dr. Sheffield at the hospital."

"Dr. Sheffield?" Jordan said, unwilling to believe the director was still at the hospital at this hour. He thought it a very odd time to discuss the outburst at the staff meeting.

"We have a problem, Dr. Keyes."

"How can I help, sir?" Jordan kept his voice low, hoping Della would drift off to sleep before he returned to the bedroom.

"The medical examiner delivered the autopsy report for that police officer who died today in SICU."

"Beamon."

"Yes, Edward R. Beamon, age thirty-three," Sheffield said, apparently reading directly from the report.

"There's a problem with the report?" Jordan probed.

"There is a problem with the medical examiner's findings, potentially a very big problem for the hospital . . . and for you, Doctor."

The knot that had been in Jordan's stomach since the voice mail message tightened again. "A problem for me? What did they find?"

"Respiratory arrest due to an overdose of phenobarbital."

Jordan lowered himself to a kitchen chair, stunned. "An overdose? How much of an overdose?"

"The chart records that you ordered one hundred milligrams at 6:00 this morning, which was administered at 6:35."

"That's incorrect, Dr. Sheffield, because—"

Sheffield talked over the top of his response. "The chart also records that another dose was given at 7:30, 8:30, and 9:30. Then you personally ordered and administered another one hundred milligrams at 9:45 this morning, only fifteen minutes after the previous injection."

"But Doctor—"

"Let me finish, Dr. Keyes," Sheffield snapped impatiently.

"Yes, sir."

"Additional doses were then given at 10:30 and 11:30, as

scheduled." Sheffield paused, as if collecting his thoughts, then continued. "Two hundred milligrams of phenobarb in less than half an hour is highly irregular for a patient in Beamon's condition. But such a dose is not often fatal. However, the report estimates that upwards of twelve hundred milligrams of phenobarb was present in the system at the time of death."

"Twelve hundred milligrams?" Jordan gasped. "Dr. Sheffield, that's impossible."

"It's right here in black and white, Dr. Keyes. I can't argue with the state medical examiner."

"There must be a mistake because I ordered a hundred milligrams an hour for antiseizure. It wasn't given, so I ordered another dose and injected it myself."

"I also can't argue with the chart, Doctor. Two hundred milligrams in a space of fifteen minutes. The SICU nurse—a Ms. Sandborn, according to the chart—remembers giving the first dose before she went off shift. She says the orders for successive doses were on the chart, and I'm looking at them right now. But somewhere in there the dosage ballooned to fatal proportions."

Sheffield did not allow Jordan to interrupt. "Unfortunately, the Beamon family has been apprised of the autopsy report, and they are understandably upset. If we don't act quickly, this thing could blow up in our face. I called Dr. Waller, and he is flying home from Santa Fe tonight. He wants you in his office first thing tomorrow."

Jordan raked his hair with his fingers. "Of course. I'll be there."

"I don't mind telling you, this doesn't look good, Dr. Keyes."

"There must have been a horrible mistake."

"Then you better help us find it, Doctor. Good night."

Jordan returned to the bedroom and dressed quickly in the walk-in closet. There was an 11:40 flight out of LAX to Portland, he knew. He had to be on it.

When he emerged from the closet, Della was standing beside the bed in her robe, arms folded across her chest. Jordan did not need to explain what he was doing. "What shall I tell Katy in the morning?" she asked distantly.

"This is a big one, Dell; this is a real big one. I have to get back tonight. I have no choice."

"I'm used to plans being canceled, Jordan. But how will I explain it to Katy? It's her birthday. She's been looking forward to this trip for weeks. You promised."

Jordan pulled on his sport jacket and picked up his bag. "Take her to Catalina. I'll call her tomorrow night."

Before Della could speak again, Jordan said, "I don't have time to get into all the details, but one of my patients died under questionable circumstances, and I need to be at the hospital first thing tomorrow to clear things up. I really wish I could stay. All I can say is I'm sorry." Then he left.

Racing on the interstate toward the airport, Jordan quickly arrived at an unbelievable conclusion. He spoke it aloud several times, and it became more frightening each time because it rang with obvious truth: "Someone killed Eddie Beamon—either intentionally or unintentionally—with an overdose of phenobarbital, and they are trying to put the blame on me."

FIFTEEN

During the flight to Portland, Jordan's mounting anxiety ricocheted between two imminent disasters—the dissolution of his marriage and the collapse of his career. A third crisis was close behind, depending on how his midnight departure impacted his relationship with Katy.

Della's revelation was more than a shock; it was an ominous threat Jordan never saw coming. His intense schedule had always been a bone of contention between them. And he understood her reticence to leave business and friends in L.A. in order to follow him to Portland. But tonight's verbal bombshell blew those concerns away by comparison. *She said she is numb inside; she senses no connection between us; she feels like I'm not there for her—not for weeks, but for months, even years. And what does she mean by no connection? She says I am there, but I am* not *there. How am I supposed to translate that?*

Jordan wasn't naïve. He knew his marriage to Della wasn't perfect. But considering the time demands of his training and career, it was a good Christian marriage. Christian couples love one another; it was a given, in good times and bad. So Jordan was equally concerned over what his wife had *not* said in their dark bedroom. *Was she working up her courage to say more when the phone interrupted our conversation? Was she about to tell me she did not intend to move to Port-*

land? Does she consider our situation hopeless? Does Della want to divorce me?

Jordan could not believe such a conclusion was possible. But neither had he expected to hear the sobering words Della uttered tonight: "I don't know how I feel for you right now. I'm just numb inside." Now that the dam had burst, what more did Della have to pour out? Jordan thought several times of the admonitions from Maggie Rusch, who sometimes talked to him like a nosy sister. It now appeared that Maggie knew more about his relationship with Della than he did.

With his marriage obviously in crisis, why was he on a red-eye to Portland? Jordan imagined Maggie would ask him this—if she ever heard about what happened tonight. The answer was clear to Jordan: triage, assigning priorities on the basis of urgency. You don't rush an MVA victim into emergency brain surgery if he cannot breathe or if his heart has stopped or if he is bleeding internally. Every trauma staffer knows the ABCs of resuscitation: Make sure an *airway* is open; make sure the patient is *breathing;* make sure blood is *circulating.* Only after respiration and circulation are stabilized is the patient ready for emergency treatment for other injuries.

Jordan was flying to Portland to stop the bleeding. As critical as things were at home, he assessed that his career was the "red blanket" need of the two at the moment. Someone was out to destroy him at Mercy Hospital. And without a career, he reasoned that he had little to offer his family. Had not Della stated only hours ago that Jordan's ability to provide for her was a sign of his love? That ability seemed to be in dire jeopardy at the moment.

As reasonable as it seemed to Jordan to get back to Portland tonight, he was aware of the risk to his marriage. He whispered a prayer that Della would still be there after his crisis at Mercy Hospital was resolved.

Jordan's plane touched down at 1:45 A.M., and he walked

into Mercy Hospital less than an hour later. He clipped his photo ID badge to the lapel of his sport jacket to get past the security guards and to defuse the curious stares of the graveyard shift, most of whom did not know him. He walked purposely into the SICU and to a computer terminal just behind the nurse's station. Two nurses on duty paid him no attention.

He pulled up the chart for the late Edward Randall Beamon, whose body was likely stored in the morgue at the state medical examiner's facility. Jordan had to see for himself if the impossible was true. Beginning at the end of the chart, he scanned the lines that detailed the last day of Eddie Beamon's life. At 12:27 P.M., the patient was pronounced dead by Dr. Oscar Ortiz, the on-call neurosurgeon. Eddie Beamon had not regained consciousness from the moment the bullet entered his brain. He died without saying good-bye to his loving mother, who was out of the SICU when her son arrested.

The preceding lines described what Jordan knew had been a frantic yet brief and futile attempt at resuscitation. He envisioned Maggie Rusch hurrying to Beamon's room from the monitor station in response to his cardiac alarm. At this point the lethal dose of phenobarbital, administered at some point in the previous two hours, had already paralyzed the central nervous system, shutting down his lungs and then his heart.

Jordan scrolled up the report and found injections at 11:30 and 10:30, as he had ordered and assumed would be given. Next he found the entry for one hundred milligrams of phenobarb he had administered personally. A few lines higher, separated from his entry by periodic readings of blood pressure and pulse rate, were three additional entries, each reporting the injection of one hundred milligrams of phenobarb, just as he had originally ordered. Higher still on the list was the original prescription with his name on it: 6:14 A.M. Right below was the first dose: one hundred milligrams of phenobarbital given twenty minutes later—by

Eloise Sandborn, just as Taylor Sheffield had reported to him over the phone. The 6:35 injection had not been on the chart at 9:45 when Jordan gave what he thought was the first dose. Nor were the three additional injections now glaring at him from the chart. He would bet his life on it.

Taking a step back from the computer, Jordan folded his arms and continued to stare at the monitor. There were three issues here, he knew. The first concerned Eloise Sandborn's "mistake." Nearing the end of her graveyard shift, Sandborn no doubt spaced-out on the first order for phenobarbital. She likely dispensed the medicine but forgot to enter it on the chart before she left the hospital. Everybody lapses on the paperwork at times, and the end of a shift is a common time for it to happen.

A few hours later, Eloise must have realized her error and entered the data on the chart, either by returning to the hospital or accessing the chart from her home computer. In order to avoid trouble, the nurse logged the time she dispensed the drug, not the time she made her entry on the chart. In between her dispensing the drug and recording it, Jordan arrived and, seeing no entry on the chart, administered an identical dose. Such an error should go on Nurse Sandborn's record. But Jordan doubted that she would own up to it, especially since the official record exonerated her.

The second issue was the subsequent doses of phenobarb that the chart declared were given as they should have been: hourly. These notes had not been on the chart this morning either. When Jordan injected one hundred milligrams into Eddie Beamon's IV line at 9:45, the chart indicated that not a drop of the drug had been given to that point.

The third issue was the amount of phenobarbital in Eddie Beamon's body: approximately twelve hundred milligrams, according to the autopsy. Seven hundred milligrams in five and a half hours would have kept him deep in dreamland, but it would not have killed him. Where did the other five hundred milligrams come from?

The thought made Jordan's skin crawl. He looked over the top of the monitor to where he had last seen Eddie Beamon. The room was tidy, dark, and quiet, ready for the next patient. It chilled him to think that someone entered that room at some time this morning, someone who looked like he or she belonged here, and delivered a fatal dose of the very drug he had prescribed to keep the Portland cop alive.

Due to restricted access into the SICU, the list of suspects was severely limited. Arleta Beamon had been in his room, and no doubt other family members had visited, if only briefly. Other police officers had been around SICU, but not many had disturbed the patient and his family in the room. Furthermore, Jordan accepted that Beamon's family and fraternity of officers would be the least adept at acquiring and delivering a fatal dose of phenobarb without being noticed by SICU personnel. And why would the people who appreciated the patient most want to kill him?

That left only two possibilities on Jordan's short list. Eddie Beamon's killer could be an outsider, such as a murderous racist or cop hater or a vengeful criminal Beamon had crossed at some point in his career. But such a person would have to be extremely resourceful and skilled to secure the drug and administer it inside twenty-four hours of the shooting. Jordan thought such a possibility highly unlikely.

Jordan lifted a hand to his chin as he pondered the last possibility. The person responsible for the overdose might have been a member of the Mercy Hospital community. Anyone in scrubs or a lab coat with an ID badge could walk into the SICU without suspicion. When the patient was alone in his room, such a person need only wait until others working the unit were distracted. He or she could inject the deadly dose into the IV port and slip out virtually unnoticed. Jordan realized that he fit those criteria as much or more than anyone in the hospital.

The realization brought another chill that localized in the pit of his stomach. He had offended a number of his colleagues in

Neurosurgery with his outspoken opinions. Was there someone among that group who was disturbed to the point of retaliation, someone perhaps on the edge emotionally and willing to punish Jordan by attempting to frame him for medical malpractice? Neurosurgeons were by nature high-strung, often possessing volatile personalities. Jordan's outbursts against the status quo had resulted in his dismissal from LAC+USC. Yet he was never tempted to harm anyone who crossed him. Had someone at Mercy stepped over that line?

"You need help with something, Doctor?"

Deep in thought, Jordan was startled by the interruption. He snapped his head around to find Nurse Eloise Sandborn standing next to him. She wore the dour, life-is-the-pits expression for which she was notorious on this floor. Having not seen her when he arrived moments ago, Jordan had assumed Nurse Sandborn had the night off.

"I beg your pardon."

"You're staring at the computer like you've never seen one before," she said, seemingly annoyed at having to explain herself. "Is there anything I can help you with?"

"No, nothing, not really," he said quickly. "I was just . . . checking a few things."

"Then do you mind if I use the machine?" Sandborn said.

"No, help yourself." Jordan took one step away, then stopped. "May I ask you a question first?"

"You're the doctor." Her cynicism was veiled, but it was there.

"Edward Beamon, the police officer in room 8 this morning. Remember him?"

"Of course."

"Do you remember my order for one hundred milligrams of phenobarbital just before you went off shift?"

"Yes." If Eloise Sandborn felt any guilt or suspicion from being questioned, she did not show it.

Jordan pressed. "And did you give that prescription before you left this morning?"

The nurse's hard gaze narrowed. "Yes, Doctor, I did," she said, almost defiantly.

The woman's recalcitrance only solidified Jordan's resolve. "And did you record that injection on Mr. Beamon's chart before you left this morning?"

"Absolutely."

"You didn't enter the prescription on the chart later in the day, sometime after you went off?"

"If I had, the time listed there would be different, wouldn't it?"

Jordan got the impression Eloise Sandborn could spar with him verbally all night and not tire of it. She was either very efficient and truthful or she was a skilled liar who could melt a polygraph with her determination.

"That's all I wanted to know, Ms. Sandborn," Jordan said at last. "Thank you." He could feel the woman's eyes boring into him as he left the SICU.

Jordan knew he should go back to his apartment and get a few hours of sleep. He would meet with Dr. Sheffield and Dr. Waller "first thing"—which in the Surgery Division at Mercy Hospital meant 7:00 A.M. On top of his other work, Jordan now had to extricate himself from what appeared to be a brutal setup perpetrated by—he hesitated to even consider the word—a *murderer.* He would need the rest.

But he found himself wandering the quiet halls of the hospital baring his soul in prayer. In the last several days, Jordan had repeatedly sought God's assistance in his personal life and his career. He had repented of his outburst in the staff meeting—which he knew was rooted in the drive to *be* the best instead of in the confidence to *do* his best. His ego had torpedoed his relationship with his superiors in Los Angeles. He had been in Portland only two months, and his attitude had reared its ugly head again. This time Jordan feared his pride had provoked someone to a heinous act.

Why had he gone off in the staff meeting? Where was the control that served him so well most of the time? Maggie would probably say his outbursts in the meeting and in L.A. were the result of some "hidden layer" in his personality. If so, why had God not pointed it out to him?

He also prayed about his relationship with Della. Obviously his obsession with a medical career had undermined what he assumed was a relatively successful marriage. In this arena, however, Jordan's prayer was more question than petition. What did Della mean by being supplanted by his other passion? Must he choose between his passion for Della and his passion for medicine?

Jordan did not know what to pray for. Short of giving up his practice in Portland and returning to L.A. without a job, he did not know how to reconnect with Della. And such a drastic move seemed incongruous with what Jordan understood to be God's call on his life to serve others through medicine. Ironically, the Eddie Beamon crisis might precipitate what Jordan would consider an untimely and disgraceful return to Los Angeles.

Ambling through the dimly lit surgery waiting room, Jordan spied a lone figure slumped like an overgrown rag doll in an upholstered chair near the corner, asleep. The large frame and blue work uniform were a dead giveaway. Either Buster Chapman had pulled the night shift tonight, or he was just too busy to go home. The janitor never seemed to leave the hospital. Jordan wondered if Buster even had an off-campus home.

Jordan quietly sat down across the room. Buster's head, with mouth agape, had flopped back against the wall. His chest heaved and fell with each deep, noisy breath. Jordan studied the sleeping giant, envious of his simplicity and tranquillity. For all Jordan's "advantages" in IQ, education, career achievements, and earning potential, he did not feel superior to big, softhearted Buster. In the long run perhaps, Buster's work at the hospital was no less meaningful than his own, especially considering the man's uncanny bedside manner. He imagined that Buster, if he had been on duty early yesterday, had shed some tears with Arleta Beamon over Eddie's unexpected death.

Watching the man doze, it occurred to Jordan that Buster Chapman, who had never been married, would make a wonderful husband. Someone so in tune with the feelings of others would likely never hear from his wife the debilitating words Della had spoken to Jordan only hours ago. If Buster were married, he would probably know how to "connect." Nor did Jordan think Buster had ever alienated himself from his coworkers by blasting their policies or competence. For a man who barely finished high school, Buster Chapman had mastered a skill for connecting emotionally with people that Jordan had somehow missed.

An open Bible lay on the lamp table next to Buster's chair. Like the Bible belonging to Eddie Beamon's mother, this one was well worn. That Buster's compassion emanated from his childlike faith in God was no mystery to Jordan. Maybe he had internalized some Bible passages Jordan had overlooked, passages that equipped Christians for cultivating love in others instead of suffocating it.

Jordan stood and approached the sleeping janitor in slow, silent steps. Reading a portion of Scripture when he got home seemed like a good idea to Jordan. He hoped it would help him sleep—just as it seemed to help Buster—and prepare him for the "inquisition" in the morning.

As Jordan neared the lamp table for a closer look at the Bible, Buster awoke with a raspy breath and a snort. Standing quickly with eyes half glazed, he rubbed his face, then focused with difficulty on his watch. "Oh boy, thanks for waking me up," he mumbled. "Dinner hour's over. Oh boy, time to get back to work. Thanks, Doctor. Oh boy." Then he collected his Bible, snapped it shut, and started off toward the elevator, a little unsteady on his feet.

"You're welcome, Buster," Jordan called after him, feeling a little disappointed at seeing the man go.

Once the elevator doors had sealed Buster in, Jordan

headed out of the building. He would read a little something from the first Gospel before he fell asleep. He thought Buster's Bible had been lying open to the book of Matthew.

SIXTEEN

Jordan arrived at the office of the head of Surgery at ten minutes to seven. He needed much more sleep than the two hours he got, but it would have to do for now. A shower, shave, a clean set of clothes, and two mugs of strong coffee helped boost his mood. Daylight also had a positive effect on him, gray though it was. There was an energy in the first hours of the day that seemed to invigorate Jordan. Today he would need that energy for more than his normal routine of mentoring medical students and ministering to patients.

Jordan had no prepared speech for Bert Waller and Taylor Sheffield. He reminded himself while driving to the hospital that his conscience was clear concerning the care of Eddie Beamon. He had successfully removed the bullet fragment, and the officer's recovery in SICU had begun nicely. The overdose of phenobarbital was not his doing, although someone seemed intent on making it look so. All he had to do was tell what he knew, trusting that his superiors respected him enough to believe him. He also hoped his disappointing behavior among the Neurosurgery staff would not be counted against him.

Dr. Waller was at his desk when Jordan walked in. The roly-poly surgeon was hunched over the editorial section of the Sunday *Oregonian.* He looked up as Jordan approached. "Aha, Dr. Keyes, I hoped you would arrive early." There was no judgment in his tone, but neither was there an assuring smile as he stood and extended his hand.

"Good morning, Dr. Waller," he said, shaking his boss's large hand.

"When did you get in?" Waller asked, motioning Jordan to a chair. "You were in Los Angeles, were you not?"

The two men sat down in unison. "Yes, L.A. Dr. Sheffield called me last night. I came back on the red-eye." Jordan did not intend to reveal that he had been at the hospital until almost three in the morning stewing over the Eddie Beamon dilemma.

"I beat you in, then. I landed about ten. I'm sorry you weren't able to spend more time with your family. I'll be glad when your wife and daughter are up here with you."

"Yes, sir, thank you." It occurred to Jordan that the fallout from Della's words last night might be just as damaging to his career as any of his foibles at the hospital. Though a bachelor himself, Dr. Waller strongly encouraged family life among his staff. Should Della decide to end their marriage, Jordan could incur further disfavor from his superior.

"I assume Dr. Sheffield brought you up to speed on the unfortunate incident with the policeman. . . ." Waller shuffled through a sheaf of papers looking for the name.

"Officer Edward Beamon," Jordan supplied.

"Aha, Beamon. Right."

"Dr. Sheffield summarized the autopsy report. He also mentioned that the officer's family is privy to the report."

Waller fluffed his mustache absently. "Mm, unfortunate. Normally we would discuss such details with the family after we got all our ducks in a row. But the law-enforcement community enjoys privileged access to the medical examiner. The Portland police and the officer's family knew the results before the report was delivered here."

"And how did the police seem about the report?"

Waller raised his hands in a gesture of innocence. "I'm sure Dr. Sheffield will give us all the details when he gets here." Then, resting on his elbows, Waller leaned forward on the desk. "I know we're going to hear your story in detail. But before our boss comes in, what is your take on this situation?"

Jordan released a long breath. The unassuming figure beholding him from across the desk belied the tireless, skilled surgeon who was responsible for directing the affairs of over one hundred surgeons, surgery residents, and med students at Mercy Hospital. If Jordan wanted anyone on his side through whatever might be ahead, he wanted this man.

"I'm disturbed about what happened and puzzled over how it did happen. I'm concerned for Officer Beamon's family and for the hospital."

Waller cut in before Jordan could say more. "But you had nothing to do with the overdose of phenobarbital found in the policeman's system." It was a question issued as a statement.

Jordan responded in kind. "Dr. Waller, I have never been more sure of anything in my life."

"Aha," Waller said, an exclamation for which he was known and mimicked around the hospital, "then you have nothing to worry about, do you?"

"If the truth comes to light, I have nothing to worry about."

"The truth will prevail, that's what I believe," Waller said.

"Yes, the truth will prevail," Jordan echoed.

"Good. Very good."

Dr. Taylor Sheffield entered the office seconds later. Usually a pleasant man to be around, the venerable hospital director appeared grim. Jordan knew he was laboring under the weight of this public-relations nightmare.

Sheffield briefly and articulately reviewed the situation at hand: the patient's untimely death, the dubious chart entries, the shocking autopsy findings, and the mounting storm of inquiry from the family and the community. As the liaison between the hospital and the outside world, Dr. Sheffield intended to know every detail about the incident. Then he and his staff would disseminate to the public only what was pertinent.

At the director's request, Jordan told his story. Having pored over the case constantly since Dr. Sheffield's call last night, he walked through the events of Eddie Beamon's admittance and treatment with minute-by-minute detail. He felt calm and positive during his report. And he purposely did not slant the story with his take on who might be responsible for Beamon's death or a possible motive. His theory of retaliation from an unbalanced member of the hospital staff would only serve to remind Waller and Sheffield of the conflict he had instigated. Jordan was confident that the truth would eventually be uncovered without him playing detective or pointing a finger.

"The SICU nurse—Sandborn—insists that she dispensed the first dose of phenobarbital and recorded it in the chart," Sheffield reviewed.

Jordan nodded.

"But when you returned later in the morning, the phenobarb injection was not on the chart."

"That's correct. Neither were three subsequent doses recorded when I looked at the chart at 9:45."

"So you ordered and injected another hundred milligrams."

"Yes."

"Did you think to check with the nurses on duty?"

"No. The injections were not on the chart, so I assumed they had not been given."

"And you gave the meds yourself instead of having a nurse do it?"

"That's correct."

"Why?"

"Because I was on my way to the airport, and I wanted to make sure the phenobarb was administered."

Sheffield continued to retrace the events. "According to

the chart, the patient received five hundred milligrams in the space of about four hours."

"But according to the chart I read at the time, the dose I gave was the first, because the previous doses had not been entered."

Waller had been listening to the exchange intently. "So where did the lethal dose of phenobarb come from?" he wondered aloud.

"Judging by the time of death, it was injected intravenously one to two hours earlier," Jordan answered.

"And what time did you leave the hospital yesterday, Dr. Keyes?" Sheffield asked.

Jordan had already explained his departure from the hospital, including the time. *Did he forget what I said, or is he trying to find a chink in my story by asking again?*

"Ten o'clock, give or take a few minutes."

"So you could have been here when the overdose was administered."

It was another way of asking the stock murder mystery question, "Where were you when the victim was killed?" Jordan assessed. But it did not come across from Sheffield as the third degree.

"Yes, it's possible that I was still on campus at that time."

"Hm." Sheffield leaned back in his chair for the first time since the interview began. Jordan guessed that he was gearing up for another line of questioning.

After a few seconds, the director returned to the edge of his seat. "Can you think of any way a massive dose of phenobarb could be administered by accident?"

Jordan had not commented on the topic because it bordered on editorializing. But he had thought plenty about it. "Since one hundred milligrams and one thousand milligrams look the same when dissolved in a syringe, yes, it could happen. A concentrated dose might have been erroneously substituted for the normal dose. Even a good pharmacy will occasionally make a mistake."

"But the odds against such a mistake are enormous, to say the least," Sheffield said, clearly expecting agreement.

"Of course," Jordan said. Dr. Waller nodded.

Sheffield searched Jordan's eyes deeply. "Is it possible that you administered the fatal dose of phenobarbital without realizing it just before you left the hospital?"

It was a slant Jordan had not yet considered. But it was logically sound. "Dr. Sheffield, I did inject a syringe of phenobarb before I left yesterday. If that syringe contained more than the requested one hundred milligrams, then yes, I administered the fatal dose."

Dr. Sheffield slid to the back of his chair again, as if regrouping for another attack. Dr. Waller sat motionlessly, chin resting on his two fists, taking in the exchange. Jordan began to feel uneasy about the rising intensity of the questions.

Sheffield reached into the leather valise at his feet and pulled out a short sheaf of papers stapled at the corner. Studying the front page for a moment, he said, "Are you aware, Dr. Keyes, that you have ordered over ten thousand milligrams of phenobarbital for your patients over the last month?"

Jordan did not like the question. It was clearly one that would be asked of a suspect. "No, sir, I do not keep track of the cumulative amounts of drugs ordered for patients. But since phenobarb is a common drug in the treatment of brain trauma, I'm sure I order quite a bit of it."

Sheffield's eyes were still on the top sheet. Jordan wondered if the man even listened to his answer. "And are you aware that hospital records account for only about seven thousand milligrams of phenobarbital administered to your patients over the same time period?"

Jordan felt invisible steam rising up the back of his neck. He could not distinguish who sparked more anger: Dr. Sheffield, for insinuating that he might have skimmed enough phenobarb from his patient orders to kill someone, or the unseen assailant, who apparently had been working overtime to prove that Jordan was the culprit.

Calming himself quickly, Jordan asked, "Dr. Sheffield, do you believe I am responsible for the death of Eddie Beamon?"

Sheffield laid the sheaf on the table and looked Jordan dead in the eye. "No, Dr. Keyes, I do not. But I want you to know what I am up against if I am to convince his family and possibly an investigative team from the Portland Police Department of your innocence. You had opportunity to deliver the overdose—either intentionally or by accident—before you left town. Your phenobarb orders over the last month don't agree with the amounts dispensed to your patients, leaving a significant quantity of phenobarb unaccounted for. And you are on probation here based on your record of behavior from Los Angeles County General. All of this information will eventually be uncovered by those seeking to know why Mr. Beamon died in our hospital under your care. I just want to have some answers when they ask me the questions I just asked you."

A little embarrassed at his initial response, Jordan said, "I understand."

"Can you give us any help here, Dr. Keyes?" Sheffield continued. "Can you think of any reason why these unusual circumstances seem to be stacked against you? Is there anything you want to tell us?"

Jordan considered his response. Someone set him up—he was now sure of it. Someone tampered with Eddie Beamon's records yesterday morning, making it appear that Jordan had carelessly overlooked the first injections of phenobarb. It was not necesarily a fatal mistake, but since it occurred in proximity to the officer's death, it would challenge Jordan's credibility in the eyes of those looking in from the outside.

The same person had also succeeded in injecting a concentrated, lethal dose of phenobarb into Beamon's veins, perhaps before Jordan left the hospital. For all he knew, the unknown assailant had loaded the syringe Jordan used with the overdose, and Jordan was his unwitting accomplice in the killing of Eddie Beamon. If that was the case, perhaps the killer deleted the first injection knowing Jordan would order another one, the deadly one.

And now additional hospital records had apparently been altered, making it look like Jordan skimmed enough phenobarb from other orders to make up a deadly batch. It was ludicrous, of course. But each additional shadow of dispersion cast upon him served to intensify the dark blot. Jordan figured that he had not seen the last of these incriminating coincidences.

But what should he tell Waller and Sheffield in the meantime? He was strongly tempted to unload his suspicions. Any of his colleagues—and he had alienated many of them with his hardheaded opinions—could be capable of this act. He could name the names of those who had opposed him most vociferously: Dr. Ortiz, Dr. Sutherland, Dr. Boorsma. But what good would it do? It might only serve to stir up more animosity against him if his suspicions became public. No, he had to stay focused on his innocence. Instead of turning over rocks looking for a killer in a lab coat, he simply had to tell the truth about his actions. The truth would set him free.

"I don't know what I could tell you," Jordan said at last. "I did not squirrel away phenobarbital from other patients in order to concoct a lethal dose. I did not knowingly dispense such a dose to Eddie Beamon. When all the facts are brought to light, I trust they will corroborate my stand."

A soft rap on the office door interrupted the conversation. Dr. Waller hurried to admit a man Jordan had never seen before. He was small and wiry with wispy, rust-colored hair and a reddish complexion. Jordan assessed that the man's slacks, sport jacket, shirt, and tie were a shade or two from coordinating. Whatever his name was, he likely had been called Red or Rusty or Carrottop by those who knew him.

"Aha, Leonard, thank you for coming," Waller said, shaking his hand and guiding him toward the last available chair in the office. "You know Dr. Sheffield, of course." Sheffield rose and shook hands. Anticipating an introduction, Jordan also stood.

Waller continued, "Leonard, this is Dr. Keyes, one of my finest neurosurgeons. Jordan, I'd like you to meet Leonard Darwin." The man acknowledged Jordan with an outstretched hand and a crooked grin. "Leonard is an attorney with Continental Health Services Comprehensive. You've been contributing a fair amount of your income to Continental since you began practicing medicine. I thought it was a good idea for you two to meet in case the Beamon family files suit. I briefed him on your situation from the plane last night. Len can do you a world of good if this thing gets nasty."

The word *attorney* turned the knife in Jordan's gut. Darwin represented the company to whom Jordan and many physicians at Mercy paid premiums for malpractice insurance. He did not know how to respond to the visitor, so he just nodded and said nothing.

Dr. Sheffield excused himself, assuring Jordan that he would keep in touch. Reaching the door, he turned to Waller. "You're going to tell Dr. Keyes about the new schedule, aren't you, Bert?"

"It's the next order of business, Taylor," Waller assured. Then Sheffield left.

Once the men sat, Waller said, "Dr. Sheffield and I have decided to move you out of clinical practice until this storm blows over. I have transferred you to Neurosurgery Team 3, which is on a research rotation. Your current patients will be assigned to other members of your present team. We think it's best that you stay out of the public areas of the hospital where you may encounter members of the Beamon family, the police community, or the media. Understood?"

Stunned at the announcement, Jordan answered rather mechanically, "Understood."

"Also, Dr. Keyes," Leonard Darwin interjected, his voice tinny and nasal, "it's best if you let us handle the investigation, if you know what I mean. There are proper channels for getting to the bottom of this—the real cause of the patient's claim and whatnot. Those channels tend to become muddy even through good intentions."

"Aha, good point," Waller said. "Leonard knows malpractice claims like you know the human brain. He'll get to the truth, believe me."

Waller stood and walked to the door, signaling that Jordan was excused from the meeting. He followed Waller out into the hall. "I know this is difficult for you, Jordan," he said. "But we'll get you through this. Keep up on your journal reading, keep your pager on, and we will be in touch."

Jordan could not bring himself to say thank you, so he just nodded and left. He was anything but thankful for being banished from his work. The research rotation was a built-in cushion for every physician, time to get away from the daily grind of clinical patient care and on-call duty. No surgeries, no rounds, no med students, no responsibilities. Other physicians might welcome the rotation as a privilege, but Jordan regarded it as a prison sentence.

Suddenly numb at having nothing to do and feeling lousy about it, Jordan struck out in search of another strong cup of coffee.

SEVENTEEN

"Sorry to hear about the policeman."

Jordan was standing in a small crowd at the coffee bar, waiting for a tall cup of Colombian blend. He recognized the New England accent before turning around. Philip Ettinger appeared dapper as always in expensive, dark wool slacks, Italian shoes, and silk tie. Even the hospital-issue lab coat seemed tailored and pressed on the elegant Bostonian.

"Thank you, Philip," Jordan returned, appreciating a sympathetic soul.

Philip called out his order for coffee, complete with "please" and "thank you." Then, lowering his voice again, he said, "Bit of a mix-up on phenobarb in ICU, I hear."

Unsure how much to disclose to his colleague, Jordan simply nodded. He received his lidded paper cup and handed over two dollars, waving off any change.

"We're going to miss you on the team," Philip said. "Hopefully it's only temporary."

Jordan was surprised that his "demotion" to research was already on the street. Then he remembered that, as acting head of Neurosurgery, Philip would automatically be in the loop on his hasty transfer. "Good news travels fast," Jordan said cynically.

"It's not good news," Philip said, mildly remonstrative. "You're being sent out to pasture until the incident blows over, we all know that. Try to make the most of it. Catch up on your reading. Polish your best lecture for grand rounds. You'll be back in the starting lineup before you know it."

"I hope so."

Philip reached across the counter to receive his coffee and pay for it. Then he offered a casual salute and set off at a brisk walk toward the surgery unit.

Hoping to avoid other colleagues who might want to discuss his plight, Jordan hurried to the sixth floor of the neurosciences building. Safely behind the closed door of his office, he dropped into the chair and sipped the steaming coffee. He could almost feel the depression settling over him. He had been relieved of his duties, shoved to the back burner. Being assigned to research was tantamount to being told to crawl into a hole and stay there. Sitting in his small office, he felt like a thoroughbred locked in the stable at the prime of his racing career.

He had two choices, he knew. He could while away the hours of his research rotation doing busywork, waiting for Dr. Sheffield, Dr. Waller, and Leonard Darwin to get to the bottom of the Eddie Beamon matter. Or he could use the imposed downtime to help prove his innocence in the officer's death. Darwin had admonished him not to interfere in his investigation, and Jordan fully intended to comply. *But there are some areas Leonard Darwin will likely not investigate,* Jordan figured, *and if I focus on those areas, I will not violate my promise to stay out of his way.*

Jordan had prayed about the Eddie Beamon dilemma sporadically since receiving Dr. Sheffield's call on Saturday night. And it occurred to him that he had extra time to pray now. But since becoming a Christian in med school, he had learned that God often chose to answer prayers in conjunction with obedient effort.

Welcoming the hot coffee in small sips, he recalled a Bible study on Acts 12. Peter was locked in prison and awaiting execution. An angel woke him up, but Peter was responsible to stand up and get ready to go. The angel opened the gates, but Peter had to walk out of the prison under his own power. Once outside, the angel disappeared, and Peter was on his own. Jordan vividly remembered the leader's summary of the study: "God expects us to do what we can do; and he will do what only he can do."

God's challenge at that time seemed to be, "Jordan, stop trying to do what only I can do." As a younger Christian, his exceptional intelligence, competence, and drive often got in the way of trusting God. Being very capable at problem solving, he tended not to bother God with anything but the seemingly insurmountable issues in his life—and only after he had exhausted his resources trying to solve them. The learning curve for including God in his day-to-day agenda had been long and difficult.

Today, however, Jordan sensed a different emphasis: "In response to your prayers, I am doing what only I can do. In the meantime, keep busy at what you can do." The impetus to stay active was just what he needed at the moment. It was the spark that kept the encroaching depression at bay.

He loosened his tie while the computer hummed and buzzed through its boot-up maneuvers. Virtually every record and byte of data in the hospital's mainframe was accessible to him via his office PC. Mercy Hospital still housed stacks and stacks of hard-copy files in the basement. But electronic data storage and retrieval would eventually turn these rooms into musty, dusty archives, unused by all but hard-core technophobes.

Jordan began his investigation by returning to the scene of the crime: the chart for the late Edward Randall Beamon. He found it as he expected. Eloise Sandborn's phenobarb entry, missing Saturday morning when he had administered another dose, was there. The nurse was likely telling the truth about her actions, Jordan thought. Someone had strategically deleted her entry and later reinserted it as part of the plot that resulted in Eddie Beamon's death.

But why? The culprit surely knew that the double dose of phenobarb was not sufficient to kill the patient. Jordan guessed that the ploy was simply to cast a shadow of suspicion on his competence. Someone could say that he carelessly doubled up on the patient's meds in his haste to catch his flight for L.A. "And why was Dr. Keyes in such a hurry to get out of town?" he imagined an antagonist inquiring. "Did he intend to be far from the scene when the lethal dose found its mark a couple of hours later?"

Jordan found it ludicrous that an unseen enemy might be trying to frame him not only for malpractice but for manslaughter or murder. Having read about other bizarre examples of the miscarriage of justice in the medical profession, Jordan would not take this seemingly groundless charge too lightly.

He printed a copy of Eddie Beamon's complete chart and placed it in a new folder for future reference. Then, pulling up a blank screen on his word processor, he documented in detail what had really happened in the SICU yesterday. It was his word against Nurse Sandborn's and the official chart, he realized, but he completed the notes just the same. He was doing what he could do. God would bring the truth to light for any who needed to see it.

Next Jordan turned to Dr. Sheffield's revelation that phenobarbital prescriptions written by Dr. Keyes for other ICU patients exceeded the actual amounts given. Circumstantially, it could be derived that he had stockpiled enough of the drug to create a small but deadly liquid concentrate that could be quickly injected into an IV port. It was another ridiculous assumption, but Jordan could not afford to let it go unchallenged.

Methodically working backward from the present, he pulled up the charts for the patients he had treated since arriving at Mercy Hospital two months ago. Being a common drug in the treatment of head trauma, phenobarbital appeared on many of the charts. For some patients, including his other recent tragedy, Trudy Aguilera, Jordan remembered writing the prescriptions. For others, he had no memory of the orders. Thankfully, it was his personal protocol to keep handwritten notes on each patient and file them when the patient left his care.

But when Jordan reached into his filing cabinet to compare the data on the electronic charts with his notes, another icy finger of anxiety ran up his spine. The notes were gone—every single sheet, even the folder he had neatly stored them in—as if he had never saved them. Jordan searched through every file in the drawer. He checked two other drawers in the cabinet. The folder had disappeared.

Closing the last file drawer more forcefully than necessary, he stood and paced the small room. It angered him that someone had actually sneaked into his office, sifted through his files, and stolen his personal property. And it unnerved him to think that this person—or *persons,* for all he knew—was so thorough and conniving as to eliminate this small but important piece of evidence. He felt suddenly exposed and defenseless, like a caged lab rat whose every action and reaction is observed by its captor.

The security and sanctity of his office had been violated. It was like waking up to find that a stranger had moved into your bedroom. All sense of privacy had been compromised. As a result, Jordan made two snap decisions. First, any shred of data he was able to find that contributed to his defense he would keep with him in a briefcase. Second, he would look for another place to continue his examination of salient data in the hospital's mainframe. There were a number of terminals throughout the neurosciences building. He would move around the building without establishing a pattern. If necessary, he would find an unused terminal in another building. He would do his best to confound whoever was intent on ruining his life.

But he would do so while trying not to draw the attention of the culprit. He would leave his office virtually intact, as if unaware that the intruder had attained access. He would spend a little time here each day as usual. But finding a way out of the net that was quickly enclosing him—at least to the extent God expected him to—would be done as unobtrusively as possible.

Sitting down again at the computer, Jordan felt as if a hidden video camera was trained on him, transmitting every move—and perhaps even his thoughts—to a secret monitor somewhere in the hospital. He tried to ignore the creepy feeling. He perused several patient charts, looking for phenobarbital prescriptions he had ordered. He found several, but some of the doses were slightly different from what he would prescribe under the conditions described. Someone had altered the charts, he knew, just enough to plant the suspicion of a significant surplus of phenobarb at Jordan's disposal. Apparently Dr. Sheffield had taken the bait.

Jordan selected eight patient charts that were clear examples of the disparity between what he had allegedly prescribed and what he would actually have prescribed. Had his notes not been stolen, the difference would have been clear and convincing. Since he had no proof, he went for the next best thing. While the charts were printing, he noted carefully for each the phenobarb dosage he normally prescribed. Perhaps he could obtain some patient charts from LAC+USC that would corroborate his methods. Hopefully, his opponent had not tampered with those records also.

Shutting down the computer, Jordan straightened his tie and slipped the documents into a soft-sided leather briefcase. It was time to find another workstation, preferably in an unused lab somewhere in this building. But first he would pay a visit to the basement in the hospital's main building on the off chance that his adversary had missed an opportunity.

The female clerk glanced at Jordan's ID badge as he entered the file stacks, then returned to her work unconcerned. Gaining his bearings in the massive floor-to-ceiling collection of patient files, Jordan located three of the charts he had just printed from the mainframe. Perhaps his adversary had not considered that the hard copies of those electronic files were tucked away down here. If the charts in the stacks did not match the phonies in the computer, Jordan's theory of tampering would gain considerable credence.

But his small hopes were quickly dashed. The file copies matched his recently printed copies exactly. Jordan pulled four more files just to make sure, but it was evident that the perpetrator had visited the stacks and replaced the originals with perfectly counterfeited seconds.

Jordan left the stacks to return to the neurosciences building. Discouraged but not defeated, he had already chosen his next step. Although the death of Eddie Beamon did not fit the pattern exactly, it was another unexpected SICU death. What did the officer have in common with Trudy Aguilera and the others who died when they should have recovered? The answer to that question—if indeed there was one—might open a doorway to the truth.

Finding a computer in a small, empty conference room on the fifth floor, Jordan set up a temporary workstation. He clicked his way to the gate of the hospital's mainframe. At the prompt for his password, he tapped in the eight letters he had used since his first day in the hospital: Katarina, his daughter's first name.

After several seconds of computer grunts, a message box appeared in the middle of the screen. Perturbed, he clicked the box away and entered his password again. The same message appeared. Beginning to churn inside with frustration and a twinge of fear, he tried again, with the same results.

Slumping back in the rickety steno chair, Jordan stared at the flashing words in the message box that seemed to taunt him—*Unauthorized Code: Access Denied.*

EIGHTEEN

"They locked me out," Jordan said aloud, staring at the flashing words on the screen. He keyed in *Katarina* at the prompt again and again, hoping he had somehow hit a wrong key but knowing he had not. The words reappeared every time, standing between him and the hospital mainframe like an armed guard: *Access Denied.* He exclaimed with greater emphasis and disbelief: "They locked me out!"

He reached for the phone to call Dr. Taylor Sheffield and complain. This was ridiculous. He had not been fired or arrested for manslaughter or placed on administrative leave. He had not been asked to surrender his ID badge or password. He could understand being rotated to research to avoid contact with the Beamon family or the media. But blocking him from the mainframe was totally unnecessary. And he would make sure the hospital director understood that.

But he put the phone down before dialing. Leonard Darwin was likely behind the lockout, he assessed. The lawyer had instructed Jordan to stay out of the investigation, to let the hospital handle it. Voiding Jordan's password was a rather crude way for him to enforce his request. But if Jordan raised a stink about it to Dr. Sheffield, the word would certainly get back to Darwin that he was not following orders. Jordan could not run the risk of crossing Darwin or Sheffield. He had to toe the line until he had enough evidence to clear himself.

A flicker of mild panic lifted Jordan to his feet, and he began pacing the small conference room. *Just when I find a thread of a lead to follow, I get locked out of the hospital's files,* he mused, raking his hair with his fingers. *How am I supposed to prove my innocence if I can't get into the electronic files on the computer?* Jordan decided to turn his wondering into a prayer. He added aloud, "How can I do it, God?"

The ideas started coming, but Jordan wasn't sure if they emanated from on high or from a very active problem-solving brain. *I could call Maggie Rusch and "borrow" her password.* Jordan dismissed the idea immediately with an audible hiss and a shake of the head. If someone discovered him hacking into the hospital's computer, it would only make him look more guilty than he already did. And what would Nurse Rusch think of him for such an unchristian request?

I could call Records and innocently request that the files I want be faxed to me, hoping they don't yet know that I am persona non grata in the electronic archives. Again Jordan shook his head. If Leonard Darwin was smart enough to delete his password from the system, he was smart enough to red-flag him throughout the hospital. As much as Jordan was tempted to gain access to the computer in some way, he acknowledged that such a move would be counterproductive to his purposes.

I could ask another hospital physician to get the files for me, someone who was discreet and sympathetic to my situation. The problem was, Jordan had alienated himself from many of his colleagues, a realization that still made him flush with shame. He might end up asking help from someone who would take delight in reporting him to Dr. Sheffield. Worse yet, he might unwittingly go to the very person who was behind the murder of Officer Eddie Beamon. Jordan could think of only one doctor he trusted well enough to ask for help: Philip Ettinger. Jordan rejected the idea immediately. He could not ask the acting head of Neurosurgery to compromise his ethics and his chances for the department chair.

Jordan kept pacing, but the ideas stopped coming. *Is that it, God? Is that all I have to work with?* Maggie Rusch came back to mind, and he stopped pacing. As an SICU nurse, Maggie had access to the computer, and she seemed to be a sympathetic, caring soul. She was also a Christian who sought Jordan out after Trudy Aguilera's death to see if he was OK and to assure him that she was praying for him. If asked, would Maggie retrieve some files for him from the mainframe?

A quick call to the SICU revealed that Maggie Rusch had Sunday off this week. Jordan sorted through a few drawers before locating a staff directory. As he thumbed through the directory to Maggie's home phone number, he quickly formulated a plan. Then he dialed her number.

"Hello." The woman's voice was heavy with sleep.

Jordan looked at his watch: 9:22. Apparently Maggie Rusch was not a morning person. "Maggie?" he said.

"Who's this?" she mumbled.

"This is Dr. Keyes—Jordan Keyes—from the hospital. I hope this isn't too early for you."

Maggie took a few seconds to process the information. "Jordy?"

"Right. I could call back later."

"No, it's all right," Maggie said, yawning. "Sam and I need to get ready for church anyway. Hey, I thought you were in L.A."

"I was, but—"

"But the police officer died and you had to come home early," Maggie finished for him.

"That's correct."

"Jordy, I'm really sorry." Maggie's consolation seemed heartfelt. "We tried our best to bring him back."

"I know you did. Thanks." Jordan was sure Maggie had

not heard about the autopsy report and inquiry into the cause of death. Unwilling to get into the topic now, he pressed on. "I apologize for calling you at home on your day off, Maggie. But I have a small, work-related favor to ask you."

"Of course, what can I do you for?"

Jordan was tempted to second-guess his judgment on what he had decided to do. But he pressed on. "Actually, I was hoping I could talk to you in person. Could I meet you—and Sam, if he can make it—for coffee somewhere?"

Maggie hesitated, then, "I have a better idea. Why don't you come over to our place for dinner after church? We're on the east side, just off Stark."

"I really hate to intrude on your Sunday dinner."

"No intrusion at all," Maggie countered. "Sunday dinner for us is nothing fancy, just lunch on the everyday china instead of paper plates. How about 12:30?"

Jordan was momentarily out of excuses. "Twelve-thirty is fine. I'll see you then." Maggie supplied directions, and he memorized them. Hanging up, he reasoned that if he thought of a better way to do this in the next hour, he would gladly call and postpone dinner with the irrepressible Maggie Rusch and her husband.

◆ ◆ ◆

Sam proudly served a meal of homemade turkey potpie, fresh spinach salad, and nuke-and-serve rolls. Maggie bragged on her husband's cooking, a hobby of his since his painful divorce six years earlier. Jordan quizzed Sam about his construction business. Sam mentioned that he was currently working at Mercy Hospital repairing water damage in one of the small buildings on the campus. Listening to Sam talk, Jordan thought he could easily become friends with Maggie's likable, devoted husband.

Receiving an after-dinner cup of coffee, Jordan launched into his topic. "Maggie, I want to hear more about the SICU deaths you mentioned the other day."

"Does this have anything to do with the cop who didn't make it, Jordan?" Sam probed, sipping his coffee.

Since talking to Maggie on the phone, Jordan had contemplated how much to tell the couple about his involvement in the death of Eddie Beamon. Realizing they would know everything after she returned to work tomorrow—including all the gossip—he had decided to tell them everything today. He did not expect to get into it quite so soon.

Jordan related the twelve-hour string of events from Dr. Sheffield's initial phone call last night to the discovery that his access to the hospital's mainframe had been denied. He explained the incriminating phenobarbital evidence that seemed stacked against him. He was careful to state the facts without defending himself or trying to elicit the couple's sympathy. They listened attentively without interrupting.

"Jordy, this is awful," Maggie said when he concluded. "You're being set up. You should tell the police."

"Maggie's right," Sam echoed, "you have to go to the authorities."

Jordan shook his head slowly. "I don't have anything to show the police. At the moment, everything points to me. I have to find something that at least sheds reasonable doubt on my responsibility for the cop's death. That brings me back to the favor I wanted to ask."

"Why me, Jordy?" Maggie said.

"For one thing, I don't know many people in the hospital I can trust, especially after the things I said in the staff meeting last week. I don't know you two very well either, but you are both Christians, and you have been . . . well, supportive."

"That's what being a Christian is all about, isn't it?" Sam said with a wink. Maggie reached to his hand on the table and gave it a pat of agreement.

Jordan nodded. "I also come to you, Maggie, because you're the one who brought up the deaths in SICU."

Maggie brushed the comment away with her hand. "I'm

sure it's just hospital talk, Jordy, kind of a morbid release valve for the pressures of the SICU."

"That's what I need to make sure of," Jordan said, leaning forward in his chair. "That's what I need to talk to you two about in confidence. Are you OK with that?"

Maggie and Sam glanced at each other, then turned back to their guest. "Sure, Jordy, we can keep a secret," Maggie said for both of them.

Jordan lifted a large manila envelope from the briefcase near his feet and placed it on the table. "A few days ago I did a little exploring in the hospital's files from my computer. I wanted to see if there was any grounds for your comment about the hospital losing an unusual number of trauma patients."

Maggie studied him again, her dour expression reflecting his. "You're serious about this, aren't you, Jordy?"

Before Jordan could answer, Sam put in, "You're worried about a malpractice suit, losing your job, maybe even criminal charges."

"Wouldn't you be—if it appeared that you were responsible for killing a patient?" Jordan said soberly.

He watched as the couple processed the thought. "I'd be a basket case," Maggie said in a whisper. Sam nodded slowly.

After another moment of silence, Maggie motioned to the large envelope and said, "So what did you find in the hospital's brain?"

Jordan explained that his brief look at the death reports only piqued his curiosity to study the medical charts of these patients, something he was no longer able to do. He concluded, "I know that fatalities happen in the OR and the SICU for a number of different reasons, including human error. But why so many here? I just want to look for a possible explanation."

Maggie and Sam waited for more, but Jordan was silent.

"You're saying that there is some substance behind all the jokes about trauma patients dying," Maggie said at last.

"I'm saying that Trudy Aguilera and Eddie Beamon fit a disturbing profile of trauma patients who made it through resuscitation only to die within days due to complications, many of them suspiciously similar. Before I take the fall for Eddie Beamon's manslaughter or murder, I want to know if there is something behind all this."

Sam narrowed his eyes with suspicion. "You mean something like euthanizing people for their organs? I thought that kind of stuff only happened in hospital novels."

"I don't know," Jordan said, shaking his head slightly. "But Maggie may be able to help me find out."

Maggie smiled. "You want me to climb into the mainframe and get those patient files for you."

Jordan felt uncomfortable about imposing. "Only if you're willing."

"So what do you hope to find in the medical files of these poor souls?" she said, eyeing the yet unopened envelope.

"Again, I don't know. But I have to look. Somewhere there exists an explanation for Eddie Beamon's death, and maybe the other deceased trauma patients can tell me something. The death reports I printed out pointed to a link, but only the full patient files will have the answer."

Maggie set down her cup and scratched her chin thoughtfully with one lacquered fingernail. "How soon do you want the files?"

Jordan shifted in his chair. "I don't want you to get in trouble, and I don't want you to lose your job."

"This is a piece of cake, Jordy. I get files all the time. Anybody in the hospital can get them—except you, of course."

"I'm serious, Maggie. If there's a risk of getting fired or anything . . . " Jordan left the exit door wide open for her.

"It's no problem. I can do it from my PC right here. I'll be glad to. Now, when do you want the files?" Then she quickly answered her own question. "Of course, you want them ASAP. Can you give me till morning?"

"Sure, but I don't want you to waste your day off."

Maggie blew off the comment with a small laugh. "Like my day off is such a big deal. Do the laundry, pay the bills, clean up the kitchen for Chef Sam. Actually, a little undercover mission sounds much more exciting. Sam, you may have to be both cook and busboy today."

Sam laughed as he stood to top off the three coffee cups. "What a slave driver," he said, winking at Jordan. Then he quickly added, "Actually, in our marriage we share most of the chores and all the fun." Then he suggested that they take their coffee into the living room.

"Speaking of marriages," Maggie said as she and Sam settled into the sofa, "how is your wife?"

The unexpected reminder of his last conversation with Della provoked Jordan to a silent sigh. "Fine, she's fine," he said, leaning back in the swivel rocker.

"Does she know what's going on up here, Jordy?" Maggie continued. "Have you told her about Eddie Beamon and the trouble you're dealing with?"

Jordan wanted to crawl into a hole. His self-appointed sister was at it again. "We didn't have much time to talk last night. I only told her that a patient died and that I had to straighten out the details," he said, fidgeting with his cup. "I had to run for the airport."

Maggie leaned forward on her elbows. "Are you and Della doing all right?"

Della's words had been with him constantly since last night, like a flashing neon sign in the back of his brain: *I don't know how I feel for you right now. I'm just numb inside.* "It's a challenge sometimes, you know, dealing with the demands of my career. But we'll be all right."

"Jordy, I'm serious," Maggie persisted. "Are you two connecting emotionally?"

Here we go again with this connecting stuff, Jordan whined to himself. *Everyone seems to know about it except me.*

"Oh boy, oh boy," Sam cut in, "Maggie the counselor is boring in. Oh boy, oh boy." Sam's rather good impersonation of Buster Chapman brought a glimmer of comic relief to the moment.

"Sam, don't make fun of Buster," Maggie scolded good-naturedly.

"I'm not making fun of Buster," Sam protested. "After all, we're fly-tying buddies."

Jordan could not mask his surprise. "You . . . you socialize with Buster?"

"Yeah, Buster and his mother attend our church," Sam explained. "He likes to fish, so I taught him how to tie flies. About once a month we head out to Eagle Creek to feed our fancy flies to the steelhead."

"And about once a month he comes over for a fish fry," Maggie added with a smile. "Buster has to be the most tenderhearted, caring person on God's beautiful earth. Just yesterday he told me he was even concerned about you, Jordy."

"What do you mean by *concerned?*" Jordan probed, not sure he really wanted to know.

"Buster said, 'I'm sad for Dr. Keyes because he's hurting a lot inside.' I'm telling you, Jordy, people like Buster who have experienced a lot of emotional pain can see it in others a mile away."

Jordan was suddenly uncomfortable about where the conversation was going. *First it's Maggie talking about a layer of sadness and pain underneath my anger. Now even the janitor is getting into the act! What do they see that I don't?*

Sam casually slipped his arm around his wife's shoulders. "You may not know it, Jordan, but Maggie and I have been through some pretty rough waters. Both of our previous marriages were disasters, and our exes were not the only ones at fault." Maggie nodded as Sam continued. "If we have learned anything over these last couple of years, we have learned to be open and vulnerable with each other in order to stay connected emotionally."

Several seconds of uncomfortable silence passed before

Jordan figured that Sam was waiting for some kind of response. He took a slow sip of coffee. "Well," he said, clearing his throat, "I guess I'm not too adept at being vulnerable. Things have been a little strained between Della and me lately. I guess she feels that I have put my career ahead of her and Katy."

It was Jordan's turn to wait for a response. He did so with another sip of coffee.

Maggie spoke next. "I know I come off as a little pushy sometimes, Jordy, but let me ask you a question: Do you feel more comfortable at the hospital than you do at home? I mean, do you connect emotionally more with your work than with your wife and daughter?"

Jordan looked away as he contemplated how to answer the question. He could think of no good reason to be dishonest with two people who had been so open and friendly toward him. After a hard swallow, he said, "I'm afraid I don't know what you mean by 'emotionally connecting.' I love my wife and daughter, and I want them here with me in Portland. But if Della says we are not connecting, then I guess we're not. So to answer your question, I suppose I am more comfortable as a surgeon than as a husband, especially since I'm not the husband and father Della wants me to be."

"I appreciate your transparency, Jordan," Sam said. "To tell the truth, it's not easy for me to be close to people emotionally. I was an abused child, and I never really learned how to love from my parents. It's as if that part of me was locked away somewhere. Maggie said I buried my capacity to love and connect when I buried the pain of my abuse. And it was Maggie who made it safe for me to come out of hiding and connect with her."

Seconds of silence ticked by again. This time Jordan decided not to add another log to the fire of self-disclosure that was burning uncomfortably close. Finally he said, "Well, thanks for your thoughts."

"We just want you to know that we're interested in you,

Jordy," Maggie returned, "not just as a coworker, but as a person, a friend."

Since Maggie appeared to be letting him off the hook, Jordan glanced at his watch. "Hey, I'd better run. Thanks for the great dinner. And thanks for the talk. I'll get that disk from you at the hospital tomorrow morning, if that's all right."

"No problem at all," she said. Sam and Maggie walked Jordan to the door. Sam grasped his hand. "Come back again, Jordan. I brew up a mean dish I call Sasquatch chili. I think you might like it."

Jordan promised a return visit and left.

Driving back to the hospital, Jordan twirled the gold band on his finger with his left thumb. He felt relieved to be away from Sam and Maggie's penetrating questions and comments. After several moments of reflection, he spoke to the couple as if they were in the car with him. "As you can tell, I'm not very comfortable talking with people about such personal matters. But for some reason I'm almost glad I came. And it wasn't just the turkey potpie."

NINETEEN

The rest of the afternoon was a waste. Banned from seeing his patients and unable to get into the hospital's computer, Jordan spent two hours in the neurosciences building trying to look busy. He read a little, but his concentration was thin. He wished he had pressed Maggie to copy the files while he waited. He could be studying them right now.

He called the Realtor to see if the owners of the Lake Oswego house had accepted his offer. She said the sellers were thinking about a counteroffer. Other medical staff in the building avoided him as if he had a communicable disease. Apparently, word of his "suspension" had made the rounds.

Finding a TV in an unused waiting room, Jordan watched a portion of a local news program. The upcoming funeral for Officer Beamon was mentioned near the top of the show. However, the anchor did not mention the phenobarbital overdose. Apparently the exact cause of death was being withheld from the media pending the hospital's investigation. The greater Portland area knew only that the bullet wound suffered by the brave officer had proven fatal. Jordan hoped the citizens would learn nothing else.

Shortly after five Jordan left the hospital. It was warm enough to open the windows in the car. Winding down the two-mile wooded slope from the hospital to the city, Jordan welcomed the fresh air and spring fragrances. Invigorated by the warm breeze swirling around him in the car, he just kept driving. Soon he was on Interstate 84 headed east out of Portland toward Mount Hood. The gathering sunset slowly transformed the distant, snow-laden mountain into a craggy mound of strawberry ice cream. The solace of the welcoming sight drew Jordan onward.

Exiting the freeway at Gresham, he found Highway 26 and headed toward the mountain. He welcomed the drive as a temporary retreat. With the wind swirling noisily around him, Jordan questioned, complained a little, and prayed. He was doing everything he knew to do, he explained to God, to save his career at Mercy Hospital. He was looking for the evidence that would exonerate him from suspicion and blame, so far without success. What was God doing in the meantime? The prison gates before him seemed formidable. He was already on his feet ready to walk through, so where was the angel to open them?

He drove through the mountain communities of Sandy, Brightwood, Zigzag, and Rhododendron. The cooler mountain air and declining sunlight forced him to close the windows. He mulled over Maggie's penetrating question about his comfort level at home. *I don't know how to connect with Della,* he lamented to God. *Until last night, I didn't even know we were not connecting. I'm doing everything I know to do. I have already lost my son. Please don't take my wife and daughter.* The ominous threat of losing Della kept him praying for several minutes.

In between his silent, informal petitions, Jordan kept returning to phrases Sam had uttered after dinner. He tried to recapture Sam's exact words: "Part of me was locked away. . . . I buried my capacity to love and connect when I buried the pain of my abuse. . . . Maggie made it safe for me to come out of hiding and connect." Every time he rehearsed the phrases, the word *buried* seemed to reverberate inside his skull. Less than twenty-four hours ago, Della had used the same word in the tear-filled lament of her unhappy marriage. "When we buried our son, I guess you buried what was left of the real you," she had said. *Does my inability to connect with Della have something to do with how I handled J. J.'s death?*

Della had also mentioned that disconnection in their relationship preceded the loss of their son. *Did I bring something into our marriage that keeps us from connecting, something from my past?* Jordan understood how the childhood abuse Sam revealed might interfere with intimacy in a marriage. But there was no abuse in Jordan's childhood. *My family was fairly close until Mom died,* Jordan argued the point to himself. *I was not physically or sexually abused. Mom inspired me until the day she died to excel in everything I did: "Make me proud, Jordan." Dad equipped me with the gift of mental focus: "Big boys don't cry, Son." Lord, did I miss something during my childhood, something that keeps me from connecting with Della?*

Reaching the ski area near Government Camp at sunset, Jordan parked the car and hiked a short distance to where he could watch the enormous pink mountain surrender to the blue shadow relentlessly advancing upon its western slope. Standing ankle deep in the snow in his loafers, slacks, sport jacket, and tie, Jordan received a few curious looks from skiers and snowboarders leaving the mountain. He couldn't have cared less. The sight was magnificent. It occurred to him that if God could conquer an 11,239-foot peak every day in such grand style, the mountains in his life right now should not be a problem.

Driving down the mountain, Jordan stopped in Rhododendron at a roadside restaurant that resembled a large log cabin. The atmosphere was quiet, and the Paul Bunyan stew was excellent. Jordan had not enjoyed such a pleasant and relaxing few hours since coming to Oregon. He thought it ironic that the brief retreat came at such a tumultuous time in his life. It was the eye in the middle of the storm, he thought, and he thanked God for it on the drive back to his apartment.

Changing out of his work clothes into comfy sweats, Jordan made the call he really didn't want to make. He considered it a moral victory that Katy, who answered the phone, didn't hang up on him for missing her birthday trip to Catalina. Cool but communicative, she described the ride on the ferry and the day of sightseeing and shopping in Avalon. Avoiding the details of the Beamon case, Jordan apologized for disappointing her and missing her special day. Katy responded, "I know, Daddy. I understand." He promised her a makeup trip in the summer. She thanked him for the birthday gifts, then said good-night and turned the phone over to her mother.

"I don't know if you are interested or not," Jordan began, "but I want to explain why I had to leave last night." Since Della did not object or hang up on him, he proceeded to tell her everything about the Eddie Beamon case, just as Maggie and Sam had encouraged him to do. He ended with another apology for leaving.

Della listened without comment through the ten-minute explanation. When he concluded, she said, "So what are you going to do, Jordan?"

"I'm going to prove that I was not responsible for the policeman's death."

"How are you going to do that?"

Jordan was still trying to solve that problem. He had not mentioned to her the other SICU deaths that had intrigued him, deaths he hoped to know more about after studying the medical charts Maggie was "borrowing" for him. "I'm going to keep asking questions and digging up records until I find the truth."

"What will you do if you find the person who supposedly set you up?"

Supposedly? Jordan retorted silently. *Do you think I'm making up this story to gain your sympathy or persuade you not to leave me? Are you as skeptical and unsympathetic as most of my coworkers? Are you tempted to believe that the death of Officer Beamon was really my fault?* Della seemed to be responding to him like many of his colleagues at Mercy Hospital had: with suspicion and subtle aversion. He suspected that she did so for the same reason he had received the cold shoulder at the hospital—he had somehow alienated her.

What is at the root of Della's suspicion? Jordan wondered fleetingly. *Is it tied to J. J.'s death in some way? Does she think I didn't try hard enough to save him? At times I have blamed myself for not finding a cure. Does she blame me too?*

Taking issue with Della's comment would not be to his advantage, Jordan judged. So he just answered the question: "I will turn the person and the evidence over to the police."

Della was silent for several seconds. Then she said, "Do you think this person intends to do more than get you fired or arrested?"

Jordan caught her meaning immediately. He wanted to take it as a sign of concern. "I don't think he wants to hurt me, just punish me and send me packing."

"But if this person killed a defenseless patient just to get rid of you, you have a sociopath on your hands. He may be tempted to kill again, especially if you crowd him. I think you ought to tell the police that much."

"They know that much already, and they probably think I'm the culprit. But I will change that very soon."

There was a long pause. "Please be careful, Jordan."

"I'll be careful. Thanks." Then he gingerly moved on to the next topic he wanted to discuss. "I've been thinking about what you said last night. I want you to know that I'm going to do everything possible to resolve things between us."

He heard Della speak away from the phone. "OK, honey, good night. I'll be in for prayers in just a minute." Then she was back on, but speaking discreetly. "What are you going to do to 'resolve things'?"

"I'm going to be more attentive to the issues you feel are important in our relationship. I'm definitely going to cut back on my work so I can be home more. I'm going to—"

"Promises won't do it, Jordan," Della interrupted. "You have made promises before only to break them. Nothing has changed."

"Della, listen to me," Jordan pleaded. "Something *has* changed. For the first time in my life I admit that I need to do something to improve our relationship. I want to—as you put it—connect with you."

Della was silent for a moment. "How are you going to connect with me?"

Jordan cleared his throat. Sam and Maggie's words about being vulnerable and his own dialogue with God on the mountain were still ringing in Jordan's ears. "I think it may have something to do with losing J. J., how I handled the pain. Perhaps there are some other issues from the past I haven't dealt with. Maybe these things have kept me from connecting with you. I want to find out."

Several seconds passed before Della spoke. "I think it would be healthy to pursue that line of thought, Jordan. But I don't want to get my hopes up only to be disappointed again."

Hope. The word seared Jordan like a red-hot branding iron. *That's what I need tonight, Della,* he thought. *If you could give me a little hope that our relationship has a chance, it would help me pursue this issue of connecting with you.* He said, "Last night I asked you a question: Do you love me? You couldn't say yes. You said you were emotionally numb. Is it true, Dell? I know I have disappointed you, even hurt you. But can you find an ember of love for me somewhere in your heart?" He knew his pointed question set him up for a potentially big fall, but he had to ask it.

Jordan heard a deep sigh. Then Della said, "I don't know how I feel right now. I'm so emotionally . . . tired. And I can't go on the way things are."

"An ember, Dell," Jordan pressed. "Is there just one ember of love still faintly glowing?" The urgency in his plea surprised even him.

Della began to cry softly. "I . . . I think so, Jordan. I want it to be there. I want my husband back. I have felt so alone."

"That's all I need to know," Jordan said, his voice constricted with a sudden swell of emotion. "Things are going to change, I promise you. *I'm* going to change. The problem is in me. I'm the one who stamped out that fire. But I want my wife back. I want that small ember of love to grow into a blaze again. I'm not sure how it's going to happen, but with God's help we're going to connect again, Dell. Just keep that ember alive a little longer."

Della was crying harder now. "I'll try," she said with difficulty, "but I've been trying for so long."

Jordan promised to keep her informed about his problem at the hospital. He told Della he loved her, then hung up before she felt pressured to respond in kind. He would hear her say those words again soon, he hoped: "I love you, Jordan."

He sat beside the phone for several more minutes. Was he really beginning to change, or had he said so to persuade Della to stay with him? No, something was different. Some kind of change was taking place. He had sensed it from the surprising knot in his throat as he talked to Della. What should he do now?

Jordan had always considered himself a problem solver. But the problems he attacked and conquered were always external, someone else's problems. Even the difficulties in their marriage Jordan had considered to be primarily Della's problem. Realizing that he was at the root of their disconnectedness, that he was the problem to be solved, was a revelation. The familiar words now had a stark and anxiety-producing new meaning: Physician, heal thyself.

I assumed that my time-demanding medical practice was at the root of our marriage difficulties. Perhaps my work is only the symptom of a deeper issue. I told Maggie that I am more comfortable at work than at home. Could I be using my work as an escape from something I don't know how to deal with? Have I buried the pain of J. J.'s death under a mountain of eighty-hour weeks at the hospital? Is the buried pain and the mountain of activity the reason I cannot connect with Della? If so, how do I fix it?

The words were before him again: *heal thyself.* Momentarily overwhelmed by a problem he did not know how to solve, he prayed: *God, Great Physician, I don't have an answer. Please help me find it. I don't want to lose my family.*

TWENTY

Jordan arrived at the hospital just before seven Monday morning and headed straight for SICU. Maggie had tucked one high-density diskette into an interoffice mail envelope and padded it with a sheaf of papers destined for the shredder. Handing him the parcel in the busy nurse's station, she said with a sly wink, "Here are the pathology reports you wanted, Doctor." Jordan went along with the act and thanked her. He felt like a spy smuggling contraband. Maggie quickly hurried off to work, and Jordan left the unit before he encountered someone who might be curious about what he was doing.

Jordan's pager buzzed on the way to his office. He recognized the caller from the readout: Dr. Bert Waller. Locking the office door, he dialed the number from his desk phone.

"Good morning, Dr. Waller," he said with all the confidence he could muster.

"Hello, Jordan. Just wanted to touch base quickly and see how you are doing."

"Fine, Doctor, thank you," he said, still trying to convince himself.

"Anybody hassling you—media, police, anybody?"

Locked out of the mainframe, Jordan felt hassled by Taylor Sheffield and Leonard Darwin. But he gathered that Waller knew nothing about it. "Nobody," he answered.

"Has the Beamon family been in touch with you?"

"No, I have not seen anyone from the family."

"Good, good. You don't need to talk to them. We will take care of all that for you."

"Anything new on your end?" Jordan probed, hoping against hope that Waller had learned something about the phenobarb overdose.

"Leonard has everything in hand, Jordan. We hope to get things ironed out on this end in short order." It was a none-of-your-business brush-off, Jordan recognized.

Jordan said, "What happens if Mr. Darwin can't get things ironed out?" He was sure the doctor knew what he was asking.

"It's out of my hands, unfortunately. Leonard Darwin and Dr. Sheffield will sort through all the data and do what is best for the hospital."

Meaning that if I am sued for malpractice or the police take me in as a suspect for manslaughter or murder, I'm out on my ear, Jordan mused uncomfortably.

"But don't worry, Jordan," Waller added quickly. "Things have a way of working out for the best, correct?"

Jordan doubted that his nominally Christian boss could quote Romans 8:28, but he responded as if Waller had. "Yes, sir, I believe that," adding silently, *Lord, help my unbelief.*

"Are you staying busy? Do you need anything?"

"I'm fine, Dr. Waller, really."

"Aha, good. I'll check back with you."

"Thank you, sir."

There was no reply. Waller just hung up. Jordan sensed that his superior was walking a tightrope. Dr. Waller seemed sympathetic and supportive personally, but Jordan knew the man had to go by the book in handling the alleged professional failure. Jordan would count on no favors from Waller in his defense. He just hoped he could continue to count on Waller's encouragement.

Jordan booted up his computer and slid the disk into the A: drive. In ten minutes he had printed a quarter-inch stack of medical files. Still uneasy about spending much time in his office, he slipped the disk into the pocket of his sport jacket, collected the hard copies into a folder, and left for the fifth floor of the neurosciences building, stopping at a vending machine long enough to buy a large coffee.

Placing the stack of papers and cup of coffee on the desk of a vacant office, Jordan shed his jacket and sat down. The stack of papers in front of him represented the last days and hours of thirty-five former SICU patients at Mercy Hospital over the past sixteen months. Maggie had copied the records in chronological order, from a seventeen-year-old skateboarder who was rushed to the ER on January 28 last year to thirty-three-year-old Officer Eddie Beamon, admitted Saturday, April 17—only two days ago.

The lines of data on each page were terse and choppy, riddled with clipped medical jargon, codes, acronyms, and abbreviations. Each cryptic line in the records represented a medical observation, a physician's order, an action, or a response to an observation, order, or action. Each page was dry, laborious reading, devoid of the pain, fear, despair, and grief that had attended each patient's struggle and eventual death.

Jordan sat at the desk scrutinizing files for the next three hours, moving only to get more coffee or go to the bathroom. Plodding through the lines of data, he meticulously diagnosed each patient and evaluated each step of treatment from ER to OR to ICU to autopsy—when one was requested. All cases involved severe brain or spinal cord trauma, so Jordan mentally performed every surgery and closely studied the follow-up treatment on each case.

The records were thorough, and Jordan had only minor disagreements about the procedures these patients received. His earlier suspicion that Mercy Hospital was a magnet for medical misfits had completely dissolved. These people knew what they were doing, and they did it well. No wonder the hospital enjoyed the reputation of a topflight trauma center in the northwestern United States.

But there was a germ of disappointment in this realization. He had hoped to find a few deaths attributed to human error: a misdiagnosis corrected too late, a botched surgery, a mix-up in prescription drugs, a tainted unit of blood, a miscommunication between physician and staff. But so far the files had documented only one physician error that might have contributed to patient death. In every other case Jordan found only the timely efforts of skilled personnel that were surprisingly and dishearteningly negated by circumstances beyond their control.

This made the mystery all the more puzzling. Thirty-five patients received state-of-the-art, lifesaving trauma care, but they all died within a matter of days. How many other trauma teams and neurosurgeons were as shocked as Jordan had been about Eddie Beamon when the patients they had so skillfully revived and repaired failed to recover? Jordan realized that a subsequent level of his personal investigation might involve locating and interviewing some of these physicians.

By noon Jordan was down to case number seventeen, a thirty-eight-year-old man named Patrick Umbertson. On Labor Day last year, Umbertson was flown by Life Flight to Mercy from Multnomah Falls in the Columbia Gorge, where he had fallen while hiking. The man sustained severe head injuries and a fracture of the fifth cervical vertebra, damaging the spinal cord. Four days after brain surgery, Umbertson was still comatose but guardedly stable. He died without regaining consciousness. Cause of death: cardiac arrest due to head and spinal trauma.

This patient was close to Jordan's age. *Tough luck for such a young guy,* he thought, allowing his eyes to stray to the personal data entered at the top of the chart. He realized that fatigue was eroding his objectivity. He didn't have time to think about the *person* on each sheet; he had to solve the *problem.* Jordan knew he should move on to the next case, but he continued to peruse the page in front of him.

Umbertson had been living in a community at the foot of

Mount Hood with the dubious name of Boring, Oregon. He thought about the young man's wife and family. *Poor lady, poor little kids—if he had any.* Jordan imagined a young woman and two school-age kids heartbroken over the untimely death of a husband and daddy.

Jordan noted that the young man had been some kind of minister. The title field next to his name contained the letters Rev., for Reverend. He found the field that reported the patient's religious preference. It read Catholic. Jordan raised his eyebrows at the thought of a Catholic priest so tragically killed. More than a family, this man had likely left an entire parish in mourning.

It occurred to Jordan that Father Umbertson was not the only cleric in his stack of charts. Leafing through pages already studied, he found the chart for Rev. Soon Kim Park, fifty-four, whose religious preference was identified as Methodist. Rev. Park had succumbed to complications after surgery to repair a brain aneurysm. *At least Fr. Umbertson and Rev. Park were prepared to die,* Jordan editorialized silently. *But how many of the others were?*

Having yielded to his curiosity already, Jordan began turning pages to investigate the religious preferences of the remaining thirty-three patients, information he had barely skimmed because it did not pertain to medical history. He began reading them aloud: "Catholic, Reformed, Baptist, Christian, Baptist, Disciples of Christ, Protestant, Evangelical, Presbyterian, Pentecostal—"

He was a third of the way through the stack when his beeper sounded, startling him. He checked his watch: 12:44 P.M. The readout displayed a number with a prefix unique to Mercy Hospital. Someone in the hospital was paging him. He dialed the number on the desk phone. When a woman answered, he said, "This is Dr. Keyes."

"Jordy, this is Maggie."

Jordan was not sure it was a good idea to stay in close touch with Maggie at the hospital. If someone found out she had tapped into the mainframe for him, she could lose her job. Worse yet, if the person responsible for Eddie Beamon's death connected Maggie with him, she could be in danger. He hoped she was not standing at a hall phone where anyone passing by could hear her talking to him.

"Yes, Maggie," Jordan said, hoping to keep the conversation short.

"I'm on my lunch break. I just called to see how you're doing."

"I'm doing fine. No one can overhear you, can they?"

"No, I'm in a safe place. I just wondered if you found anything?"

"Like what?"

"Like the reason these patients didn't make it."

Jordan resumed surveying the religious preferences of the patients as he talked. "No, I haven't found anything. The charts look to be in order." *Assembly of God, Protestant, Protestant, Catholic, Nazarene.*

"Yeah, from what I can see, these people were cared for by the book."

Jordan stopped turning pages. "You looked through these charts?"

Maggie laughed. "They're only medical files, Jordy, not classified documents. I made a backup disk and hard copy just in case. I spent a couple hours last night leafing through the charts while Sam watched the Trail Blazers game on TV. Two heads are better than one, you know. I thought maybe I could be of some help."

"Maggie, I didn't really expect you to help me. Don't feel obligated to get further involved. It's kind of my problem, if you know what I mean."

"It's no bother, Jordy," Maggie said, "I'm glad to help. And I might notice something you miss. Are you OK with that?"

Jordan was not totally OK with it. He was concerned for Maggie's safety, and he was afraid she might unwittingly leak his intentions to Dr. Waller or Leonard Darwin. But he knew he had to trust her. "I'm OK with it. But I want to keep these charts—"

"Between us," Maggie finished for him. "My thoughts exactly. No problem, Jordy. I'm very discreet."

"I hope so."

"Now if I should happen to find something interesting or unusual in these charts," Maggie went on, "do you want me to tell you about it, or are you like a lot of doctors who would rather have the nurse butt out of the diagnosis?"

Jordan surprised himself with a smile at Maggie's observation. "If you find anything that might get me off the hook, I want to hear about it."

Maggie agreed and reminded Jordan that she and Sam were praying for him. Jordan suspected that their prayers were as much directed at his relationship with Della as with the dark cloud hanging over him at the hospital.

Returning to the sheaf of charts on the desktop, Jordan remembered what he had been looking at when Maggie called: religious preference. Was he mistaken, or had he yet to find a chart without a stated religious preference? He quickly flipped through the files he had already scanned. All of these patients or their families had aligned themselves with a segment of organized Christian religion. Jordan thought it odd that there were none marked atheist, Mormon, Jehovah's Witness, Buddhist, Scientologist or simply left blank.

Continuing through the rest of the stack, Jordan looked only at the box identifying religious preference. Every patient claimed to be a Christian of some kind. Even the chart for his patient Eddie Beamon identified him as Missionary Baptist. At a time of crisis, Jordan knew, even the most irreligious patients often cry out to God and reclaim a religious association from their past. Yet Jordan was astonished to find a large sample of trauma patients 100 percent Christianized—especially in the state of Oregon, one of the least churched in the nation.

An unbidden memory suddenly materialized. Jordan and Della were at the hospital, admitting their son, J. J., for what would prove to be his last stay. The last thing Jordan wanted to do was to sit at the admitting desk and verify the information on their son's file. Jordan had sent his wife on to J. J.'s room while he finished the necessary business.

"What is Jeffrey's religious preference?" the admitting clerk asked.

"He's only eight years old," Jordan snapped, brittle from months of stress over his son's decline. "He doesn't have a religious preference yet."

The clerk had tried to calm him by being saccharine sweet. "I understand, Dr. Keyes, and our thoughts and prayers are with you and your son. Perhaps we might put your religious preference for him."

So J. J. became a Presbyterian eight days before he died, without ever really knowing what a Presbyterian was.

Jordan overpowered the memory by forcing himself back to the charts in front of him. He had seven more charts to examine, and a quick check determined that all seven were identified as Christians. Not all of them were really committed to Christ, he knew. Many of them, like his son, had likely been tagged people of faith by their distraught family members.

After another minute of reading, Jordan gave up. Tucking the charts into his briefcase, he set out in search of the fastest way to satisfy his demanding hunger.

TWENTY-ONE

Jordan downed half a microwave burrito and a can of Pepsi while looking through the remaining charts in a different office. Turning the last page, he sighed and shook his head. He had learned nothing from the charts except that a very high percentage of trauma patients at Mercy—an amazing 100 percent in this sample—made a claim to Christian faith. As interesting as it was, this fact moved Jordan no nearer to clearing his name in the Beamon case. He needed something more.

Tossing the rest of his burrito in the waste can under the desk, Jordan leaned back to think. Somewhere in cyberspace or deep in the mainframe's archives there had to be proof that the charts of Eddie Beamon and a number of his previous patients had been altered. Such documentation was the shortest distance between suspicion of incompetence or manslaughter and the truth. But where to look?

An ominous question overshadowed the daunting task: Why look in the first place? If such a record had ever existed, it did not exist now because someone did not want it to exist. That person had orchestrated Eddie Beamon's death and positioned Jordan to take the fall. Whoever was clever enough to do the deed was clever enough to cover his or her electronic tracks.

The pager snapped Jordan out of deep thought. It was the

same number Maggie had called from an hour ago. He dialed back immediately.

"What about the blood work, Jordy?" Maggie said after Jordan identified himself.

"Blood work?" Jordan questioned.

"Did you notice the orders for blood work on those charts I gave you?"

Jordan rubbed his forehead. "What blood work?"

"I was looking over the charts again and noticed the blood samples that were taken."

"Of course there was blood work for these cases. You know it's standard procedure."

"Not that blood samples were taken, just how many," Maggie explained. "How often do you need to take a sample from one patient?"

"There are no minimums or maximums," he said. "You take blood every time you want a reading of what's going on in the system." As he spoke, he pulled the stack of files back in front of him on the desktop next to the phone.

"Well, it just seemed to me that each of these patients lost a lot of blood in the name of screening. I just wondered if it seemed strange to you."

Jordan quickly perused the orders on several pages as she spoke. He had noticed the number of screenings last night and attributed them to thoroughness. He thought no differently now. "No, nothing seems out of order."

"OK," Maggie said resignedly, "just a thought."

"I hope you're keeping those charts under wraps," Jordan added quickly.

"No problem, Jordy. I lock them up when I'm not working."

"And you're not talking to anyone else about them?"

"Not a soul."

"Good."

"Speaking of talking to someone," Maggie inserted in her sisterly tone, "did you tell your wife about all this yet?"

"We talked last night."

"And?"

"I can't go into detail right now," he explained tentatively. "When we have a chance to talk, I'll tell you and Sam about it. Your comments yesterday were . . . well, helpful."

"How about tonight? Sam is going to throw some halibut on the barbecue."

"Hey, I wasn't trying to beg another dinner."

Maggie laughed. "We enjoy having people over. Besides, we have to make sure you're eating well until Della moves up."

"I don't know if I—"

"Six o'clock. We'll be watching for you." Then Maggie hung up before Jordan could protest further.

Wondering what to do next, Jordan spied a stack of old charts he had pushed to a corner of the desk. Maggie had used this wad of discarded paper to pad the envelope and conceal the diskette. On a whim, he pulled the stack closer and began to page through a series of last year's charts. There were at least a hundred charts in the stack. Ignoring name, presenting condition, and treatment, Jordan focused on only one field: religious preference. He simply wanted to find out how the general hospital population compared to the thirty-five unanimously Christian trauma patients who died over the last sixteen months.

Flipping through files, he recognized many of the designations he had seen last night: Protestant, Catholic, and a variety of denominations ranging from African Methodist Episcopal to Wesleyan. But they were interspersed with a significant number of patients—about half, he guessed—whose religious preference was not Christian: Buddhist, Shinto, Jewish, atheist, Islam, Unitarian, Mormon, or not identified. This more correctly represented the general population in a state ranked forty-fifth in the nation in church attendance, he assessed. How unusual that the thirty-five deceased SICU patients were all associated with some kind of Christian religious group—not an atheist or Zoroastrian among them.

He continued flipping through the charts, keeping mental tabs on the religious preferences of patients. The spread seemed to hold: about 30 percent indicated no religious preference, about 50 percent Christian religious groups, and 20 percent non-Christian religions, including one self-avowed Satan worshiper. Jordan did some quick math in his head. According to the law of averages, about ten of the thirty-five SICU patients he studied should have had no religious preference, another eighteen should have been Christian, and seven should have been other religions. How could the averages be so skewed when it came to patients in SICU?

Jordan stood and stepped to the window of the small office on the sixth floor. The forecasters had promised the residents of western Oregon a beautiful spring day with temperatures in the mid sixties, virtually no air pollution, and zero chance of rain. These were the kinds of days Oregonians ballyhooed as the best living conditions in the country: clear, green, and healthful. The color and splendor during the months of April through October made you forget the other five cold, wet months of the year, the locals had assured Jordan.

The beauty of the new day and the promise of a glorious spring did nothing to lift Jordan's mood. For all the beauty of these surroundings and the promise of a revived career at Mercy Hospital, someone did not want him here. And if Jordan did not find a way through the facade of guilt arrayed against him, that someone would get his wish.

Returning to the desk, his eye fell on a small sticker attached to the desktop where a computer monitor had once stood. The sticker read Computer Technical Support, Ext. 4431. Jordan had seen the same sticker on several desks around the hospital, but not having needed technical support, he had ignored it. At this moment he wondered if the hospital's computer department could somehow help him resurrect purposely deleted or altered charts. It was a slim hope, but more substantial than anything else at the moment.

Checking the hospital directory, he discovered that Computer Technical Support was in the basement of the main building. Stuffing the original sheaf of charts into his briefcase, Jordan slipped on his jacket and headed for the main building, case in hand.

The computer support office was tucked into a corner of the basement several hundred feet from the elevators, behind the sprawling Medical Records Department. The hallway was a little darker due to a few burned-out fluorescent tubes, and scuff marks on the walls and floors were more frequent than on other floors. Jordan assumed that this area of the hospital was among the last to receive maintenance attention since it was so far from the public.

The first door Jordan approached contained the mainframe computer. The door was locked, but a window in the door provided a good view of what he judged to be a remarkably small machine for handling the electronic data of a substantial hospital. He could also see that the room was neat and spotless.

The office next to it was another story. The door was propped open and the lights were on, but when Jordan stepped inside, the occupant was gone. He marveled at the piles of electronic gear littering the desktop, bookcases, and three mismatched chairs—coils of wire, boxes of parts, stacks of disks and CD-ROM cases, manuals, and nondescript jumbles of computer accessories. The sounds of whales communicating came from the speakers of a PC mounted on the desk. Another PC on a credenza behind the desk displayed a game of chess in progress on the monitor. The computer was apparently playing itself.

"Can I help you?"

Startled, Jordan turned to find a young man in his early twenties standing in the doorway. "I'm looking for one of the computer techs," he said.

"That would be me—the *only* computer tech around here this week," the kid said with an unusual hand gesture pointing to himself.

"Where is everybody else?"

"'Everybody' is four of us," Turk said. "One is on vacation, two have the flu—at least that's what they say. It's hard to keep help on the job these days."

The kid had made a sad attempt at professional apparel. The long sleeves of his off-white shirt were rolled up past his elbows, and his dark tie sported a pattern of fluorescent orange smiley faces. Rumpled khaki trousers—no belt—and blue canvas deck shoes—no socks—completed the ensemble. "Something wrong with your computer? All you had to do was call. We have voice mail down here."

"No, no computer problems," Jordan said. "Just looking around."

"You must really be lost. The dungeon isn't one of the featured stops on the hospital tour."

Jordan smiled at the humor, eager to make a friend of the young man. "I'm Dr. Keyes, Neurosurgery," he said, thrusting out his hand. "Just been at Mercy a couple of months."

"Whoa, brain carver, big job," the kid said. He accepted the hand awkwardly, as if unfamiliar with the social graces. "I didn't think you guys had time to sit around and shoot the bull with computer geeks."

"I'm on my research rotation," Jordan said, hoping the kid was as ignorant of his situation as he seemed.

"They call me Turk," the young man said with another nebulous hand gesture. "Turk DeVrees. Only been around here a couple of years myself."

The odd first name seemed to fit. Jordan suspected that Turk was sometimes ridiculed as a computer nerd, someone who could build a powerful computer blindfolded but had no idea how to dress for public view. Yet Jordan had high regard for people like Turk who could navigate and repair a computer's brain as skillfully as he repaired a human brain.

Turk emptied one of the office chairs of its contents, loading another chair to overflowing. He offered the chair to Jordan, then sat down in his squeaky swivel chair.

"You work full-time for the hospital, Turk?" he said.

"Yes and no," Turk said with a quirky smile. As he spoke, the kid fiddled with a short strand of wire from a pile of junk on his desk. "I put in about sixty hours a week here, but I actually work for myself. I'm an independent Mr. Fix-It for computer systems. But the hospital is my only client right now, so I keep a lot of my stuff here."

"You troubleshoot the whole system?"

"Yep, me and my team. When a hard drive crashes, they call Mr. Fix-It. When a modem goes haywire, they call Mr. Fix-It. When Eunice in Radiology accidentally deletes her solitaire program, she calls Mr. Fix-It."

"And the mainframe?" Jordan probed, jerking a thumb toward the next room.

"Mainframe, terminals, and the network that ties them together—I do it all, man. Troubleshooting, maintenance, upgrades, change-outs . . ."

"You take care of the mainframe." Jordan sounded impressed.

"Oh, I've been known to call in a factory rep when Maxine goes super nutsoid on me, but I handle just about everything else."

"Maxine?"

Turk eyed Jordan over the top of the plastic-rimmed glasses slid halfway down his nose. "Maxine the Mainframe," he said with a droll smirk. "My main squeeze, my girlfriend. Treat her with respect and tenderness, and she fulfills my wildest dreams. Ignore her, slight her, and she becomes a banshee. For better or worse, for richer or poorer, in sickness and health, Maxine is my woman."

Jordan chuckled at Turk's description, and the response brought a smile of pleasure to Mr. Fix-It's boyish, acne-pocked face.

"Maxine handles a lot of data, I bet."

"Tell me about it," Turk said in mock complaint. "Maxine hears all and sees all. I've had to rent a bigger house just to accommodate her memoirs."

"What do you mean?"

"Data backup," Turk said. "Every fifteen minutes Maxine automatically copies all her files to a writable compact disc. Takes all of 2.7 seconds to copy every byte of data in the entire system. Every night I take home the day's CD, label it, and add it to my collection."

"Every fifteen minutes?" Jordan said, curious. "You mean the computer replaces the old data with new data every quarter hour?"

"No, it adds new data every fifteen minutes. Only program of its kind, far as I know. I wrote it myself."

"What's on those CDs?" Jordan was suddenly very serious, leaning toward Turk in his chair.

Turk glanced at him. "Everything," he said with obvious pride. "Maxine sees all and hears all, Doc, remember? If it passed through the system, Maxine captured it and saved it to CD every quarter hour."

"Patient files?"

"Patient files, financial records, logs . . . anything, everything."

"Are you saying that you can select any day in the last week or month or—?"

"Twenty-two months, actually," Turk finished for him. "I developed the system when I first came on board. And I'm a pack rat, so I keep every CD."

"You can pull a CD off your shelf for any day and find minute-by-minute additions to a patient's file?"

"Mr. Fix-It at his best, Doc," Turk said.

"Why did you set up the computer this way?" Jordan pressed. "I mean, is it hospital policy?"

"Policy schmolicy," Turk retorted. "I did it to protect my own rear end. Hardly anyone around here knows about

Maxine's memoirs, or even cares, for that matter. But suppose you say to me, 'I lost a file from last April, Mr. Fix-It. I have to know what I did for Patient X and when I did it. Get me that file.' Do you think I'm going to be very popular if I say, 'Tough luck, Doc, it's all lost in cyberspace'? No, I keep everything so I can keep this contract."

Jordan felt a flood of hope surge through him. This was a providential meeting. "Turk," he said forcefully, causing the kid to stop playing with the wire, "how soon could I see a file on one of your CDs?"

Turk cocked his head. "You've only been here two months, and you've already lost something?"

"This is kind of important to me," Jordan said, purposely downplaying both the desperation and hope he felt.

"Give me the date, and I can bring the CD tomor—"

"No," Jordan cut in, his heart suddenly racing. "I mean how soon today? I'll buy you lunch. I'll pay you for your time. We can take my car. I need to see some charts as soon as possible."

Turk studied the doctor, assessing his need. "So what's it worth to you, Doc?"

If this had been official hospital business, Jordan assessed, he could likely get Turk fired for suggesting an under-the-table payoff. But he needed Turk no matter what the cost. "How about fifty bucks for your time and trouble?"

A smile of contentment brightened the kid's face. "OK, Doc," he said, "you're the boss. Give me a minute to button up the office; then we can go dig out these charts of yours."

As Jordan's Lexus emerged from the parking garage and turned toward the city, neither occupant noticed that the car was being followed at a distance by a dusty, cream-colored Suburban.

TWENTY-TWO

Turk lived in Vancouver, Washington, thirty minutes from the hospital, just across the Columbia River, Oregon's northern border. The kid opted for drive-in burgers he could eat on the way. Mr. Fix-It could not afford to be away from the hospital very long, even though his extended lunch hour would earn him fifty dollars.

Jordan was just as glad not to sit through a restaurant meal. He was in a hurry to see Turk's records for the last two days of Eddie Beamon's life. If they really existed, and if they confirmed what he knew to be true, that Eloise Sandborn's phenobarb injection was strategically deleted from and then returned to the chart, he would take a copy of the CD to Dr. Waller and Leonard Darwin immediately. Jordan also would look at several other patient charts that were altered to make it appear that he was squirreling away a deadly cache of the drug.

Turk's small, rented, wood-frame house was in a dumpy old section near downtown. The living room looked much like his office: a combination computer store warehouse and trash dump. Three computer systems and assorted paraphernalia occupied one entire wall. Shelving on the other walls was piled with cables, monitors, computer magazines and manuals, hundreds of CD cases, and assorted electronic parts in no particular order.

"What dates are you looking at, Doc?" Turk asked without a hint of embarrassment over the state of his quarters.

Jordan had been thinking about it on the drive north. He wanted every shred of data on Eddie Beamon, from admittance through post-mortem. He practically knew the file by heart, but he wanted to see the quarter-hour changes that did not appear on anything he had seen. "For openers, last Friday and Saturday, April 16 and 17," he said.

Turk left the living room. Jordan furtively followed him far enough to get a peek into the bedroom where the kid had stored Maxine's memoirs. The walls were lined floor to ceiling with wooden shelves that bowed under the weight of thousands of plastic CD cases. Jordan could see two additional computers and more boxes and piles of stuff on the floor. Jordan was thankful he was not asking for a CD from a year ago, as he wasn't sure Turk had a reliable system of organization and storage.

But Turk came out a minute later with two cases in his hand. He loaded the first CD into the drawer of one of the living room computers and sat down in an old plastic deck chair that listed to the right. In seconds the search field and prompt were on the screen. "Name of the patient?" Turk said, fingers poised over the keyboard.

"Beamon—*B-E-A-M-O-N,* first name Edward."

Turk snapped his head around. "The cop?"

Jordan nodded. Comprehension materialized on the kid's face. "Did you screw up and kill a cop?" he blurted.

"No, Turk, but somebody screwed up. That's why I need to check these charts."

"I heard about the big hit of phenobarb," Turk said, his countenance suddenly clouded with anxiety, "and I really don't want to get involved. I need this job." The kid squirmed on the chair as if wanting to bolt.

"You're doing nothing wrong, Turk," Jordan said in a calming tone. "You're just pulling some old hospital charts for me. And I'm paying you fifty dollars for your effort. I have the money with me."

"You must be the doc whose password was just revoked. You're not supposed to be messing with Maxine."

"I'm not messing with the computer. I'm looking at old charts that are no longer in the computer."

Turk hovered in indecision, so Jordan played his trump card. "It's worth a hundred to me to get a look at these charts."

"You'll give me a Franklin for this?" Turk said, obviously tantalized.

"As soon as I look at the charts and get any copies I need."

Turk paused only briefly. "All right, but let's do the deed and get back to the hospital."

Jordan dragged a battered folding chair through the floor debris and sat down just behind Turk's left shoulder. At the kid's command, the computer located Eddie Beamon with a humming whir punctuated by soft clicks. The screen flooded with the data of Beamon's admittance to Mercy last Friday afternoon at 2:46 P.M. Jordan's heartbeat quickened with anticipation. "I can take it from here," he said to Turk.

The computer genius yielded his chair to the brain surgeon. "Use 'page down' and 'page up' to move between time increments," he instructed, "or scroll through them with the mouse."

Jordan said nothing, homing in on the data glowing on the screen. He scanned the chart carefully in quarter-hour segments. He found it identical to what he remembered about the patient's treatment in the critical hours after he removed the bullet from Beamon's brain. Nothing in the chart was missing or suspect.

He removed the first CD and inserted the one for Saturday, April 17. He could hear Turk tinkering with something behind him, staying near enough to watch over his equipment while trying not to meddle in the doctor's search. Scrolling through the predawn hours of the patient's care, he found it in perfect order. Slowing as he approached the time of his first visit to Eddie Beamon's room on Saturday, he watched carefully: 0545, 0600, 0615. There was his first order of phenobarbital. Two more clicks on the page down key: 0630, 0645. There was Eloise Sandborn's compliance with the first order. He kept paging down: 0700, 0715, 0730, 0745, 0800. The record remained untouched, and the 7:30 dosage appeared as well.

He kept going expectantly: 0815, 0830, 0845, 0900, 0915, 0930—*There it is!* he exclaimed to himself. The nurse's entry disappeared from the log. At some time between 9:15 and 9:30 A.M. last Saturday, someone had opened Eddie Beamon's chart and deleted Sandborn's entry. The chart now appeared as Jordan had found it several minutes later that morning: as if the morning's phenobarb injections had not occurred. A tide of confidence and relief welled up within him. *I knew I was right. The nurse's entry was not there when I did my later rounds.*

Continuing to scroll, he saw his entry for the phenobarbital he personally injected just where he had inserted it last Saturday. And after three more taps, Nurse Sandborn's entry mysteriously reappeared on the chart. Whoever deleted the line before 9:30 reinserted it after 10:30. It was too strategic to be a coincidence. The two blips in the chart had been planned around Jordan's visits to the SICU that day. "Yes!" he exulted aloud.

Turk said, "Find what you are looking for?"

Jordan barely heard him. He was focused on a column of eleven-digit numbers that did not appear when he pulled up charts in the hospital's computers. Every line item on the chart was headed by one of these numbers. "What are these numbers, Turk?"

The kid leaned over his shoulder. "ID codes," he said. "The first seven digits contain Maxine's hardware and software codes. The last four digits identify the person responsible for each entry on the chart."

"Why don't these numbers appear on a regular chart?"

"Nobody cares about Maxine's signature except me. And since the doctors and nurses key in their name and password for every order, the ID code is just for Maxine's benefit."

Jordan looked at his order for a phenobarb injection. His last name was on the line, but there was also an eleven-digit number ending in 4651. "But I don't enter a four-digit number when I log on. I have a password."

"Of course, but you don't want your password showing up on all the charts where anyone could see it. Maxine doesn't speak words—she speaks numbers. So all the passwords are translated into digits."

Jordan stared at the four-digit number beside Nurse Sandborn's entry at 9:30. The code was 4664. Then he scrolled back to 6:45 A.M. and checked the entry. Sandborn's name was on that line, but the four-digit ID number was different: 6991. He looked at earlier entries on the chart during Eloise Sandborn's shift. Every line with the name Sandborn also contained the ID code 6991. Then he returned to 10:45. It was the only other entry where Sandborn's name was accompanied by the number 4664.

Jordan sensed a jolt of hope. If his adversary had a number, he also had a name. "Whose number is this—4664?" he asked.

Turk studied the number on the screen. "I know a lot of them, but I don't recognize that one offhand."

"Can you find out?"

Turk seemed reluctant. "Yeah, I guess."

"First, I need a copy of the Beamon chart from this CD," he said, rising from the chair. "Then I want to look at a few more while you track down 4664."

Turk sat down, loaded a blank CD-ROM into another drawer in the computer and input the commands. The copy was ready in seconds.

At Jordan's direction Turk pulled another dozen dated CDs out of his library. As Turk retreated to another terminal to search for the identity of 4664, Jordan located the charts of ten previous patients. As expected, Maxine's meticulous records clearly exposed tampering with other phenobarbital prescriptions. Several numbers had been slightly increased to allow suspicion that Dr. Jordan Keyes had been collecting a deadly dose of phenobarbital over a period of time. The discrepancies could not be more clear. Even more telling, every adjusted entry occurred at the hands of the person identified by the number 4664.

Jordan carefully copied the ten charts onto the CD containing Eddie Beamon's chart. He was quietly elated at the answer to his prayer. The proof of his innocence was clear in the data he would take with him today.

Turk, who had been pecking away at another computer, swiveled his chair toward Jordan. "Something's fouled up somewhere," he said, scratching his head. "I keep entering 4664 and getting the wrong answer."

"What answer?"

"Dr. Will Kopke."

"But he died skiing last year."

"Right."

The words came to Jordan's lips, but he would not speak them, because Turk did not need to be burdened with them: *Then someone who knows Will Kopke's password is trying to ruin me. Someone who knows Will Kopke's password is responsible for the death of Eddie Beamon. And since I don't believe in ghosts, that someone is still at large in the hospital.*

Before Jordan could ask another question, Turk said, "Hey, man, I've got to get back to the hospital."

Jordan had what he needed, and he was satisfied. He would relate to Dr. Waller the strange appearance of the late Dr. Kopke's ID code. Waller, Sheffield, Darwin, and the police could take it from there. Jordan would be happily back to work.

Turk locked the house as they left. Before they pulled

away from the curb, Jordan retrieved his billfold. "Like I said, I want to pay you for your trouble, Turk," he said, taking out a fifty, two twenties, and a ten and handing them to him. "This has been a great help to me. Maybe I can tell you about it someday."

Turk, who had been subdued while Jordan made his copies, brightened. "Hey, glad to keep ex-presidents in circulation," he said. Turk handed the CD to Jordan and took the money in the same motion.

A block and a half away in the cream-colored Suburban, a powerful telephoto lens caught Jordan and Turk in a tight close-up through the windshield, and the Nikon camera attached to it recorded the transaction in ten rapid-fire exposures.

TWENTY-THREE

After parting company with Turk in the hospital parking lot, Jordan went straight to Bert Waller's office. "I'm sorry, but Dr. Waller is not in the hospital today, Dr. Keyes," Shirley, the department administrator, called out to him as he passed by her desk.

Jordan stopped and turned. "Where is he? When will he be back?"

"The University of Washington Medical Center. A genetics conference. He comes back late tonight."

Jordan dropped his head and blew a dejected sigh. Then he asked, "Do you have a pager number for him?"

"Yes, but I'm not allowed to give it out," Shirley said. "If it's an emergency, I could page him for you."

Jordan could not in good conscience label his findings an emergency. But the sooner Dr. Waller knew about the CD he had obtained from Turk and the strange appearance of Will Kopke's ID code, the sooner he could walk out from under the cloud of malpractice and manslaughter and get back to work. Besides, Dr. Waller had been supportive and encouraging; Jordan wanted him to hear the good news as soon as possible.

"It's not an emergency, Shirley, but I need to talk to him. It's very important."

"Dr. Waller usually checks in with me a couple of times a day," Shirley said. "Perhaps I could ask him to call you then."

Jordan agreed and recited his cell phone number to her, underscoring that it was important. Then he said, "Do you know how I might get in touch with Leonard Darwin?"

"I *can* give you that number, Dr. Keyes," Shirley said, accommodatingly. She wrote Darwin's office number on a slip of paper and handed it across the counter. Jordan expressed his thanks and left.

Hurrying to his office, Jordan inserted the CD into his computer. He sent Eddie Beamon's detailed chart to the printer, requesting two copies. He did the same with the other ten charts he had copied. Then he copied all the files from the CD onto duplicate floppy disks. He had already determined it wise to keep a backup of the data—both on disk and hard copy—in a separate location from the CD. He sealed one disk and hard copy in a large envelope, addressed it to his apartment, and dropped it in the hospital's outgoing mail slot. He hid the other disk deep in a file cabinet in another sixth-floor office. The other hard copy and the CD from Turk's house went into his briefcase, which would stay with him.

While working on the backups, Jordan decided not to contact Leonard Darwin until after he talked with Dr. Waller. Darwin had been the most insistent about Jordan staying out of the investigation. Jordan thought it best to go through the chain of command on this, which meant talking to Waller, his superior, first. Except for Della, Sam, and Maggie, no one would know of his windfall discovery.

Waiting for a call from Dr. Waller, Jordan halfheartedly perused several journals to pass the time. He left the hospital at 5:30 without hearing anything. Once in the car, Jordan checked his voice mail. Being out of the loop at the hospital, he expected few messages. There was only one. Bubbling with triumph, Virginia the Realtor reported that the sellers had decided to accept his offer on the Lake Oswego home. She requested that he come to the office tomorrow and sign the papers.

He still had time to call Della. "I have some good news," he said when Della picked up her cell phone. He was halfway over the Hawthorne Bridge on his way to Sam and Maggie's northeast Portland home.

"OK," she said, more enthusiastic than during their most recent conversations.

Jordan described his providential meeting with Turk DeVrees and the saving discovery of eleven detailed files. He decided not to cloud the issue with mention of Will Kopke and ID code 4664. "I still don't know how the phenobarb overdose happened or who gave it," he said, "but at least I can prove I was not responsible. So I'm off the hook."

"That's good, Jordan," Della responded, sounding genuinely pleased.

"I want to make it up to Katy—and to you, of course—for being so preoccupied with this crisis."

"That would be important for Katy," Della said. Jordan waited to hear Della express what it would mean to her, but she said nothing. Hurrying on to his other piece of good news, he told her about the Realtor's message. "I want the house in both our names, so I will overnight the papers to you for your signature. Will you send them right back?"

"Sure, whatever you want. I would like to hear more, but I'm with the Parade of Homes people now." Jordan said a hasty good-bye, unable to determine if Della's feelings for him had changed since their last conversation.

Sam and Maggie greeted Jordan at the door. They looked cool and comfortable in summer shorts and polo shirts, even though today's temperature had topped out at only sixty-six degrees. Anything in Oregon over sixty degrees was summer weather, Sam joked. Jordan felt overdressed in his professional attire.

Maggie supplied Jordan with a glass of lemonade. "I hope you don't mind, but Buster will be joining us for dinner. He loves Sam's fish dinners."

"Buster the janitor?"

"The only Buster I know," Maggie said, laughing.

"Fine with me," Jordan said, still a little surprised that the couple had taken on Buster as a project of their care.

As Sam fired up the gas grill on the small patio, Jordan related to his hosts the meeting with Turk and the discovery of backup CDs from the hospital's mainframe. "As soon as I can present the evidence to Dr. Waller," Jordan concluded, "I should be back to clinical duty. I hope to hear from him sometime this evening." Maggie and Sam rejoiced with him about the providential turn of events.

The halibut was ready to take off the grill when the doorbell rang. Maggie opened it to find Buster Chapman's hulking frame filling the doorway. He wore baggy cutoff jeans, knee-high athletic socks, white high-tops, and an orange Oregon State University T-shirt. "I hope I'm not late for the fish fry," he said with disarming boyish enthusiasm as he entered. "I love Sam's fish like ice cream."

"You are right on time, Buster," Maggie assured him.

"Oh boy, Dr. Keyes is here. Hello, Dr. Keyes. Do you like Sam's fish dinners too?"

Jordan had to smile at the purity and innocence. "I'm sure I will, Buster."

Conversation over Sam's halibut dinner was about fishing. Buster packed away two large Alaskan halibut steaks and all the trimmings while recounting several fishing trips he and Sam had enjoyed. Buster's hands only left his fork long enough to demonstrate the size of the largest steelhead or bass he pulled in on each trip. Jordan, who said very little, enjoyed the lighthearted table talk.

Maggie served cookies and lemonade in the family room, where Buster and Sam sat down at a small table to tie flies. Sam started Buster on a project, then turned to Jordan, who had taken a stool at the breakfast bar. "We're waiting to hear how it went with you and Della," he said.

Jordan glanced at Buster, who seemed thoroughly absorbed in his task. He relaxed a little, figuring that the topic would be of little interest to Buster.

"We had a good conversation last night," Jordan said with a measure of enthusiasm. "Thanks to the two of you, I think we made a little progress toward connecting."

"In what way?" Sam probed. Maggie was listening from a maple rocker near the fireplace.

"I spent some time last night thinking about what you said, Sam. You mentioned that a part of you was locked away when you buried the pain of your abuse. You said it caused you to disconnect emotionally from people, especially those you loved."

Sam nodded as he monitored Buster's progress.

Jordan continued. "Last night I began to wonder if the same thing has happened to me. Two years ago we lost our son to leukemia. Maybe I haven't fully dealt with that loss. Maybe I'm retreating into my medical practice to keep from dealing with the pain from these events. I mentioned the possibility to Della last night. She thought I should pursue the idea."

"You may be on to something, Jordy," Maggie put in. "During counseling, Sam and I discovered that traumatic losses, like our abusive backgrounds, need to be mourned, and those who mourn need to be comforted for the hurts to be healed."

"Blessed are they that mourn: for they shall be comforted," Buster recited from the table, still thoroughly absorbed in the tiny fly taking shape in his massive fingers. "St. Matthew, chapter five, verse four, King James Version."

Maggie grinned at the timely interruption. "In case you didn't know, that is Buster's favorite verse," she informed Jordan. Jordan flashed on the recent middle-of-the-night encounter with Buster in the surgery waiting room. The worn Bible on the table had been opened to Matthew.

"If you don't deal with the pain of your tragedies like the verse says," Maggie continued, "you end up stuffing it somewhere, and that can cause all kinds of problems. It did with Sam and me."

"But I vented my grief," Jordan said. "The night J. J. died, I found a closet in the hospital and told God all about it. I asked him to take away the terrible sense of loss and pain I felt."

"Did you tell anyone else how badly you felt?" Sam asked. "Was there someone there to share God's comfort with you?"

"Like I said, I told God," Jordan said, feeling a little penned in by the questioning.

"Then what did you do?" Maggie pressed gently.

Jordan sighed. "After the funeral, I put it behind me. I had a practice to get back to."

"And Della?"

"She grieved for months. I don't think she's over it yet."

"Did you comfort her?" Sam said.

"I tried. I reminded Della that God in his wisdom knew what he was doing by taking J. J. I told her that we had to move on with our lives, that we still had Katy and our friends and our work. I even suggested that counseling might help her get over her grief. My efforts to fix things didn't seem to help much."

"May I make an observation, Jordy, based on what Sam and I have been through?" Maggie continued before Jordan could nod his assent. "Pain and grief are not things you fix; they need to be mourned and comforted. Paul said it in Romans, I believe: 'Rejoice with those who rejoice; mourn with those who mourn.'"

Sam joined his wife at the rocker and placed a hand on her shoulder. "Let me tell you what that verse looked like for Maggie and me. When I was a kid, my alcoholic father used me for a punching bag. I still have the scars to prove it. Early in our marriage, anytime Maggie would correct me in some way, I would get defensive and hostile. One day she invited me to tell her about the pain behind my reaction. When I began to talk about my father's abusiveness—" A sudden swell of emotion interrupted Sam's story.

Maggie placed her hand on his and continued. "When Sam described the way his father had treated him, I broke down in tears. All I could see was this cute, innocent boy bruised and bleeding from his father's fists. I said to him, 'I hurt so badly that little Sammy had a father who beat him instead of protected him.' We cried in each other's arms for several minutes."

Sam picked up the story. "I know God used Maggie that day to share his comfort with me, just like the Bible talks about. But it didn't happen until I told her about Dad. That's what I mean by mourning your hurt and allowing someone to mourn with you and comfort you. Opening up to Maggie and receiving comfort through her has brought us so close together. We continue to get closer every time we mourn our hurts and comfort each other. My inner pain is less intense, and I'm enjoying greater victory over my selfishness." Maggie affirmed her husband's testimony with a nod.

Buster Chapman, who was so involved with his project that he seemed not to be listening, turned to Jordan. "Hurts go away when somebody hurts with you, Dr. Keyes. That's what Mama says."

"Buster knows what it's like to be hurt, don't you, buddy?" Sam said.

"Oh boy, Sam, yes I do."

"Tell the doctor what you told us about your mama and your hurts."

Buster set aside his tools. "When I was a little boy, the kids in my school, they . . . well, sometimes they hit me and threw things at me. They called me Big Dummy and Godzilla and other names I'm not allowed to say.

"When I came home from school, Mama said, 'Were the kids mean to you today?' I said, 'Yes.' Then she said, 'Come over here and let me take the hurt away. Hurts go away when somebody hurts with you.' Then Mama and me, we cried. And you know what happened, Dr. Keyes?"

Intrigued by the simple, touching story, Jordan almost ignored the anticipated response. "What happened, Buster?"

A small tear trickled down Buster's cheek. "When Mama talked to me and cried with me, my heart didn't hurt so bad. Mama said it was God coming in to take the hurt away."

Jordan rubbed his chin for several thoughtful seconds. "You have a very special mother, Buster," he said.

"I love my mama, don't I, Sam?" Buster wiped his cheek with the back of his hand. Sam smiled and nodded.

"Now you know what makes Buster the most compassionate employee at Mercy Hospital," Maggie said to Jordan. "He's there to hurt with people and make the hurt go away."

Buster turned to Jordan again. "Do you have a very special mama, Dr. Keyes?"

Jordan shifted uncomfortably on the stool. "My mother passed away when I was nine years old."

Buster's face clouded with sadness. "Oh boy, Dr. Keyes, you didn't have a mama to make the hurt go away. Oh boy."

Jordan averted his eyes as the spotlight suddenly shifted to him.

"How did your mother die?" Maggie probed gently.

"Ovarian cancer."

"Losing your mother when you were so young, that must have hurt you terribly."

Jordan heard the words in his head as clearly as his father first spoke them: *Stop your crying right now, Jordan. You're a big boy, and big boys don't cry. Mother is with God in heaven, and that's a happy thought. I don't want to see another tear or hear another sad word about it. Make her proud, Jordan, just like she said.*

Along with the words came the familiar inner ache, as if someone had plunged a fist into his abdomen and stripped him of a vital organ. Jordan had felt the same ache the day his mother died and again on the day of her funeral. He yearned to tell his father how badly he hurt inside, but he could not. He had never told anyone, not even Della. *Big boys don't cry.*

All Maggie wanted at this moment was a simple word from Jordan acknowledging that the tragic loss of his mother at age nine had been difficult, painful. But it was not that simple. Jordan knew such an admission would bring him uncomfortably close to the tide of emotions he had carefully controlled for thirty years, a flood he had channeled into his work to earn his mother's pride.

For an instant Jordan saw Della, separated from him by the boiling black sea. Her face was passionless. She was mouthing the words above the roar: "I'm just numb inside, Jordan. . . . I'm just numb inside." The realization flashed before him: *Disconnected from Della by a pain never acknowledged and never comforted. Disconnected by fanatical devotion to work intended to bury the pain. Disconnected over our lost son because our grief was never shared, never healed. Is this the first step to the change I promised her? Is this the first step to reconnecting with Della?*

Jordan held steady. "Yes, I lost something very special when Mom died," he said evenly. "I remember watching as they closed the lid on her casket. It was like a part of my life had been cut out of me and laid in the casket with her."

As he finished the sentence, Jordan's eyes fell on Buster. The big man's face was contorted into a mask of sadness. Large tears coursed from his eyes to his chin. "Oh boy, Dr. Keyes, I'm so sad for you." Then he stood and approached Jordan in several small, childish strides. Dropping to one knee, Buster wrapped two burly arms around Jordan's torso in a bear hug. Burying his face in the doctor's chest, Buster blubbered, "I'm so sorry you lost your mama, Dr. Keyes. I'm so sorry . . . so sorry."

A brief, involuntary shudder rattled through Jordan's bones. He knew he was very near a precipice he had carefully avoided for thirty years. He fixed his eyes straight ahead and clenched his teeth as the torrent of comfort swept around him. Not knowing what to do, Jordan spread his arms tentatively around the massive, heaving form clinging to him and patted Buster gently.

From the corner of his eye, Jordan saw Sam and Maggie clinging to each other and weeping at the tender scene unfolding in their family room. Something very good was happening to him, Jordan knew. The muscles in his face grew taut. Swallowing hard, he squeezed his eyes shut, but not before one small tear escaped and rolled down his face.

◆ ◆ ◆

Bert Waller finally called from his car phone at 9:40 P.M., after Jordan had returned home. The head of Surgery was en route to Portland after the brief conference in Seattle. He seemed relieved to hear about the files on the CD. Jordan sensed that his boss's relief was tempered by the fact that he still had the Beamon family and the public to deal with. Waller wanted him in the office tomorrow morning at seven. If everything looked good, Jordan could rotate back to "active duty." It was the best news yet from what had turned into a very good day.

TWENTY-FOUR

At 6:15 Tuesday morning, while driving to work, Jordan received a call from Maggie. He thanked her again for the evening without mentioning Buster's emotional outburst. She had something else on her mind.

"I was looking over the charts last night before bed, Jordy," she began. "Something fishy is going on with the blood work on these patients."

"What's so fishy about it?" Jordan probed.

"All thirty-five of these patients had blood work processed in our labs during their treatment."

"That's standard procedure, Maggie. You should know—"

"Let me finish, Jordy," Maggie cut in insistently. "All of them, including your patient Beamon, also had blood work processed outside the hospital during their brief treatment. If you ask me, that's weird. Why would you need a second opinion on a blood screening, and why would you go outside to get it when Mercy's lab is one of the best?"

"Where did you get that information? It isn't on the chart."

"I did a little extra checking in the mainframe," Maggie said, obviously proud of having taken the initiative.

"Where in the mainframe?"

"Lab files," Maggie said. "The initial blood work was done here for these people, but other samples were sent out to another lab in Wilsonville."

"Wilsonville? Where's Wilsonville?"

"Suburb just south of Portland. A lot of high-tech firms there."

It seemed a bit odd to Jordan that lab work was going outside the hospital, but he was not alarmed. "Different hospitals have different protocols. I don't know much about the Mercy lab. Could even be a blind study. We did them all the time in L.A.—take a bunch of random samples, number them, screen them for something, send them back."

"It just seems odd to me, especially since no lab reports came back from Wilsonville."

"No reports?"

"Not that I could find."

Jordan guided the car through the sharp, wooded curves, ascending the hill to the hospital. "I wouldn't waste a lot of time on it if I were you, Maggie. The Wilsonville lab must specialize in something we don't do down here—advanced HIV screening, drug tracers, whatever."

Maggie was silent for several seconds. "Well, you sure know how to spoil somebody's fun," she said at last, sounding deflated.

"Sorry," Jordan said, smiling. "Hey, I have to go. I'm pulling into the parking garage and have a meeting with Dr. Waller at seven."

"That's super. Let me know how it turns out."

"Will do. Thanks."

Jordan paced outside Dr. Waller's office for fifteen minutes before his boss arrived. "Jordan, good to see you again," Waller said, gripping his hand firmly, "hopefully under more pleasant circumstances. Come on in and show me what you have," he said, leading the way into his office. "Dr. Sheffield and Mr. Darwin will be along shortly." Jordan took the side chair next to the cluttered desk. Waller moved several piles of papers and books, clearing a space on the desktop between him and his guest, before sitting down.

Without a word, Jordan retrieved the hard copy of Eddie

Beamon's chart from his case. He had already highlighted the discrepancies associated with phenobarbital and ID code 4664. He added to the stack the charts of ten other patients from whom he had allegedly skimmed enough phenobarb to concoct the lethal dose. The discrepancies in these charts and Kopke's number were also highlighted. Laying the sheaf of papers in front of Waller, Jordan watched him absorb the data.

"Aha," Waller said after almost two minutes, still studying the chart. Then he eyed Jordan over the rims of his half glasses. "The record appears to be quite clear. Where did you find it again?"

Jordan rehearsed the story of meeting with Turk and finding out about "Maxine's memoirs."

"I didn't know our computer could do such a thing," Waller said. He added with a chuckle, "Of course, there's quite a bit I don't know about computers."

"Sorry I'm late." The man's voice came from behind Jordan. He knew who it was without turning around.

"Leonard, I'm glad you could make it," Waller said, standing. "You remember Dr. Keyes, of course."

"Hello again, Doctor," Darwin said, all business. Jordan stood and shook Darwin's hand.

Dr. Taylor Sheffield trailed Darwin into the room a few seconds later and nodded a superficial greeting. Jordan wondered if the two men had come together and entered separately to avoid the appearance of friendship. He would have preferred to settle the issue with Waller alone and be on his way. Both Darwin and Dr. Sheffield had seemed adversarial toward him in their previous meeting.

"As I mentioned to you on the phone, Leonard, Dr. Keyes has found something tucked away in the hospital's brain," Waller said, passing the stack of documents to the lawyer and waving him and Sheffield to chairs on the opposite side of the desk. "It doesn't solve our problem with the family of the late Mr. Beamon, but it suggests that Jordan here was the victim of some shabby record keeping."

Sheffield cut in front of Darwin and took the sheets, ignoring Waller's invitation to sit. The lawyer leaned over Sheffield's shoulder to study with him. Waller excused himself to call Shirley and check a few schedule items for the day. Jordan sat down and watched the two men scrutinize the charts.

Finally, Sheffield said, "Where did you get this data, Doctor?"

Jordan was sure the director had already heard the details from Waller. "The hospital's head computer tech, a kid named Turk DeVrees." Waller was still talking to Shirley on the phone, half turned away from the two men.

"And where did DeVrees get it?"

"He programmed the hospital mainframe to automatically back up its data on CD-ROMs every fifteen minutes. He keeps the CDs in case he needs them. He has hundreds of them, all catalogued by date."

"How did you find out about these backups?" Darwin asked.

Jordan said, "I met Turk yesterday down in the basement." Waller hung up the phone and turned to the conversation as Jordan continued. "We got to talking, and he told me about his backup system."

"So you went with DeVrees to his house in Vancouver, where he retrieved this chart on CD-ROM and made copies for you," Sheffield said, indicating the sheets in his hand.

Jordan's skin suddenly flushed. He had said nothing to Waller about going to Turk's house, and he had talked to no one else about the episode. "How did you know that?" Jordan bored into the director, standing to meet him at eye level.

"Yes, what are you getting at, Taylor?" Waller added, still seated.

Dr. Sheffield nodded to Leonard Darwin, and the lawyer retrieved a large envelope from his briefcase and laid it on the desktop in front of Waller. "Take a look," he said.

Jordan leaned over the desk as Dr. Waller lifted the flap

and pulled out the contents. There were ten eight-by-ten, black-and-white photographs, close-ups of two men, Jordan determined at first glance. The lighting in the photos was poor, but the resolution was excellent. It took only a few seconds for Jordan to realize that he was looking at Turk DeVrees and himself. The series of photos clearly showed a CD-ROM case and currency being exchanged between the two men.

Jordan's spine turned to ice at the sight. Waller spoke first. "What is this, Leonard?" Jordan could not believe the wise doctor had missed the implication, but he sounded as if he had.

"I'll tell you what it is, Dr. Waller," Jordan said, fighting a tide of disdain for the sneaky lawyer. "I asked Turk DeVrees to take some time off at noon yesterday to make me a copy of the CD. He was away from the hospital for about an hour and a half, so I offered to pay for his time. That's what this is," Jordan said, tapping the photos emphatically with his finger. "I am giving Turk a hundred dollars to thank him for his time, and he is giving me a copy of the CD."

"One hundred dollars, Dr. Keyes?" Darwin said, his tone clearly suggesting that the reward grossly outweighed the service rendered.

"I was very grateful for Turk's assistance," Jordan said, turning to face the lawyer. "Remember, Mr. Darwin, my career is in jeopardy. This detailed chart exonerates me. It was the least I could do."

"I think you could have done much less, Doctor," Sheffield interjected, irritated. He began pacing the room.

Jordan felt his blood begin to boil. "Why did you do this, Darwin?" he demanded, waving toward the photos. "Why did you tail me like a spy? I thought you were on my side. The chart clearly shows that I treated this patient by the book. And it shows that someone using Dr. Kopke's password fooled with the charts in an attempt to incriminate me. You're making me out to be some kind of thug."

Leonard Darwin's countenance softened, as did his tone. "Forgive me, Doctor. I don't mean to sound like your enemy, because I *am* on your side. First, you need to know that I did not take these pictures, nor did I have you followed. Apparently, someone working for the Beamon family wants badly to make a malpractice or manslaughter rap stick. Second, I—"

"Then how did you get these photos, Leonard?" Waller interrupted.

Darwin thought for a moment. "I can't say, because I don't really know. They were delivered to my office by courier late yesterday. There was no name or return address."

"Aha," Waller responded without approval or disapproval.

Darwin swung back to Jordan, and his serious expression returned. "The second thing you need to know is that I am not trying to make you look like a thug. Pardon me for saying so, but you are doing a very good job of that yourself. You know what the Beamon family attorneys will contend about these pictures, don't you? That you paid Turk DeVrees to create a bogus version of Eddie Beamon's chart, one that corroborates your story. Or they may say that you paid DeVrees to alter the original chart."

"But I didn't," Jordan insisted. "He just made a copy for me, and I thanked him for it."

"That's not what it looks like, Keyes," Sheffield snapped, still pacing. "There is something else you need to know about this kid DeVrees. He's a small-time bootlegger—copying music CDs and software programs for fun and profit. We've known about it for a few weeks, and the courts will likely hit him with a nasty fine eventually. We will fire him before that happens. But it makes your CD here look even more suspect."

Jordan dropped his head and hissed his disappointment.

Darwin continued. "How things look is very important to your case, Doctor. I asked you the last time we met to let us handle everything. Episodes like this one with DeVrees are what I hoped to avoid. We can still get you out of this mess, but you just made my job a lot harder."

Jordan was mortified, both by the pictures and their implication and by his misjudgment of Leonard Darwin. The last thing he wanted to do was delay the resolution of the Eddie Beamon dilemma. But it appeared that he had. He considered for a moment reiterating the issue of Dr. Kopke's password, but he knew what Darwin would say: The number 4664 on the charts means nothing in light of Turk DeVrees's skill at altering computer data.

Jordan dropped into his chair with a sigh. "I'm . . . I'm sorry," he said, head bowed.

Dr. Waller, who had been a silent spectator to the exchange, spoke next. "I had hoped to rotate you back into the starting lineup today, Jordan, and I know that's where you would rather be. But, under the circumstances, I think it is best that you remain in the lab for a few more days."

From the corner of his eye, Jordan saw Dr. Sheffield nod his approval. "I understand," he said, unable to cover the disappointment in his voice.

"Leonard will get this knot untangled, Jordan," Waller assured him. "Leonard is a good man."

Jordan said thank you, not really sure what he was thankful for.

Leonard Darwin sat down long enough to brief the doctors on what would happen next. The Beamon family had not yet filed a malpractice suit, he said, but he expected the action before the weekend. Jordan only half listened as the lawyer described how he would respond. Dr. Waller stood to listen, obviously needing to be somewhere else. The head of Surgery excused himself and left before Darwin finished. Sheffield exited with him.

"By the way, Doctor," Darwin said, "a detective from the Portland Police Department will be contacting you in a day or two. If I were you, I'd stick with what happened *inside* the hospital and leave your contact with Turk DeVrees out of it."

Jordan nodded disconsolately.

At the attorney's request, Jordan relinquished the CD Turk had prepared for him. Darwin did not ask him about a backup copy, so Jordan said nothing about the disks and hard copy he had kept. The attorney wished him luck and left.

Jordan sat alone in Waller's office for several minutes. The surging hope he had felt yesterday had drained away. And it was his own fault. In his eagerness to wriggle out of the quicksand of the Beamon accusation, he had only managed to sink deeper into the quagmire. Instead of returning to rounds and surgery today as he had hoped, Jordan faced days—possibly weeks—of further inactivity as Leonard Darwin sought to extricate him from the dilemma.

Clouds of despair hovered near. But Jordan knew he could not allow himself to be immobilized by them. He had to remain active. He had to do something to help without causing himself more harm. He stood up quickly, fearing that if he did not, his depressing circumstance would strap him to the chair. There was a way he could help solve the Eddie Beamon problem without interfering with Leonard Darwin. But he would need help.

TWENTY-FIVE

Jordan went looking for Turk DeVrees. When he reached the kid's office in the back corner of the basement, it was dark and locked. In the adjoining room, which was also locked, he saw Turk's beloved Maxine efficiently handling the computing chores of Portland Mercy Teaching Hospital.

Realizing it was not quite 8:00 A.M., Jordan anxiously paced the quiet, musty basement halls waiting for Turk to show up for work. After the discouraging personal defeat in Dr. Bert Waller's office, Jordan's options seemed to have dwindled to one: He had to find out who was using the late Dr. Kopke's password to ruin him. And since Turk DeVrees held the key to Maxine's hidden treasures of hospital information, he needed to see Turk again and explore what Maxine could tell him about the person using 4664. And he had to do it before Turk lost his job at the hospital and disappeared.

But Turk did not show. At nine Jordan pulled out his cell phone and dialed Turk's home number, which he found on a business card he had picked up at the kid's house. Still pacing the basement halls, he listened to more than a dozen rings before tapping the phone off. He was surprised that an electronics wizard like Turk had no answering machine or that his machine could be broken or turned off. The realization fed an uneasy suspicion Jordan did not want to acknowledge.

He then dialed the hospital's phone number and connected to Turk's office extension. He could hear the phone ring inside the kid's office. At the tone following Turk's voice-mail announcement, he said, "Turk, this is Dr. Jordan Keyes. Please call me as soon as you get this message. It's very important." Then he left his phone number.

To save time, Jordan decided to run over to the Realtor's office and sign the papers for the house he had bought, giving Turk an opportunity to arrive at work. Returning to the hospital a little after ten, Jordan was disappointed again. Another call to Turk's house also proved fruitless. Jordan dialed the hospital's personnel office, but they knew nothing about the kid's whereabouts, only that he had not reported for work or called in sick.

Earlier questions returned to badger Jordan, thoughts he wanted to dismiss but could not. *Why would Turk turn up missing today of all days—just when I need further information from him? Is it because he is the gatekeeper to Maxine's vast memory of activities at Mercy Hospital? Are there other people just as surprised as I am at the existence of such a treasure of CD-ROMs? Is Turk's sudden absence the result of someone hoping to quickly shut down access to Maxine's memoirs? Is Turk in some kind of trouble as a result of helping me—trouble with the hospital, the Beamon family's lawyers, the police, or someone else?* The last question brought a chill: *Does Turk's odd disappearance have anything to do with the person behind ID number 4664?*

Jordan spent the next two hours in the small conference room on the fifth floor of the neurosciences building. He reviewed again the eleven charts he had brought to Dr. Waller's office this morning and carefully documented in writing his deductions. Every ten minutes he dialed extension 4431, but he left no new messages for Turk.

The Portland detective showed up unannounced just after noon. Sgt. Lyle Bohanon was youthful, polite, and laid-back, so much so that Jordan wondered if the detective was capable of giving anyone the third degree. Bohanon showed no signs of animosity toward someone he might have considered the potential murderer of a fellow officer. He listened to Jordan's story attentively, jotted down a few notes, thanked Jordan for his time, and left after only twenty minutes.

After printing his documentation and slipping it into his briefcase, Jordan returned to Turk's office in the basement. The door was still locked, and there was no sign that anyone had been there since Jordan's last visit. He made a snap decision: *Since Turk won't come to me, I will go to him.*

It took him forty minutes to reach Turk's neighborhood in Vancouver because of a wreck on the interstate bridge. Instead of driving directly to the house, he parked on a quiet side street two blocks away. Approaching the house cautiously on foot, Jordan surveyed the area for anyone watching Turk's front door with binoculars or a camera. He saw no one suspicious.

Moving a little closer, he paused to survey the cars parked within eyesight of Turk's old house. Satisfied that the phantom photographer from yesterday was not around, he went to the door. After several solid raps with his knuckles, he called out, "Turk, are you OK? This is Dr. Keyes." No response. Traffic noise from the street overpowered anything he might hear from inside. He rapped again, harder this time. "Turk, are you there? I just want to talk." He listened for a response. Nothing. Waiting for a momentary lull in the traffic, he put his ear to the door. No music or sounds of movement came from inside.

Jordan could not leave. The treasury of information he desperately needed to explore was just inside this door. When Turk returned, Jordan wanted to be here. But he could not camp out on the kid's doorstep. Turk might see him first and avoid him. Worse yet, the person or persons opposing Jordan might spot him, and there might be more incriminating photographs. He had to think this through.

Walking back out to the curb, Jordan noticed a

mom-and-pop donut shop across the street and a hundred feet to the east. Seeing a break in traffic, he jogged across the street and ordered a tall coffee to go. Waiting for his order, he dialed Turk's hospital number again. No response. After paying for and picking up his cup, he changed his mind about going back to his car. Sitting down at one of the small tables, he had a clear view of Turk's front door across the street.

Sipping the hot coffee, he flashed on Maggie's interesting word from earlier this morning: *fishy.* Things were indeed fishy around Mercy Hospital, Jordan agreed. Eddie Beamon dies, and no matter how well Jordan defends himself, the finger of blame seems to find him. Fishy. A frizzy-haired computer genius comes out of nowhere with hard evidence of Jordan's innocence, but the kid turns out to be a minor-league software pirate who disappears. Fishy. Someone had tailed Jordan, spied on him, and photographed him as if he were a drug dealer or a terrorist. Very fishy. For good measure, all of the trauma patients who died at Mercy Hospital over the past sixteen months were self-proclaimed Christians. Very fishy indeed. Jordan had heard before he moved that the Northwest was a little weirder than the rest of the country, that people up here marched to a different drummer. But he never expected the culture to affect the medical profession so much.

Jordan stared at Turk's place between the occasional cars passing by outside. What he was thinking right now was equally fishy. He wondered how securely the house was locked, how easily he could get inside. The other day the kid had opened the door with a single key and no dead bolt. How hard could it be to force the door open or bust a rear window and snatch a box of CDs before the cops showed up? Jordan shook his head at the ludicrous thought.

As much as he disliked the idea, Jordan had plenty of time to burn. He would stay here and wait for Turk until the shop owners kicked him out, if he had to. He bought a newspaper from the rack outside and read it from front to back, keeping one eye on the house. He spent the next hour and a half in the sunshine with his jacket slung over his shoulder, walking the sidewalks near Turk's place as unobtrusively as possible, always with a clear view to the front door. No one came near the house.

At about five o'clock he stepped into the small market next to the donut shop to buy an apple and an orange. Standing in the shadows outside, eating his small dinner, he was tempted to pack it in and go home. Turk might never show, and even if he did, he might not agree to grant Jordan access to his library of backup CDs, even though Jordan was prepared to pay him more money. Yet the slim chance of Turk's reappearance kept Jordan from leaving, despite the boredom and sense of futility. So he returned to the donut shop for another coffee and a cinnamon roll.

When darkness fell, Jordan hurried to his car and pulled it around to the side street just east of the market. From this new vantage point, he had a clear view of the house while being less conspicuous than on display in the well-lit donut shop. The house was completely dark, but a street lamp at the curb shed enough light on the yard that Jordan was sure he would see someone approaching the front porch. Rolling up the windows against the evening chill, he settled in to wait and watch.

As the hours passed, Jordan's thoughts returned often to the incident in Sam and Maggie's family room last night. The image of Buster's hulking, quivering form clinging to him, the sound of his sobbing, and the undeniable warmth of the moment were indelible in Jordan's memory. He had been ushered to the threshold of something both terrifying and inviting. Della had given him a glimmer of hope for their future together. Sam and Maggie—and Buster—had provided impetus for him to step through the door. Jordan prayed for courage to do so when the time was right.

Just before ten o'clock he visited the rest room in the

donut shop, which was ready to close. By eleven he began to question the value of staying much longer. The neighborhood was dark and quiet, and his concentration was wearing thin. He blinked hard at any movement he perceived in Turk's yard—which turned out to be a cat or the shadows of tree branches moving in the breeze.

At midnight, with traffic almost nonexistent, Jordan feared that a police patrol car might stop to see why a clean, late-model Lexus with Oregon plates was parked on the dark side street at this time of night. And with no police in sight, he also feared becoming the target of a gang of car thieves. Yet he stayed and watched.

At 12:40, the shadows near the back of the house changed slightly. Jordan sat up and focused on the apparent movement. Then he saw it: a two-legged figure near the back of Turk's tiny lot, moving slowly but deliberately toward the house. Heart instantly pounding, Jordan slipped silently out of the car and followed the shadows to the corner of the little grocery store. One hundred and fifty feet away in the dead of night, Jordan could not tell if it was Turk or someone else. But it was definitely a person in dark clothes now crouching beneath one of the side windows.

Jordan hesitated in indecision. Should he call out to the person, hoping it was Turk? Should he get closer for a better look? Should he just watch to see what happened? He did not want to scare Turk away by moving too fast, nor did he want to lose him again after waiting so long.

The sound of breaking glass and a small flash of light made the decision for him. The match light beside the house briefly illuminated the figure. It was not Turk but a slight, dark man with closely cropped hair and beard. The man touched the lighted match to a cloth fuse protruding from a bottle, then quickly tossed the bottle through the broken window. The explosion of the firebomb brought an orange glow to every window in the small house.

"No!" Jordan yelled, sprinting across the deserted street

toward the house. Surprised by the onrushing stranger, the bearded man froze beside the house, apparently unsure of whether he should prepare to defend himself or flee. But Jordan aimed for the front porch, launched from his hiding place by the terrifying image of young Turk being engulfed by flames in his bed.

Scaling the small wooden porch in a single leap, Jordan threw his shoulder into the door. The wood cracked under the blow, but the door did not open. "Turk, wake up!" he yelled, pounding on the door with his fist. "Fire! Fire! Turk, get out!" He lifted his foot to kick at the door lock, but the bearded man rammed him from behind, and they both fell heavily to the floor of the porch. Meanwhile, Jordan could hear the hissing, crackling fire spreading through the interior of the house.

Springing to his feet, Jordan grabbed the man—who was smaller and lighter than he—and spun him around. In the dim light he caught a brief glimpse of the man's face—sharp features, Middle Eastern appearance. The small man flailed wildly with his arms, but Jordan wrestled him to the side of the porch and pushed him off, where he tumbled into a scrawny bush. Jordan braced himself for another attack. The bearded man scrambled to his feet, ready to charge the porch again. But seeing the mounting flames behind the curtains, he smiled triumphantly before disappearing into the darkness on the run.

After four violent kicks near the lock, the door burst wide open. Pausing only to lift his coattails over his head for protection from swirling embers, Jordan entered the burning house. By the light of the flames, he saw that the living room and kitchen were unoccupied. During his brief visit yesterday, he figured that the back bedroom was Turk's quarters. Rushing down the smoke-filled hallway, he found the room and pushed open the door. Flames had yet to reach the room, but a cloud of smoke followed Jordan in, seeking an escape route to the outside.

Jordan stumbled through the dark room, calling for Turk

until the smoke provoked a coughing fit. He felt around the room—bed, dresser, closet, floor. Turk was not there. Staying on his knees, he retreated to the hallway. A quick glance proved that Turk was not in the tiny bathroom. It was time to get out before the smoke overcame him.

The only room left to check was the first bedroom, which Turk used to store most of his backup CDs. One wall and part of the ceiling were already seared and smoking, ready to erupt into flames. The mounting heat would melt the CDs in the room before the fire could consume them. This was the reason for the firebomb, Jordan realized: to destroy Maxine's vast memoirs. The bearded man was not after him or Turk; he was out to destroy the CDs, and he had run because he was sure he had succeeded.

Jordan did not pause to evaluate the consequences of his sudden decision. Scrabbling into the room on all fours, he began pulling handfuls of boxed CDs from the shelf and throwing them into a plastic waste can. With the smoke burning his eyes, he could not read the labels. Guessing that Turk filed the CDs chronologically from left to right, he picked from the right end of the shelf, hoping to get some from the last two years.

Before he could fill the waste can with CDs, Jordan was driven from the room by the mounting heat, blinding smoke, and live embers touching exposed skin. Dragging the waste can behind him, he fumbled his way, crouching and crawling, through the hall and living room to the front door. Outside he found a small knot of onlookers from the neighborhood, mesmerized by the conflagration. One of them had found a garden hose beside the house. The weak stream of water directed onto the roof did little to slow the advancing flames.

Sirens wailing in the distance announced the imminent arrival of the Vancouver fire and police departments. Fire crews would likely fare no better at saving the structure than the civilian with the hose, Jordan judged.

"I checked all the rooms," he yelled to the people above the din of the flames, "and there's no one else inside." A large, gray-haired lady in a chenille bathrobe applauded weakly, then returned her gaze to the fire. No one seemed concerned that he was carting spoils out of the building.

Unwilling to get involved with the police, Jordan eased away from the scene and returned to his car, stashing the plastic waste can of CDs in the backseat. The first emergency vehicles arrived as he backed the Lexus slowly down the side street, lights off, then headed for the interstate bridge. At some point he might feel free to tell the police about the small, dark-skinned arsonist. But not now.

Jordan's jacket reeked of smoke, and his trousers were torn at both knees. As the numbing adrenaline dissipated in his system, he began to feel the pain. His hands and knees stung from the abrasions he received while scrabbling over the floor. His shoulder and hip throbbed from the collision with Turk's front door and his brief skirmish with the mysterious bearded attacker. Jordan was sobered to realize that proving his innocence and saving his career was quickly turning into a matter of life and death.

TWENTY-SIX

Jordan stopped at his apartment just long enough to collect a change of clothes. Replaying the events of the night as he drove, he was confronted by a real and valid fear. Anyone desperate enough to firebomb Turk's home—with or without the kid inside—was capable of greater harm. The arsonist, who Jordan figured was only a pawn in the plot against him, had seen his face. *He may also know where I live,* Jordan surmised with a chill. *I better not stay here tonight, not even to take a shower.*

But who was actually behind the firebombing? Clearly someone else who knew about Turk and his cache of CDs. Perhaps Turk had more enemies than Jordan knew about. Or perhaps someone Jordan had trusted with the information had carelessly—or purposely—leaked it to whoever commissioned tonight's attack. He did not believe that Maggie, Sam, or Buster would knowingly disclose what he had shared in confidence—at least he did not *want* to believe it. And he could not conceive that his superiors at Mercy, including Leonard Darwin, could be involved in such a scheme. Jordan resisted the idea that the people he trusted and depended upon must be considered suspects in the plot against him.

Arriving at Mercy Hospital just before 2:00 A.M., he hoped to get to the locker room outside the surgery wing to shower and change before being noticed in his soiled, torn clothes. He had transferred a total of thirty-one CDs from the waste can to a gym bag, into which he also placed his clean clothes. The CDs appeared in good order, and they were all from this year or last. As soon as he cleaned up, Jordan intended to find a computer somewhere and begin looking through them for Dr. Will Kopke's signature ID code.

The locker room appeared empty when he entered. He had just opened his locker and begun to disrobe when a figure in dark clothing swept around the corner, heading in his direction. "Hello, Dr. Keyes. Kind of late for you to be at the hospital, isn't it?"

Buster Chapman, in his navy blue work shirt and pants, was toting two large, stuffed canvas bags over his shoulder, dirty scrubs destined for the laundry. Seeing the doctor, he dropped the laundry bags for a moment of conversation.

"Hello, Buster," Jordan said, relieved to see someone who was no threat to his safety or his career. "I had a late . . . appointment, you might say."

"Oh boy, you tore your good pants there, Dr. Keyes," Buster exclaimed in boyish wonder, pointing to the tattered knees. "Did you hurt yourself, Doctor? Are you OK?"

"I'm fine, Buster, thanks," Jordan said. "I just took a little fall."

Buster lamented the torn wool-blend slacks as a great loss. Jordan guessed that Buster owned only one pair of "church pants," perhaps the most expensive item in his wardrobe and costly to replace on his meager earnings. "Is there anything I can do to help you, Dr. Keyes?" he concluded.

Jordan reached out and patted the janitor's arm. "You have done quite a lot for me already, Buster. You're a good friend. I can't think of anything you can do to help me except keep being my friend."

"Oh boy, I can sure do that, Dr. Keyes," Buster beamed. "Mama told me to be a good friend to everybody."

"I'm sure your mother is very proud of you."

"Oh yes, Mama is very proud of me." Buster's return gaze turned wistful. "And I think your dear mama is proud of you, Dr. Keyes."

Jordan weighed the words for a moment. "I would like to think she is," he said hopefully.

"She is, Dr. Keyes. I know it," Buster said, smiling broadly and nodding vigorously, "because she loves you. Mama says that kinfolk and real friends love us just because. We don't have to do anything for it."

Buster chatted for a minute more, then he tossed the laundry bags over his shoulder and went on his way. Jordan stood under the nozzle in the empty shower room for twenty minutes, allowing the hot water and steam to minister to a collection of scrapes and bruises. He decided not to tell his superiors about last night—at least not yet. Dr. Waller might be sympathetic, but he also had a responsibility to Taylor Sheffield and Leonard Darwin. There was no need to tell Waller something he could not tell the others. And since Philip Ettinger was also in the loop by reason of his role in Neurosurgery, Jordan would not burden him with his findings yet, even though he longed for his colleague's moral support.

Jordan knew he would eventually tell Della about his harrowing experience in Vancouver last night. But there was no sense concerning her with the problem until he could also share the solution. Perhaps one of the CDs would point him directly to the guilty party, and the issue could be resolved.

Dried and dressed in clean clothes, Jordan felt the full force of fatigue. Attempting a detailed examination of charts on the computer would be fruitless. So he located a vacant call room—temporary sleeping quarters for on-call trauma personnel—locked himself in, and crashed hard.

Three hours' sleep was not enough, but Jordan forced himself to get up at six anyway. He turned on the TV as he shaved and dressed. The early-morning local news carried a fifteen-second story about Turk's house fire. According to the reporter, the owner was not in the house at the time of the blaze and had not yet been located. She did not mention Jordan's appearance at the scene.

After a stop at the coffee bar, Jordan sequestered himself in the neurosciences building with the cache of CDs rescued from the fire. The smell of smoke emanating from the open bag was a sobering reminder of his close brush with death only hours ago.

He organized the thirty-one CD boxes on the desktop chronologically, beginning with the earliest date: April 8 of last year. The CDs seemed to fall into groups of three or four consecutive days followed by a gap of several days up to a month or more. The pattern made sense to Jordan, remembering how he had hastily grabbed CDs in handfuls from several different shelves. In the most recent batch of five CDs, two were duplicates of those Turk had copied for him on Monday. It did not matter to Jordan since he had a different target for this search.

Booting up the computer, Jordan loaded the CD from April 8, just over one year ago, into the drawer. After experimenting a little, he discovered the search function Turk had built into his backup system. At the search prompt, he keyed in Will Kopke's ID code: 4664. Then he clicked on "Find Next." In less than a second a message box appeared declaring, "No matches found." It told him that Dr. Kopke—or anyone who was disposed to use his password—had not written a single patient order at Mercy Hospital on that date.

Jordan pushed away disappointment by reminding himself that doctors don't write orders every day. Perhaps Dr. Kopke was lecturing on April 8 or conducting grand rounds or attending a conference away from the hospital. He pulled the CD from the drawer and loaded in the next one: April 10. The search for 4664 bore the same results: nothing. He also came up empty for April 11 and 12, the last two CDs in the first stack.

The next CDs in sequence were April 29, 30, May 1, and 3.

Jordan struck gold on April 30. The search for ID code 4664 took him first to the chart of a thirty-seven-year-old male patient, a head trauma MVA victim. The name of the patient—Herbert Warren—seemed familiar. Jordan pulled out the sheaf of hard copy charts Maggie Rusch had obtained for him. Leafing through several sheets, he found Warren's chart. He was one of the collection of head trauma patients who had died after successful brain surgery. The chart listed Dr. Will Kopke as the attending physician. Kopke had performed the surgery and directed the recovery of patient Warren until the man's untimely death in the SICU.

Recalling the other curious discovery from his study of the charts, Jordan checked Herbert Warren's religious preference. It was Methodist. He also remembered Maggie's insistence that something was "fishy" with the blood work, a point he had dismissed as inconsequential. On a hunch, he scrolled through the chart looking for blood work orders. There was only one for Warren on April 30, the date of the patient's accident and surgery, which was perfectly normal.

Jordan pulled a legal pad out of the desk drawer and entered at the top 4664. He headed four columns on the sheet: Date, Patient, R.P. —for religious preference—and Blood. He entered the information from his first encounter with Dr. Kopke: 4/30, Warren, Methodist, 1. Continuing through the Warren chart in fifteen-minute intervals, Jordan noted Kopke's involvement with the patient the rest of the day. Everything seemed to go by the book, including orders for mannitol, used to combat brain swelling.

Returning to the 4664 search, Jordan found that Kopke had no other surgeries on April 30. He rounded on several other patients—none of whom had come through the trauma center—and dismissed one from the hospital. It had been a rather quiet day for Jordan's predecessor, about whom he knew so little.

Encouraged to be finally getting somewhere, Jordan stayed on Will Kopke's trail. He tracked 4664 in CD after

CD. His first interest was to see if Kopke's ID code appeared alongside someone else's name, as it had for Eloise Sandborn in Eddie Beamon's chart. It never did. Kopke's number in Turk's CDs always accompanied Kopke's name in the official hospital charts.

Jordan paid particular attention to the religious preference of each of Kopke's patients and the frequency of blood samples taken. Kopke's name and number appeared for patients with every type of religious preference, from Christian to Eastern religion to cult to none. But it seemed that orders for blood samples were more frequent in those identified with some kind of Christian group. And from this group, as he had discovered earlier, Jordan found two more patients who had died in the SICU. Dr. Will Kopke was the attending physician for both.

Jordan knew he was looking at puzzle pieces, not the whole picture. He had observed Kopke's actions for only a few days in the treatment of a group of patients. The gaps in the CDs often occluded one or more of the three major phases—how the patient presented and was diagnosed, how the patient was treated, and the eventual outcome. It was unavoidable, he realized, considering the conditions under which he collected the odd lot of CDs. So he kept moving forward and filling pages on the pad.

In November, Will Kopke's name and ID code disappeared from the hospital's charts. He was the attending physician for four patients on November 17, but in the next CDs in sequence—November 21, 22, and 23—his patients were under the care of other neurosurgeons: Ettinger, Sutherland, Boorsma. Then Jordan recalled that Kopke's fatal skiing accident on Mt. Hood occurred around that time. *Will this be the end of 4664,* Jordan wondered, *until "Dr. Kopke" suddenly materializes in the SICU to tamper with some of my patient charts and slip Eddie Beamon an overdose of phenobarbital?*

He breezed through five CDs from December and another

three from January of this year. No matches appeared for 4664. Dr. Will Kopke was clearly out of the picture. The first CD in February, ten days before Jordan began work at Portland Mercy Teaching Hospital, was the same. The next CD was dated eighteen days later, and the search for 4664 was again successful. Kopke's ID appeared in the chart of one of Jordan's first patients, an MVA victim. Jordan had prescribed an injection of 90 milligrams of phenobarb. But according to Maxine's see-all-tell-all records, 90 milligrams was abruptly changed to make it appear that Jordan had ordered 160 milligrams instead. The name entered for the order was *Keyes,* but the ID code was 4664. It was the first of several secretly altered charts that Jordan had discovered.

Jordan stared at the characters on the monitor, disturbed. It was as if Will Kopke had come back from the grave to punish him for taking his place. First, the charts were changed to create suspicion that Jordan had collected enough phenobarb to kill Eddie Beamon. Then the falsified charts were mysteriously brought to the attention of Leonard Darwin. Someone at the outer fringe of sanity might suggest that the ghost of Will Kopke, jealous that a successor had taken his old job, was making life miserable for Jordan.

But Jordan knew that his real adversary was very much alive and well and working at Mercy Hospital. For some reason, this person wanted him out of the way, and he was not above dishonesty, destruction of property, and murder to accomplish his purpose. If Jordan could not locate and expose this sick individual, his career and possibly his life were in dire jeopardy.

Jordan forced himself back to the task, a skill he was very good at: diagnosis. Examine the symptoms long enough and closely enough, and you will find the root cause of the patient's problems. He had to continue to gather data about 4664 and the mysterious SICU deaths at Mercy. Somewhere in the data God had allowed him to collect Jordan expected to find the disease at the center of his personal crisis.

Jordan methodically worked through the remainder of the CDs. Kopke's number appeared four more times, all in charts where Jordan's phenobarbital orders had been altered. He was disappointed not to find a CD for April 10 or 11, the two days Trudy Aguilera was under his care. He was curious to see if 4664 appeared anywhere in Aguilera's chart. But that record and scores of others Jordan could not rescue from Turk's library had been vaporized in the burning house.

Having been hunched over a keyboard and mouse in front of the monitor for three hours, Jordan stood to stretch the kinks out of his shoulders and upper back. He had filled several pages of the legal pad with observations, both in columns and otherwise. He had cross-referenced his notes with the hard copy charts of thirty-five trauma patients who had died in SICU over the past sixteen months. Pacing the small office space, a curious profile came into focus.

The Tough Luck Club, he labeled them cynically. *A group of almost three dozen patients over the last year and four months who would have been better off never coming to Mercy Hospital for help. Having been transported to the finest trauma center in the Northwest, they should have lived, but instead they died.*

A grim pattern crystalized as Jordan paced.

Mr. X is critically injured in a motor vehicle accident and rushed to Mercy Trauma Center. As Mr. X is wheeled into the ER for brain surgery to save his life, an emotionally shaken Mrs. X answers a few questions for the admitting clerk. "Religious preference?" the clerk says. "Oh, we're Christians," Mrs. X says. "We attend the Baptist church." The clerk asks, "So your religious preference is Baptist?" Mrs. X answers, "That's right." The clerk types *Baptist* into the admittance form. Mr. X's religious preference will be entered on his permanent chart.

Strike one. All twenty-five members of the Tough Luck Club at Mercy Hospital were at least nominally Christian.

There was not a Buddhist, Mormon, Scientologist, atheist, or agnostic among them. Trauma patients of the non-Christian or no-preference variety were certainly treated at Mercy, and some of them died. But in this sampling of Kopke's patients, a far higher percentage of them lived to be dismissed from the hospital.

Patient X survives emergency surgery and is transferred to the SICU. No doubt Buster Chapman tearfully rejoices with Mrs. X and her family in the waiting room. But a casual scan of Mr. X's chart reveals a subtle anomaly that becomes significant only when compared with the charts of other patients in his category: an extra blood sample.

Strike two. As Maggie had pointed out to him, Jordan found that more blood samples were extracted from the Christian patients processed through the Trauma Center than from patients identified as non-Christian or non-religious. It was not a large difference, but it was consistent. Furthermore, a quick survey suggested that a significant number of Christian patients who survived the Trauma Center and SICU were also subjected to extra blood tests. Maggie believed that many of these samples were processed outside Mercy Hospital, at a pathology lab in a city called Wilsonville. It was something Jordan intended to look into.

Oblivious to blood samples and other facets of his care, the sedated Mr. X, still in critical condition, recuperates in the SICU. Surgery was successful. The prognosis is guardedly good. The worst seems to be over.

Strike three, you're dead. It had happened to thirty-five patients since the beginning of last year—all identified as Christians. Their deaths were attributed to cardiac or respiratory failure brought on by complications of their injuries. Yes, other patients died in the SICU—several. Yes, Christian patients survived the SICU and went home healed—a fair number. But for people like Mr. X, a Christian who was subject to more blood samples, the risk of death in the SICU was significantly higher than for any other group.

Trudy Aguilera fit the profile. She was the latest unfortunate inductee into Mercy's Tough Luck Club. Eddie Beamon almost fit the profile, except his death came as a result of a phenobarbital overdose purposely administered; the autopsy had proved it.

That was the final indignity foisted on the members of the Tough Luck Club: no autopsy. Except for only three—Trudy Aguilera being one—these patients went to their graves without a comprehensive postmortem exam to pinpoint the cause of death. And when autopsies were performed, they were done so by one man: Dr. Joseph Wiggins. It was Jordan's overreaction to this indignity that precipitated a falling-out with his colleagues. And he suspected that this falling-out had something to do with the death of Eddie Beamon.

Jordan stopped pacing. He had to talk to someone about this, and he knew who. He quickly looked up the phone number and dialed.

TWENTY-SEVEN

"Jordy, do you realize what you're saying?" Maggie said, just above a whisper. Her face had lost some color during Jordan's story.

The pair sat at a corner table in Ragamuffin's Deli in northwest Portland. Maggie's shift started at 1:00 P.M. today, but she had eagerly accepted Jordan's invitation to meet him for an early lunch. Sam was up to his elbows in his repairs at the hospital or he would have joined them. Jordan had told Maggie everything about Turk, the incriminating photographs, last night's fire, and the CDs he had rescued. He had also summarized his conclusions about the Tough Luck Club. Neither of them had touched their sandwiches.

"You're saying that somebody at Mercy Hospital has been quietly murdering trauma patients for over a year."

Jordan nodded slowly. "Yes, I guess that's what I'm saying."

Maggie continued, "You have wandered into some deep yogurt here, my friend. If you're right, you have made somebody at Mercy very nervous. Somebody wants you out of the picture before you can ask any more questions. Are you aware of that?"

Jordan nodded again. "Yes, I'm aware. But I needed to hear someone else say it. It's too crazy, too bizarre. Stuff like this doesn't happen in real life, not in my life anyway."

Maggie's expression was deathly serious. "Who is behind all this? Any ideas?"

"Will Kopke, obviously."

Maggie wrinkled her nose in disbelief. "That's not funny, Jordy. The guy has been dead for five months."

"I know, but up until his accident, Kopke seemed the most likely candidate. He lost more patients than anyone else last year. His ID code keeps showing up in the most suspicious places. He may be gone, but people keep dying in SICU."

"Someone else around here knows Kopke's password?"

"Apparently."

Maggie was more tentative about her next question. "Someone who did not like the way Dr. Kopke operated—no pun intended—and took over for him?"

Jordan read her meaning. "In other words, the skiing accident was no accident. Another person was involved—perhaps more than one."

Maggie shrugged. "What do you think?"

Jordan looked away pensively. "I think this is too bizarre."

"Who could it be? Who wants you out of here?"

"Could be almost anyone in Neurosurgery. I have succeeded in alienating a lot of people."

"Anyone in particular?"

He had been thinking about that. "Oscar Ortiz and Mark Sutherland appeared the most upset about my argument over the lack of autopsies. They have clearly avoided me ever since. But their displeasure is obvious. Maybe it's someone quietly going about his business hoping not to draw attention to himself."

"Any ideas who?"

Two names immediately came to Jordan's mind. The first was Taylor Sheffield. Was the hospital director hard-nosed and suspicious because of his concern for Jordan and the hospital, or did he have a secret to hide? The second name was Leonard Darwin. The lawyer had produced the photographs that captured Jordan giving money to Turk in exchange for CDs. Where had he gotten them? Could he be setting Jordan up for the big fall? Were he and Sheffield somehow behind the unexplained SICU deaths? They were the only other people in Waller's office when he told his superior about Turk's records; then the kid's house went up in flames.

Unwilling to name them as suspects in Maggie's hearing, he answered, "I'll have to think about that."

Maggie took a bite of the small mound of pasta salad next to her sandwich. Then she said, "You have to tell the police, Jordy." She used her sisterly tone, the same one she used when counseling him about his relationship with Della.

"No, not yet. Whoever is behind this has taken great pains to set me up as the bad guy. The police will find it difficult to regard me as innocent when Will Kopke's ghost has made sure I look so guilty. No, I need to uncover this guy. He's not perfect—he already proved that. I think the collection of backup CDs was a big surprise to him, and that's why he torched Turk's house. I just have to find another chink in his armor."

"You think he left himself open in another area?"

"He's only human," Jordan said.

"Do you have any idea what you're looking for?"

Jordan nodded. "I have a couple of things I want to check out this afternoon."

Maggie leaned closer. "I'll help you, Jordy. Sam is willing to help too."

"I appreciate that, Maggie," Jordan said, "but knowing too much could be dangerous for both of you. I don't want anyone else to get hurt."

Maggie came back quickly. "But if you up and disappear while you're playing Lone Ranger, nobody will know where to look for you."

Jordan knew she was right. "I won't do anything foolish, Maggie. And if I run into trouble, I'll call for help."

Maggie acquiesced quickly, like a concerned sister who had met her match in a stubborn brother. "Is there anything you want me to do?"

"Two things," he said. "First, keep an eye on the SICU, but don't call attention to yourself. Check the charts of any patients who are identified with a Christian group. Look for blood work orders. Take note of the doctors and nurses working with these patients. Do you feel all right about doing that?"

"No problem," Maggie said. "And don't worry about me. I can take care of myself."

"Second, if I should suddenly disappear, you and Sam go straight to the police with what we have discussed." Jordan paused a moment. "Then call Della and explain everything. She knows some of this, but not everything. OK?"

"Of course. But you need to check in occasionally. I'll keep my phone with me."

"Sure. Good idea. I'll call."

After a few bites of his sandwich, Jordan gave Della's number to Maggie, left cash for the bill, and excused himself. He was apprehensive about his next two stops. But the sooner he unmasked Will Kopke's "ghost," the better.

◆ ◆ ◆

Dr. Joseph Wiggins's office was strategically located only a few blocks from the Oregon state medical examiner's building, east of the Willamette River. The semiretired pathologist, who had restricted his practice to private autopsies, kept his name and number on file with the larger hospitals in town. Whenever family members of deceased hospital patients sought a postmortem outside the narrow criteria of the medical examiner, the hospitals often sent them to Wiggins.

The office was at the rear of a small, one-story medical building that was built in the sixties and apparently last repainted in the eighties. Jordan had worn his lab coat and hospital ID badge into the office to gain immediate recognition, and it worked. "Good afternoon, Doctor. May I help you?" The matronly receptionist, sitting behind a counter that stretched the length of the small waiting room, was all business. Three fragrances struggled for dominance in the room: formaldehyde, mildew, and the receptionist's floral perfume.

Jordan read the nameplate on the counter and put on his most pleasant, agreeable, disarming self. "Hi, Leona. I'm Dr. Keyes from Mercy Hospital."

"Oh yes, the Aguilera case," the receptionist said, warming to the unexpectedly pleasant approach. "I have a copy of the report for you right here." She began flipping through a stack of folders. "I mailed the statement to you instead of the family. That's what you requested, right?"

"Yes, and I'll take care of that today if you don't mind." Jordan reached for his wallet.

"We never mind getting paid ahead of the due date," Leona said with a small laugh. "It's a rarity these days."

Jordan glanced over the report while Leona billed his credit card for services rendered. It was what he expected. "Is Dr. Wiggins in today?" he asked casually, scribbling his signature.

"Yes, do you have a question about the report?"

"No, not really. I'm new to Portland, and I'd just like to meet him—if he can spare a minute." It was the reason Jordan had come to the office, but he hoped it sounded like an afterthought.

Leona seemed to like his attitude. "Of course. Let me see what he's up to at the moment." Then she headed toward the lab, and Jordan waited, anxiety mounting.

He considered Dr. Joseph Wiggins a key player in the drama unfolding around him. For the past sixteen months, Wiggins was the only one afforded an opportunity to examine the corpses of patients who died in the SICU at Mercy Hospital. He had not examined many, according to the hospital records, because very few families had requested postmortems. But when they did, the bodies came here because Wiggins was virtually the only show in town. And every autopsy report supported the cause of death determined by the attending physician at Mercy.

The possible implications were frightening. Killing a patient—whether you call it a mercy death or cold-blooded murder—is child's play for anyone who can use a syringe. A substantial injection of potassium short-circuits electrical conductivity to the heart. When patients in the SICU experience cardiac arrest, it is almost always prompted by their traumatic injuries. The medical examiner accepts the physician's cause of death without question, and the body is buried with the incriminating potassium being undetected in the victim's system.

But what happens if the family requests an autopsy after the medical examiner declines to perform one? To a trained pathologist, the deadly potassium would be as obvious as a bullet hole through the head. The autopsy report would starkly refute the hospital's claim of death due to injuries—unless the report was falsified. With the cooperation of a private pathologist, someone at Mercy Hospital could get away with murder even when an autopsy was requested.

Was Trudy Aguilera a case in point? Was she the latest victim of a mysterious killer at Mercy Hospital? Had Jordan's brash push for a private autopsy unwittingly attracted the killer's attention? And was Joseph Wiggins an accomplice in this dreadful, sick plot? Jordan hoped a few minutes with the man might provide some answers, though Jordan knew he had to continue to play the role of the naïve visitor. Would Dr. Wiggins also be playing a role?

"Dr. Keyes, welcome to Portland." Wiggins was lanky and square-shouldered, draped in a pale green lab coat that stretched to his knees. A tan face, crowned by a full head of white, wavy hair, witnessed that Wiggins found plenty of time in his semiretirement for visits to a sunnier climate. He stretched out a welcoming hand.

"Thank you, sir," Jordan said, shaking hands firmly. "I hope I didn't interrupt your work."

"No problem at all, Doctor," Wiggins said. "Unlike you, I can walk away from the operating table for a half-hour coffee break, and my patient is no worse off when I return."

Jordan laughed politely at the well-worn pathology humor. Wiggins did not invite him back to the lab, nor did he offer a chair or a cup of coffee. Jordan got the message: This unscheduled meeting would last only a few minutes.

Wiggins said, "Leona reminds me that you paid for the Aguilera postmortem personally."

"Yes, sir, that's correct."

"I must say, I'm impressed at the depth of your commitment to patient care."

Jordan smiled at the compliment. If Wiggins suspected him of snooping, he was very good at concealing it.

Determined to make the most of this brief window of opportunity, Jordan started asking questions. Taking care to sound interested and inquisitive and not accusatory, he asked about Wiggins's procedure in general. Wiggins was cordial but brief with his answers. Then Jordan turned to the report for Trudy Aguilera and casually posed one strategically planned question.

"Was there a trace of illegal drugs in the system, such as marijuana or cocaine, perhaps too small to mention in the report?"

"I don't exclude anything, Doctor. If it was in her system, I put it in the report."

"So you found nothing out of the ordinary?"

"That is correct, just as I stated in the report."

Jordan did not want to overstay his welcome or appear too nosy. He thanked Dr. Wiggins for his time, shook his hand again, and left.

Joseph Wiggins walked straight to the private phone in his office and dialed a pager number from memory. Punching in his number at the prompt, he hung up and waited. In two minutes the phone rang.

"Keyes was just here," he told the caller.

"What did he want, Joseph?"

"What do you think: He was checking me out." Wiggins fiddled nervously with the phone cord as he spoke.

The person on the other end was silent for a moment, then asked, "Do you think he knows anything, Joseph?"

"I don't know what he *knows,* but I think he *suspects* too much." Wiggins swore. "This man could be more trouble than Kopke. I don't like it. You've got to do something."

The words coming back to him were spoken calmly with assurance. "Don't worry, Joseph. I'll handle it."

"That's easy for you to say. Keyes hasn't been in your office sniffing for trouble."

Another pause. "If it will make you feel any better, why don't you take another little trip? No one can fault a semi-retired pathologist for jetting down to the Yucatan for a week of sunshine."

"I just may do that."

"Go ahead, Joseph. Enjoy yourself. I'll call you when things have quieted down."

"When will that be? I like Mexico, but I never intended to spend the rest of my life hiding down there."

"Don't worry, Joseph," the caller repeated. "I'm on top of it."

TWENTY-EIGHT

Jordan walked nonchalantly to his car in case Dr. Wiggins was watching him. He pulled away from the office as if on a leisurely Sunday afternoon drive, but his mind was racing, and his gut was churning. The brief visit had convinced him that Dr. Wiggins was an accomplice to Will Kopke—or whoever was playing the role in his absence. Wiggins had not reported the presence of marijuana in the young woman's system. Roberto and Esther Aguilera, Trudy's parents, had lamented that their daughter sometimes used marijuana when she was with her boyfriend. She had smoked a joint on the day of the accident, they knew. The substance would have been evident in a thorough postmortem exam. Dr. Wiggins did not find it because he likely had not even looked. There was no need to do the work of a thorough autopsy if you intended to falsify the findings.

The autopsy report was bogus, and the evidence was conveniently buried in Trudy Aguilera's grave. In order to get at it, the state medical examiner and Portland police would have to get involved. At this point, Jordan's request to exhume the body for a second autopsy would only bring further attention to himself. He needed to find at least one more piece of this complex puzzle before going to the police to prove he was the scapegoat in the death of Eddie Beamon.

Working his way back to Interstate 5, he turned south

toward Wilsonville. As he drove, he dialed Maggie's portable phone. The nurse reported that she was very busy and unable to talk for more than a few seconds. Keeping her voice low, she said a stroke victim was admitted to SICU this morning, a woman whose chart identified her as a Lutheran. Standard blood work had been sent to the hospital lab, but no other orders for samples had been given.

"Who is the attending physician?" he asked.

"Dr. Ettinger. Sorry, I have to go, Jordy. I'll keep my eyes open." Then she hung up.

As the cerebrovascular specialist, Philip Ettinger was usually the point person in the treatment of emergency stroke victims at Mercy Hospital. Hearing Philip's name mentioned, Jordan again thought about confiding in him. Philip could possibly fill in some of the gaping holes of background for Dr. Oscar Ortiz or others on the staff who might be against him. But Jordan quickly came back to the same roadblock. Sharing his suspicions with Philip Ettinger would place Philip in an awkward position with his superior, Dr. Waller. As much as he wanted an ally on staff, he had to wait until he had more evidence. Jordan hoped his next stop would be as fruitful as the first.

After fifteen minutes on the freeway, he took the Wilsonville exit. Following the main drag for a couple of miles, he drove through a retail district and approached a quieter industrial section. At the far end of a number of small industrial parks, he found the building he was looking for: Hematech Laboratories. It was larger and more impressive than he had expected, certainly not a hole-in-the-wall, fly-by-night operation. He guessed that Hematech was a viable pathology lab serving Portland area medical offices and clinics too small to support an in-house lab. If there were illegal or unethical activities occurring inside this building, it was likely the work of individuals, not the lab as a whole. Jordan was banking heavily on this conclusion being valid.

Pulling into a parking space in the lot among two dozen

other cars, Jordan solidified his strategy. It was important that he look like he belonged here and knew what he was doing. The lab appeared small enough that a receptionist would know everyone working here. Yet it was large enough that there would be visitors—medical personnel doing business with the lab. The receptionist would doubtless know some of them but not all of them. Jordan would play the role of a confident, purposeful visitor.

He waited fifteen minutes until another car pulled into the parking lot. When the two occupants got out and headed for the main entrance, Jordan, still looking "official" in his lab coat, stepped out of the Lexus and casually followed them up the steps, briefcase in hand. Once inside the lobby, Jordan was quietly elated to find no receptionist. The persons entering ahead of him had taken one of two corridors leading away from the lobby. With his heart in his throat and a mask of confidence on his face, Jordan turned down the other corridor.

He passed one open doorway but did not look inside because the light was on. In his peripheral vision he noticed someone at a desk, facing a computer monitor away from the door. The next door was open, but the room was dark. Risking a quick glance, Jordan turned inside. It was a small office with the tidy desktop of an obsessive-compulsive personality or someone gone for the day. The computer was on with a screen saver image of stylized bouncing *H*s—Hematech's logo—displayed on the monitor.

An empty office with a computer ready to be used—it seemed too easy. It had to be providential, so Jordan did not hesitate. He turned on the light and closed the door just enough to block the line of sight from the corridor to the computer. It would appear less suspicious than trying to explain why a visitor had locked himself inside an employee's office. At least with the door open, someone might believe that he was borrowing the computer to check his e-mail.

It took him a few minutes to figure out the filing system on the computer. Locating the search prompt, he entered Trudy Aguilera's name. The search led Jordan to a lab report dated April 10, the day he had performed two craniotomies on Ms. Aguilera. It had been a Saturday, and the report on the monitor revealed that the lab work was performed in the evening. *Is this the new thing in lab services—open weekends and evenings for your convenience?* Jordan wondered. *What's next—a drive-in window for blood tests?*

Jordan scanned the report on the screen. It was a different format than he was used to. It was not a standard blood screening; it was something more. The format and abbreviations were foreign to him. But this was not the time or place to figure them out. Retrieving a blank disk from his briefcase, he slipped it into the A: drive and copied the Aguilera file to study later in privacy.

He had been in the building eight minutes. So far, so good. Referring to the sheaf in his briefcase, he entered name after name from the Tough Luck Club. Every search pulled up another codified report that Jordan quickly copied to disk.

"I thought you called in sick today, Kristen—"

Jordan turned to see the young woman coming through the door, a look of surprise on her face.

"Oh, you're not Kristen," she said. Since she was not wearing lab apparel, and since she looked barely out of high school, Jordan took her for an entry-level filing clerk.

Jordan smiled and took control from where he sat. "You're right, I'm not Kristen. I'm Dr. Keyes. And who might you be?"

"I'm Debbie. Do you know Kristen?" Debbie looked confused and a little suspicious.

"No, I'm just borrowing her workstation for a couple of minutes. I hear she's out sick today."

Debbie didn't know what to think. It was all over her face. Did this doctor work in the lab? Did he have the right to be in Kristen's office? Would it be disrespectful to ask what he was doing here?

Jordan stayed on the offensive. "What do you do here at Hematech, Debbie?"

"I'm a temp, actually," she said, warming to the interest shown. "So is Kristen."

Jordan relaxed a little inside. "Secretarial? Filing?"

"Filing mostly."

"Well, I don't want to keep you from your filing, Debbie," Jordan said, ready for her to move on.

"It's my break," she said. "It's three o'clock."

Jordan forced a laugh. "I especially don't want to keep you from your break. Good talking with you." He turned back to the computer, hoping she would take the hint.

Debbie backed out of the room on cue. "OK. Bye."

Urgency spurred Jordan to move quickly. Would the young temp pass the word that there was a strange doctor in Kristen's office? He did not like playing a spy in enemy territory. He had to get out before facing another curious or suspicious Hematech employee.

Working quickly, he summoned and copied four more files. He had lost count but guessed there were ten or eleven now on the disk. He wanted more. He wanted every report Hematech had done on these patients. But better to get out with something than get caught with everything.

Backing out of the search engine until the desktop display returned to the monitor, Jordan stuffed the disk and sheaf of charts into his briefcase. Having barely disturbed the office environment, he turned off the light and headed toward the lobby. A lab-coated tech turned the corner, headed in his direction. Jordan smiled and nodded. The tech said hi and swept by him, obviously in a hurry. Fighting off an impulse to run, Jordan strode through the lobby and out the door to his car.

Finally behind the wheel, he looked for anyone who might have followed him out of the building. He saw no one.

Releasing a long, nervous breath, he started the car and wasted no time getting out of the parking lot and turning toward the freeway.

He did not notice the old, cream-colored Suburban sitting at the curb fifty feet away from the Hematech driveway. When Jordan's white Lexus was out of sight, the Suburban roared to life and eased away from the curb. The driver, a small, olive-skinned man with a short beard, was content to follow at an unobtrusive distance.

TWENTY-NINE

Late afternoon freeway traffic and a load of pipe dumped on the freeway turned a twenty-minute drive into an hour-and-a-half ordeal. Jordan arrived at the hospital at five-thirty and went straight to SICU to find Maggie Rusch. The unit was nearly full, and Maggie was very busy in the room of a combative patient who had just pulled out his IV and nasogastric tube. Jordan succeeded in catching her eye as a means of checking in, as she had suggested. She nodded and kept working.

Two neurosurgeons were seeing patients in the SICU at the time. Dr. Oscar Ortiz walked past him without a word, flashing a proud look that communicated, "I'll be glad when you're gone, troublemaker." What did he know about the real cause of Trudy Aguilera's death? How well had he known Will Kopke? Was there something more sinister behind Ortiz's look—something he was hiding?

Philip Ettinger was rounding on his latest patient, seventy-two-year-old stroke victim Dolores Walker, the Lutheran woman Maggie had told Jordan about over the phone. Philip emerged from room 5 while Jordan regarded the departing Dr. Ortiz. "How goes the battle?" he said, grabbing Jordan by the shoulder.

"I'm beginning to see light at the end of the tunnel, Philip, thank you," Jordan said, wishing he could tell him more.

"Wonderful!" Philip exclaimed. "The malpractice suit is being dismissed, I take it? You will be back to your patients soon?"

"Hopefully yes, on both counts. I think we're getting to the bottom of some things."

"That's a great weight off your shoulders, I'm sure."

Jordan was relieved that Philip did not press him for details. "It will be soon, I trust," he said. Then on a whim, "Do you have time for coffee?"

"Good idea, Jordan, but I'll have to take a rain check," Philip said, his New England accent turning *Jordan* into *Jawdin.* "I'm a bit behind on rounds, and I'm on call tonight. I want to finish up my day's work and sneak away for a quick nap before the night people start injuring one another."

Understanding Ettinger's concern completely, Jordan nodded. "You have pulled a lot of call shifts lately," he said.

Ettinger sighed. He looked weary. "As you know, we're a little shorthanded these days. The buck stops here, I guess."

Jordan felt a little sorry for Philip. When Dr. Waller had rotated Jordan to research because of the Eddie Beamon case, the acting head of Neurosurgery took the brunt of the increased workload. "Hang in there, Philip. Help is on the way."

"Very glad to hear it," Ettinger said, making for the exit. "Let's have that coffee soon, shall we?"

Jordan nodded as the tall neurosurgeon strode away quickly.

He looked to see if Maggie had extricated herself from the difficult patient. But she and another nurse were still attempting to sedate and stabilize him. Jordan didn't really need to talk to Maggie, but she had been adamant—and rightly so—about him staying in touch with someone. Perhaps later in her shift she would have time to talk. He would like to bring her up to date on this afternoon's discoveries.

Retreating to the neurosciences building to study the Hematech disk, Jordan found all the computers either occupied or out of order. With Turk DeVrees in hiding or halfway across the country by now, the hospital's computer system was temporarily in the hands of temps. It also meant that Maxine's intimate, quarter-hourly memoirs of the day's events were likely not being copied to CD-ROM. It didn't matter to Jordan. The CDs he had rescued from Turk's burning house had clearly exposed the activities of someone using Will Kopke's password. All he had to do was find out who that person was. At some point Dr. Joseph Wiggins might be persuaded to help him identify the elusive Will Kopke.

Out of other options for the moment, Jordan decided to use his own small office on the sixth floor. Locking himself in, he booted up the computer and loaded the disk. Opening Trudy Aguilera's report from the Hematech files, he again wondered at its meaning. The fact that he could not readily identify the precise nature of the report was no large concern. Medical technology was upgraded daily. It was difficult enough for Jordan to keep up with the changes in his own field of neurosurgery, let alone advances on other fronts, such as hematology and pathology. The report glaring at him from the monitor obviously reflected a new means of studying and/or reporting on blood samples.

Jordan printed the Aguilera report in order to study it more closely. There were two pages filled with blocks of numbers in neat columns and ranks. The codified headings were unknown to him. He printed two more of the eleven reports he had copied. Laying them side by side on the desk, he looked for similarities. There were a few—higher numbers in one block or column, lower numbers in others. But ignorant of their meaning, Jordan could not see why they would be of any value to his quest. Printing the rest of the reports only swamped him with more numbers that meant nothing to him.

It was eight o'clock, and Jordan knew his blood sugar was low. The law of diminishing returns was in full force; the reports would make increasingly less sense to him until he found something to eat. Slipping the disk and printouts into his briefcase, he locked his office and headed to the cafeteria for a salad to bring back, toting his briefcase along with him as usual.

Twenty minutes later he stepped off the elevator and turned down the long hall leading to his office with chicken-salad-to-go in hand. After only a few steps, he stopped abruptly. Halfway down the hall, his office door stood open. Parked next to it was a janitor's cart stacked high with an array of cleaning tools, supplies, and an industrial-sized trash barrel.

Jordan chilled with suspicion. *Why would someone show up to clean just when I am away for a few minutes? Why clean my office at all, since I am rarely here to clutter it? Or perhaps the office is not being cleaned at all, but searched.*

The clerical people on the floor had long since gone home, so the hall was vacant and quiet. Jordan approached the open door stealthily. But before he peeked inside, Buster Chapman stepped through the doorway, startling them both. The big janitor had a bottle of window cleaner in one hand and a cleaning cloth in the other.

"Oh boy, you scared me, Dr. Keyes," Buster said. "I thought you went home already. I saw you leave with your briefcase."

"I just went down to the cafeteria for some dinner," Jordan replied, studying the janitor's face for signs of guilt over a break-in being foiled. He saw only wide-eyed surprise from the sudden encounter, from which Jordan's heart was still pounding.

"You keep your office real clean, Dr. Keyes," Buster said with a little laugh. "I just washed the glass on your door and your bookcases." He lifted the supplies in his hands as proof.

Convinced of the man's innocence, Jordan said, "Thank you, Buster. If you are finished now, I'll get back to work."

"Yes, sir, Doctor," Buster said, stashing the bottle on the

cart and tucking the cloth into his back pocket. "Everything is clean as a pin. Have a good evening. I hope you don't have to work too late."

"Me too, Buster." Jordan moved past him into the office and unloaded his hands. The janitor headed down the hall accompanied by the squeaking casters on the cart and jingling wad of keys on his belt. Having barely sat down, Jordan jumped up and hurried to the doorway under the impulse of inspiration.

"Wait a minute, Buster."

Buster turned around quickly. "Yes, sir, Dr. Keyes. Something I can get for you?"

"No, just a question."

Buster obligingly walked back to the doorway where Jordan stood.

Jordan said, "Did you know Dr. Kopke very well?"

"The doctor who died?" the big man said.

"Yes, Dr. Will Kopke, the neurosurgeon."

"He didn't talk to me, Dr. Keyes—not like you do. He was always too busy." The expression on Buster's face communicated that his relationship with Kopke had been distant at best.

"Did Dr. Kopke work closely with other doctors on the staff?"

Buster furrowed his brow trying to remember. After a moment of thought, he said, "He worked with all the doctors, just like you do, Dr. Keyes."

"Did he have any friends among the other doctors—you know, someone he spent a lot of time with?" Jordan would have been more specific if he thought it would do any good: *Someone with whom Kopke might have shared his password?*

Buster was silent as he thought about the question. After a few seconds, Jordan switched from short-answer to multiple choice: "Dr. Ortiz? Dr. Boorsma? Dr. Sutherland?"

"I don't remember, Dr. Keyes," Buster said at last, wearing a blank look.

"No problem, Buster. I just wondered if you knew something about him."

Buster brightened. "I know one thing."

"What's that?"

"Your office used to be his office," Buster said proudly, as if he had solved a great problem. "And he was not very tidy, Dr. Keyes—not like you."

"Thank you, Buster," Jordan said, smiling. "Now I guess we had both better get back to work."

"Yes, sir."

Jordan spent the next hour puzzling over the thirteen reports he had obtained from Hematech Labs. The only thing he knew for sure was that they were not standard blood screenings for diseases, poisons, or foreign and illegal substances. The samples sent to Hematech by Will Kopke and colleagues using his password had been studied for some other purpose.

He pulled up Hematech's Web site on the computer. Leafing through the informational pages, he found nothing unusual about the Wilsonville laboratory. But one word caught his attention—a word he had read past a number of times because it had not seemed to apply to the patients he had been investigating: *genetics.*

In the midst of a frantic effort to save the life of a critically injured patient, who could possibly be interested in some kind of genetic study? he wondered. *What's the point? What was Dr. Kopke thinking? What was he into?*

The response that first came to mind surprised Jordan. The dawn of the third millennium had revealed an interesting and even bizarre side to some otherwise normal people. He had read of a few physicians who were committed to saving the world from alien invasion by conducting secret DNA tests on unsuspecting patients. Jordan was sure Oregon had its share of alien seekers. Had Will Kopke terminated the lives of patients he determined to be enemies through some harebrained genetic measuring stick? Were there others at Mercy

Hospital carrying on Kopke's mission? It was entirely too far-fetched to believe. But the possibility that the reports before him were genetic in nature captured his interest.

Maggie called. It was a zoo in the SICU, so she could not talk long. She thanked him for checking in with her and asked what he had found out.

Unwilling to be specific over the phone, he explained that the puzzle was slowly coming together. "That's about all I can say right now," he concluded, hoping Maggie got his meaning. Then he asked, "And how is your new patient, Mrs. Walker?"

Maggie was appropriately vague in communicating what Jordan wanted to know. "She's doing just fine. No change in her condition." Jordan got the interpretation: *No further blood tests have been ordered on the elderly Lutheran woman.*

She continued, "I'll be going home at ten. Are you OK with that?" Translation: *Do you realize I won't be able to watch Mrs. Walker all night?*

Jordan checked his watch: 9:45. "Sure, no problem. I'll talk to you tomorrow." Jordan said good-bye and tapped off the phone. He was not very concerned about Dolores Walker. She was Philip Ettinger's patient, and Philip was on call tonight. If someone ordered anything for her care, Philip would hear about it.

Stepping outside his office, Jordan slowly paced the quiet hall for about an hour, pondering saner implications of the Hematech reports being some kind of genetic studies. He thought about Trudy Aguilera. Someone using Will Kopke's password had obtained a sample of her blood and sent it to Hematech. It was examined the same day, and a report was prepared for someone. The next day Trudy Aguilera died suddenly. Only at Jordan's insistence did the family request an autopsy. And that autopsy, Jordan had been convinced earlier, was a sham. Joseph Wiggins was covering up the fact that Trudy Aguilera had been murdered just like almost three dozen other Christian patients over the last sixteen months.

But why and by whom? Did the genetic study uncover a secret disease that could be eradicated only by euthanizing the patient? Was there a demon-inspired physician at Mercy Hospital systematically snuffing out the lives of defenseless people of God? The ideas seemed as ludicrous as the alien theory. Yet it remained vital that Jordan find an answer. The clock was ticking. A malpractice suit and possible criminal charges could be only hours away.

Shoji Ozawa. The name was suddenly before him. Jordan's fellow resident at the University of Southern California Medical Center was in genetics. Shoji and his wife, Kathy, had been very supportive when J. J. was sick. Jordan had not talked to Shoji in months, but Dr. Ozawa was still at LAC+USC.

Back at the computer, Jordan wrote a quick e-mail to his former colleague asking him to look over the Hematech reports and interpret them if he could. Then he attached the electronic reports from the disk to the note and sent the package to Shoji's e-mail address. Perhaps by tomorrow the assistant professor of genetics at the USC med school could shed some light on the reports Jordan had lifted from Hematech Lab.

Jordan's cell phone sounded. He noticed that it was 11:30, far too late for a social call. He answered with trepidation, "This is Dr. Keyes."

"Doctor, this is Kim at the hospital switchboard." There was urgency in her tone.

"Yes."

"I just received a call from your landlord—a Mr. Gillette. Your apartment complex is on fire, Doctor. He said it started in your unit. The fire department—"

Jordan did not wait for more. He scooped up his growing collection of files, stuffed them into his briefcase, and took off for the parking garage on the run. Tires squealed as he exited the garage and accelerated toward the city. He barely noticed the cream-colored Suburban pulling away from the curb directly behind him as he left the hospital property.

Seconds later he approached the top of the two-lane road that wound through the woods to the city below. Reluctantly he decelerated to negotiate the curves alongside the steep, rocky incline. That's when he noticed the bright headlights closing quickly behind him on the otherwise dark and deserted road. The driver of the large vehicle—the Suburban from back up the road, Jordan guessed—seemed to be in a greater hurry than Jordan was. And he didn't seem to care what—or who—was in his way.

The Suburban rode the Lexus's bumper through the first turn. With no time for fear, Jordan accelerated through a short straightaway, trying to gain a few feet of separation. But the Suburban stayed with him. Jordan instinctively braked hard to pull his car into the next tight turn, then he braced for the collision he expected from the rear. *Jesus, help me! He's crazy!*

At the last second, the big rig swerved to Jordan's left side, the inside of the turn, and the two vehicles roared through the curve together, tires howling. But at the next straightaway, the Suburban did not relent. A violent hit on the driver's side slammed Jordan against the door, dislodging his grip on the wheel. He stood on the brakes to force the Suburban by him. But the unseen driver also braked hard to stay alongside.

Jordan had just regained the wheel when the Suburban rammed him again from the side. Glass from the door's window exploded over him, and the caved-in door pushed him into the center console. Jordan was powerless to control his careening car. In a flash of time, Jordan knew he had been set up. His apartment was not on fire. The call to the switchboard was a ploy to lure him onto the road. The Suburban was not manned by a drunk or lunatic strung out on drugs.

This diabolical encounter was intended to end the life of the meddling Dr. Jordan Keyes. *God! Save me, God!*

The third vicious collision sent the white coupe into the guardrail. The momentum carried it over the precipice, and the car tumbled down the steep, mountainous slope.

THIRTY

The damp cold stirred Jordan to consciousness. Eyes still closed, he reached to pull up the blanket. But there was no blanket, and the simple act of reaching brought pain. His groggy mind struggled for a logical explanation: *I have fallen out of bed and hurt myself.*

Other senses slowly awoke, and his initial theory quickly faded. There was more pain, acute pain—his left shoulder, ribs, and hip, and a pounding headache. The odors surrounding him were not from his bedroom: gasoline, damp earth, burnt rubber. There was a strange taste in his mouth, but a taste he knew. Blood. And there was total silence. *Something very bad has happened. I must be seriously hurt. I am not in a safe place. And I'm alone.*

The pain along Jordan's left side grew in intensity as he gradually woke up. Eyes still closed, he moved his right hand to explore his surroundings. He felt cold, damp plastic and metal, then something rough and sharp—*broken glass!* He forced his eyes open and was not surprised to find himself in the dark. With his pupils already dilated, he began to interpret the black and gray shadows around him.

The car is on its side, but I am still buckled into my seat. I can see through a space where the door should be. It's nighttime, and outside there are trees. My skin is cold and wet from the dew. I've been in a wreck, perhaps hours ago.

But I'm not on a highway. I'm in the woods somewhere. The car flipped or rolled into the woods.

Am I really alone? Was anyone else injured? "Hello, anybody." The words came out weak and garbled. Jordan listened but heard no response. "Somebody. Please. I am *not* OK." Nothing. *Dear God, where am I? What happened? Help me.*

Convinced that he was alone, Jordan knew he must try to move, try to get to a hospital. The opening above him, where the passenger's door had been, seemed the most likely way out. But the slightest movement with his left arm produced a jolt of pain to his shoulder that made him cry out. *Possible dislocated shoulder, fractured clavicle, fractured upper humerus—or all three,* he assessed with a grimace. Unbuckling the safety belt with his right hand, he gingerly rolled onto his back, the first motion in trying to stand up. The limp left arm fell away of its own accord, and Jordan moaned loudly, tears of agony filling his eyes.

Grasping the left wrist with his right hand, Jordan slowly moved the injured arm to the front of his body and struggled into a sitting position. He unbuckled his belt, pulled it from his pants, and buckled it into a loop. He slung the circle of leather around his neck and placed his limp arm inside it. With the improvised sling in place, he pulled himself into a crouch, favoring his injured left hip, which stung with pain. Then he slowly stood on unsteady legs.

Even in the darkness, the view out the car's doorway was sobering. The Lexus was totaled, with a door and other mangled parts strewn up the steep hillside. Had the trunk of an old, sturdy fir tree not stood in the path of descent, the car might have tumbled even farther, perhaps violently enough to kill him. Jordan breathed a prayer of thanks at the realization that his had apparently been the only car involved.

Resting his left arm carefully on the car, Jordan took stock of his other injuries. Nearly dry blood caked one side of his face. He had been unconscious for an hour or two, maybe longer, he surmised. The source of the blood was a scalp laceration, which he found by feeling through his matted hair. The wound had stopped bleeding, which was another cause for thanksgiving. Had the cut been more severe, he could have bled to death without regaining consciousness.

Apart from the obvious injuries to his left side and a possible concussion, Jordan's other injuries appeared to be minor: contusions from bouncing around inside like a rag doll, abrasions and small lacerations from contact with broken glass or exposed metal. Thankfully, both legs seemed to be free of fractures and ligament damage. Ducking back into the collapsed cabin, he groped for the medical bag he kept behind the front seat. One thousand milligrams of ibuprofen or aspirin would certainly help ease his painful symptoms. But the bag was gone, likely thrown from the car during its tumble down the hill.

Jordan stood again. He did not know where he was, nor did he remember what had happened. His cloudy thinking was limited to his painful injuries and the need to find help. The cell phone was gone, but it didn't matter. Jordan could not tell a 911 operator where he was anyway. He tried to cry out, but the pain in his side prevented him from drawing a full breath. *Broken ribs, possible punctured lung,* he thought. He had gotten himself into this predicament alone, perhaps by falling asleep at the wheel. So he apparently would have to get himself out. The road had to be somewhere up the hillside. Perhaps there was a road below him too. Going downhill would be easier and faster, but it was a gamble. He had to go for the sure thing. He decided to climb.

The relatively easy task of climbing out of the car sapped his strength and left him dizzy. After pausing two minutes to regain his equilibrium, he started slowly up the dark, steep, wooded hill. He inched his way, pulling at tree limbs and bushes with his good hand. Every small, cautious step brought pain, and with each pain came a gasp or a moan. The increased circulation caused his head to throb terribly, and his scalp wound started bleeding again. *You don't have to get up to the road in five minutes,* he admonished himself, *you just have to get there eventually. Take your time. Ration your strength. Watch your footing so you don't fall.*

Strobe flashes of Jordan's memory returned as he climbed. At first he recalled only frightening sounds: the wail of rubber on the pavement, the deafening thunder of the car rolling down the hill with him inside, the shattering of windows. Then he remembered the terror of crashing through the guardrail. He had not been asleep at the wheel, he knew. Something had happened on the road that had caused him to lose control. *Was there an animal in the road? Did another car swerve into my lane?*

Jordan had to rest often for fear of passing out. During an early stop, he cinched his tie around his head to hold his handkerchief—a makeshift compress—snugly against the cut on the side of his head. During one moment of rest he heard a car pass on the road above. Encouraged by hope, he kept moving upward.

A big Suburban—white or yellow or beige—with high-riding tires. I was on my way to the apartment. The driver purposely ran me off the road. The fresh page of memory caused Jordan to stop climbing. *It was no accident; it was a planned attempt to kill me. And except for the grace of God, the driver of the big Suburban would have succeeded. He followed me down the hill from the hospital. He knew exactly where to force me off the road. Did I ever get a look at his face? Will I remember it if I did?*

A new concern quickened Jordan's heartbeat. *Where is the guy who tried to kill me? Is he waiting for me on the road above? When I try to flag down a passing car, will it be the Suburban that stops?* Jordan had no choice. He must keep climbing. He would be as careful and quiet as possible approaching the road. If the Suburban was there, he would move laterally through the brush until he could reach the road in safety.

But the road was deserted. Exhausted and sore from the climb, Jordan sat in the roadside gravel. Even in the darkness, the guardrail displayed the frightening signs of violent impact where Jordan's white Lexus had gone over the side. *Did no one passing by notice the damaged guardrail and stop to look?* he wondered. *Did no one care that there might be someone lying injured at the bottom of the hill? Where are the Good Samaritans in the world today?*

Jordan knew he should get up and start walking toward the hospital. But which way? He could not remember. He was losing it, he knew. His body had taken a terrible beating. He had lost some blood, and he was dehydrated. The perspiration from the climb was evaporating, and he was shivering. He was powerless to help himself. He could go no further. *I can't do it, Jesus,* he prayed, consciousness ebbing away. *If I just rest, someone will come.* Slumping to the gravel, Jordan blacked out. His last thought was another memory fragment from his ordeal. A brief glance into the Suburban, a shadowy face, a dark-skinned man with a beard.

◆ ◆ ◆

Lights, voices, activity—seemingly far away—stirred Jordan to the surface of consciousness. "Sir, I'm with the Portland Fire Department. You're going to be all right now. Stay with me, sir. Can you tell me your name? Where do you hurt, sir?" Jordan could not think of his name. When he tried to say so, nothing came out. He was being moved, and the pain was intense. *Don't touch my shoulder! Don't move me! I need something for the pain! Please!* But the words never reached his lips.

There was fuzzy recognition of what was happening to him, a comforting familiarity. Vital signs being checked and called out. A body board being slipped under him, straps cinched into place, head and neck immobilized in a brace.

Knowledgeable medical people were talking to him, caring for him. Then, finally, warmth—a blanket thrown over him, shelter from the cold inside the ambulance. And with the warmth came another wave of unconsciousness.

◆ ◆ ◆

Louder voices, more voices, brighter lights. "Dr. Keyes, you're in the Trauma Center at Mercy Hospital," someone was saying. Jordan was on a gurney in motion. "Your car went over the side less than two miles from here. Everyone is amazed that you got back up to the road by yourself. But you can relax now, Doctor. We take care of our own. You get first-class treatment all the way."

Jordan struggled toward full consciousness as the trauma team swarmed over him, removing his clothing and evaluating his injuries. "Keyes, you got yourself all banged up, man," a booming voice near him announced.

Opening his eyes with difficulty, Jordan looked into the broad, reddish face of trauma surgeon Otto Gebhardt. "Otto, my shoulder," Jordan said as clearly as possible.

"Your left shoulder, yes, we noticed," Gebhardt said. "Classic football injury, Keyes. You forgot to wear your pads, didn't you? Separated shoulder, busted clavicle, and some cracked ribs is my guess, plus assorted contusions and abrasions. I'll let you know about your shoulder and ribs as soon as I see the plain films. You also smacked your noggin a good one. I may want to run you through CT just to make sure you didn't spring a leak in there."

"Call Ettinger," Jordan said with difficulty.

"Yes, I believe Philip is on call tonight. I'll call him if your CT warrants."

"No, Otto. Call Ettinger now, please. I need to see him *now!*" Jordan tried desperately to inject urgency into his slurred request. He could not wait for a CT scan to see Philip. Someone had run him off the road in order to kill him. That someone might already know he had survived the crash and might try again. Jordan needed someone on his side, someone he could confide in.

"Now Dr. Keyes, I'm the doctor here tonight, OK?" Otto scolded him good-naturedly. "It's been a pretty quiet night so far, and Dr. Ettinger is probably conked out in a call room. You don't want to wake him up at three in the morning just to tell him you bumped your head, do you?"

Jordan was in no position to argue, so he chose not to. He did not want to seem unreasonable with Otto and his team. "OK, no problem," he said, grimacing at the pain on his left side. "But I could use some Demerol when you get a chance."

"Demerol it is, Dr. Keyes," Otto said agreeably, "just as soon as we take a few candid snapshots."

Jordan endured the exam as cooperatively as possible, gritting his teeth at frequent stabs of pain in and around his shoulder. He recognized a few faces working in his trauma slot: the radiologist, a couple of residents and nurses. Here he was, naked beneath a flimsy paper sheet. But he was too distracted by pain to be embarrassed.

Trauma surgeon Otto Gebhardt returned with X-ray films in his hand. Standing with him at the gurney was Dr. Donald Jurgen, the on-call orthopedic surgeon, eyes still puffy from recently interrupted sleep. Jordan knew why Don Jurgen was there. "Bad break, I'm afraid, Keyes," Otto began, lifting the films to the light over the gurney so Jordan could see. His left clavicle was broken in two places. "Dr. Don will take you to the OR in an hour or so and put you back together with pins and screws. He'll also pop your shoulder back in place. But first I want to scan your noggin. You have a concussion, for sure. Just want to make sure it's nothing worse."

"Right," Jordan said, "go for it." He knew the value of the CT scan in uncovering potentially fatal bleeding in the brain. "Don't forget my nightcap."

Otto nodded and ordered a moderate intramuscular injection of Demerol. The drug began to ease the pain and blur Jordan's world almost immediately. He remembered being rolled to CT and scanned, and he remembered Otto saying the films looked good—no bleeding.

As he was being prepped for surgery, Philip Ettinger appeared at his side. "I hear you took a nasty tumble, my friend," he said, resting a comforting hand on Jordan's good arm.

Jordan fumbled to get the words past lips and tongue that functioned like they were swollen three times their normal size. "You're supposed to be asleep."

Philip smiled. "You should know that being on call and sleep don't often mix. I was in SICU when word came about your accident. I'm just glad you're all right."

"Philip, listen," Jordan said, trying to whisper. "It was no accident. Somebody ran me off the road . . . tried to kill me . . . old yellow Suburban."

"Yes, I'm sure they did," Philip said, amused.

Philip was humoring the dopey surgery patient, and Jordan knew it. He had done the same thing to patients under the influence of drugs who confided in him that they had been abducted by aliens. "I'm serious, Philip. It was a guy with a beard. . . . Iranian or Arab or something . . . same guy who torched Turk's house."

"Yes, I know, Jordan. You can tell me all about it after surgery."

A nurse appeared next to Ettinger. "Dr. Keyes, they're just about ready for you in the OR. Before you go, I need one little piece of information for your chart."

Jordan tried to focus on the woman, who was dwarfed standing next to Philip Ettinger.

"What is your religious preference, Doctor?"

Sudden concern and fear gripped Jordan. "No," he said. "No, no."

"You don't understand, Dr. Keyes," the nurse said, speaking louder to aid comprehension. "It's not a yes-or-no question. I need your religious preference. Are you a Protestant? Catholic? What?"

Consciousness fading again, Jordan insisted, "None. No. Leave it blank."

The nurse turned to Ettinger with raised eyebrows. Philip said, "Perhaps later." She nodded, then turned back to the patient.

"We have a number for your wife on file, Dr. Keyes. Shall we call her for you?"

"Yes," Jordan said eagerly, "please call Della. But tell her not to worry."

As Jordan was wheeled into the operating room, Philip Ettinger walked with the nurse back to her station. "Sandy, I know Dr. Keyes's wife fairly well. If you will give me the number, I will make the call."

Sandy sighed her relief. "I appreciate that, Doctor. I hate making these calls." She tore off a square of paper on which she had written Della's number in Los Angeles. Ettinger took the scrap, and the nurse hurried off to her next duty. Walking down the hall toward the elevator, he casually wadded the paper in one hand and dropped it into a trash bin.

THIRTY-ONE

Someone touching his bed brought him out of his sleep. Having flirted with consciousness briefly in the recovery room, which he faintly remembered, Jordan awakened this time knowing where he was before opening his eyes.

The person at his bedside was not a nurse, he determined. The nurses he knew hurried through their chores with little concern that they might wake the patient. The person in his room right now was not working but waiting, trying to be quiet. The occasional gentle touch on Jordan's right arm was a caring touch. And Jordan heard sniffing, as if the person near him was concerned about his plight to the point of tears.

Della is here! he thought. Rolling his head to the right, he forced his eyes open.

"Dr. Keyes, you're awake. Oh boy, I'm so happy to see you awake. I was worried that . . . " Buster's words trailed away as he began to cry, the unashamed emotion of a child confiding sorrow or pain to a parent. All the while the big janitor, as if he were the comforting parent, continued to pat Jordan's arm gently.

"You were in a bad crash, Dr. Keyes," Buster said after the brief surge of tears, wiping his eyes with his handkerchief. "The paramedic said your car rolled down the hill almost two hundred feet. He said you climbed the hill by yourself, all busted up like that. Oh boy, Jesus really helped you, Dr. Keyes. I'm so glad Jesus saw you down there and helped you."

Buster's simple report brought Jordan's situation into focus again: the menacing Suburban, the terrifying crash, the painful climb up the hill, the Emergency Room, and the middle-of-the-night surgery. He explored the area of his left shoulder lightly with his right hand. The pain under the dressing as well as the throbbing in his head told him he was due for medication.

"Where am I, Buster?" he said.

"Room 441, Dr. Keyes."

"And what time is it?"

The answer came from the doorway before Buster could reply. "It's almost five-thirty in the morning, my friend. Good to see you awake." Philip Ettinger walked to Jordan's bedside. Buster quickly excused himself to get back to work.

Philip continued, "Your surgery went very well, as expected, Jordan. The steel in your collarbone may set off a few airport metal detectors in the future, but Jurgen tells me you will regain full use of your shoulder and arm in time. The other bumps and bruises—including a minor concussion—will take care of themselves with rest."

"And with a little Demerol," Jordan added, wincing.

"I'll write the order right away," Philip said. He walked to the small computer on the left side of the bed. After a brief flurry of keystrokes, he said, "Done. The nurse should be here in a couple of minutes."

Philip looked dog-tired, but Jordan implored, "Will you close the door and sit down for a couple of minutes—please?"

"Of course." Philip returned to the right side of the bed, pushing the door closed on the way, and took the chair Buster Chapman had recently vacated.

"I know I rattled off some crazy-sounding stuff last night about being run off the road and—"

"Not a problem, my friend," Philip cut in. "We have all been exposed to patients who are in delusion from pain or medication. Don't worry, you didn't talk about old girlfriends or reveal any family secrets."

"I'm not deluded, Philip. I was telling the truth," Jordan said with conviction. "I know it sounds crazy, but I was purposely run off the road last night by someone who was waiting for me when I walked out of the hospital."

"You're serious, aren't you?" Philip said soberly.

"I couldn't be more serious. And what happened on that road last night is just the latest episode in a very dark story with implications that reach deeply into this hospital. I know you're tired, Philip, but please listen to what I have to say."

"Of course, Jordan," Philip said.

Trying to ignore the mounting pain, Jordan quickly summarized the story—the altered medical charts, the revealing CDs from Turk's house, the string of seemingly related deaths of Christian patients, Will Kopke's ID code linked to the death of Eddie Beamon and others, Joseph Wiggins's bogus autopsy report on Trudy Aguilera, the puzzling blood screenings at Hematech Labs.

Strength waning, Jordan concluded, "The guy in the Suburban who tried to kill me last night was the same guy who burned down Turk's house Tuesday night. It's all connected, Philip; I'm sure of it. That stroke patient of yours—the Lutheran woman—may be in jeopardy. I think you need to tell the police before something disastrous happens to your patient—or me."

Philip leaned forward in his chair. "I want you to know that I believe you, Jordan. And no one is going to hurt you or my patient, Mrs. Walker, I assure you. A personal friend of mine is a retired Portland police detective. I'll call him this morning and ask how to proceed—strictly confidential and off the record. Perhaps in a few hours, when you're a bit more rested, he will come over and talk to you."

"But a lot can happen in a few hours, Philip," Jordan objected, wincing in pain.

"Nothing is going to happen," Philip insisted, standing. "I won't leave the hospital until we get some direction from my detective friend. And I'll keep an eye on you and Mrs. Walker. In the meantime, you need to rest—no visitors. I'll get the nurse to bring your Demerol." He started toward the door.

Jordan stopped him with a question. "Philip, did someone call my wife?"

Ettinger turned at the door. "Yes, I did," he said. "I called while you were in surgery. Woke her up, I'm afraid. But I was sure you wanted her to know."

"Yes, I wanted her to know. What did she say?"

"She was upset, of course, and she cried a little. I told her you were out of danger, that the surgery was time-critical but rather routine. She said she would try to get on a plane this morning—nine-thirty or ten, I think. She could be here around noon."

Jordan relaxed a little. "Thank you for calling her, Philip."

"You're entirely welcome," Philip said with a warm smile. "I'm looking forward to meeting Della in person. You rest now. I'll mind the store, and we'll talk when you feel a little better." Then he left the room.

Jordan knew he should check in with Maggie and Sam Rusch before the Demerol put him back to sleep. He pulled his head up from the pillow to look for the bedside phone. There was none. Patient phones were a patient option, he recalled. He dropped his head back to the pillow. Since Philip was now up to speed, Maggie and Sam could wait, he reasoned.

Minutes later the nurse entered the room with twenty-five milligrams of Demerol, which she injected into Jordan's IV. He thanked her and asked that a phone be connected as soon as possible. She agreed.

The Demerol was swift and effective. Relaxed and gradually distanced from the sharp edge of pain, Jordan drifted back to sleep.

◆ ◆ ◆

Dr. Philip Ettinger found a vacant office near SICU, locked the door, and dialed a number outside the hospital. "It's worse than we first thought," he said calmly. "He knows everything."

"Everything?"

"I just spoke with him. He is convinced—"

"The accident that put him there was unnecessary, Dr. Ettinger." The interrupting voice was stern and authoritarian.

"Unnecessary perhaps," Ettinger acquiesced, "but expeditious."

"It may have seemed expeditious to you, but it was not wise. You failed to seek my counsel."

"Yes, sir. Of course."

"And who is this foreigner you have employed?"

"You mean Saba," Ettinger said.

"He is an outsider, a threat to the secrecy of our important work."

"With Dr. Kopke gone, we are somewhat shorthanded," Ettinger argued. "I cannot control Keyes without Saba's help. He knows little of our work."

"The success of our noble service to humanity hinges on discretion, Doctor," responded the voice on the other end of the phone.

"Saba is discreet," Ettinger countered. "I pay him plenty to be discreet."

"Whatever he knows is too much, Dr. Ettinger. Send him away."

"Very soon. At the moment he is very useful to me because of what Keyes knows."

After a brief silence the voice said, "Exactly what does Dr. Keyes know?"

"He knows that Dr. Wiggins falsified the autopsies, although he has no hard evidence. He has also discovered Dr. Kopke's ID code in numerous charts of deceased patients. And he likely suspects that Dr. Kopke was once involved closely with us."

"The CDs secreted away by the computer technician. The CDs no one knew about."

"No one, except DeVrees and then Keyes," Ettinger said.

"And where is DeVrees?"

Ettinger wished he had a better answer. "He has disappeared. Saba cannot find him."

"Will he come back to haunt us at some time, Philip?"

"Doubtful, sir. Turk DeVrees has other troubles. I don't think we will see him again."

"And his cache of incriminating CDs is destroyed?"

"Yes, sir, except for the ones Keyes rescued from the fire," Ettinger said.

"And where are the surviving CDs, Philip?"

Ettinger paused. "Strewn over the hillside, I suspect."

"Then you must send your friend to find them and destroy them."

Ettinger said, "Whether we destroy them or not, Dr. Keyes still knows what he knows." His comment provoked silence on the other end of the phone. He continued, "With this in mind, I submit that Dr. Keyes is a candidate for a merciful termination."

"Another *fatal* accident, perhaps?" the listener offered cynically.

"Keyes may prove to be genetically tainted like the others," Ettinger advanced.

"Do you know for sure? Has he been screened?"

"Not yet, but I will see to it this morning."

"And if the screening is negative?"

Ettinger responded cautiously, "In Dr. Keyes's case, I suggest we make an exception."

A few seconds ticked by. "I cannot approve, Doctor. We

have only terminated those found to be genetically tainted and spiritually qualified."

"Keyes is different from the others," Ettinger argued. "His condition is not critical. His passing will seem less suspicious now than later."

"Dr. Keyes's 'mistakes' will effectively take him out of the picture," the voice argued. "I have seen to that."

Ettinger sensed that the point was no longer open to debate. "All right, I will send a sample."

"Thank you, Philip. And please inform me of the results before you take action."

"Yes, sir, I will."

Ettinger hung up the phone feeling harried. The "noble work" of his superior had changed since Jordan Keyes had arrived at Mercy Hospital. Too many things had gone wrong. Too many surprises threatened to turn a quiet mission of mercy into a public spectacle. Immediate corrective measures were necessary, no matter what the DNA test revealed. Ettinger's superior would eventually realize this. Until then, someone had to act.

Returning to the nurse's station, Ettinger pulled up Jordan Keyes's chart on the computer and entered an order for an additional blood sample to be sent by courier to Hematech Labs. He attached Dr. Donald Jurgen's name to the order. When the nurse came by, he told her about it, saying he was conveying Dr. Jurgen's wishes.

"Dr. Keyes requested a phone in his room," the nurse said. "Is there any reason I should not hook it up for him?"

"Not a good idea quite yet," Ettinger said. "He needs peace and quiet more than he realizes. No phone and no visitors."

"Sure. No problem."

Ettinger left for his morning rounds. He had not slept in twenty-six hours, but he could not let down until he resolved the issue of Jordan Keyes. And it *would* be resolved in a few hours, Ettinger determined, no matter what his secret colleague thought about it.

THIRTY-TWO

Jordan awoke with a surprisingly clear head. Judging by the natural light flooding his private room and the moderate pain he felt from the Demerol's decreasing effect, he had been out for a couple of hours or more. His first thought was to talk to Della. He wanted her to know everything about what had happened to him before she left for the airport. And he wanted to warn her to be careful when she got to the hospital.

But when he checked the bedside table, the phone he had ordered was not there. He did not like the feeling of isolation—alone in the hospital room without a phone, movement restricted by his injuries and an IV line taped to his arm. The man in the Suburban must know by now that his victim had miraculously survived the violent tumble down the hillside. What if he decided to finish the job? Jordan did not feel capable of defending himself. Philip Ettinger might be watching out for him, but could this mild-mannered New Englander stop someone bold and vicious enough to run a driver off the road?

Jordan had to prepare himself for anything, and that meant getting dressed. Finding the bed controls, he elevated himself to a sitting position. He sat on the edge of the bed for a minute, waiting out the dizziness and new shocks of pain in his shoulder. Adjusting the sling for maximum support of his left arm, he gingerly stood, supporting himself by gripping the bed rail with his right hand.

The light-headedness returned, so Jordan leaned against the bed and waited for it to pass. Then he grabbed the portable IV pole and began shuffling toward the closet, rolling the pole in front of him. Pain from surgery and his other injuries was strong but bearable. He would need another dose of medication in an hour or two. But he hoped to be in a more secure location by then.

Reaching the closet, he found it empty. *Wake up, dummy,* he remonstrated himself. *Your slacks, shirt, and jacket were torn and stained with dirt and blood. They're probably still in a plastic bag in the ER or somewhere.* A quick survey of the room turned up no other possibilities for clothing, not even a robe. For the moment at least, he was stuck with the flimsy hospital gown that covered his front to the knees and no more. He would not be wandering far in this costume.

After three minutes on his feet, the room began to float around him. Jordan felt the blood leaving his head, and his heart began to pound. He moved carefully back to the bedside and sat down, perspiration oozing from his pores. While resting, his eyes fell on the bedside computer, and his thoughts turned to the charts of the SICU victims he had studied. Jordan's injuries and treatment did not require time spent in Intensive Care. But he was still a patient at Mercy Hospital. Was there anything on his chart he should be concerned about?

Strength ebbing from him by the second, Jordan pulled himself up again and approached the monitor. Manipulating the keyboard with one hand, he summoned his chart to the monitor. Everything seemed in order until he reached the final two entries. Shortly after Jordan received his dose of Demerol this morning, Dr. Jurgen had ordered a blood sample. And minutes later, apparently after he was already asleep, the nurse took blood.

Why take an extra blood sample on me? Jordan pondered. *Is Dr. Jurgen acting out the part of the late Will Kopke? Am I the next patient at Mercy Hospital to die unexpectedly after successful treatment?* The fearsome possibilities further weakened his knees, and the room began to spin again. Had he been more than three steps away from the bed, he would have collapsed. Laid out flat on the bed, Jordan caught his breath while the revolving room slowed and finally stopped. *As long as I am trapped in this room, I am vulnerable,* he thought. *But if they don't know where I am, my chances of survival are greatly increased. I have to get out of this room—just as soon as I can gather my strength.*

He was about to drift into unconsciousness from fatigue when he heard the door of his room slowly open. If it was the olive-skinned man with the beard slipping in to finish him off, he had picked the perfect moment. Jordan did not have strength enough to cry out, let alone defend himself.

Rolling his head toward the door and opening his eyes, Jordan found Buster Chapman standing quietly next to the wall, watching him. "Oh, Dr. Keyes, I didn't mean to wake you up," he said apologetically. "I'm going home now, so I came by to say a little prayer for you. The nurse said I could come in for a minute if I was quiet. Oh boy, I'm sorry. You need your rest. I'll come visit you tomorrow."

"No—wait, Buster," Jordan said, stopping him before he could open the door. At this moment he did not see a simple, compassionate hospital janitor. Buster Chapman was nothing less than a guardian angel. "Come over here, please."

Buster obediently came to the bedside.

"Buster, will you do me a very large favor before you leave?"

Buster's face brightened at the prospect. "Of course, Dr. Keyes."

Jordan explained in simple terms that he had to move to somewhere else in the hospital without telling any of the doctors or nurses. "It's very important, but I can't tell you why just now," he said, hoping his guardian angel was trustworthy.

"You don't look very strong, Dr. Keyes," Buster said with obvious concern. "How can you move somewhere else?"

"I can move if you will help me, Buster. But it's a secret, and it's OK if you can't do this for me."

"Oh boy, I love secrets, Dr. Keyes," Buster said with a mischievous gleam in his eye. "I can help you, and I won't tell anybody."

Jordan outlined the crazy plan that had come to him only seconds before he verbalized it to Buster. He cautioned the big man to secrecy again, then sent him to complete his errands.

After Buster left the room, Jordan summoned the nurse with the bedside call button. She entered the room, surprised that Jordan was awake. Acting much better than he felt, he requested a breakfast of juice, coffee, oatmeal, and dry toast. The nurse said she would have it sent up right away.

Jordan said, "I asked for a phone a couple of hours ago."

"I know," she said, "but Dr. Ettinger wanted you to get some sleep."

"Well, I had a good nap," Jordan said, forcing a smile. "Will you bring me a phone now, please?"

The nurse hesitated, then, "I guess that would be all right."

"By the way, have you seen Dr. Ettinger lately?" he probed.

"Not for a couple of hours. He's on rounds, I believe."

"If you see him on the floor, will you send him in, please?" Jordan needed more than Buster Chapman as his ally. Philip might think his plan was foolish, but he wanted him to know what he was doing.

The nurse nodded. "Of course. Back with your breakfast in a minute. Back with the phone in two."

Jordan was not hungry, but he nibbled his toast and sipped his coffee while waiting for the nurse to plug in his phone.

When she left the room, he dialed Della's home number. He got the machine but hung up without leaving a message. She was no doubt on her way to the airport for her flight to Portland. He waited for another dial tone and tapped in the number for her cell phone.

Della's businesslike hello was a sweet and welcome sound to his ear.

"Dell, it's me."

"Hello, Jordan." He was surprised at the absence of concern in her voice.

"Are you on your way to LAX?" he said.

"No," she said, her tone adding, *Why would I be going to the airport?* "I'm on my way to Agoura Hills. I have a meeting with the Parade of Homes people."

Jordan's heart sank. Apparently she had little interest in flying up to visit him. He was in the hospital after a terrifying attack on his life, and his wife was going about her decorating business. "Didn't Philip Ettinger call you this morning?"

"Philip who?"

"Philip Ettinger. He's a neurosurgeon up here and a new friend. He said he talked to you this morning about what happened."

"I never talked to him. He must have left a message."

Jordan wondered if he was hallucinating from pain and fatigue. "No, he said he talked to you personally. He said you were going to fly up today. He said that you cried when you heard about last night."

"Jordan, I didn't talk to anyone from the hospital this morning," Della said, concern overtaking her tone. "What happened? What's wrong?"

Confused over the apparent communication mix-up, Jordan told Della about his accident and surgery. He was straightforward about his accident not being an accident. But he minimized the ongoing threat to his life, hoping to keep his wife from greater worry.

The shock and alarm in his wife's response was a welcome sign. "You have to tell the police, Jordan."

"I will—soon, I hope. But I still need more evidence."

"I'm coming up," Della insisted. "It's 8:45. I can be at the airport in time for a 10:30 flight. I'll call Mother and have her take care of Katy."

"This means a lot to me, Dell," Jordan said, feeling an unexpected knot of emotion in his throat. "But don't come to the hospital, because I don't know where I will be. Better yet, just wait at the airport until I call."

"I'm on my way."

As Jordan hung up the phone, the brutal truth hammered him with successive, painful blows. *Philip never called Della. He wants me to think that Della is on her way to Portland. Philip lied to me. He cannot be trusted. I must get out of here now!*

Barely able to breathe from suffocating fear, Jordan activated his patchwork plan. He pushed his tray of food to the edge of the bed table until it toppled to the floor with the noisy crash of broken glass and the clatter of plastic dishes on linoleum. To make sure the nurse was alerted, he pushed his call button.

The nurse hurried into the room and surveyed the mess on the floor. "We had a little accident, it appears."

"Sorry," Jordan said. "I'm a little clumsy this morning."

"No problem, Doctor. I saw Buster and his cart down the hall. I'll get him."

Right on schedule, Buster! Jordan exulted silently.

Moments later the janitor wheeled his cart into Jordan's room. "Oh no, Dr. Keyes, you dropped your food tray," he said.

Instead of explaining the mess as part of his scheme, Jordan ignored it. "Swing the door closed, Buster." He did as instructed. "Did you bring the scrubs?"

Buster produced the green cotton shirt and pants, clean and folded from the locker room, and handed them to Jor-

dan. Then he started to clean up the spilled dishes and food.
"No time for that right now, Buster," Jordan said, sliding out of bed on the side away from the broken glass. "I need you over here to help me get dressed."

Buster held the pants while Jordan stepped into them. Then, using his left hand from the sling, Jordan carefully pulled the IV out of his right arm and secured a cotton-padded Band-Aid over the puncture. As much as he needed the nutrients and Demerol, it would be difficult to cart the bag and line wherever he went.

With Buster's help, he removed the sling and gown and then slipped into the green shirt. His shoulder screamed at him as he worked his arm through the sleeve and repositioned the sling. The expense of energy and the pain from moving around were taking a toll. Jordan's head throbbed, and his heart pounded. His breathing was shallow, and his knees began to buckle. Grabbing onto Buster with his right hand, he said, "Help me get on the cart, then take me someplace where no one will look for me."

Buster looked at the cart, puzzled. "But you won't fit on the cart, Dr. Keyes."

"Put me in there," Jordan said, pointing, "in the trash barrel. Then clean up the mess and get me out of here."

Moments later, Buster Chapman emerged from room 441 and pushed his cart down the hall toward the elevator. Hunkered in the large trash barrel with the hospital gown for cover was Jordan Keyes. By the time they reached the elevator, Jordan had passed out.

◆ ◆ ◆

Philip Ettinger's resolve had grown during his long rounds. Every minute Jordan Keyes was alive increased the chances that the secret work in the SICU over the past two years would be uncovered. On his way back to Jordan's room, he stopped by his office to prepare a syringe of potassium. Hopefully, Jordan would still be asleep. If not, he was due for another serving of Demerol, and the syringe now in the pocket of Philip's lab coat would pass for Demerol.

Ettinger strolled past the nurse's station, smiling at the two nurses. Pushing into the patient's room, he stopped, dumbfounded. The bed was empty, as was the bathroom. Dr. Jordan Keyes was gone.

THIRTY-THREE

For the second time today, Jordan awoke in pain not knowing where he was. Only this time, even after opening his eyes, he could not immediately identify his surroundings. He was lying on his back on a narrow cot, the kind used in a patient's room when a relative asks to spend the night. But the room was dark and small with cardboard cartons stacked floor to ceiling around him. The air was heavy with the scent of industrial-strength cleaning fluid.

Sitting up and finding himself dressed in ill-fitting green scrubs, Jordan remembered that he was a fugitive. His accomplice, Buster Chapman, had apparently secreted him in a musty supply room somewhere in the hospital. He had a dim memory of Buster helping him climb into the trash barrel to escape his room. Somehow he had been transferred from the barrel to the cot, but Jordan did not remember it happening.

"Buster?" he called out in a soft voice. There was no response. He stood cautiously to test his legs and explore his small cell. The only entrance to the room, a windowless door, was locked to the outside. Shelves lining the walls were neatly arranged with cans and bottles of cleaning supplies. Stacks of facial and toilet tissue in large cartons had been pushed aside to make room for the cot.

Woozy from standing, Jordan returned to the cot. The

hard sleep had done him some good, but his shoulder and incision still throbbed painfully. He would need some medication soon. It would take some creative problem solving to get hold of something more powerful than aspirin without showing his face at the pharmacy and asking for it. And showing his face around the hospital was not an option until he determined the extent of Philip Ettinger's involvement in the incredible plot to get rid of him.

Philip was involved, all right. His obvious lie about talking to Della this morning proved it. But how deeply involved was he? Had Philip been in league with Will Kopke and Joseph Wiggins to secretly terminate the lives of innocent, defenseless patients at Mercy Hospital? Had he assumed the grisly work after Kopke's unfortunate death? Had Philip taken the project by force by putting Kopke out of the picture? Was he behind the murderous actions of the small, bearded man?

Philip Ettinger was certainly a prime suspect in the strange affair. He had known Dr. Kopke as well as anyone in Neurosurgery. If Kopke would have shared his password with someone—either intentionally or unintentionally—it could have been Philip Ettinger. And Philip was the last person Jordan would have thought might be against him, until he caught the man in a lie this morning.

Or was Philip merely a pawn in the sordid SICU murders? Was he trying to protect someone else? Jordan thought of Taylor Sheffield and Leonard Darwin, who had seemed anxious and adversarial after he had gotten involved with Turk DeVrees and the CDs. He thought of Dr. Oscar Ortiz and other staff members in Neurosurgery who had distanced themselves from him. Having appeared detached from the antagonists, was Philip really part of them? Was he the head of the bizarre and deadly scheme? How many physicians were involved in the conspiracy to euthanize patients?

The next nagging questions centered on why. Why would any member of the healing profession, sworn to preserve life under the Hippocratic oath, intentionally take lives? Why would patients identified as nominal Christians be targeted for euthanasia? And why kill patients who had so recently escaped death?

Jordan had no answers. And despite the personal attack on his life last night, he could not yet prove that those who had painted him as the negligent physician were in fact the murderous culprits. Philip and whoever else was involved had covered their tracks well. Jordan had to collect more puzzle pieces, and the doorway to the answers he sought seemed to be guarded by Philip Ettinger. Jordan needed a strategy for extricating himself. But a mind cloudy from the brain rattling he had experienced and a shoulder seared with pain distracted him from what to do next.

Jordan heard a key slide quietly into the door lock. Someone was about to enter, someone hoping not to be heard. Forcing himself to his feet, Jordan ducked behind a stack of cartons. He might not be able to defend himself well, but he wanted the advantage of seeing the intruder before he or she saw him.

Peering around the cardboard corner, he saw Buster Chapman slip into the room with a brown bag in his hand. Buster closed the door quietly behind him and moved toward the cot, which was partially blocked from his view by another stack of cartons. Jordan stepped out of his hiding place to meet him.

"Oh, Dr. Keyes, I thought you were still asleep. Are you feeling better?"

"Maybe a little better, but not well," Jordan said. "Does anyone know where I am? Does anyone know you brought me here?"

"Oh no, Dr. Keyes," Buster said with a Cheshire cat grin, "it's a big secret, like you said. And I keep good secrets." Then, holding out the bag, he said, "I thought you would be hungry, since your oatmeal went on the floor. So I brought you some more breakfast."

Disarmed by another outpouring of kindness from the janitor, Jordan took the bag and sat on a corner of the cot. "Thank you," he said, feeling very grateful at the moment that he was not alone in hiding. He was not hungry, but he knew he must eat if he was to accomplish anything today in his defense. He must eat and rest—and get something soon to hold back the mounting pain.

Jordan opened the bag to find three Danishes and two six-ounce cartons of orange juice. "I'll be happy to pay you for these—if you can wait until I locate my wallet."

"You don't need to pay anything," Buster said, sitting on the other end of the cot. "Helga in the kitchen saves the pastries for me. They are a day old. I hope you don't mind."

"I don't mind at all," Jordan said, taking a bite. It occurred to him that Buster had been up all night working and should be in bed asleep by now. "I appreciate all your help this morning, Buster. But if you need to go home now, I can probably take care of myself." He had to say it, and Jordan hoped he was right about being able to take care of himself.

"Do you want me to go home now, Dr. Keyes?" Buster said. He appeared ready to do whatever Jordan wanted him to do, as he had so far in his escape from the hospital room.

Buster's selfless caring challenged Jordan to replace his usual self-sufficiency with vulnerability. "If you can stay, I could really use your help. But if you need to get out of here . . ." Jordan did not know how he would manage alone, so he could not finish the sentence.

"Sure, I can stay," Buster said. "I really want to stay, if you want me to."

"Yes," Jordan said, relieved, even though he did not know what his next move would be.

The throbbing in his left shoulder increased as he ate, provoking an involuntary frown. He felt Buster's hand rest lightly on his good shoulder. "I'm so sad about your car crash, Dr. Keyes," the big man said, his eyes instantly moist with tears. "Oh boy, your shoulder must hurt real bad."

Jordan was again the grateful recipient of the janitor's simple expression of comfort. Buster knew he was hurting and cared enough to say something—to the point of tears. His words were certainly not complicated or deep, but they seemed to ease the emotional weight of Jordan's predicament.

Jordan relaxed under the wave of Buster's unambiguous kindness. His thought seeped out in words, "You really know how to connect with people, don't you, Buster?"

The big man's brow furrowed, signaling a lack of comprehension. "You need me to connect something for you, Dr. Keyes?"

Jordan smiled inside at Buster's interpretation. "No, nothing." Then a simple prayer found its way to his thoughts, and he prayed: *God, give me a heart like Buster's for Della and Katy.* Then he said, "Thank you, my friend. Thank you for breakfast. Thank you for staying with me."

"You're welcome, Dr. Keyes. Is there anything else you need right now?"

Jordan thought a moment. "Yes, I need a phone. Is there a phone in this room?"

"It's just a supply room," Buster said, shaking his head. "There's no phone in here."

"What building are we in? What floor are we on?" Jordan quizzed.

"We're on the ninth floor of the main building, the cancer wing," Buster said.

"Is there a phone nearby, in one of the other rooms around here?"

"I don't know. I guess so. Do you want me to find one?"

"Yes, find a phone that I can use without being seen by anybody, if possible; then come and get me."

Buster stood, eager as always to help. "Sure, Dr. Keyes." Then he left the room as quietly as he had entered.

Jordan forced himself to finish one of the pastries and a carton of orange juice. Pain medication was becoming a high priority. But first he had to determine for sure if Philip Ettinger was really at the center of the bad things that had happened to him and to other patients at Mercy Hospital. And the easiest way to do that, he realized, was to ask him personally.

THIRTY-FOUR

Instead of finding a room with a phone, Buster did even better. He found a spare phone to plug into the unused jack in the supply room. He assured Jordan that no one noticed what he was doing.

Jordan dialed the hospital's main number and had Philip Ettinger paged. In less than two minutes, he was on the line.

"Jordan, where are you? You disappeared from your room, and no one saw you go. After the story you told me, I was beginning to fear you had been kidnapped."

The worry in Philip's voice sounded genuine, but Jordan was cautious. He ignored the question about his location for the moment. "I'm doing all right, Philip," he said.

"You're in no condition to leave the hospital, my friend."

"I never said I left the hospital."

"You're still here?"

"Yes, I'm still here."

"Where, Jordan? I'll send a wheelchair for you. You just had serious surgery. You need to rest, man."

"Don't worry about me, Philip. I'm doing fine." It was a generous stretch of the truth, Jordan knew, but he didn't want Philip to think he was entirely vulnerable. "My mind is a little fuzzy, Philip. Did you tell me earlier that you called my wife and told her about the accident, or was I hallucinating?"

Ettinger did not answer right away. "Why? Did you call her?"

Clever response, safe response, Jordan thought. "Yes, I tried calling her at home."

"And did you talk to your wife?"

"She wasn't home." That much was true, but Jordan couldn't lay all his cards on the table right now. "Is she on her way to Portland?"

"Yes, I'm sure Della is on her way. When I talked to her early this morning, during your surgery, she said she would fly up sometime this morning. Would you like me to pick her up at the airport?"

"You talked to her personally?" Jordan asked.

"That's right."

"You said she cried a little, as I recall."

"A little, yes. But she sounded fine. She's a brave lady."

"Yes, she is," Jordan said. "And you wouldn't mind picking her up?"

"Of course not. My pleasure. But I would like to see you settled in first. You probably could use another shot of Demerol."

Ettinger was right. The wound in his shoulder cried out for relief. "Perhaps you're right, Philip. Why don't you send a chair for me? I need to rest."

"Wise choice, my friend," Philip said, sounding pleased. "Where are you?"

"Oncology, ninth floor. I'll wait at the nurse's station."

"I'll send somebody right up."

"Who will you send? A candy striper?"

"No, a hospital aide."

"Thanks, Philip. I'm really hurting. I guess I tried to do more than I should have."

"It's all right," Ettinger assured. "You will feel much better after some medication, my friend." Jordan scowled at Philip's glib reference to being his friend.

Buster was right there listening to Jordan's side of the

conversation, but he did not seem alarmed at what he heard. Nor did he ask about it after Jordan hung up the phone. Jordan gave the janitor a few concise instructions, emphasizing that their secret must remain intact. Buster immediately went to work.

◆ ◆ ◆

Eleven minutes later one of the two elevator doors on the ninth floor opened, and a man wearing the white shirt and pants of an orderly emerged pushing an empty wheelchair. He rolled the chair down the hall to the nurse's station and looked around for the patient he was supposed to pick up. He found no one. He asked the nurse if she had seen anyone waiting for transport, but she had not.

Puzzled, the man pushed the chair to the far end of the hall, looking for his intended passenger. Then he headed back toward the elevator, stopping at each doorway to look for a patient waiting for a ride. No one was.

He returned to the elevators where the janitor was busily cleaning the metal doors with all-purpose cleaner and a soft, folded cloth. Approaching the janitor, he said, "I'm looking for a patient who needs a wheelchair. He was supposed to be in the hall by the nurse's station. Did you see him?"

The aide was from a foreign country, Buster surmised, because he had rather dark skin and an accent. And this man was small like some foreigners are, at least a foot shorter than Buster. He was probably new at the hospital too, Buster thought, because he knew almost everybody at Mercy. He had never before seen this small aide with the strange accent, dark skin, and a thick, closely cropped beard.

"No, I didn't see anybody," Buster answered.

After another long glance down the hall, the aide pushed the chair onto the elevator, and the door closed behind him.

When the foreign man disappeared, Buster heard Dr. Keyes whisper from his hiding place on the janitor's cart. Buster nodded, then pushed the elevator's down button.

When the door opened, he rolled his big cart inside. Using the wad of keys on his belt, he switched the elevator to express mode—no stops for other passengers. Then he tapped *B.* The doors closed, and the elevator began descending toward the basement.

THIRTY-FIVE

Turk's office in the back corner of the basement had not been occupied since his disappearance two days ago. According to Buster, the hospital had called in temps to troubleshoot computer problems in the hospital until Turk's team returned to work. But no one had been inside Turk's office, not even Buster.

"There are some very bad things going on in our hospital, Buster." Safely locked inside the office with the mini-blinds to the hallway drawn and a small desk lamp for light, Jordan felt a need to tell Buster a little of what was going on. The naïve but caring janitor was sticking his neck out to hide him and help him. Jordan owed Buster at least a cursory explanation. "I think someone in the hospital has been causing patients to die."

Buster seemed unfazed by the idea. Surrounded by shadows in the office, he appeared larger than normal.

"And somebody is upset that I know about it. This person also caused my accident. He wants to kill me."

"Do you want me to go get Lavelle?" Buster asked, always ready to help. Lavelle Goodwin, a former New York City policeman who retired to the Northwest, was head of hospital security. Jordan had been reluctant to go to security with his notion, unsure of who might be in collusion with the killer.

"Not yet," Jordan said. "I have to find out a few more things before I tell the police. But I wanted you to know what my secret was about. You could be in danger by staying with me. It's all right if you want to go home now. I appreciate your help, but I feel safe here."

"If you have to go somewhere, how will you get there?" Buster's face mirrored concern. "No, Dr. Keyes, I need to stay with you. I'm the only one who knows the secret. I have to stay with you in case you need me."

Jordan had never thought much about guardian angels. If they did exist, he had reasoned, they were invisible spirits doing their jobs apart from human knowledge. But Buster's timely appearance, pure heart, and selfless loyalty caused Jordan to wonder if God had disguised one of his heavenly agents as a janitor especially for him.

"Thank you, Buster," Jordan said, humbled. "I guess I need help more than I care to admit." Characteristically, Buster said nothing.

The knowledge that Philip Ettinger was involved in a plot to murder patients had left Jordan stunned and sullen. Questions peppered his mind: Who was this man at the core—a fiendish sociopath, a demon in disguise? How had his thinking become so polluted that he could justify a secret scheme of physician-assisted homicide? How had he fooled his colleagues, and perhaps himself, for so long? And what enabled him to convincingly act the part of a friend while simultaneously plotting to end Jordan's career and life?

As much as these questions begged for answers, Jordan had a higher priority: stopping Ettinger and exposing his plot before the madman silenced him. But to do so Jordan needed a clear head and freedom from the invisible ax blade of pain assaulting his shoulder. And with this realization, Jordan remembered something that could help.

"Buster, would you go get something for me?" he said.

"Sure, Dr. Keyes."

"I want you to go over to my office. But make sure nobody sees you go in and nobody sees you come back here. Can you do that?"

"Yes, sir, I can," Buster answered with confidence.

Jordan described the locked cabinet in his office where he kept a stash of backup supplies for his traveling medical bag—including a few disposable syringes of painkilling Demerol. He explained where to find the hidden key to the cabinet. Buster left, locking the office door behind him. Jordan listened until he could no longer hear the janitor's cart rolling in the hallway.

The digital desk clock read 10:43. Hopefully Della was aboard a flight to Portland. He yearned to be with her. He had important things to tell her, things about himself, about them, and about the pain they each had been carrying. But most of all, he did not want her to be alone at a time like this. Buster's profoundly simple words and example conveyed wisdom Jordan had previously overlooked. Pain had to be shared in order to be comforted and healed. Apparently, he had to receive comfort before he could give it, and now he must give it in order to find himself. Jordan considered how his wife must be feeling right now, and it saddened him that he was not there to comfort her.

Aware that he needed more help than Buster could supply if he was to bring Philip Ettinger into the light, Jordan picked up the phone and tapped nine for an outside line. Not exactly sure of the number, it took him four tries to reach Maggie and Sam Rusch's home.

"This is Jordan," he said in response to Maggie's hello.

"What's happening? I'm just heading out the door for work." Her tone communicated that she had heard nothing of last night's events.

The insistent pain in his shoulder pushed him past any pleasantries. "I'm in trouble, Maggie, and I need help."

"Jordy, what's wrong? You sound awful. Where are you?"

The concern in Maggie's response touched him with reassurance. In several brief, halting sentences he summarized the terrifying events of the past twelve hours. Maggie gasped at the description of his crash, rescue, surgery, and escape from the hospital room. Without mentioning Philip Ettinger, Jordan explained that he had uncovered telling details of the plot to kill SICU patients and to eliminate him.

Without a pause to receive sympathy or questions, Jordan rushed into a list of specific needs to help him make his case to Waller, Sheffield, and Darwin. It would take some time to get everything accomplished, but he urged her to hurry, even to get Sam to help her if possible. Then he elicited a promise of caution and secrecy. Maggie soberly agreed and hung up.

Confident that Maggie would eventually arrive with concrete evidence to present to his superior, Jordan dialed Dr. Waller's extension. He was disappointed but not surprised to be connected to voice mail. "Dr. Waller, this is Jordan Keyes. I must see you immediately. Please call extension 4431 as soon as you receive this message. It is extremely urgent—a matter of life and death."

Distracted by the knifing pain in his shoulder and the pounding headache from the concussion, Jordan snapped off the desk lamp and eased himself to the floor behind the desk, out of sight from the office door. He could not afford to drift off to sleep. But he had to conserve his dwindling strength for a few more hours. So he lay as still as he could in the darkness to rest and wait for Buster's return with the Demerol.

◆ ◆ ◆

Philip Ettinger and the man he knew only as Saba were alone together in Bert Waller's office. Standing beside the desk, they saw Waller's message light blink on. Ettinger immediately entered Waller's security code, thankful the old man was never too careful about who was watching when he entered his code. As he waited for the message to play, he hoped Jordan was checking in with Waller. It would save him the time of searching the hospital.

"Extension 4431—that's the computer geek's office in the basement," Ettinger said. "Keyes could not have made it easier for us." He turned to the small, olive-skinned man at his side. "Get down there immediately and take care of him before he ruins everything." As he spoke, Ettinger pulled a syringe from the pocket of his lab coat and held it out.

"But your boss insisted that you inform him when the doctor was found," Saba said without reaching for the syringe.

"I pay you well, Saba," Ettinger said sternly. "Do as I say and be quick about it."

Saba received the instrument and secreted it in the pocket of his white shirt. "As you wish, Doctor," he said impassively. Then he left for the elevators.

◆ ◆ ◆

Lying on his back in the dark office, Jordan tried not to move. Even shallow breaths caused his arm to move slightly, sending sharp jolts of pain through his shoulder and clavicle. And every heartbeat made his head throb painfully. He considered with greater sympathy so many of his patients who had to gut it out through the pain while waiting for the next dose of medication.

Concentrating on what he must do was almost impossible. When Dr. Waller returned his call, Jordan would have to logically and lucidly pull the evidence together, evidence that pointed to a series of murders at Mercy Hospital over the last sixteen months. But at the moment, the information he had compiled fluttered around in his brain like scraps of paper in a whirlwind. Lab reports, autopsy reports, patient charts, ID codes—none of it made sense right now. If he was going to get through this, he would need help.

Jordan was acutely aware of his utter dependence on others. Without Buster Chapman he could not have eluded Philip Ettinger and his bearded little goon. He needed Buster now to bring the medicine that would allow him to defend himself to the men who held his career in their hands. And without Maggie and Sam Rusch, Jordan would be unable to gather the vital puzzle pieces for his defense. The thought sparked the memory of a verse he first read in a Bible study during med school shortly after becoming a Christian. It went something like, "How silly it is to think that one part of the body would say to another part, 'I don't need you.'"

Jordan needed Della more than anyone, more than he had allowed himself to admit. Jordan had dedicated his life to serving God through his profession. And the greater his success as a neurosurgeon, the more meaningful his ministry to God had seemed to him. But at this moment, a successful, ministry-oriented career in medicine seemed meaningless apart from the journey-mate God had given him. It was not the journey that had been so painful for him, he realized; it was traveling the road alone that had left him—and Della—so empty.

I would be better off working as a hospital janitor and at peace with Della than becoming a world-renowned neurosurgeon without her. The thought startled him, but Jordan was defenseless against its inherent truth. Della said her love had grown cold because Jordan had become so distant and dispassionate. Anything Jordan achieved in medicine could not change that. Success and meaning to God were not career issues; they were relationship issues. Without peace at home, paradise on earth was unachievable.

The pain distracted Jordan's thinking, but it seemed to expedite his praying. His inner cry for help reached far beyond his immediate need for safety and deliverance. He found himself praying for Della, especially that her cold, wounded heart would survive until he was able to confess to her his misplaced priorities.

After only a few minutes, Jordan's brief, heartfelt petition was interrupted by the sound of the doorknob being tested. Seconds later a key was inserted into the lock, tried unsuccessfully, and withdrawn. Jordan held his breath. He did not expect Buster back so soon, nor had he heard the cart in the hallway outside. And it was unlikely that a hospital employee just happened to be passing by this office near the dead end of the basement hall. Someone wanted in.

With difficulty, Jordan sat up and turned his body so he could peek around the corner of the desk with one eye and see the door. The second key inserted into the lock worked, and the door quietly opened. A figure stood in the open doorway for only a few seconds before stepping inside the office and locking the door behind him. But the brief image rocked Jordan with fear. It was the small, dark, bearded man. The last thing Jordan saw before darkness returned to the office was the glint from the syringe the man pulled from his shirt pocket.

THIRTY-SIX

When the overhead light snapped on, Jordan knew any attempt to hide would be futile. He pulled himself quickly to his feet, hoping to keep the desk between himself and the man who had already terrorized him twice.

Jordan felt betrayed. The man facing him had not come to the basement on a whim. Someone had identified Turk's office as a hiding place. It was likely a slip of the tongue by Buster Chapman, whom Jordan now judged incapable of keeping a secret. The only other possibility was Maggie Rusch. Had Jordan been unwittingly sold out by a devoted and helpful friend?

The attacker remained by the door and eyed Jordan with the air of a conqueror. "You are a remarkably resilient man, Dr. Keyes," he said with a thick accent. "I am amazed that you survived your unfortunate accident. Saba never fails."

The bearded man took one casual step toward the desk. Saba was no fool, Jordan thought. He need only maneuver his wounded prey into a corner while blocking the path to the door. Having only one arm to defend himself, Jordan would be no match against his more agile attacker. Once subdued, he would likely be injected with the same potassium solution that had killed so many defenseless patients in SICU, including Trudy Aguilera.

Jordan regarded the man warily. Then he cried out, "Help! I need help in here!"

"You are a clever man, Dr. Keyes," Saba said, inching closer to the desk. "But you made two tactical errors that cause me to wonder if your head injury is more serious than you think. First, you flee to a place where your cries for help cannot be heard. This is the hospital's basement, Doctor. Nobody comes down here. Your hiding place has turned out to be your own death trap."

Jordan cried out again, "Please help! Call security!"

Saba moved closer to the desk, unconcerned about the vain ruckus. "Second, you disclose your location on voice mail, where anyone can intercept it." The diabolical grin returned to the man's face. "I am afraid your brain injury is severe, terminal. But do not worry, Doctor. I have come to put you out of your misery."

Out of options, Jordan snatched up the desk lamp and threw it at Saba. But the cord was attached to the desk, and it fell harmlessly to the floor before reaching the target. He hurled a flurry of items from the desktop in the man's direction: a cheap plastic desk organizer full of pens and paper clips, a technical manual, another book, a small box of disks. While the disks were still in the air, Jordan broke around the short side of the desk for the door.

Catlike in response, Saba leapt across the room and lunged at Jordan, catching him in the right hip. The momentum of the blow threw Jordan to the carpet, and he shrieked at the explosion of pain in his shoulder. But in panic for his life, he rolled quickly onto his back and kicked violently upward, keeping the man at bay.

Saba grabbed an umbrella by the door and began flailing at the kicking legs. Each blow brought a new sting of pain, but Jordan kept kicking until his leg strength gave out. Then Saba was astride him, pinning Jordan's free arm to the floor with his knee and gripping his neck with small but powerful hands. Disabled by pain and fatigue, and powerless under his attacker's weight, Jordan struggled for breath. But the man's hands closed around Jordan's neck, and the black tide of unconsciousness swirled nearer.

With the first loud *thwang* overhead, the assailant's hands relaxed and fell away from Jordan's neck. With the second blow, producing the same sickening sound of metal colliding with flesh and bone, the attacker collapsed on top of him with a moan. Frantically gasping for air, Jordan pushed the limp body away to find another man standing above him. In his hands was the metal folding chair he had used to knock Saba unconscious.

It took several seconds for Jordan to identify his rescuer. "Turk!" he exclaimed, still fighting for air. "Where . . . did you . . . come from? How did you . . . get in here?" Turk DeVrees had let his beard grow to short, scraggly stubble. He wore a soiled ball cap pulled low over his head. Dressed in dark, baggy clothes, he looked more like a homeless street kid than a computer genius.

Laying the chair aside, Turk lifted a ring choked with keys. "No problem getting in. I used to work here, remember?" he said wryly.

Saba moaned and moved. As Jordan pulled himself into an office chair, Turk retrieved a roll of duct tape from a desk drawer. Working with the quickness of a rodeo calf roper, he pulled Saba's hands to his back and joined them with several lengths of tape at the wrists. Then he lifted the groggy attacker into the folding chair and secured him with yards of tape binding his torso to the chair.

A small trail of blood trickled from Saba's scalp behind his ear and down his neck. His head bobbed and rolled as he slowly regained consciousness.

Turk knelt beside Jordan's chair. "Are you all right, Doc?"

Jordan made a quick inventory. His neck burned from the choking, but the adrenaline surge from the attack had momentarily dulled the pain in his shoulder. From all he could tell, he was no worse off from the brief scuffle. And he was very glad to be alive. "Yes, I'll be OK—thanks. What are you doing here?"

Turk tossed the roll of tape aside. "I came to the hospital to find you. That's why I look like this—" he gestured to his costume—"so I wouldn't be noticed by certain other people who work here. I'm walking down the hall upstairs, and who should I see but this jerk. I remember he's the guy who torched my house the other night."

"You saw him do it? You were there?" Jordan said with surprise.

"I figured whoever was out to get you would take a shot at me," Turk said, nodding. "So I staked out my own place. I saw you, too. You're some kind of crazy man, chasing off an arsonist and running into a burning house."

"I was afraid you were still inside," Jordan explained.

"That's what I figured. Thanks, man. Anyway, I see this guy upstairs a couple of minutes ago, but he doesn't recognize me. I see him get on the elevator and drop to the basement. So I decide to follow him down here and take a couple of swings at him—you know, a little payback."

"I'm glad you did," Jordan said, feeling no sympathy for the tough little man who had almost killed him.

"What are you doing down here in my cave, Doc? And what's with the scrubs and the sling?"

"It's a long story, Turk, but this guy is right in the middle of it." Jordan jerked a thumb toward Saba, who slumped in the chair with glazed eyes.

"And his boss is part of it too, right—Ettinger?"

"You know about Ettinger?"

Turk lifted his hands in a sign of innocence. "Hey, I don't know much, and I like it that way. I'm already in enough trouble outside the hospital, thanks to what Ettinger dredged up on me. That's why I'm on my way out of town—permanently. But Ettinger and his trained baboon here are into something ugly. And they're not in it alone."

"You mean Kopke?"

"Kopke, yeah, him and Ettinger were tight, all right—until the guy ran into a tree on Mt. Hood. But there's somebody else. I don't want to know about it, but I thought you might. So I brought you this." Turk reached into a deep pocket in his baggy pants, produced a single disk, and held it out. Jordan took it.

Saba began muttering curses at the two men. Turk casually pulled another length of duct tape off the roll and slapped it across the man's mouth.

"What about this disk?" Jordan said.

"It's from my private collection. I took the good stuff out of the house before this loser tossed in his firebomb."

"What's on it?"

"A little something else from Maxine's memory that Ettinger doesn't know about. I'm not sure where the data fits into the stuff going on around here, but you might find it helpful. Take it with my compliments."

"You came here today just to give me this disk?" Jordan said.

Turk pulled dark glasses out of his pocket and slipped them on, adding to his disguise. He seemed eager to leave. "You did right by me, Doc—paid me well for services rendered, ran into the burning house looking for me. And you didn't treat me like a cross-eyed computer nerd."

Jordan was humbled by another act of helpfulness he had not sought. "I don't know what to say, Turk. Thanks."

"My pleasure, Doc. Are you going to be OK if I leave this with you?" Turk nodded toward the subdued Saba.

"Sure, I'm fine, Turk. I'll take care of him."

"I have to get going," Turk said. "I have to log some serious miles toward the far side of nowhere. Take care."

"God bless you, Turk, and thanks."

After a cautious check of the hall, Turk left, locking the door behind him. In order not to be surprised again, Jordan wedged the office chair under the doorknob. He was tempted to run after Turk and find out where he was going. He owed the kid a greater debt of gratitude than just a thanks. But Turk would likely choose to disappear into the landscape for now. Jordan hoped God would allow their paths to cross again.

Jordan retrieved the plastic syringe from his captive's shirt pocket and laid it on the desk. He checked the bonds and found them ample to keep the small man immobilized. Then he inspected the laceration on the man's scalp, which had stopped bleeding. "You'll need a couple of stitches for that cut," he said without sympathy. "But I'll let the county jail's infirmary handle it later. In the meantime, you're just going to sit here for a while. I have some work to do."

Saba attempted a glare of defiance, but he still looked a little dopey from the blows to his head.

As the adrenaline drained from Jordan's system, ravaging pain returned to his shoulder in force. If Buster did not return soon with an injection of Demerol, he might be driven to go looking for him.

The disk Turk had brought for him was adequate distraction for the moment. Sitting down at the desk and working one-handed, Jordan booted up the computer and loaded the disk into the A: drive. As he did, he heard a key in the lock again. The unlocked door held fast against the office chair. A soft rap on the door followed.

Peeking through the mini-blinds, Jordan saw Buster Chapman waiting to enter. His cart was not with him. "Who's that, Doctor Keyes?" the janitor said with surprise, staring at the man who was duct taped to the chair. "He was pushing the wheelchair upstairs."

"This is the man who tried to kill me last night," he said.

"Should I get Lavelle now? Should I call the police?"

"Soon, Buster," Jordan assured him. "I have a few things to pull together first. Did you bring something for me?"

Buster proudly produced a small plastic box from his pocket. Inside were three one-hundred-milligram syringes of

Demerol ready for injection. "Thank you, Buster," he said. It took Jordan only a few seconds to empty fifty milligrams into his left arm. Then he returned to the computer and started scanning the data Turk had saved for him. Buster pulled up a chair and assumed the role of Saba's personal guard.

It took Jordan several minutes to figure out what he had. At first the columns of numbers made no sense. When he finally recognized what kind of records they were, a light of understanding began to dawn. He continued to survey the data until one unavoidable fact began drumming into his consciousness with sobering force. Jordan sat back, stunned by the truth of what he had found. It was the final piece of the puzzle. It was the source of the murderous plot he had already uncovered in the SICU. The records had led him to a name.

Picking up the phone, Jordan dialed an extension in the neurosurgery lab. He was relieved to hear Maggie's voice on the other end of the line. She had been waiting for his call right where he had asked her to wait.

"Did you get everything?" he asked eagerly.

"Yes," Maggie said. "I pulled Sam away from the Sheetrock for a while, and we got it all. Can you tell us what this all means, Jordy?"

"Very soon. But first I want you to fax everything to me." Jordan recited the number for Turk's fax machine. Then he gave her another precise order and hung up.

The fax machine began humming almost immediately, and sheet after sheet slid into the tray. With each new document the picture became clearer. In a matter of minutes the puzzle was complete. Jordan's mounting relief was tempered by the sobering truth of what he had just learned.

Jordan took a legal pad from the drawer and wrote a quick note. Below the note he added a short list of names. Pointing to the names on the pad, he said to Buster, "I want you to go find each of these people and show them this note. Will you do that for me?"

"Sure, Dr. Keyes," Buster said, scanning the names. "I know these people. I can find them for you."

"Good. When everyone has seen the note, come on back here."

"OK, I'll be back." Buster left the office with the pad under his arm.

Turning back to the phone, Jordan dialed the switchboard for a page. In less than a minute his party was on the line.

"Hello, Philip," he said. "This is Jordan."

Silence at first. "Jordan, I'm surprised to—"

"I'll bet you are surprised," Jordan cut in. "You sent your associate to kill me again, but he failed again."

"Jordan, don't be ridiculous. You're hallucinating. Your concussion must be worse than we first thought."

"I'm not hallucinating about being run off the road last night. And I did not imagine the physical assault at the hands of the same man a few minutes ago."

"Jordan, listen. I—"

"No, you listen to me, Philip," Jordan interrupted forcefully, his anger mounting. "Your triggerman is sitting in front of me, tied to a chair with a mile of duct tape. If you want the job done right, it looks like you'll have to do it yourself. I'm still in Turk's office, and it's just me and your bumbling accomplice."

The phone clicked off. Jordan pursed his lips, hoping he had not tipped his hand too soon. Then he sat back to await Philip's arrival.

THIRTY-SEVEN

Philip Ettinger wasted no time getting to the basement. He closed the door behind him but did not lock it. Jordan sat behind the desk in Turk's old swivel steno chair. The welcome effects of the painkiller were beginning to take hold. Saba, now fully awake, squirmed restlessly in his bonds.

Ettinger was impeccably dressed, as always, but the shadows on his face testified that he had been deprived of sleep for some time. Also missing from Ettinger's countenance was the welcoming warmth of friendship he had displayed toward Jordan in recent weeks.

"You're too smart to invite me here without alerting others as to your whereabouts," he said, standing in front of the desk with hands resting in the pockets of his lab coat. "And I'm sure you did not subdue my associate here without help. So I am not about to fall into your trap by getting rough with you so others walk in and see me as the bad guy. That's why I have an associate, though his failure in your case troubles me." Ettinger glanced at Saba with disdain. Saba averted his eyes.

Jordan did not respond. Ettinger continued, "In point of fact, Keyes, I don't need to lay a finger on you to finish what Saba could not. You seem to forget that you are not very popular around here. Ask anybody in the Neurosurgery Division. You are a rebel and a troublemaker, another California hotshot come to push your weight around and set people straight.

"And you are negligent in your practice of medicine. Hospital records clearly show that you are guilty of manslaughter in the case of Officer Beamon. You stashed away phenobarb and killed a cop with it. No, I don't have to kill you to get you out of my way, though I must admit it would be preferable. All I have to do is call security and explain that I found you here, deranged and dangerous, pummeling this poor aide."

"Allow me to make that call for you, Philip," Jordan said, reaching for the phone. He tapped in an extension and waited. Ettinger stood watching. His expression mirrored mild surprise and curiosity.

"Security? May I speak with Lavelle Goodwin, please?" Jordan said into the phone. "Lavelle, this is Dr. Keyes. I have a security problem to report. . . . That's correct. A hospital aide physically assaulted me. . . . Yes . . . I'm in the basement—the computer technical support office. . . . Yes, the aide is still here. He has been restrained. . . . Thank you, Lavelle. And will you please bring the nurse who is there in your office? . . . Very good, Lavelle. I'll be waiting for you."

"Nice try, Keyes," Ettinger said with a sneer as Jordan returned the receiver to its cradle, "but you are already in too deep. I have seen to that."

Before Jordan could respond, someone rapped on the door, then opened it and looked inside.

"Mr. Darwin, come in please," Jordan said, standing.

The malpractice attorney, wearing his trademark mismatched slacks, sport jacket, and tie, took one hesitant step into the room. "I was in the parking lot, just leaving the hospital," he explained, eyes flitting questioningly between Philip Ettinger and the man tied up in duct tape. "Sheffield paged me—told me to meet him here. Something about the policeman's death."

"I was hoping you would come," Jordan said. "I expect Dr. Sheffield and Dr. Waller shortly. Come on in."

Darwin took another cautious step inside. The questions

were obvious in his expression: *What is going on here? Why is that man restrained with tape? Do I really want to be here?*

"If you don't mind, Mr. Darwin, I'll save my explanation until everyone is here," Jordan said reassuringly. "By the way, have you met Dr. Philip Ettinger?"

Ettinger looked uneasy, as if he suddenly realized that he had walked into the wrong party. "Just leaving, actually, Mr. Darwin," he said, offering a weak hand as he sidled toward the door. Darwin was still captivated by the sight of a man gagged and taped to a folding chair.

"I think you ought to stay, Doctor," Jordan said forcefully. "You will be very interested in what I have to present." Ettinger stopped in his tracks. Jordan thought he would have made a run for the elevator, except such a response would have appeared very suspect to the wide-eyed lawyer.

At that moment, Taylor Sheffield and Bert Waller entered the room, followed by Buster Chapman. Sheffield was wearing one of his expensive tailored suits and a glower of disapproval. Waller, in green scrubs, had obviously come directly from surgery.

"What kind of a circus are you running down here, Dr. Keyes?" Sheffield demanded after seeing the prisoner. "And what are we supposed to make of this?" He held up the pad Jordan had sent with Buster to announce the impromptu meeting.

Jordan ignored the director's questions while he instructed Buster to round up a few more folding chairs for their guests. Buster slipped out of the room to get the chairs.

In the meantime, Philip Ettinger stole a glance at the note on the pad. "So you promise to introduce us to the person responsible for the death of Officer Beamon," he said. "Do you expect us to believe that this aide was responsible? Or have you called us here to confess what we already know—that you screwed up and killed the cop?"

Jordan sat on the corner of the desk, unruffled by

Ettinger's snide questions. "Gentlemen, I beg your patience until the last of our guests has arrived. I will explain everything, and my data is conclusive."

"Who else are you expecting, Jordan?" Dr. Waller asked, motioning to the pad still in Sheffield's hand. "We are the only ones on the list here."

"I have someone coming down from security—Lavelle Goodwin. And one of our SICU nurses will be with him."

"I'm due back in surgery in thirty minutes, Dr. Keyes," Waller said, uncharacteristically brusque. "This had better be important."

"This is vitally important, not only to me and each of you, but to Mercy Hospital and its patients. I'm sure that what I have to say will be worth the inconvenience to your schedule."

Buster returned with metal folding chairs and set them up around the desk in the suddenly crowded office. But no one sat down until Maggie, Sam, and hospital security officer Lavelle Goodwin entered moments later. Following Lavelle into the room was another man in jacket and tie, taking his place at the back of the room with Maggie, Sam, Lavelle, and Buster. Jordan and the man exchanged nods.

"As you all know," Jordan began, standing beside the desk, "the unfortunate death of Officer Eddie Beamon last week cast a shadow of suspicion on me and my skill as a physician. Each of you—Dr. Sheffield, Dr. Waller, Dr. Ettinger, Mr. Darwin—has been summoned here because you are involved in my case. I can prove to you conclusively today that I was not responsible for the overdose of phenobarb that killed Officer Beamon.

"Furthermore, I have come across certain information that strongly suggests that Beamon's death was not the result of someone's negligence. Rather, it was an intentional, cold-blooded act designed to impugn my career, remove me from Mercy Hospital, and possibly terminate my practice of medicine altogether."

"Are you asserting that someone killed that policeman for the express purpose of blaming you?" Sheffield interjected, openly incredulous.

"Yes, sir, I am. And when I began digging into the incident and putting the facts together, the attack on me turned personal and ruthless." Jordan briefly described his accident at the hands of the olive-skinned man bound to the chair in the corner of the office.

"Are you saying that this man here," Sheffield said, pointing to Saba, "murdered the policeman and almost killed you?"

"This was the man who crashed into my car last night and intended to kill me minutes ago with this." Jordan held up the syringe he had confiscated from Saba. "But I do not believe he is at the heart of the plot."

Ettinger cut in to address his colleagues. "In addition to a dislocated shoulder and fractured clavicle, Dr. Keyes suffered a serious concussion during his accident. I am very concerned about his mental and emotional state. He left his room this morning without being released by Dr. Jurgen, and he has been flitting around the hospital like a crazy man, avoiding those who want to care for him." Then, turning to Jordan, "With all due respect for your painful ordeal, I recommend at least twenty-four hours of bed rest before you attempt this taxing endeavor."

The dripping condescension in Ettinger's words soured Jordan's stomach. *Of course you want to put this off, Philip,* he thought, *because you are going to look very bad after I say my piece. You are trapped, and you know it.* Jordan beat back the temptation to lash out at him. The evidence would speak for itself.

"Actually, gentlemen, Philip is right," Jordan said. "I feel terrible, and I'm still a little fuzzy upstairs. But my mental and emotional state at the moment does not dilute the facts I am prepared to share with you. So I will simply show you the data I have found, and you can draw your own conclusions. Fair enough?"

His logic was irrefutable, so no answer was given.

Jordan held up the disk of Eddie Beamon's detailed charts copied by Turk DeVrees and handed a hard copy of their contents to Taylor Sheffield, who sat between Waller and Darwin. He pointed out the highlighted number 4664 and explained its relationship to the disappearance and reappearance of the phenobarbital injections.

Then he produced a sheet listing all the hospital ID codes assigned to hospital staff members and passed it to Sheffield. "ID codes are stored in the hospital's mainframe computer next door. When a physician or nurse makes a chart entry using his or her unique password, that person's name is entered on the chart. But the mainframe logs the action using a four-digit code that most staff members never see. Number 4664 belongs to Dr. Will Kopke. Dr. Kopke, of course, has been gone for five months, but someone used his password to tamper with Eddie Beamon's chart, making me appear negligent."

"It could be a computer glitch," Leonard Darwin advanced. "They're not perfect, you know."

"And anyone could have become privy to Will's password and used it," Ettinger put in, "even you, Dr. Keyes."

"Anything is possible," Jordan conceded. "For the moment, however, the computer record shows that Will Kopke's number is associated with an unusual sequence of entries on Eddie Beamon's chart. Furthermore, this is not the only place where number 4664 turns up in questionable circumstances."

Handing Sheffield a sheaf of reports from Mercy Hospital's pathology lab, Jordan explained that someone identified as 4664 directed that blood samples from scores of trauma patients be sent to an independent pathology lab in Wilsonville. The patients selected for these independent samples all claimed religious affiliation with known Christian groups. Jordan supplied Sheffield with the documentation. Leonard Darwin and Bert Waller leaned in to peruse the pages with him. Philip Ettinger sat with arms folded, staring at the stack of documents on the desk yet to be presented.

"Why were these people selected for this special screening?" Jordan continued. "I had to visit Hematech Labs in Wilsonville to find out, because none of the reports were returned to our lab."

"Hematech? They specialize in genetics, don't they?" Taylor Sheffield's irritation had evolved into genuine curiosity.

"That's correct," Jordan said. "I was able to obtain eleven reports of blood samples submitted to Hematech by 'Will Kopke.' The reports turned out to be DNA studies. I'm not up on genetics, especially the latest developments. So I had a friend in L.A. look at the studies for me. He teaches genetics at the USC Medical Center. Here's the report I received from him within the past hour." Jordan handed over another short stack of papers.

Jordan sat on the edge of the desk while Sheffield scanned the data. The Demerol had taken the edge off his pain, but it had not increased his stamina. He felt very weak.

"The Turnbull marker," Sheffield said with surprise mixed with disdain. His eyes were fixed on the sheet in his hand.

"What's a Turnbull marker?" Darwin wondered aloud, craning his neck for a better look at the report in Sheffield's hand.

"About four years ago, a research scientist named Eli Turnbull made what he thought was a breakthrough discovery," Jordan explained. "Turnbull isolated a gene marker that he linked to a number of forms of aggressive, incurable cancer. His initial claims drew rabid interest in the medical community, which first thought that this aged, relatively unknown researcher had opened the door to a cancer cure. But in a matter of weeks his findings were discounted by others in the field, and Eli Turnbull dropped out of sight as quickly as he had appeared."

"Spurious data," Sheffield muttered, still scanning the report. "The man was a quack."

Jordan nodded.

"So there never was a Turnbull marker?" Leonard Darwin probed. "It was just a hoax?"

"The marker exists, all right," Jordan said, "but geneticists are divided on what it means. Turnbull's theory, however, has been disproven."

"So what's the point?" Darwin asked.

Jordan continued. "Even though Dr. Turnbull's discovery was discredited, he attracted a tiny but loyal following in the scientific community. My friend in genetics writes that Turnbull and his disciples are holed up in some lab somewhere trying to prove his theory and cash in on a cancer breakthrough. Every so often Dr. Turnbull presents a new paper at an obscure futurist's conference, usually to an empty room."

"He is the quintessential mad scientist, Leonard, if you ask me," Sheffield said.

Leonard Darwin took the sheaf of Hematech reports from Sheffield's hand. "What does a no-account quack have to do with these reports?"

Jordan paused a moment. "The gene marker Eli Turnbull insists is linked to cancer appears in the DNA of each of these eleven patients. According to Turnbull and his disciples, incurable cancer was imminent and inescapable for these patients. They were the very people Eli Turnbull wanted to warn and to help."

"So what about these patients?" Darwin pressed, waving the reports. "Did any of them turn up with cancer?"

Jordan glanced at Philip Ettinger, whose face mirrored cool defiance. "We will never know, Mr. Darwin," Jordan said, "because every one of them died unexpectedly in our Surgical Intensive Care Unit shortly after their DNA studies were performed."

THIRTY-EIGHT

Sheffield picked up the questioning. "They all died? How?"

"What you would probably expect," Jordan explained. "Various complications from their presenting condition. At least that's what was entered on their death certificate."

"Could there be something else? Were autopsies performed?" Sheffield bored in.

"No autopsies were required for these patients because the cause of death was ostensibly related to their injuries. The families of three patients requested autopsies, and the hospital referred them to Dr. Joseph Wiggins."

"Joseph is a good man," Bert Waller put in.

"And the results of those autopsies?" Darwin said.

"Each confirmed the original cause of death."

"What are you getting at, Keyes?" Sheffield pressed, showing impatience. "If Eli Turnbull's theory is a futile grasping at genetic straws, what's the point of these reports from Hematech? More importantly, what do they have to do with the death of Officer Beamon?"

"Before I answer, Dr. Sheffield," Jordan said, "I need to share one more piece of information from our mainframe, something brought to my attention just today."

Philip Ettinger snorted with contempt. "Not another dubious contribution from that mercenary computer tech?"

Jordan answered, keen to Ettinger's sense of panic at the

noose of evidence closing around his neck, "Turk DeVrees provided the information, but the data came straight from our mainframe. It concerns the passwords we all use. For any transaction entered on the hospital computer, our passwords key the ID code that is entered on hospital data. The computer knows everyone's password, of course, and passwords can be retrieved if you know where they are stored."

Placing the sheet in Sheffield's hand, Jordan said, "Will Kopke's ID code, 4664, was responsible for the blood samples sent to Hematech and for the aberrations on Eddie Beamon's chart. Dr. Sheffield, this sheet lists all the ID codes and passwords from our mainframe. You may be interested in the password linked to number 4664.

Sheffield ran his finger down a list of figures until he found 4664. His eye jumped to the corresponding word in the list of passwords. Leonard Darwin strained to see the data.

Looking up with an expression of bewilderment, Sheffield said, "Turnbull. The password is Turnbull."

Jordan nodded. From the corner of his eye, he saw Philip Ettinger purse his lips and begin to fidget. The irrepressible Maxine had thrown him another curve by revealing information he assumed was buried deep in her vast memory.

"Dr. Sheffield, here's my point," Jordan said. "I have become convinced that there are closet disciples of Eli Turnbull at Mercy Hospital—at least two. Except our Turnbulls—who use the ID code 4664—have taken their interest in those afflicted with the Turnbull marker to the extreme, something that would likely make old Eli gasp in disbelief. These people have taken it upon themselves to play God in the life of patients whose DNA contains the marker.

"Our Turnbull devotees have been submitting patient blood samples to Hematech Labs for at least sixteen months—perhaps longer. I was able to obtain only eleven lab reports, but there are many more in the Hematech computer system. I'm sure the staff at Hematech have no idea how their routine genetic screenings were being used.

"Patients from Mercy Hospital who were screened for the Turnbull marker have a unique profile. They were all from Surgical Intensive Care. Though often in extremely critical condition, all were good candidates for recovery. And, curiously, all professed to be people of Christian faith—at least they identified with Christian churches or groups. By contrast, SICU patients who were members of an eastern religion, a cult, a New Age group, or who claimed no religious preference were not screened."

"Are you implying, Dr. Keyes, that someone in our hospital is killing patients because they claimed to be religious?" The whine of disbelief in Sheffield's tone was edged with horror.

"Not exactly," Jordan said. "I believe the people responsible for these deaths were motivated by what they perceived to be a much higher calling. Impacted by the dubious work of Eli Turnbull's group, they were moved by acute concern that some people of religious faith are genetically predisposed to terminal cancer. So at some point prior to last year, Eli Turnbull's disciples at Mercy Hospital began screening so-called Christian SICU patients for the marker. No harm done there. Blood work for numerous procedures is common, and genetic blind studies in need of samples are popping up everywhere.

"However, these people were apparently convinced that the supposedly Christian patients were destined to suffer the ravages of an incurable disease, bringing immeasurable heartache and pain to themselves and to their loved ones. They may have regarded the critical injuries suffered by these patients as God's merciful intervention, sparing them from future agony—mercy that our expert trauma care reversed.

"For example, my former patient Ms. Aguilera was critically injured in a motorcycle accident that killed her boyfriend. Had it not been for emergency brain surgery, she would have died within an hour of her arrival at the Trauma Center. Unknown to me at the time, a blood sample from Ms. Aguilera, an avowed Roman Catholic, was sent to Hematech Labs. The report, which is in the collection of reports you are holding, Dr. Sheffield, shows that the Hispanic woman has the Turnbull marker.

"I believe at least two people at the hospital were moved with a twisted measure of compassion for Ms. Aguilera. I believe they regarded the emergency medical treatment that saved the woman's life as a tempting of fate. I believe they quietly—and in their view, mercifully—ended Ms. Aguilera's life with a secret lethal injection, intending to spare her and her family the future pain indelibly written into her genetic script. They have killed at least thirty more supposedly Christian SICU patients over the last sixteen months."

"But where does the religious preference fit in?" Darwin said, appearing stunned. "If you're going to euthanize cancer victims, why do so to religious people and not to others?"

"I don't know the answer to that question, Mr. Darwin," Jordan returned. "Perhaps our suspects are secretly anti-God or anti-Christian. Perhaps they were convinced that these people were ready to meet their Maker. I hope to know the exact answer very soon."

"Mercy killings at Mercy Hospital?" Leonard Darwin breathed the sad irony aloud.

"In the eyes of these people, yes—mercy extended to critically injured patients who were better off dead, people like Trudy Aguilera."

"A noble effort of deduction, Dr. Keyes, but you are forgetting something." Philip Ettinger was now sitting erect in his chair. The worry on his face had been replaced by a glint of triumph. "Your patient, Ms. Aguilera, was subject to a postmortem examination. And I believe you stated that at least two other allegedly euthanized victims had been examined by a pathologist in private practice. Did those autopsies detect the presence of a lethal substance?"

"No, Dr. Ettinger, they did not. That is because Dr. Joseph Wiggins, whom the hospital recommends for independent postmortems, was in league with those at the hospital who were lethally injecting patients like Trudy Aguilera. Whenever an autopsy was requested by the family, Dr. Wiggins conveniently falsified the report to confirm the original cause of death. He may be a sympathizer with Eli Turnbull or just an unethical physician turning a few extra bucks."

Dr. Waller remained stoic and quiet at the charge that Wiggins, a "good man" in his estimation, was in collusion with a murderer.

Turning to Dr. Sheffield, Jordan continued. "The autopsy issue is the point at which our murderers' quiet, efficient ministry of mercy began to unravel. Following the death of Ms. Aguilera, I was upset that the body was not examined postmortem. I not only sounded off to my colleagues about it, I talked the family into a private autopsy—and paid for it myself. Dr. Wiggins, of course, confirmed the cause of death: complications from severe head trauma. I know beyond all doubt, however, that further examination of Ms. Aguilera's remains will reveal a lethal substance in her system."

"Preposterous, utter fiction," Ettinger muttered loudly enough for Jordan to hear.

He ignored the aside. "My curiosity apparently provoked some panic among this murderous band. The overdose of phenobarbital and subsequent evidence incriminating me in the death of Officer Beamon was an attempt to get me out of the picture. When I got even closer to the truth, this man—" he motioned toward Saba—"was commissioned to kill me, first by running me off the road, then by coming at me with this." He displayed the syringe loaded with potassium.

Dr. Sheffield spoke up. "I must agree with Philip's response, Jordan: This sounds preposterous. If you are set to accuse someone, then do so, and let us or the police check it out."

Jordan returned the syringe to the desktop and retrieved yet another sheaf of printouts. "Again, the mainframe computer supplies a vital bit of data. Not only does it recognize and store passwords and ID codes linked to user activity, it also knows where that activity originates. Every PC in the hospital has a unique electronic signature. So every transaction with the mainframe is internally stamped with the PC's encoded make, model, and serial number. The sheets in my hand identify the computers that were used to order blood samples and to tamper with Officer Beamon's chart."

Dr. Sheffield opened his hand to receive the documents, but this time Jordan did not give them up. He leafed through several pages briefly to review the highlighted markings. Then he returned the sheets to the desktop to address his small audience.

"Two computers in the hospital were used to enter physician orders under the ID code 4664. The first computer currently is assigned to me. I inherited my office and workstation from my predecessor, the late Dr. Will Kopke. Prior to Kopke's death, most of the blood samples sent to Hematech Labs last year were ordered from his computer. Apparently Dr. Kopke or someone with virtually unlimited access to his computer was actively involved in the mercy deaths of a number of SICU patients.

"Following Dr. Kopke's fatal accident last fall, the blood samples were no longer ordered from the computer in my office. The evidence is circumstantial yet convincing that Dr. Kopke was indeed involved in the plot, because with his death the center of operation moved to another computer in the hospital. That computer belongs to Dr. Philip Ettinger."

Ettinger jumped to his feet, fists planted on hips, face suddenly crimson. "I am outraged at such an accusation, Dr. Keyes. I don't know about where you come from, but we share our equipment around here. My computer is available to a number of people in the Neurosurgery Division every day. I resent being implicated in the macabre fantasy you have foisted on us today. And I resent being accused as the murderer you have invented."

Jordan stood and came around to the front of the desk, only a few feet from him. Ettinger's dark eyes were wide and intense, like those of a cornered animal weighing the options of fight and flight. Jordan had always regarded Philip Ettinger as too refined and genteel to fight. But at this moment he sensed great potential for physical harm from the tall man who was slender and bookish, but not weak. Jordan did not want the confrontation to lead to a brawl, abbreviated though it might be by the presence of others who would intervene. And he did not want a clash with Ettinger to dull the final point of his presentation.

"Yes, I understand that the hospital's PCs are accessible to a number of staff members, Philip," he said with measured calmness. "I am merely stating that your computer's signature appears on the orders for blood samples sent to Hematech. Will you allow me that observation?" The occupants of the room were hushed, with every eye appraising the distance between Jordan's face and Philip's clenched fists. Yet as silent seconds passed, the futility of a physical confrontation seemed to register on Ettinger's face. He sat down without answering.

Jordan leaned back to a half-sitting position on the desktop. Returning to the sheets in his hand, he addressed Sheffield again. "The most critical item concerns the reports prepared by Hematech for the blood samples in question. The person who received those reports should know something about the identity and motives of the person or persons who use the password *Turnbull.*

"The reports themselves do not tell us where they were sent. But our computer remembers every incoming fax received by the PCs in the hospital. Again, according to the computer's records, only one computer at Mercy Hospital has received faxes from Hematech Labs over the past sixteen months." Jordan drew a long, silent breath. "And that computer is in the office of Dr. Bert Waller."

During most of Jordan's presentation, Dr. Waller had seemed politely disinterested and impatient. He typified the task-oriented surgeon for whom even a necessary meeting was a waste of valuable surgery time. As the eyes of the hospital director and the attorney turned toward him, he remained impassive, as if he had not heard his name spoken.

"Bert, you knew about these reports?" Sheffield said, clearly disbelieving it possible.

Dr. Waller did not move or blink—staring through the walls as if lost in thought. Jordan did not want to say any more. He owed his superior the opportunity to give an explanation. He hoped the man would make a clean breast of it. If he would not—or if he *could* not, believing he and the "ministry of mercy" in which he was a participant were somehow above human law—the information yet in Jordan's hand would undeniably refute him.

"Bert, what about these reports?" Sheffield insisted. "What about the DNA studies? Did you know about them? Did you authorize them?"

Bert Waller remained statue-still for several moments. Then his face erupted into a cherubic grin, as if deeply pleased. Lifting his glowing face to Jordan, he said, "Do you know what it feels like, Dr. Keyes, to be used as an instrument to deliver people from pain and grief? Of course you do. Anyone who practices the healing arts has sensed the exhilaration of saving a human life by interposing his God-given skills between human tragedy and death. It's what we live for, isn't it, Dr. Keyes? It's what keeps us doing what we do eighty or ninety hours, week in and week out.

"Well, I have found a greater thrill, Doctor," Waller went on, eyes glistening with tears. "I have tasted the supreme ecstasy of interposing my medical skills not between tragedy and death but between people and the pain hurled at them by fate and the devil himself. Can you imagine how it feels knowing that your one simple, compassionate act of mercy has averted heartache, misery, and grief for untold numbers of people? Can you understand what it means knowing that a beautiful young woman will be spared the torture of a cancer that will literally eat her away to nothing? Can you estimate the fulfillment I have tasted, knowing that a man permanently scarred and disabled from an accident will be spared the double tragedy of prolonged suffering that we cannot cure?"

Waller was not engaging him in a conversation, Jordan knew. There was no need to respond, only to listen and lament that a gifted healer had been deceived into believing that ending a human life could be something other than heinous and wrong.

"And what would you give, Dr. Keyes, to ease the torment of the individual who faces a year or two of blinding pain? What would you give to bring peace to that person's heartbroken family, to spare them the futile, crushing financial burden? Better yet, what would you give to quell that torment and heartbreak before it erupts? This is the ultimate healing art: to stop the hurt before it happens. It is the ultimate and final expression of mercy."

The room was a tomb of silence. Taylor Sheffield and Leonard Darwin were stunned as much by Waller's triumphant demeanor as by his chilling confession. Maggie, with Sam holding her, stood at the back of the room, smothering a cry of shock with her hand. Eyes blinking rapidly, Philip Ettinger would not look at anyone. Even the fidgety Saba was suddenly still.

"Dr. Waller," Jordan said at last, his voice just above a whisper, "Trudy Aguilera was only twenty-eight years old. She loved her parents, her brothers, her sisters. She was a strong young woman who had survived a terrible accident and lifesaving brain surgery. She had no signs of cancer. The presence of the Turnbull marker was no threat to her health. Trudy Aguilera had a life of promise ahead. But you took it away from her. You took that woman's life, Dr. Waller."

"Aha, that's what you don't understand, Doctor," Waller returned, as assured and levelheaded in his tone as Jordan had ever heard him. "Fate—or God, if you prefer—took that girl's life in the motorcycle accident, not me. Fate or God saved her from her cancerous future stamped into her genetic code. You pulled her back, Dr. Keyes, because you didn't know any better. You're a very good doctor and a very good Christian, but you have a lot to learn about life and death and mercy. The only thing I took from your patient was the insurmountable pain that lay ahead for her and her family. It was the same for all the others. And since they had apparently made peace with their Maker, they are all in a better place. Those who had yet to come to terms with him, we left alone so they might do so."

Leonard Darwin nodded slightly, his question about religious preference answered.

"Dr. Will Kopke was involved in your work, correct, Dr. Waller?" Jordan continued. No one else in the room moved or spoke, for fear that the solemnity would shatter before the full truth was disclosed.

"Will was a good man, Jordan," Waller said, nodding. "We were like-minded in our respect for the genius of Dr. Eli Turnbull, genius you people will never begin to appreciate."

"Turnbull is as wild as the March Hare, Bert," Sheffield said, visibly trembling at the sudden revelation, "but he has never advocated killing patients."

Waller shrugged away the comment as of no importance. "Dr. Turnbull is an intellectual genius but an emotional and spiritual imbecile. He has no concept of mercy."

"And Dr. Wiggins?" Jordan said, recalling that he was also a "good man" in Waller's estimation.

"A convenient and thankfully unconscionable associate to our ministry of mercy."

"Dr. Waller, *you murdered defenseless patients."* Jordan emphasized the sobering words without raising his voice one decibel. "Dr. Wiggins falsified autopsy reports and lied to families who placed implicit trust in him. How can you talk about mercy? How can you talk about ministry?"

"I don't expect you to understand, Jordan," Waller said condescendingly. "You are so absorbed with the religious box you're in that you have no capacity for universal truth. You are so concerned with good that you cannot see the greater good. Yours is a common problem. Our simple ministry would have continued unnoticed had it not been for the limited vision and obstinate cooperation of an associate who—"

Ettinger's chair toppled backward with a crash as he sprang toward Jordan. With one swift motion the lanky neurosurgeon subdued Jordan and secured him as a shield between himself and the others. Ettinger grabbed the syringe from the desktop and held it aloft, aiming the needle at his hostage's neck.

"Stay back or I will kill him!" Ettinger warned, a demonic glare underscoring his threat. "I can do it. I *will* do it, if necessary. I have already eliminated one physician for getting in my way. I have no problem killing another one."

THIRTY-NINE

No one moved. The syringe poised only inches from the hostage's neck effectively nullified for the moment the fact that the attacker was cornered and outnumbered. Jordan froze in Ettinger's grip, eyes locked on the plunger of the syringe aimed at him.

"You murdered Dr. Kopke?" Taylor Sheffield gasped.

"A conveniently prearranged skiing accident," Ettinger answered with a fiendish glare. "The man had usurped my place."

Sheffield muttered a disbelieving curse.

Ettinger eyed the man in the back of the room standing next to Sam and Maggie Rusch. "You're a police officer, right?" he demanded.

The man moved his hands slowly away from his body and the pistol holstered under his gray tweed jacket. "Lyle Bohanon, detective with the Portland Police," he said. "If you just put down the needle carefully, we can talk about—"

"I'm not interested in hostage negotiations, Detective. I just want to walk away from this hospital," Ettinger snarled. "And if you try to play hero, this man's death will plague your conscience for the rest of your life."

"No problem, Doctor," Bohanon said in his most assuring tone. "We can work this out. Just be careful with that needle."

Expressions of shock and fear across the room were contrasted by a look of righteous indignation on Bert Waller's face. "You are a worthless failure, Philip, a Judas," he said with disdain. "You failed me, you failed yourself, you failed our mission of mercy. You have no future in medicine or in life. You would do better to plunge that needle into yourself. Your impudence, greed, and impatience have not only brought down your career in medicine, they have effectively terminated our ministry of mercy."

"It was *your* mission of mercy, Bert, not mine," Ettinger snapped. "You are as crazy as that old lunatic Turnbull. I helped you and Kopke put patients to sleep because I thought it was my ticket to my rightful position as the head of my department. With that on my résumé, I could have moved up to Harvard or NYU or Johns Hopkins. But you and Kopke and now Keyes made the mistake of tampering with my destiny. My career may be over, but I'm not going to death row with you."

Jordan sensed mounting rage in the rough grip of his captor. "I think Dr. Waller is wrong, Philip," he said, hoping to prevent a physical outburst that could plunge the needle into his skin. "You are not worthless. You are of great value to God. No matter what happens here today, you are a person of infinite worth to him."

"Save the altar call, my friend," Philip cut in cynically. "Your greatest service to me and to yourself right now is to escort me to the parking garage. Let's start moving. Everybody just stay where you are, or I will use this syringe. I swear it."

Jordan thought he had prepared for this eventuality. Before Ettinger had entered the office, Jordan had found a key chain with a tiny can of pepper spray while rummaging through Turk's desk. Not knowing what to expect during their confrontation, he had hidden the small can in the sling supporting his injured left arm in case he needed to defend himself. But when Ettinger grabbed him, the can had moved inside the sling, sliding down near his elbow and out of reach.

Jordan did not want to leave the room with Ettinger. The dark side that had emerged from him in the last few hours was terrifying. Philip Ettinger had killed patients with lethal injections, and he had arranged the death of a colleague, perhaps through Saba. How desperate was he to escape? Jordan did not want to find out by pushing Philip to his limit.

Ettinger emphasized his intention to leave by tightening the grip around his captive's arm and torso until it sparked a flash of pain and a moan. Jordan had to cooperate, while biding his time and waiting for the chance to reach for the pepper spray.

When Ettinger began edging Jordan toward the door, Saba sounded off behind his gag and squirmed violently in his chair. Ettinger ignored his nonverbal demand for release. Everyone else stayed put, eyeing the treacherous syringe hovering near Jordan's neck. Sam and Maggie clung to each other, faces drawn with fear for their friend. Even Detective Bohanon backed slowly away from the door, giving wide berth to the two men moving as one.

"Open the door for us, Buster," Ettinger demanded. The janitor, white with fright, complied, then stepped quickly away. "I do not want to hear this door open behind us," Ettinger threatened. Then he pulled Jordan through and kicked the door closed.

The staff parking garage was adjacent to the basement, accessible by a door near the elevator. The detective would likely call in backup, Jordan thought, and they might never get out of the garage. Perhaps the Portland Police Critical Response Team had already been called in, waiting for Ettinger with guns trained on the door into the basement.

"You don't need me anymore, Philip," he said as Ettinger pushed him hurriedly through the empty hall. "Just run for your car. I won't follow you."

"You are all the insurance I have, my friend," Ettinger

said, forcing him onward. "If there are any surprises waiting for us in the garage, I need you close at hand."

Rounding the corner, they encountered an elderly woman with a walker and her husband waiting for an elevator. "Good morning, folks," Ettinger sang cheerily as he pushed Jordan by them.

"Good morning," they replied in unison, thoroughly distracted by the unusual sight of one doctor with a syringe in his hand practically carrying another doctor to the garage door.

As Ettinger threw open the door to the parking garage and pushed his hostage through it, Jordan feared being mowed down by a hail of police bullets. He had seen law enforcement programs in which officials insisted that terrorist demands would never be honored, even if it cost the lives of hostages—the sacrifice of the few for the many. At this moment Jordan prayed that the Portland police would err on the side of caution.

But there were no police in the garage. Ettinger tightened his grip on Jordan and rushed him past a dozen cars until they reached a forest green Mercedes sedan. Released momentarily while Ettinger reached for his keys, Jordan was tempted to bolt. But Philip Ettinger was disturbed and trapped. In Jordan's state, Philip could catch him in a few steps. What would prevent him from following through with his threat to use the syringe of potassium one more time?

Opening the driver's door, Ettinger ordered, "Get in and climb over to the other side. Hurry!" Jordan slipped into the driver's leather bucket, then clambered over the center console to the passenger's bucket with Ettinger and his deadly needle right behind him. But before the door was closed, the sound of squealing tires could be heard in the garage. One car and maybe more were moving fast in their direction.

A new fear flashed hotly through Jordan's veins. Was he about to become the helpless victim in a high-speed chase?

Did Philip Ettinger think he could outrun the police? Terrifying images in his memory goaded Jordan to avoid another crash at all costs.

After slamming the door, Ettinger transferred the syringe to his left hand to insert the key in the ignition and fire up the engine. As he did, Jordan unobtrusively slipped his hand deep into the sling, located the tiny can, and positioned his finger over the trigger. The bawling tires in the garage grew louder. Panic and perspiration obvious on his face, Ettinger reached for the gearshift with his right hand.

Jordan acted. Withdrawing the can from his sling, Jordan thrust it at Ettinger's eyes and depressed the trigger. A burst of liquid pepper spray hit Ettinger in the right eye as the car slipped into reverse. Howling with surprise and pain, he reacted instinctively. His right hand flew to his eyes, and his legs stiffened, involuntarily tromping the accelerator to the floor. The Mercedes screeched backward from its parking space, slamming into the rear end of the new Explorer parked behind it.

Jolted by the impact, Jordan had only an instant to avert two grave and immediate dangers. The deadly syringe was still in Ettinger's hand. Jordan expected him either to lash out blindly in the direction of the passenger's seat or to slam the car into drive and try to ram his way out of the parking garage. Neither option appealed to Jordan's heightened sense of self-preservation. So before Ettinger could do either, Jordan threw open the door, dove to the cement floor, and rolled.

As he did, the Mercedes bolted forward, engine roaring, tires screaming and smoking. The blinded driver again failed to clear the impediments in the garage, this time crashing head-on into a huge cement support column. Blue-and-white patrol cars squealed to a stop on either side of the suddenly mangled and immobile Mercedes. In just a few seconds, the police had subdued and handcuffed Philip Ettinger. Only then did Jordan begin to feel the slashing pain in his shoulder and notice that his scrubs and sling in that area were stained with his blood.

◆ ◆ ◆

Ninety minutes later, Jordan was back in the hospital bed he had escaped from six hours earlier. Portland Police Detective Lyle Bohanon and hospital security chief Lavelle Goodwin had visited him in the Trauma Center shortly after his incision was resutured. Philip Ettinger, Bert Waller, and Saba were in custody, and the box of evidence from Turk's office had been secured for the district attorney's office, including the syringe retrieved from Ettinger's totaled Mercedes.

When Jordan expressed his concern about Della's imminent arrival at the airport, Lavelle took the project as his own. He promised to meet her at the gate and bring her directly to the hospital.

Dr. Sheffield and Leonard Darwin had also stopped by before Jordan left the Trauma Center. They expressed their shock and regret about what had happened to him, and they apologized sincerely for their suspicion and distrust. Sheffield practically begged Jordan not to leave the hospital over the incident. He instructed Jordan to take as much time off as he needed to fully recover from his injuries. He even offered him the use of his late-model Cadillac Sedan DeVille—his "second car"—until the Lexus was replaced. Having lost the head of Surgery and the acting head of neurosurgery in one morning, Sheffield was clearly desperate to retain the services of an outspoken but intelligent and resourceful neurosurgeon.

"What did you tell Dr. Sheffield about staying on?" Maggie probed after he told her about the visit. She and Sam had come in when they found out that Jordan had been sewn up and returned to his room. The discussion turned to Sheffield's comments after several solemn minutes reflecting on the deception that had seduced Bert Waller and Philip Ettinger to commit murder in the name of mercy.

"I told him I'd think about it," Jordan said, still a little fuzzy-headed from another dose of pain medication. "Today is not a good day to make a decision about the next ten or fifteen years of my life."

"Would you even consider leaving?" Sam put in. "I mean, you have only been here a couple of months."

Jordan took a sip from the straw in his water glass. "I decided on Mercy Hospital a few months ago, but I . . . I did so without considering my wife's thoughts—more importantly, her feelings—on the matter. Della has a new business in L.A., and she and Katy have their friends. I need to revisit the issue of Portland with my wife. In fact, Della and I have a lot to talk about."

There was a glimmer of pride in Maggie's broad smile. "That's great, Jordy. That's really great."

Jordan smiled, then looked away thoughtfully for several moments. "In twelve years of marriage, I have given Della everything I thought she needed. I worked hard to get through residency and establish my practice because I wanted to provide a nice home for her, to shower her with things she wanted. You two have helped me see that, while meeting some of Della's wants, I have failed to provide what she really needs: me.

"Della is a wonderful person, and I have been so wrong not to make our relationship a priority. I never knew how important it was that I give her myself, my heart. I guess, down deep, I have been afraid that if I really gave myself to her I would lose her like I lost my mother and J. J. Thank you both for showing me how to deal with my pain and fear."

Buster Chapman's large frame filled the doorway. "Are you OK now, Dr. Keyes?"

"Come on in, Buster," Jordan said, summoning him with his right hand. "Yes, I'm doing fine. I may even convince Dr. Jurgen to let me go home later today."

Buster came to the bedside and comforted Jordan with a

simple pat on his good shoulder. The man's face was haggard from lack of sleep, and a pall of perplexity was visible in his furrowed brow. "Why did our doctors kill the patients, Dr. Keyes? Those people didn't hurt anybody." Buster's chin trembled slightly as he blinked away small tears.

It occurred to Jordan that Katy would likely ask him the same question someday soon. His answer to her would need to be as sensible and uncomplicated as his explanation to the compassionate man who had unwittingly taught him so much about dealing with people in pain.

"They made a terrible mistake, Buster. They thought they were doing something good for people when they were doing something very bad. They thought they should decide when patients live and die instead of letting God decide that. They forgot how important it is for a doctor to help everyone get well. They forgot how important it is to live."

Buster grappled with the difficult words for a moment. "The devil played a bad trick on them," he said at last, wiping a tear from his cheek with his thumb.

The theological implications of Buster's simple statement begged a response. Why do decent, intelligent people do bad things? And how do moral people arrive at the place where something as wrong as murder becomes right in their eyes? The complicated issues of sin, satanic influence and deception, warped human thinking, and free will are not fully served in the statement "the devil made me do it." But for now, a simple answer would have to suffice. "Yes, the devil tricked Dr. Waller, Dr. Kopke, and Dr. Ettinger," Jordan said. "And what is worse, they let him do it."

Someone else entered the room, but Buster's large frame blocked Jordan's view. A quick hand signal from Maggie cued the janitor to step back.

Lavelle Goodwin, wearing a father-of-the-bride grin, ushered Della to the bedside. There were no tears in her dark eyes, but Della's sober countenance telegraphed her relief at finding her husband well. She gripped Jordan's right hand

and kissed him lightly on the lips. "I can't believe what Lavelle has been telling me," she said. "You could have been killed."

Jordan had been waiting for her to walk in the door; nevertheless, he was stunned at the touch of her hand and her subtle, familiar fragrance. "It's all over now, Dell, and everything is going to be fine," he said, thinking far beyond recovery from his injuries.

Maggie, Sam, and Buster edged quietly toward the door, but Jordan would not let them go without an introduction. "I owe my life to this man," he said as Della shook Buster's meaty hand, "and I can't tell you how helpful Maggie and Sam have been in getting me through this ordeal. Thank you all, very much." After the brief exchange, Maggie herded her husband, Buster, and Lavelle from the room.

Jordan knew he must rest if he hoped to be released from the hospital by late afternoon. But Della had many questions, and he did not want her to leave. She pulled a chair to the bedside and sat down. Jordan held her hand to keep her near while he recounted the details of the story Lavelle had started as he drove her to the hospital.

"I'm going to be off for a few weeks, and I want to come home with you," he concluded. "I want us to spend time together. I want to see the home you're doing in Agoura Hills. I want to hear your plans for the decorating business."

"All right," Della said guardedly. "That would be good."

"And I want us to talk about Portland. This may not be the place for us right now. I want to hear what you think about it and feel about it . . . so we can decide together."

Della nodded slowly, as if expecting a punch line. There was none.

"There are other things I need to share with you, Dell," Jordan continued, more subdued, "personal things, painful things. It will be difficult for me, and it will take me some time. But I want to open up to you because I don't want you to be alone anymore."

Della's eyes misted slightly. "All right, Jordan, I guess we can work on that." After a long breath, she said, "Then I had better get you a ticket to L.A. while you rest. When will you be ready to fly?"

The idea had barely dawned in Jordan's brain before he spoke it. "I don't want to fly home, Dell; I want us to drive to L.A. together. Katy can stay with Grandma, can't she?"

Della was shocked. "Drive? Jordan, it's a thousand miles to L.A."

"Just you and me, Dell. We'll take two or three days. We can spend the night in San Francisco, eat dinner on Fisherman's Wharf. How often do we get a chance like this?"

"What about your shoulder?"

"I can drive one-handed. You can drive. No problem."

Della could not subdue a growing smile of surprise. "You're really serious. What's gotten into you?"

"I just feel it could be a great time for us."

"But your Lexus is totaled. We don't have a car up here."

"I just happen to know where I can get my hands on a silver Caddy, and all we have to buy is the gas." Jordan laughed as he said it, and it felt very good.

FORTY

Two and a half weeks after the accident, Jordan had recovered well enough to get along without the sling. There was still some tenderness in his shoulder and around the incision, so he had to avoid sudden movement and take care not to bump into things on his left side. But he was sleeping much better, and he was able to tackle a few minor chores around the house on the days Della was at work.

Sitting on the patio waiting for Della to change clothes, Jordan realized it had taken him just as long to prepare mentally and emotionally for what he would do this afternoon. It was Mother's Day, and they had been home from church long enough to eat a light brunch. Katy was spending a few hours with the church youth group taking flowers to neglected mothers in a nursing home. Jordan would take Della, Katy, and her parents to Mother's Day dinner at the Chart House later in the day. In the meantime, Jordan and Della would be alone for almost three hours. He had asked her to change into casual clothes because he wanted to take her for a short drive.

Basking in the spring sunshine as he waited, Jordan reflected on the time he had been home. In his view, the long drive from Portland had gone reasonably well. Conversation had been a little contrived at times, and there were sustained periods on the road when neither of them had anything to say. But Jordan had not expected the distance between him and Della to dissolve in two days. As Della had blurted out on the phone one day, there was a part of him that was gone, that she could not reach. Jordan knew it would take some time to open up to her, face his pain, and heal emotionally.

Being off work and at home for all this time had been torture for Jordan. Conditioned for fast-paced, high-stress twelve-to-sixteen-hour days, his transition to temporary househusband and Mr. Mom had taxed his self-discipline to the limit. He yearned to be in the hospital—any hospital—doing something productive in the field he loved. Gamely fighting off the urge, he channeled his energies into projects at home, which were particularly challenging when done one-handed. He was up early every morning to help prepare breakfast and get Katy off to school. On the days Della's work took her out of the house, Jordan replaced leaky washers, weeded the front flower beds, installed a new water purifier for the kitchen sink—any little chore he could handle to make their home, which was still on the market, more salable.

Jordan also used his forced downtime for long sessions of Bible reading. Maggie and Sam Rusch's penetrating questions and comments had brought him up short about the emotional chasm he had created in his relationship with Della. He longed for the blessings that openness and vulnerability with his wife would bring. Furthermore, Buster Chapman's example of tender care for hurting patients and their families had exposed Jordan's glaring ignorance of the concept of compassion. So on the afternoons he was home alone, Jordan took his Bible out to the patio and began reading through the Gospels.

He had never noticed before how important relationships were to the Savior. Jesus Christ was the Creator of heaven and earth, the Lamb of God come to take away the sins of the world. Yet he loved and needed the rough-hewn men called to be his disciples. Jordan marveled at the tender words *whom he loved* used to describe Christ's close friends at Bethany: Mary, Martha, and Lazarus. It intrigued Jordan that the Master apparently retreated to Bethany to be with them, especially when he was under pressure. Perhaps even Jesus found a portion of his Father's comfort waiting for him there.

Jordan was also astounded at the description of Jesus that so frequently recurred: "Jesus was filled with compassion." The shortest verse in the Bible, he noted, the easiest for anyone to remember, referred to Christ's heart of compassion: "Jesus wept."

Every afternoon session in the Gospels ended with several minutes of spontaneous, heart-searching prayer. "God, I don't feel in my heart the compassion I read about in your Word, the compassion that seems to flow so freely from people like Buster Chapman. Am I a hopeless case? Has my intellect and scientific bent permanently calcified my heart to the needs of others? Am I incapable of exercising compassion for my wife and daughter?

"I can't believe you would let Maggie, Sam, and Buster cross my path if I were a lost cause. So I ask you now to perform major reconstructive surgery. Cut away the dead, insensitive tissue within me. Transplant your sorrow and compassion to this cold heart of mine. Awaken new sensitivity in me to Della's concerns and needs. Help me care about her the way you care about her."

In only two and a half weeks, Jordan found it difficult to quantify how God was answering his prayers. But he continued to give his attention to Della and Katy when he was with them. He asked them to share their thoughts and concerns about moving to Portland, and he listened for what they felt as much as to what they said. The more room he created for them to express their apprehension, the more his wife and daughter seemed willing to share. And the more they shared, the easier it was for Jordan to determine how he could help them make the transition.

After seventeen days of off-and-on discussions, the family

had not reached a decision. But it did not bother Jordan as much as he thought it might. He found the process of getting to know Della and Katy gratifying in itself.

In the meantime, Jordan had periodically talked with Dr. Taylor Sheffield in Portland by telephone. Bert Waller and Philip Ettinger had been arraigned in Multnomah County Municipal Court on numerous counts of murder in the second degree. They were being held in the county jail without bail. Joseph Wiggins had fled the country, but a warrant for his arrest had been issued. Portland detectives had launched into what promised to be a long and grisly investigation of SICU deaths at Mercy Hospital. In the meantime, Dr. Waller maintained that his murderous actions were both merciful and morally justified.

During each conversation, Sheffield probed Jordan about when he would be back to Mercy Hospital. Jordan had no answer, so he kept the director at bay by bragging on his Cadillac and how well it performed on the L.A. freeways.

"Is this too casual?" Della stepped into the sunlight on the patio modeling tailored white shorts, a flowery sleeveless top, and sandals.

"No, you're perfect, Dell," he said, standing. Jordan had changed into shorts and a polo shirt.

"Where are you taking me, Jordan?" she probed. Her subtle grin told him that she found pleasure in the mystery.

"Someplace I should have taken you months ago," he said as they walked to the Cadillac. "It's not a big surprise, Dell. I hope you're not disappointed."

Jordan drove southwest toward Santa Monica. He stayed off the freeways because he knew Della preferred to travel surface streets. "Freeways are all right when I have to get somewhere in a hurry," she had once told Jordan, "but when I'm not in a rush, I'd rather take a slower, more scenic route." He purposely avoided the freeway today, hoping to convince her that he was not in a hurry, just content to be with her.

He turned off Pico Boulevard and wound through the back streets to a serene, rolling, fifteen-acre plot of grass surrounded by a wrought-iron fence stretched between brick columns. Large oaks and elms shaded much of the verdant carpet. The plot was within a mile of the Pacific Ocean.

"This is the cemetery, Jordan," Della said, almost whispering.

Jordan did not respond until they had driven through the gate and parked on a shady knoll. The grass around them was dotted with modest headstones and grave markers, many decorated with bouquets of cut flowers. There were a few other visitors on the grounds, but none near Jordan and Della.

"You talked as if we had never been here before, Jordan," Della said, sounding perplexed. "We have been here several times. Our son is buried here."

Jordan was silent for a moment. "Yes, we have been here before, but not for this reason. Actually, there are three reasons why I wanted us to come here today. It's Mother's Day, and I thought you might want to spend a few minutes at J. J.'s grave."

"You said we were coming later today, on our way to dinner. We were going to bring flowers."

"We will, with Dad and Mom and Katy. But I wanted us to be here alone together first . . . for two other reasons."

"What reasons?"

Jordan rubbed his lip nervously. He had rehearsed his words countless times in his head. Actually speaking them to Della was so foreign to him, more difficult than he had anticipated. But he wanted to do it for her and for them.

"The night of Katy's birthday party, you told me that you didn't know how you felt toward me, that I had shut you out of my life. You said that we never really connected. Do you remember?"

"Yes."

"Another time you said that I had buried the real me when we buried J. J., right?"

"Yes."

Jordan swallowed hard. "Dell, I have come to realize how right you were, how self-centered and distant I have been. I brought you to the cemetery because I want to change that, beginning now. That selfish man you were married to, well, he has begun to change. The man you thought you married, the one you always wanted to connect with, is finally beginning to emerge.

"Dell, I want you to tell me right now how deeply my selfishness has hurt you in the past. I want to hear about the pain I caused by ignoring you, taking you for granted, making my work a priority ahead of you. I have come here to listen to you. Take all the time you need. I want to hear everything."

Della stared back at him as if dazed. "Jordan, what's come over you?"

"It's hard to explain, Dell. I just know that I have hurt you deeply, and I want to see those emotional wounds healed. It's the most important thing in the world to me. So, please, talk to me about your hurt and disappointment."

Della was silent for nearly a full minute, and Jordan waited. She began haltingly, speaking in generalities about feelings of loneliness, abandonment, self-doubt, and depression. Quelling the urge to interrupt her and defend his actions as he had many times before, he remained silent and attentive, allowing his eyes to look deeply into hers.

When Della began to relate specific occasions of hurt from their years together, her tears began to flow. She spoke of a special romantic encounter she had prepared for him one evening, only to eat the veal parmigiana alone by candlelight and bury the new negligee deep in her bureau before he arrived home four hours late. She recounted four distinct occasions when Jordan had failed to return her calls from the hospital and how unimportant she felt. And the stories continued.

With each sad memory Della expressed, Jordan's heart

broke a little more. He knew that he had caused much of her disappointment and sadness, but for the first time, he began to feel sorrow for the hurt he had caused. As the stories poured out, Jordan imagined that Jesus himself was sitting with them in the car, listening and weeping over Della's pain. Tears began to flow from Jordan's eyes, but he urged his wife to continue.

After nearly a half hour of sad stories and tears, Jordan and Della fell into each other's arms. "I'm so sorry . . . so sorry," Jordan sobbed, tears pouring down his face into Della's hair. Brokenhearted, he could say no more for several moments.

As the wave of sorrow began to recede, Jordan held Della at arm's length to restore eye contact and say clearly what his outburst of tears had prevented him from saying. "Della, I have been so wrong for causing you such pain. I feel so sad for that beautiful, caring young wife who was repeatedly ignored and spurned by her insensitive husband. Your stories break my heart because I love you. You do not deserve to be treated so coldly." He steeled himself against another swell of emotion. "My dear Della, will you please forgive me?"

Della pulled him close, and they cried hard together for another minute. Only then could she get the words out: "Yes, I forgive you, darling. Thank you, thank you."

When they stepped from the car several minutes later, a pleasant, ocean-scented breeze greeted them. Jordan led Della by the hand down the gentle grassy knoll dappled with sunlight penetrating the trees. They stopped in front of a simple brass marker that read: *Our Beloved J. J.—Jeffrey Jordan Keyes,* followed by two dates barely eight years apart. They stood over the marker in silence, hand in hand. Softly rustling leaves overhead muted the distant sounds of other visitors in the cemetery.

"There's another reason I wanted to be here with you alone today," Jordan began, voice quavering slightly. "I have never told you how I feel about J. J.—I mean . . . about his death. As you know, I haven't felt very comfortable sharing my feelings. I guess when J. J. died I buried my pain with him. Losing J. J. also stirred up the memory of Mom's death, another pain I didn't know how to express. After losing my mother and then J. J., I guess something inside me shut down for fear of losing someone close again. My unwillingness to acknowledge my sense of loss over J. J. has driven this wedge between us. I am the reason you feel so disconnected. But I don't want anything to keep us from being together, being one."

Della allowed him a thoughtful moment before she said, "I very much want to know how you feel, Jordan. Go ahead, darling. Take all the time you need."

His hand trembled around hers. "I tried to save him, Dell," he began, voice cracking, "but I failed. I did everything I knew to do, but I couldn't save him. And I miss . . . our little boy . . . so much." Another gale of tears pulled them together in a prolonged, sobbing embrace.

"I have felt so bad for you since J. J. died, Jordan," Della whispered between sobs. "You worked so hard to find a cure for his leukemia, and I love you for that. I know you took his death as a personal defeat. Maybe that's why you have been unable to grieve. It's not your fault, darling. I miss him too. I'm so sorry you lost your only son. But it's not your fault."

"And I'm sorry our little boy isn't here to wish you happy Mother's Day," Jordan said in a broken voice. Then they held each other and cried.

◆ ◆ ◆

Driving back to the house an hour later, Jordan and Della shared several pleasant and humorous memories of J. J. Then Della abruptly changed the subject. "I really enjoyed traveling with you from Portland. I would like to go with you when you drive the car back. Maybe Katy could come with us."

"I'd like that."

"Have you made a decision about returning to Mercy Hospital?" Della said.

Jordan shook his head. "I had hoped we could make that decision together."

"But you want to go back, don't you?"

"Yes, but I'm not going back without you and Katy, and I won't ask you to leave your business and friends if you don't want to."

"What will you do if I say I'm not ready to move?"

Jordan paused. "I'll find something down here—L.A., Orange County, Ventura County."

"But you bought a house in Portland already."

"The deal isn't airtight. We can get out of it."

This time Della was silent for a moment. Then, "The Cadillac has to go back to Portland regardless."

"Right."

"Since I'm going up with you anyway, it wouldn't hurt to take a good look at this dream house you found."

Jordan smiled. "No, it wouldn't hurt at all. I'd like to show it to you."

"Then I don't think it's a good idea to make a decision about Portland until I see the house," Della said, reaching over to touch his hand. "I happen to know a good decorator, if you need one."

about the author

◆ ◆ ◆

After nearly sixteen years in pastoral ministry, Ed Stewart sensed God's call to use his gift for writing in full-time Christian service. He began his new career as a Bible study curriculum editor for a major Christian publishing house in Southern California. In 1986 Ed became a full-time freelance writer and book editor, working in partnership with numerous Christian leaders to produce ministry-related books and Bible study materials. He has written or assisted in writing nearly one hundred Christian books and study guides.

Ed's involvement in Christian fiction began with the publication of two books of short stories and a novel for youth coauthored with Josh McDowell. These works were followed by Ed's best-selling action/suspense series, *Millennium's Eve, Millennium's Dawn,* and *Doomsday Flight.* He teamed with Josh McDowell again to write the best-selling political thriller *Vote of Intolerance.* Today Ed maintains a full schedule of Christian fiction and nonfiction writing.

Ed and his wife, Carol, make their home in a suburb of Portland, Oregon. The couple is active in a large church and in their small care group. They have two grown children and three grandchildren.